The Broken Circle

LINDA BARRETT

DEDICATION

For young parents without parents of their own.
This story is for you.

Cover art by Melyssa Naujoks

www.purplegirldesign.blogspot.com

E-book and print formatting by Web Crafters

www.webcraftersdesign.com

Copy Editing by Amy Knupp

www.blueotterediting.com

PART I
DARK DAYS

CHAPTER ONE

January 2009
Boston

A knock at her grad school apartment door pulled Lisa Delaney away from Commonwealth of Massachusetts vs. Torcelli Construction. Eyes burning, she rubbed her lids while, from her iPod, she heard Bryan Adams insist that everything he did, he did for her. Old song. Easy words. If the man really wanted to impress, he could take her contracts exam in the morning.

She pushed away from her desk, covered in law books and case briefs, and rose from her chair, stretching, bending and groaning. Her knees creaked like an arthritic old lady's. Shaking her head, she emitted a long sigh and promised herself a gym visit the next day—after the exam.

A second knock echoed, this time more impatiently.

"I'm coming. Hang on." Nimble again, she rushed across the room and opened the door.

Her eyes widened, her stomach began to roil as she looked at two uniformed state troopers, snow melting on their jackets, cop faces in place. Her thoughts raced with possibilities. Classmates? Mike? Oh, please, not Mike.

"Are you Lisa Delaney?"

She stared at bad news and froze. All of her. Nothing worked. Not her mind, tongue, or breath. Perhaps her heart had stopped, too. One man coughed. The other repeated the question.

"I-I'm Lisa."

"Are your parents' names Robert and Grace Delaney?"

Oh, God, yes! Her heart raced at Mach speed, but she couldn't feel her legs at all. "What happened?"

"May we come in, Ms. Delaney?" Taller cop.

She nodded and pulled the door wider, but the knob slipped through her sweaty hands and she lost her balance.

"You might want to sit down."

As though moving underwater, she struggled into the closest chair.

"I'm afraid there's been an accident on the turnpike," began the quiet-till-now officer. "A fatal accident."

"Not…not my…my parents?" She barely got the words out before the officers' sympathetic silence answered her question.

"But that's impossible! I just spoke to my dad…"

"When was that, ma'am?"

When? When? "I think…maybe…last…last night…." Her voice drifted. Daddy had been checking up on his eldest, his numero uno child, joking with her about an apple a day. Staying healthy. A convenient excuse to call. To keep in touch with the one who'd left home. She'd understood his M.O. a month after arriving at school. Sweet, loving man. A man with a phone.

"Wh-what…?" Her throat closed.

The cops seemed to understand her intent. "The official investigation is ongoing, but according to preliminary reports, the other driver lost control of his vehicle and did a one-eighty."

"Drunk? But…but it's the middle of the week." As if that fact could change things.

"The driver's blood alcohol was normal."

"Then what…? The road…?"

"Icy conditions contributed. The temperature drops at night, and your folks were approaching at just the wrong moment. There were no survivors. I'm very sorry."

She nodded. *No survivors? Mom and Dad?* She wanted to cover her ears.

The other officer looked at his notes and said, "The Woodhaven police are with your brothers and sisters."

Oh, God, the kids… She had to get back to Woodhaven!

Standing quickly, she was hit by a wave of nausea and fell back into her chair. She doubled over, hand on her stomach. The phone rang, startling her further. She stared at the instrument, half-buried by textbooks, reached forward, and slowly lifted the receiver. "Hello?" she whispered.

"Lisa! Lisa! The police are here. Mom and Dad were in an accident. You have to come home! Now! I'm scared."

Jennifer. Her social butterfly teenage sister whose life revolved around boyfriends, best friends, and having fun. Except, not tonight. In the background, she heard the cacophony of younger voices crying and talking at the same time. She heard little Emily's high-pitched wail. "When is Lisa coming?"

"Hang on, Jen." She took a breath and looked at the officers. "There are four of them. Emily's only seven.

My twin brothers are nine. Jen's sixteen. I've got to get there—a hundred miles—and I don't own a car." She couldn't afford one and didn't need one in a city with mass transit.

The troopers nodded, and she spoke into the phone again.

"I'll be there soon, Jen. As soon as I can. Maybe William and Irene can stay with you meanwhile." Her fiancé's parents lived across the street.

"They're not home. They went to Miami to see Mike play. Didn't you watch the game yesterday?"

"Of course I watched, but I didn't know his folks flew down." Mike had subbed for the starting quarterback and played an entire quarter. It was only his first year, but now the Riders were in the play-offs.

"So, Jen, you need to be in charge now until I get there. You and the kids sit tight and wait for me." She glanced toward the window, where falling snow was reflected by the light of the streetlamps.

"It might take a little while," she added. "It's a big trip, and the roads are bad…" What was she saying? Her parents had just been killed on those roads. "Jen, honey, let me talk to one of the officers there."

Her hand shook as she gave the receiver to the state cop. "Ask if they told the kids the truth."

In seconds, he shook his head. "Not yet. They're getting a social worker in on it."

She raised her eyes to his. "Please tell them not to do or say anything until I get there. Okay?"

Perspiration trickled from every pore. She shivered and sweated until finally her stomach lurched. Running into the bathroom, she vomited until nothing remained. Then she brushed her teeth, packed her suitcase to the brim, and snapped it shut. The sound focused her, and she inhaled a deep breath. *Be strong, be strong…*

One of the troopers held the door open. Her gaze skimmed the small apartment. She'd been happy there and ecstatic at being accepted into the program. She glanced at her textbooks before locking on to her college graduation photo. Her parents stood on either side of her, their smiles wide.

"Oh-h… One second." Her own future was now uncertain. Dropping her suitcase, she darted to the wall, took down the picture, and tucked it under her arm. Their dreams and her dreams might have to wait awhile.

#

Michael Brennan needed three days to get home to Woodhaven and to Lisa. It seemed like three years.

He tossed his luggage in his parents' front hall, turned around, and headed directly across the street. The Delaneys lived in a two-story wood-framed house with a front porch similar to his and to all the other homes on Hawthorne Street. He'd grown up there, but Lisa and her family had moved in over four years ago in June, right after her high school graduation. He'd graduated from a neighboring high school that same year. Their paths hadn't crossed until the evening his mother baked a cake and insisted their family welcome the new neighbors. Moaning and groaning, he'd given in, and the Brennans had gone to visit the Delaneys.

When Lisa opened the door and walked outside, he'd almost tripped up the front steps. One glance and he couldn't speak. His brain froze, too, as if a lightning bolt had slammed him head to toe. Big violet eyes, long, dark wavy hair, and a killer smile. A friendly smile. *Who wouldn't have fallen in love with her?* But he'd been the lucky one, the lucky guy who'd relished every single day since Lisa Delaney had first appeared at that front door.

Now her sidewalk needed shoveling. The streets had been plowed since the storm a few days ago, the walkways, too, but snow had fallen again yesterday, and surfaces had turned icy. He flexed his shoulders and entered the house. He'd take care of the snow after he wrapped his arms around her…if he could find her.

The Delaney house was packed. He recognized Lisa's aunts and uncles from out of -town, and all the neighbors, of course. Lisa's closest friends, Sandy and Gail, were there, too. Either they'd stayed all day or had just come from work. He waved and searched for his mom.

"Where's Lisa?"

"I'm glad you're here, Michael," she said, giving him a quick kiss, "but don't expect too much from Lisa. She's overwhelmed as…as we all are." Irene Brennan gazed up at the ceiling, indicating the second floor. "She's got the kids with her. The funeral's tomorrow, and she wants time alone with them."

"Alone doesn't include me."

He took the stairs two at a time, sensing the glances, the sympathy of the visitors as he made his way up. He appreciated their support, but they didn't have to worry. Surely, he could handle whatever he found. Surely, he and Lisa could handle it together.

He paused in the hallway at the top of the stairs. Each of the four bedroom doors stood ajar, but he could hear nothing. He started to push the first door open when, from the end of the corridor, he heard Lisa singing quietly, "Too-ra Loo-ra Loo-ra, Too-ra loo-ra lie…"

Was she trying to put the kids to sleep at five o'clock in the afternoon? He slowed his pace and walked the last few steps before knocking softly and entering the master bedroom. Lisa sat on her parents' bed, leaning against the headboard, the twins dozing on either side of her, little Emily sleeping on her lap. Jennifer lay across the foot of the bed, also sound asleep. He took it all in and understood that day and night had no meaning to them.

"Lisa..." A whispered prayer.

Her red-rimmed eyes brightened, her arms opened, and he was there. Kissing her and gently shifting one little brother lower on the mattress. She began to cry, her tears mingling with his as he rained kisses, and his tension melted simply by holding her in his arms. Tears flowed as he continued to embrace her and grieve while remembering Grace and Robert Delaney.

They'd been wonderful neighbors, wonderful parents, and good friends with his folks. The Delaneys had worked so hard to finally become "owners" instead of "renters," and celebrated their move to Hawthorne Street each time they'd made a mortgage payment. Lisa had told him how her dad would brandish the check and twirl Grace around the kitchen every single month. With their growing family, it had taken them fifteen years to afford their own home.

"How long can you stay?" Lisa whispered.

"He can't," mumbled nine-year-old Andy, rousing slightly. "He has to go to the conference championship game. And maybe to the Super Bowl."

"But not yet," Mike said, rubbing the boy's head with affection, but focusing his gaze on Lisa. "I'll be here for the funeral tomorrow. You won't be alone. Then I'll be back in a week. One short week." Which might feel like an eternity to Lisa.

"I'm glad, but-but everything has changed," she said, pulling a tissue from the nearby box and blotting her face. "We need to rethink our plans."

"The basics haven't changed," he replied quickly. "I love you, Lisa Delaney. And don't you forget it."

Her eyes shone. She pressed his hand, her fingers narrow and delicate around his broader ones. "I love you, too, but-but…." She sighed and glanced at the assorted children. "I'm not sure what's going to happen next," she said quietly.

"I am," he said. "I'm going to kiss you again."

And he did. When she kissed him back, when she lingered and leaned against him, he almost collapsed with relief. She was *the one* for him. No matter what. Her needs, the kids' needs….

"We'll sort it out when the time comes," he said. "I'll support you in every way I can." The logistics would no doubt be complicated, but he had faith that he and Lisa could do anything as long as they did it together.

She offered a wan smile. "I know you'll do your best, but you have commitments to the team. You're so talented! We all know you're being groomed as a starting quarterback, maybe even next year. So I think, for both our sakes, I need to handle this-this family situation by myself."

No, she didn't, but her brave effort tore a corner of his heart. "I think you're right about my place in the team," he said slowly, "but that's in our favor. The money's good." He'd worked hard with his coaches, and his natural talents had been recognized. His dream career loomed just over the horizon.

"I must be weird," said Lisa. "I never think about your salary. Even your first year minimum is like make-believe Monopoly money to me. It doesn't matter. I'm just so…so proud of you."

Men cry. Even big football players. But once that afternoon was enough. His throat ached as he swallowed to stem more tears. Lisa needed him to be strong.

"Have I ever told you about my conversation with your dad at the end of the summer you moved to Hawthorne Street?" he asked. "It was right before I went off to Ohio State on my scholarship."

"All Daddy told me was that you were too big for your britches, but he was laughing."

A surge of love and a wave of sadness—both raced through Mike. The words sounded exactly like something Rob Delaney would say. And the laughter–well, laughter was the norm in Lisa's family. Her dad loved to tell a good story and could imitate the comedy greats and their jokes. Rob had been a natural "on stage," and no one had a bigger heart.

"Before I left for college," Mike continued, "I told him I was going to marry you someday."

"You've got to be kidding! We were only eighteen. We'd just met that very summer." For a moment, her expression lightened. She tipped her head back, and her eyes met his. "And what did he say?"

"He said that I'd better treat you like gold—always. And I promised I would."

"O-o-h…." Despair once again etched her face. "Our lives… everything..."—she waved her arm— "has changed. I can't-I *won't* hold you to any promise."

"You have no vote." He kissed her again, vowing to keep that promise. Loving Lisa was the easy part. Building a solid future together…well, that goal might be more difficult to reach now. Lisa was in no condition to make any decisions. Their next steps would be decided by him.

His gaze rested on each of the youngsters, one at a time. Four sweet, innocent children. Without warning, his heart started to race, and his palms became covered in sweat. Fear. Like Lisa, he was almost twenty-three, and deep down, he was scared, too. He had no experience with kids, not even a younger brother or sister. But he wouldn't give himself away, wouldn't let Lisa know. A quarterback led with confidence on the field. Now he had to do the same at home.

CHAPTER TWO

On the day after the double funeral, the Delaney living room was still filled with visitors. Lisa's head pounded as she sat on the couch, trying to face her new reality, the fallout hitting like buried landmines in a war zone. Yesterday, in the crowded church, the normally shy little Emily had jumped from the front pew and run down the center aisle as soon as she'd spotted the two caskets. They were closed, but the child had understood…and she'd screamed, then begged, "Mommy, Mommy! Get up, get out of there! Please, get up."

Lisa would never, ever forget that heartbreaking scene. She'd gone after Emily, of course, had held her tightly, and gotten punched and hit on whichever part of her body the child could reach before she collapsed against her. Mike had tried to take the little one. Her two aunts—Pat and Sally—had tried to help. But in her despair, Emily had clung to Lisa.

The funeral was over, so what was she going to do now? What should she do? Images from yesterday kept invading her mind, however, postponing thoughts of the future.

At the cemetery, Jen had said, "They'll be too cold here. It's so cold today, Lis, how can we just…just leave them…?"

And Lisa had wondered if the younger kids thought she had all the answers. She was a kid herself. She knew nothing!

She'd watched in silence as the coffins were lowered into the hard ground, their graves side-by-side, and wanted to scream just like seven-year-old Emily, *Don't go! Don't leave us!*

Instead, she'd grabbed a shovel and was the first of her family to drop earth into the graves. She'd acted on impulse, but it felt right. She'd looked at Jen.

"We'll tuck them in tightly, and they'll keep each other warm." Her voice shook, and her throat hurt as she spoke the surprising words that came to her. Then she handed the shovel to her sister who dropped more earth on the coffins. Then to Andy. To Brian. And finally, to Emily, whom she helped.

"Will you tuck me in tonight, Lisa?"

"Of course, I will." She understood once again, that for Emily in this crises, no one else would suffice but Lisa.

In the living room, memories of the funeral made her headache worse, and she winced. Immediately, Gail appeared with aspirin and a glass of water.

"Thanks." She took the tablets eagerly. "How did you know?"

"We've been friends forever. I just know." Gail leaned over and brushed a kiss on her cheek before returning to her self-imposed chores of clearing away empty coffee cups or taking coats from new arrivals. Gail and Sandy were the best friends a woman could have, but Lisa longed for Mike. He'd left that morning, bestowing kisses, hugs, and promises to be back next week. Lisa wished she could hide under the covers until then.

But now, her mom's sisters were walking toward her, looking as if they wanted to talk. Lisa pointed at the sleeping Emily and put her finger over her own lips.

Her aunts nodded, motioning Lisa to follow them to the kitchen. Carefully, she rose and made sure Emily still slept. She glanced at the boys, glad to see them chatting with their uncles.

Jen was already seated at the long Formica kitchen table when Lisa arrived with the two older women.

"What's going on?" the teen asked, her eyes laser-focused on her sister.

Lisa shrugged and looked at her Aunt Pat and Aunt Sally, stalwart, loving, and wearing their worry and fatigue for all to see.

"We need to-to discuss…," began Aunt Sally. But her mouth trembled in a way that Lisa was becoming all too familiar with.

"About the future," added Aunt Pat.

"I'm not ready for that," said Lisa. "One day at a time is all I can handle." That's what Mike said to her when he'd left that morning. *One day at a time.* She thought it was good advice.

"I know, honey. I know," said Aunt Pat. "But a week will go by, then another. And we need a plan."

A plan? She was drowning. She couldn't think while she was gasping for air. "Later." She waved her arm. "Later on."

Aunt Sally took her hands, squeezed them. "Try to listen, Lisa. Concentrate. You're a smart girl, and now you need to be strong as well. Strong enough to think about tomorrow. You, too, Jen. So pay attention."

She loved them, trusted them, but she wanted Mike with her. Sighing, she finally said, "Okay."

"Uncle Steve and I can stay with you this week, and then we need to get back to Hartford. We closed the store, but we have to re-open soon. Aunt Pat and Uncle Ted will leave tomorrow for Maine and then return in a week, so you'll have some support here."

Ahh. She got it now. "But none of you can stay with us forever," said Lisa. "Is that what you want to say?"

"I wish we could, honey. I wish we could all move to Woodhaven, but that's just not possible. So, we've come up with another idea."

A significant glance passed between the two women, and Lisa sat up straighter, her headache forgotten. An unease filled her as she forced herself to pay close attention. "What?" she asked. "What's your idea?"

Aunt Pat reached for her hand again while Aunt Sally held Jen's. "We thought the best thing to do now is for the twins to live with Uncle Ted and me," said Pat, "because we have boys, too, and they could be like big brothers to Brian and Andy." Her aunt leaned closer. "And then, of course, Jen and Emily could live with Aunt Sally and Uncle Steve. We all think this makes the most sense."

Sense? They were way ahead of her with their plan. But…it wasn't a bad one. If the younger ones were safe with loving relatives, then Lisa could return to Boston. Get her degree. Her parents would approve. Wouldn't they? Sighing, she silently admitted she couldn't know for sure.

"We'd love to keep you all together," continued Aunt Sally, "but, well, neither of us have a mansion, you know? So, it's just not feasible. But in the summer and holidays, we'd all visit."

"And you, Lisa, could return to school." Aunt Pat had jumped in again, her words echoing Lisa's idea, relighting a tiny ember of hope. "Gracie would want that. She was so proud of you, darling. Maybe not this semester, but whenever you feel ready."

Boston and law school seemed far away at the moment, but it wasn't impossible. Maybe soon, in just a little while, she could fan that banked ember to flame again. Oh, yes. Her aunts' plan could work for her.

"In the meantime, you can stay with either of us," said Sally, "or with Mike's parents right across the street. We've already mentioned the possibility to Irene, and she'd welcome you. The football season's almost over for this year anyway, and Mike will be home again soon."

They'd already spoken with Mike's parents about splitting the kids up? Without asking her? No, no, no. Not right. She held up her hand. "Stop. Wait. Now you're going too fast for me."

Silence descended as her relatives acquiesced. But before Lisa could ask a question, Aunt Sally spoke again.

"We know you and Mike have your own plans for the future… and we know how much your dad and mom loved him, honey. They'd want you to marry when the time is right." Sally patted her hand. "We like him, too."

She and Mike had planned to wait until she graduated and took her bar exam. Two-and-a-half years out. Law school was very demanding. She'd be an awful wife if they rushed a wedding, with no time to set up house, go to his games or even cook a decent meal!

Lisa glanced at her sister. Jen hadn't said a word yet, which was very unlike the teen. The girl usually had an opinion about everything. Her pale complexion, wide open eyes, and raspy breath, however, said it all without a syllable being uttered. Jen had been shaken up. The aunts meant well, but Jen was not happy with their surprising plan. At least not now. Maybe she'd change her mind later when she got used to the idea. The seed was planted. Time to back off.

"I'm not sure about this," said Lisa, returning her attention to the women. "It's a lot to take in, and I need time." She glanced around the familiar kitchen, so empty without her own mother, without her life-of-the-party dad. Tears pooled and overflowed. "Jen and I can't think about anymore big changes right now."

Everyone at the table started blowing their noses and wiping their eyes. Her aunts were kind and loving, but Lisa, too, had a voice in the matter. She hadn't considered the possibility of splitting up her siblings. And now, she simply didn't know the best thing—or the right thing—to do. At least, not yet. *When in doubt, wait.* A piece of advice from her mom. She'd follow it.

#

Lisa wanted everyone gone. Back on the couch, she looked at friends, family, neighbors and Jennifer's entourage. The world had shown up to support the Delaney children. Lisa knew it, appreciated it, but her earlier headache had returned and become chronic. She blamed her aunts' plan for part of it. But there was more. Other questions about the kids, the house, school, money, a car, and insurance entered her mind, and her thoughts scattered in all directions at once.

Worst of all, she couldn't mourn privately with her sisters and brothers. Emily claimed Lisa's lap every time she sat down. With the many distractions in the house, maybe the seven-year-old thought her big sister would disappear, too.

Emily wriggled next to her and pulled at Lisa's hand. "Please. Let's go."

Lisa stood. Em had barely spoken since her outbursts at the funeral. Crying? Yes. Hugging? Yes. Shadowing Lisa? Yes. But speaking? Not much.

"Where do you want to go, sweetheart?"

"Out."

They slipped on their coats and stepped onto the front porch. "It's cold out here," said Lisa, wrestling with the child's buttons.

"I don't care."

"Then I don't care either." She put her arm around the little girl and heard the door open behind them. Brian and Andy stood there, winter jackets on.

"Hi, boys." Lisa smiled at the twins. Their sunny natures usually made everyone smile or laugh along, that is, when they weren't in trouble. These days, however, there was nothing to laugh about. "Decided to join us?"

"Yeah," said Brian, stepping forward. "With no one else around. Me and Andy were talking…

"Andy and I," she corrected automatically.

"…and we want to know," the boy continued, "if we hafta live all the way up in Maine with Aunt Pat and Uncle Ted."

"And…and…" Emily's words stuck in her throat. She began to sob. Lisa held her tightly, but glanced toward her nine-year-old brothers.

"Nothing's been decided," she said.

"Jen told us. And then we heard them talking," said Andy. "Jen and Emily are going to Hartford with Aunt Sally and Uncle Steve, and we're supposed to live in Portland. I know they're Mom's sisters, but…"

"But that stinks!" Brian interrupted.

Her heart sank. She saw where this was leading, but had no definite answers for them or for herself. She needed to buy time. "It seems to me that everyone's been talking way too much," she said, making an effort to lighten her tone, "except for us. Where's Jennifer?"

"Right here," said the teen, stepping over the threshold. "I didn't see any of you inside, so I figured something was up. And I also figured out what I'm doing, so no one has to worry about me for very long."

Lisa's eyes narrowed as she studied the girl. "Is that right?" This was the Jen she was used to, creative with ideas, passionate with opinion, and often acting before thinking ahead. Whatever she had on her mind would be a doozy.

"In six months, I'll be seventeen," began Jen. "I did some research, and at seventeen, I can be emancipated from my family and live on my own. I can get a job. I mostly do what I want now anyway, you know-hanging out with my friends."

Lisa didn't believe that last part for a minute, not with their hawk-eyed parents.

She looked from one child to the next. And the truth stared back at her. Four precious lives. Four worried faces, one touched with attitude. She saw four frightened children trying to articulate their fears. To her. The oldest. In their eyes, she was the adult. The thought almost broke her. Sure, she'd had household responsibilities while living at home. However, Gracie was the captain, totally in charge. How in the world had Lisa's mom handled five children?

Lisa had no idea how to be a mother. Not even how to begin. And the kids were waiting.

Mom! Dad! What should I do?

Was there a right or wrong? She needed the wisdom of Solomon here. She needed to think! "It may be," she began slowly, "that we have some choices."

Before she could say more, little Emily tugged on her hand again, and in a clear voice said, "Then I choose you. I choose my house. I choose Massachusetts. I choose Andy and Brian and Jennifer and me – everybody together. For always."

"Me, too! Me, too." The twins nodded so hard, Lisa winced. "Easy, boys, easy," she crooned, stroking their heads, and looking at her sister. "What about you, Jen?"

"It doesn't matter what I want, or what they want," Jen said. "You and Mike can't live here after you're married, so staying here is a ridiculous option."

Mike! Fear landed in the pit of her stomach. She hadn't thought about him at all during this discussion. Did Mike Brennan truly have a vote in this life-changing decision? Her sisters and brothers were *not* his responsibility. And who took priority for Lisa? The kids or Mike? With four children, how could she and Mike build that solid future they'd envisioned?

She stared at each child in the small circle. After a week of numbing grief, of walking around like a robot, of listening to theories and maybe's, another truth smacked her with hurricane force.

The kids wanted *her*. Not Aunt Sally and Uncle Steve. Not Aunt Pat and Uncle Ted. They'd chosen her. A seven-year-old. Two nine-year-olds. And a teenager. She remembered diapering the little ones when they were babies, reading picture books and singing lullabies to them. She loved them all. But God almighty, she also loved Michael Brennan!

"We'll be good, Lisa," said the once-silent Emily. "Can't you stay with us just until we grow up? You're so smart and you're already a grown-up. Twenty-two-and-a-half is old. You can be the mother, like Wendy in Peter Pan."

Four sets of unblinking eyes stared into hers. The younger ones didn't understand yet that no one could take their mother's place, not even a much-loved older sister. Theirs wasn't a Neverland adventure, but a nightmare none of them had chosen.

"Here's what I'm going to do," said Lisa, holding out both arms and wrapping her siblings in a group hug.

"I'm going to search the house for what's called a Last Will and Testament or any other instructions Mommy and Daddy might have left for us if a terrible thing happened. Like it did. Sometimes parents write those things down."

"They do?" asked Andy, his voice filled with wonder.

"It would be a piece of paper," she began slowly, "telling us what to do if they weren't here anymore." And the bottom-line decision would be her parents' decision, not hers. If they had left instructions, then Lisa's conscience would be clear. She loved her siblings. That was not in question. But what about her own plans with Mike and her career? All just around the next corner. Maybe she was selfish to hope for a way out. Her aunts seemed not to think so, however, with their offer to take the little ones and allow Lisa to continue her schooling. Maybe her folks would also prefer the kids go with Mom's loving sisters.

"In the meantime," she said, "remember this for now and forever: we are the Delaneys, and nothing will ever change that!"

#

A long, high-pitched scream shattered the night. "Mom-my!"

Lisa's heart raced as she ran into Emily's room, to the bed, and gathered the child to her. But Emily, lost in her own nightmare, shook her off. "I wa-want Mommy," she hiccupped. "I want Mommy."

"Shush, honey. It's Lisa. I'm here with you." Finally, Emily's body relaxed enough for Lisa to cuddle her. Her eyes opened slowly. "I want Mommy." A flat statement.

"I know, Em. I know. I want her, too."

The child snaked her arms around her big sister and held tight. "But now I have you, don't I? I love you, Lisa."

"And I love you." She kissed Emily's cheek and inhaled her little sister's sweet scent. So innocent. When the overhead light went on, a lightbulb in Lisa's mind blinked, as well. She and the children were a family, not to be scattered like leaves in the wind. She'd never be the mom Grace had been, but she'd try. A corner of her heart shredded as she silently said good-bye to the future she'd planned. A future with Mike Brennan.

Andy, Brian, and Jen crowded through the doorway.

"We heard her screaming," said Jen.

"Did you find the will yet, Lisa?" Andy's voice.

"What did it say?" asked Brian.

She hadn't had time to start. "It doesn't matter after all," said Lisa. "I-I did some thinking. And even though I don't have a lot of experience in being a mom, if that's what you all want, then I vote the five Delaneys stay together."

She had to cover her ears with all the hooting and hollering that followed. "Shush. Your aunt and uncle are sleeping."

"Not anymore." Aunt Sally and Uncle Steve stood in the doorway. "What's going on? That was Emily crying, wasn't it?"

Lisa rose from the bed. "She's fine now. As for the others…well, you might not approve, and we do very much appreciate how you and Aunt Pat are willing to help out, but we just voted to stay together." She turned back to her siblings. "Right?"

Four distinct nods.

"Oh, dear, Lisa. I'm not sure. You're barely out of childhood yourself. Let me talk with Pat and Ted and we'll see."

Brian interrupted. "I hate 'we'll sees.' That's the worst answer in the world."

"Bri—pipe down." Lisa turned back to her aunt. "I love you, Aunt Sally, but in this case, my brother is right. There's no 'we'll see.' None of us really know what my parents' wishes would be. And staying together seems right to me."

No way would she voice doubts and fears to her relatives. She had to project strength.

When they were all back in their own rooms, Lisa sat on her bed, lips quivering as she thought about Mike. She silently said good-bye to the man she loved. To the man who loved her. To the man she could have leaned on. Oh, yes. He would have provided a strong shoulder, but the timing was wrong.

Mike's career was just starting, but nothing was guaranteed. Bad luck in college with a broken leg had cost him in the draft. He had to prove himself more than ever, and she couldn't, she wouldn't hold him back by foisting emotional crises on him. In the NFL, his elite opportunity wouldn't wait.

She'd get a job—maybe teaching history—in one of the high schools. She'd keep the family going and was thankful Gracie had insisted Lisa have a practical backup plan. Law school had seemed so out of reach at the time. Truly, a dream.

She walked to the window and peered into the night sky.

I'm scared, Mom. Help me.

CHAPTER THREE

"I love you, Lisa. Put the ring back on your finger. Please..."

After a week with the team, Mike was back in Woodhaven, in the middle of another disaster. Stars twinkled in the cold night sky outside, but inside Lisa's kitchen, the facets of her engagement ring twinkled in the palm of her outstretched hand. He'd placed the ring on her finger seven months earlier after their college graduations.

"Our lives have changed," Lisa continued, and he wondered at the calmness in her voice. "The plans we made…they won't work anymore. The kids are a huge responsibility, and they're *my* responsibility. Not yours. I can give you the freedom you need." She met his gaze, her violet eyes now black and…blank. "The NFL is a once-in-a-lifetime opportunity." She moved her hand closer, the ring on her palm. "Take it."

He didn't move. Wouldn't make it easy.

"Don't you understand?" she asked, her voice rising, her expression more animated. "The kids are mine. Forever! I can't give them away when they challenge your sanity…and they will. Trust me, they will. Chaos is normal. Take the ring."

Mike studied her clenched jaw, listened to her strained voice, saw her shadowed eyes. The symbol of love rocked in her trembling hand.

Ignoring her request, he deliberately placed his own hands behind his back, his gaze steady on Lisa's face. "It's not returnable. The kids will be *our* family. Your kids are my kids. They like me. I like them. We'll get married sooner than we'd planned, that's all. How about this summer, after they finish the school year? Then we'll all move to Boston."

The words tripped off his tongue as quickly as the thoughts entered his head, but as he spoke, he realized every idea made sense. At least, to him. His plan could work for all of them. Typical quarterback. Creative and quick.

But Lisa shook her head. "You don't understand…" She paused, her mouth tight, and he pounced with the ace he'd been holding back.

"You need me, Lis," he said quietly. "Have you forgotten how much I'll earn?"

One look at her outrage and he wished he'd never spoken. "I-I didn't mean it like that…" he floundered.

She tossed the ring on the floor and seemed to grow inches taller. "The Delaney kids are not charity cases. My parents managed with five, and I'll manage. And as far as your career, what about concussions? ACL tears? Nothing's guaranteed, Mike."

He inhaled deeply and nodded. Injuries happened on the field, so why refute it? "The Delaney kids are the best, the smartest, funniest, most loveable kids around…especially the oldest sister."

He stepped closer, wrapped her in his arms, and, when he felt her stiff body finally lean against him, almost collapsed in relief. She loved him. That was all that mattered.

"Nothing's changed between us, Lis. You're worrying too much. We'll figure everything out little by little, and we'll do it together."

"You make it sound so reasonable," she began, "but it's not. You didn't sign on to raise four kids. Kids who've been hit hard, who are grieving hard, just as I am. It isn't fair to you. You've got only one brother, and an older one at that, so you don't know what it's like to 'babysit' for real. To supervise homework, to make sure they've eaten, bathed, dressed. To make sure they have enough. To tell the truth, I don't have the hang of it, either."

"Maybe not at this moment, but you will. The intrepid Lisa Delaney knows how to carry the ball straight into the end zone." At last, he got a smile out of her.

"Touchdowns may take a while," she said.

We're near the goal line right now, baby. He brushed kisses all over her cheeks and along her neck. "Together, we can take on anything."

"Maybe. Maybe not."

He didn't understand her hesitation, but he'd never confronted a predicament he couldn't figure out. He kept his arms around her, simply held her, letting her know he was there. But also ready to pry. "I know you're scared, sweetheart. I know. Just remember one thing—you're not alone. I'll discuss these plans with the kids, too. We'll have a…a family conversation."

She pressed against him. "Then you should know the biggest hurdle first. They want to stay here in Woodhaven."

He hadn't counted on that but was sure he could talk them around eventually. "The place doesn't matter in the end, does it? Being together does."

He heard her sigh, felt her lean farther into him before moving away, her posture still straight and tall.

"You know that. I know that. We'll see." She stared hard at him. "But if I have to choose, Mike, I'll choose Woodhaven. I don't want to do anything to shake the little ones up again, to make things worse. As if…" She sighed.

Woodhaven today. Boston tomorrow. Location was a temporary situation. He could handle it. "I understand."

She blinked rapidly, her mouth quivering. "And there's something else…"

He smelled her fear and drew her close again. "Whatever it is, we'll intercept it, take it down. Just talk to me."

She nodded. "I've had to petition the court for custody of the kids. After Jen and I told my aunts and uncles we wanted to stay together, they were going to file their own suit—for my own good, they said. Fortunately, I was able to convince them not to." She peered up at him, offering a tiny smile, the first he'd seen in a long time. "I was always a good debater in high school."

"And very modest," he joked, glad to lighten the mood. The proposed custody procedure shocked him. He'd seen for himself the love and affection among Lisa's family. "I don't understand. I'd think they'd be satisfied simply to help you out, stay in touch, visit regularly…"

Her sad chuckle made him wince and hold her tighter. "Well, they wanted more. They said if the kids lived with them, I could stay in school. They said it's what my mom and dad would have wanted."

She stepped back and gripped both his forearms, her fingertips turning white.

"How can they possibly know what my parents would have wanted? Did they ever ask? All I know is that when Emily cries at night, she calls my name. And when the boys have questions, they run to me. And the other night—after they'd gone to bed—you know what I saw when I checked on them?"

He shook his head. *Let her talk. Let her get it all out.*

"My dad's sweater! Andy and Brian were together in one bed, wrapped in my dad's gray mohair sweater. The one my mom knit for him."

Mike's stomach knotted. Beads of sweat covered him, and he shivered. This was heavy stuff.

"As for Jen," said Lisa, "well, I don't know what to say or do. Her first day back at school was a nightmare, and she described hell as the five minutes between classes when all the memories flooded her."

Tears rolled down her face, and he gently wiped them away, but her words continued to flow. Had she held all her thoughts inside until he returned?

"Jen's ordinary, safe life is over," said Lisa. "She's like a yo-yo, running back and forth between her friends' homes and our house. But mostly ours. My social sister is afraid to turn her back on us. I…I'm worried about her." Her breath came hard, gasping.

"Easy, easy," he murmured, kissing her temple, stroking her back.

But it seemed she wasn't finished yet. She stepped aside, her gaze burning. "If actions speak louder than words, does it sound like my brothers and sisters want to be sent away from me, from each other? So I filed the damn petition quickly in case my aunts change their mind."

He'd known the Delaney kids since Emily was a toddler and her big brothers had entered kindergarten. Jennifer had been twelve when she'd moved onto

Hawthorne Street. The children played together, fought with each other, looked out for one another, and even sang together as they cleaned up the kitchen after dinner. Rob and Grace had started that routine to make time go faster as they worked. Their voices blended in a sweet chorus.

Mike had known better than to join in and spoil the effect. He'd always waited until afterwards, when the noise began. Oh, yeah, the Delaneys could make a lot of noise, definitely more than his family did, each person voicing an opinion about everything. That's when he loved being with Lisa's family the most.

"Go to court, baby. Get the kids legally, and we'll make a life together. All of us. One family." He kissed her and murmured, "It'll work out as long as you and I are a team."

Finally, her eyes gleamed. "The L and M Team? Or the M and L Team?"

He grinned. "Whichever you want, sweetheart."

She scooped up the ring from the floor and replaced it on her finger.

Touchdown.

#

The little ones were finally sleeping; Jen was in bed probably with her headphones on. Another school day awaited each of them in the morning. Mike had reluctantly left a little while ago as he'd done every evening since returning to Woodhaven. Lisa insisted he go home—also reluctantly—and always watched from the front window as he headed across the street. After he'd turned and waved, she allowed the curtain to fall. She'd wanted him to stay, hold her and make love with her, but they'd both agreed to be careful about late-night visits. They'd do nothing that could create doubt about Lisa's judgment and her ability to claim the children. Social workers might question the neighbors, and rightly so.

That night, for the third time since the funeral a month ago, Lisa sat on the floor in front of her parents' bedroom closet and pulled open the bottom drawer of a metal file cabinet. When her folks were alive, she'd never dream of digging into their private papers. But now she had no choice. She wanted to find a will or some other custodial directive before the court date next week.

She'd spent recent days searching every bedroom and coat closet, every nook and cranny in the basement and attic in this quest. If a will existed, the decision about her brothers and sisters would be out of her hands.

She'd never go back on her word to her siblings, but this first month alone had been… She shook her head as her memories swirled. *Difficult* would be too easy a word. *Impossible* was better. To be expected, of course, but she wondered if she could handle it. Besides the cooking and cleaning, the crying, sobbing, shouting, but most of all, the questions. Why? Why? Why? She tried to save her own tears for when she was alone. No question her own life would be easier if her siblings did live with their relatives.

She pictured herself back in her grad school apartment, where exams were all she worried about. She'd been happy. Challenged. Excited by the city. Being in Boston had been her first venture away from home, her first taste of the real college experience, living on a vibrant campus instead of commuting from her house each day as she'd done as an undergrad.

On top of all that, she and Mike had wonderful plans for their future. He'd be the starting QB for the Boston Riders and she'd be a practicing lawyer. *Mike*

Brennan. Her rock-solid, funny, smart, talented, and ambitious boyfriend. And so loving. She'd had it all.

Idiot! Did she think returning to campus would make her forget this tragedy? Erase the grief?

Tears welled as her fingers crawled through each manila folder—car, insurance, mortgage—plus a fat, weighty, mailing envelope labeled "recipes." She wasn't looking for secret recipes—the ones her mom used were in the kitchen—and had bypassed the envelope on her prior searches. But now she shrugged, opened the flap, and reached in.

Two old-fashioned black-and-white school notebooks. And a legal-sized envelope with the words *Last Will and Testament* handwritten on it. The shock made her gasp, and her hands trembled as she brought the three parcels to the bed. Sinking into the mattress, she tore open the envelope and skimmed the contents before slowing down to proofreading speed.

She saw nothing. Nothing of significance. The will was a store-bought blank document that her parents had filled out. Each one naming the other as their one hundred percent beneficiary. The lines asking about custodians for minor children had been left blank. No lawyer's signature. Just two witnesses whose names Lisa didn't recognize, which made sense when she checked the date: 1997.

Twelve years ago, Lisa had been ten, and Jen, four. The boys and Emily hadn't been born yet.

A useless piece of paper. She let it fall to the floor and rested her head in her hands. No magic "get out of jail" card existed. The only direction to move was forward as she'd planned.

#

Five minutes later, Lisa placed the notebooks on the kitchen table and put up a kettle of water. Maybe a cup of hot tea would calm her down.

She opened one of the notebooks. The pages were dated and covered with writing. Her mom's handwriting. Short stories? A journal? Scanning the dates, she selected the earliest—1975.

Dear Diary,
My mother doesn't understand anything. I'm twelve years old, and she doesn't trust me to go on a date!

Despite her anxiety, Lisa chuckled. Her mother's voice rang true and so clearly in her head she could have been in the kitchen with Lisa. Sighing, smiling, but wanting to cry, Lisa remembered feeling the same way about Grace, her own mother.

She fixed her tea and continued reading. And saw her mother grow from young teenager to young adult.

I met such a nice boy today when my friends and I went swimming at the lake. His name is Rob Delaney. So cute! Curly black hair, dark eyes, and a smile that made my heart race...and ache. He asked for my phone number, and I gave it to him. I wonder if he'll call.

Lisa didn't have to wonder. Her dad often joked that he fell head-over-heels in love with her mom, and that's why he had a scar on his forehead! But now the joke made her breath hitch. She could drown in memories, and that wouldn't help her or the kids at all.

She paged quickly through the second book. The entries became less frequent, but she paused over one dated during her mom's pregnancy with her.

Robbie and I are pregnant! We weren't sure how soon this would happen because I have only one ovary, so we are thrilled. We always wanted a large family— three, four, or even five children. I'm not sure that will really happen, but we are counting our blessings with this first. Boy or girl—we don't care. Please, God, a healthy child.

Very few entries followed. Her mom was probably too busy, but not too busy to share her thoughts with each new child. With Jennifer: *A sister for Lisa! How wonderful to have a sister. Almost seven years apart, it's true, but love transcends time.*

And when the boys were born: *We've been blessed with two healthy sons! Small but feisty. Robbie is ecstatic, but I want to see the babies gain weight. Money is tight, but we'll manage. Robbie signed up for overtime. Buying a house of our own seems out of reach, but we're doing fine in the rental house. Handling twins will be a challenge. Fortunately, I can count on Lisa to help. I'm very proud of her. So smart, so pretty and talented. She's everything a mom could wish for, and she's never let me down.*

Tears streamed down Lisa's face as she read. Grace's presence filled the room, filled her. *I'm trying not to let you down now, Mom.*

2002
Five are enough! Little Emily has rounded out the family. Who could have guessed that Rob and I would actually wind up with five when we thought our first was a miracle? We've been blessed with beautiful children, and my wish for them is to grow up together, loving, learning, playing, and knowing that they'll be friends

forever. No matter what the future brings, I want them to know that family ties are unbreakable.

Lisa reread the last paragraph over and over, pausing each time on the words, *my wish for them is to grow up together.* A quiet peace filled her. She'd made the right choice.

The following page was blank. Instinctively, Lisa picked up a pen:

February 19, 2009—one month post-accident
Dear Mom,
Your sisters want the kids, but I'm fighting to keep your children together. I know after one short month that mothering is not easy. However, I think I can figure it out as I go along.

We're going to family court in two weeks. Pat and Sally are going to offer their homes, but my God, the little ones have already lost you. I can't let them lose each other, too.

Mom…Dad…I'm scared. It seems I'm always scared these days.

She began to doodle. A heart with initials inside: M.B. + L.D. Quite the artist.

She smiled and laid her head on her arms. Love would have to be enough. Thinking about Mike relaxed her now. Her mind eased. If he were with her, perhaps she'd be able to sleep—finally. Taking a deep breath, she forced herself to go upstairs.

She quietly opened the first bedroom door. The ceiling fixture in the hallway provided enough light for her to identify her brothers, one in the top bunk, one in the bottom one. Two blond-haired imps, legs sprawled, blankets kicked awry in similar fashion. An arm moved above. A leg moved below. A restless sleep for both. She paused, simply to hear them breathe.

Emily's bedroom was empty, and Lisa quickly glanced into her own room, expecting to find her youngest sibling there. Em had joined her many nights during the past month…but Lisa's room was vacant, too. Moving faster, she swung Jen's door open and saw no one. Which meant they had to be…

She entered her parents' room, which she'd left almost two hours ago. The window shades were up, and pale moonlight revealed the sleeping pair. They lay spooned on their sides, Jen's arm wrapped around her little sister, both girls her little sisters. Lisa's eyes filled. She ached to jump in with them, to touch, to feel, to know that the Delaneys were still a family. She leaned over and brushed a kiss on each forehead.

I'm here. Everything will be all right. She wouldn't admit how scared she was. Not to them.

"Mom?" A murmur, before Jen sat up. "Oh. It's you. I thought…I-I forgot… Ohh…."

"Yeah, Jenny. I know. Sometimes, when I'm asleep, I forget, too. And then…"

"…and then it's worse when you get up and remember. It hits like a bomb right into your stomach."

"Exactly."

"I-I… Oh. I just hate everything. Everybody. Why us, Lisa? Why us? Why did they have to die?"

She wasn't God. "Wrong place. Wrong time, and it sucks."

"Damn right it sucks. It's just not fair!"

Amen and amen.

Lisa inhaled deeply. "I need you to be strong next week. In court. We need to show everyone that we're both ready and able to take a step forward." Her voice dropped. Who was she kidding? She was more frightened than Jen.

"That judge better say we can stay together," said Jen. "He just better."

"Or what?" Her sister was an emotional teen with the typical hormonal explosions, and God knew she certainly had reason to be off-the-wall now. But Lisa needed a heads-up.

"Or…" The girl's mouth tightened, her chin jerked upward. "I've got ideas that don't include living in Hartford with my relatives. And that's all I'm saying."

A sharp pain began throbbing in Lisa's temple. That bottle of aspirin was becoming her best friend.

CHAPTER FOUR

Light shone from the kitchen, surprising Mike when he entered his house after saying good night to Lisa. His parents were usually asleep by now, and he headed down the hall, wondering briefly at their change of routine but dismissing it as inconsequential. No one involved with the Delaneys had remained fixed on normalcy. His own thoughts focused almost entirely on Lisa, especially now. Their earlier conversation had shaken him up more than he'd let on. He'd hated leaving her alone with her imagination. They'd made a pact about discreet behavior, however, and he'd stick with it, unless *she* changed her mind.

His mom and dad smiled, then yawned, their mugs of tea on the table half-consumed. A familiar scene.

"Couldn't sleep?" Mike poured himself a glass of milk and sat down. "I think we'll come out all right next week. Lisa will get the kids."

Silence was the only reply. His mother squeezed his arm, earning his closer attention. He examined her face and saw how a month of grief and worry had taken its toll. Dark circles under her eyes, lines around her mouth where none had been, hollows beneath her cheekbones. She'd lost weight. His usually trim mom couldn't afford the loss. He glanced at his dad.

"She needs to eat more. Some whole grain..." The words left his mouth before he realized his dad looked no better. William's robust complexion appeared sallow, and his normally high energy level a mere memory. Both his parents had aged during the last month, and suddenly, a frisson of fear arced through Mike, causing him to choke on his drink. His parents were mortal, too. Dear God...if he reacted this strongly to a shadow of possibility, how was Lisa able to cope at all?

His dad patted Mike's back, then his hand as though Mike were still a child. "Milk. A good choice for a growing boy."

He stared at his worried father and bit back his immediate retort. Joking would be better. "If I grow any more, Dad, I'll be a linebacker, not a QB. But we both know that's not going to happen. I'm done in the growing department. I'm not a boy anymore."

"But you're so young..." Irene protested, shaking her head and looking as though she'd cry again.

"I'm a man," he said, "with man-size responsibilities. You're the ones I'm worried about. Maybe you need some sleeping pills...?"

"Your mom and I will be fine," William said quickly. "We, uh, just need a little more time to...to adjust." He shook his head, murmuring to himself, before looking at Mike again. "We did wait up for you, though, to discuss...the future. It can't be put off any longer."

Mike leaned back in his chair. "Lisa and I have already discussed everything, but if you have any good ideas, I'm listening."

"You know we love Lisa and the children," Irene said. "We still can't believe Gracie and Robert..." With a trembling hand, she reached for the ever-present tissue box. "Well...you know."

Yeah. He did know. Just being with Lisa and the kids reminded him without a word being said. The Delaney house was eerily quiet now, all the noise of family reduced to whispers. Shadows marked every face, eyelids blinked hard. He glanced at his mom's tissues. In the house across the street, similar boxes sat on tables in every room except they were in different colors. He noticed details like that. A quarterback had to notice physical details and behavior. He had to know his team well, had to read them as easily as he read the sports pages in order to be a good leader. Everyone said he'd been born with those skills, but he still had to prove them.

"But, Mike, *you* are our son."

"What?" His folks stared at him with puzzled expressions. "Sorry, my mind was elsewhere."

His dad sighed. "Focus, Mike. We're talking about Lisa and the kids."

He focused.

"You're our son," William repeated, "and it's our job to protect you. And the truth is, Michael, you need protection now. You need time. Time to think."

"Lisa, too," Irene said quickly.

Where were they going with this? "There's nothing wrong with my brain, Dad."

"Well, let's see..." William began slowly. "You're on the cusp of an extremely demanding career, an exceptionally physical career, and a public one, at that. You're still proving yourself, and if you're distracted on the field by personal problems, you not only could be hurt, and hurt badly, but you'd also let your teammates down, not to mention the coaches who believe in you. You won't even be twenty-three until June. Too young to handle that NFL spotlight as well as this huge tragedy." William stared in the direction of the Delaney home. "Frankly, I don't know if there is a right age to handle this, but if there were, I don't think it would be twenty-two."

Mike pushed his glass away and stood. "You must have been brainwashed by Lisa's aunts and uncles. Well, forget about them. You know I've loved Lisa from the moment we met. And she loves me just as much. That's all that matters."

"Oh, your feelings are not an issue," his mom said quickly, and for a moment, he was comforted. "We're just suggesting you wait awhile. That's all." Irene rose from her chair and hugged him. "Give Lisa and the children a chance to settle in. The little ones have just returned to school, so let them find their way. And then figure out what you want to do."

Nice in theory, but he was dealing with real people who needed him immediately. A family who needed a clear plan to regain their equilibrium. "I've already figured it out." He took a breath. "Our plans have changed. We're getting married this summer, before my preseason exhibition games in August. We'll move to Boston immediately after the wedding. Even you have to admit that a hundred-mile commute to Woodhaven each day is more than I can handle."

His folks stared at him as though he'd spoken Chinese.

"So soon...?" His mom's trembling voice ended in a squeak.

"This isn't about the driving!" protested William. "It's too much responsibility. All of it. You're both too young. And you're not financially ready. Wait a year or two, until you're a starting player, until your career's more established. We'll help. We'll be right here for the children if they stay together, right here on Hawthorne Street."

Mike grabbed the back of his chair and leaned toward his parents. "Lisa and I discussed the same thing... She wanted to break the engagement. Wanted to 'set me free.'"

They hadn't known. How could they? Their curiosity, surprise, and incipient *hope* revealed in their expressions showed him where their feelings lay. He had to set them straight. "Breaking up with Lisa will never happen. She's the only one for me. Always has been. If I postponed our lives now, she'd feel abandoned. I won't do it. She and I have to begin by depending on each other."

"But...but she mentioned applying for a teaching job at the high school," said Irene. "And I just learned someone in the history department is going on maternity leave March first. Lisa can probably step in and get a full-time assignment for next year, too. Teachers are always coming and going."

He didn't question her facts. His mom was one of the secretaries at the high school. A source. "Lisa's licensed by the commonwealth and can work anywhere," replied Mike. "She'll find a job in Boston if she wants to work, but I'm going to make sure she goes back to grad school as soon as possible."

He headed toward the stairs, then paused and turned back to his parents. "I know you're trying to help, and I love you both. But if you can't be supportive in court next week, then stay home. Please."

#

Lisa rapped her knuckles on the kitchen table during breakfast on Saturday morning, the last day of February—two days before the court hearing.

"Family meeting," she announced.

"Huh?" Brian tilted his face toward her, confusion evident, milk and Cheerios plopping from his spoon.

She smiled at her little brother, an imp who could coax a laugh from the most solemn people, and scanned the circle of faces. "Now that I've got your attention"—she took a breath—"here it is. We go to court on Monday. We don't know what the judge will say, or if he or she will even make a decision right then."

She'd done some research on family court procedures and adopted the mantra of "forewarned is forearmed." She'd be ready to handle the possibilities—soften a blow, argue a point, or explain the judge's ruling—even a postponement—on a child's level.

She could hear them breathe. Each one individually, from Emily's quavers to Jen's controlled inhalations.

"That's not necessarily a bad thing," Lisa added, stroking her youngest sibling's hand. "But I'm thinking we need a plan in case the judge sends a social worker to the house." Another strong possibility.

Jen scowled. "We don't need any social worker..."

"That's beyond my control," said Lisa.

"And don't talk that way to the judge," said Brian, his eyes wide as he stared at Jen. "He won't like you, and then...then he'd give you to Aunt Sally, and..."

Emily began crying. "No, no, no."

"Enough!" said Lisa, noting her imp had a vivid imagination. "No one's going to Aunt Sally unless the judge thinks I can't handle the four of you."

Quiet reigned for a moment until Andy asked, in his thoughtful manner, "But *can* you handle us, Lisa?" And because identical twins were not necessarily identical in every way, and her brother deserved an honest response, Lisa said, "I don't know for sure. But I'm going to try my hardest."

Andy nodded once, his eyes solemn. "When I grow up, Lisa, and make a lot of money, I'm going to give it to you for school. So you can be a lawyer again."

"Me, too," said Brian. "Hey! I got an idea. You take care of us now, and we'll take care of you later."

The boys fist-bumped each other; their faces, alight with eagerness and pride, as though they'd discovered gold, made Lisa laugh so hard she hurt. She grabbed them around, kissed them until they squirmed away, carbon copies once more—at least at that moment.

Jen reached for a pad and pencil. "We have to clean the place up today and keep it clean." She pointed at her brothers. "Including under your beds and your closet floors. Then we all have to sort the laundry in the basement and put it away. From now on, every Saturday is linen change and laundry."

"Thanks, Jen. I'll do the meal planning and shopping." Sudden fatigue slammed Lisa as sleepless nights caught up. "I-I really can't do everything by myself," she whispered. "Even Mom, who could whip up a meal in five minutes, had us help her…"

"She used to call you her lieutenant," said Brian, "didn't she? Before you went to Boston."

Your lieutenant still needs you, Mom. "She did. She sure did. And now, you're all my army…I guess. Because if we're to live on our own, in a proper way, everyone needs to help out."

She nodded at Jen's automatic note-taking. "Mom always said between your organizational skills and math skills, you'd rule the world."

Jen's unexpected sobs came slowly at first, then heavy and hard, a sorrowful song with no end. Once more, Lisa realized that raw emotions could high-jack them anytime and anywhere. But hopefully not in court.

#

Lisa wore a suit and low-heeled pumps for the court appearance. Professional attire. If she dressed the part, she'd have an edge. If the judge ruled against them, it wouldn't be her fault. Living defensively—thinking defensively—was becoming a habit.

She sat directly in front of the judge's bench, the little ones between her and Jen, who sat at the far end. Each child was scrubbed, shiny, and neat. Jen was at her best, no talk of emancipation. There was too much at stake to be flippant.

Mike had driven them to the courthouse and now sat directly behind them, in the same row as her aunts and uncles, while his parents sat several rows back.

The judge, a woman, had been pretty smart so far, asking the kids about school and sports and what they liked best. Either a getting-to-know-you process—which seemed to work—or a gaining-trust process before the killer questions came. To Lisa's surprise, however, the judge called upon their relatives next.

As she listened, she winced. She had to admit her aunts were eloquent and sincere in expressing their love for their sister's children. Their homes and wallets were open to them. They made it sound like fun. The twins would be little brothers to their older cousins. Jen and Emily would have full attention of two loving adults whose own children were away at college. Her uncles confirmed every idea, demonstrating couples united in their plans.

Andy squeezed her hand. "I don't like this," he whispered.

Lisa studied each sibling. They might have been young, but they weren't stupid. Their collective brave front was back, the judge's prior friendly conversation forgotten. Identical pale complexions revealed freckles in startling relief, and her heart sank for them. Two losses! If the judge was truly swayed by their aunts' presentation…

Oh, God, she couldn't bear the kids' pain. She had to be proactive. Nothing else mattered. Not law school, not money worries, not cleaning a house, not lack of a car, not Mike, not anything except keeping the family together.

When her aunts and uncles headed toward their seats, Lisa stood. "Your honor, my relatives may have good intentions, but my sisters, brothers, and I have something to say, too."

Jen rose. "We have a lot to say."

Emily raised her hand. "I cleaned my room, even under the bed."

The judge grinned. "I bet you did a great job."

The child nodded. "And so did Brian and Andy. Lisa said boys have to clean, too."

"Smart sister," said the judge.

"I know," said Emily. "She's old enough to be smart."

Lisa heard the laughter and the sob from her aunt Pat and wanted to gather sweet Emily into her arms and hold her forever. She'd bet her aunt wanted to do the same.

The judge gazed at Emily and smiled. "Are you finished now?"

"Okay. But I want Lisa."

"I'll write that down," said the judge, holding up a pencil.

Emily's smile melted Lisa's heart. She turned to the judge.

"And I want them all." She took a breath. "Your Honor, in your years on the bench, you must have witnessed an extraordinary array of family circumstances. Custody battles, abuse, neglect, drug use, foster care. Issues that needed resolution in a court to ensure the safety and well-being of the children involved." She paced three steps to the right and looked up again.

"We, Delaney children, may not be an ordinary family, either. But we are safe. We are a healthy family, with a home and a full refrigerator. And as Emily indicated, we've gotten the chores worked out, too." She walked back to her starting point.

"But a family is about more than chores. It's about love and loyalty and knowing where you come from." This time she stepped toward the bench, closer to the woman with the gavel.

"The five of us in the first row are the children of Grace and Robert Delaney. Our hearts are broken. Oh, God, how they're shattered! But we share common memories of them. And when we do, we cry and we laugh. But I think that's okay.

"We share what we've learned from them. Hard work, education, and music. You should have heard my dad sing. To say we miss our mom and dad terribly is too mild a statement. But here's my point—we are their family even though they're no longer with us here on earth. I know they'd want us to stay together. And we want to make them proud."

She was drained, had no more words to offer. But then heard one quiet word from the second row.

"Bravo." Mike's voice. Her eyes met his, and she saw the pride, the gleam. She knew she'd done her best. And if she had, her life was going to change forever in every way imaginable. Her stomach twitched as butterflies danced a wild tarantella.

#

She'd spoken from her heart and head, but before the judge called a recess, she asked questions. About today, tomorrow, and the future. About the engagement ring on Lisa's finger and Michael Brennan, who was in the courtroom. About his relationship with Lisa's parents.

"Her folks made me welcome, and once we were older, I promised her dad that I'd treat her like gold." He leaned forward in his chair. "I intend to keep that promise."

"Thank you," said the judge before banging her gavel.

One hour to mingle with her relatives, hear their pleas to reconsider, and then take hope as they assured her of support if the judge ruled in her favor. "We won't abandon you, Lisa. We love you. We only want what's best for all of you."

Mike's parents had joined them. "We do, too," said Irene, "and we think your ideas make more sense. Lisa's capable, but our son's career is just starting. How can he give the time and attention four grieving children and a new wife would need?"

Silence among her relatives.

Surprised silence from Lisa. Mike hadn't said a word to her about his parents' attitude. Was this something else she'd have to deal with?

"Your point is noted," said Mike. His nostrils flared but his tone was controlled. "As is your presence. Why did you ignore my request to stay home if you couldn't help?"

Irene reached to touch him. "Don't be angry. Grace and I were so close, but we never spoke about a possible tragedy like this. She was a fierce mother, however, and she'd want what's best for her children."

"Do you have an insight that we don't?" asked Sally.

Irene shook her head. "Sadly, no. I don't know what they'd want. I don't know what's best for their children.

I only know what's best for mine! And it's not…not…this." She waved her arm to encompass the youngsters.

Jen's complexion whitened, her expression blank. Brian had turned his back. Andy studied his mom's friend, and Lisa swore she could hear his gears turning. But it was Emily who asked, "Don't you like us anymore?"

"Of course she does," said Lisa quickly. "It's just that she loves Mike more. He's her son." A door clanged shut in her mind. No support from the Brennans. Despite all the food trays, visits, and words of encouragement, when crunch time came, the Delaney kids hadn't made the cut.

The judge reappeared, and everyone returned to their seats, first standing and then sitting as directed. The woman rattled some paper and nodded slightly at Lisa before addressing Jen, Andy, Brian, and Emily.

"I listened carefully to what you told me, and I heard you. You each said you want to stay together even though you have wonderful choices with relatives who love you. Is that right?"

Four heads nodded. Emily said, "I love them, too."

"I'm glad to hear that, Emily," said the judge. "Keeping families together is the court's greatest goal, if at all possible. Your sister"—she turned toward Lisa now—"has argued her points eloquently." Focusing again on the children, she said, "So, I want you all to help her. Keep your rooms clean, do your homework, and behave. Or Mr. Brennan will toss you into the end zone."

The boys giggled and looked back at Mike, their eyes adoring. Mike was becoming their go-to guy, and Lisa understood she was going to gain custody of her sisters and brothers.

She'd accomplished what they'd all wanted. And yet, with that realization, a bone-chilling fear swept through her, as cold as an Arctic wind, and the butterflies danced again.

Her parents had made it look so easy, but in the last month, Lisa had learned that caring for her siblings would be difficult, physically and emotionally. Only yesterday, she'd been a teenager herself!

The judge stared at her. "You're very young and inexperienced to take on this responsibility, Ms. Delaney, but your brothers and sisters trust you. The court, however, is uneasy about simply dismissing this case—this family—into the world without supervision. Therefore, a social worker will be assigned to monthly home visits for the next six months."

The order seemed reasonable. Had Lisa been the judge, she might have done the same thing.

Her Honor leaned forward. "Ms. Lisa Delaney—the court has decided that you, and you alone, will be granted legal guardianship of your siblings until each of them reach majority age of eighteen years. The court realizes that Mr. Brennan cares about the children. Perhaps one day he'll be their brother-in-law. However, at this point, he will *not* have legal authority. The issue may be revisited in the future at your discretion."

She understood. Any legal involvement for Mike would have to be initiated by her.

The judge resumed. "It is the court's hope that from the pain and chaos of loss, a family will be maintained and grow stronger over time. Your relatives support you, which is not a small thing. The children will need all the love and reassurance they can get. And so will you.

"And as an aside, Ms. Delaney, it is the court's opinion that you will make an excellent lawyer one day."

Lisa's breath caught. She blinked back tears as a ray of hope brightened her heart. One day…one day. For herself. For her parents. She'd make them proud.

The judge lifted her gavel. "The four minor Delaney children remain in the custody of their adult sister, Lisa Delaney." Bang, the gavel spoke.

Terror, relief, happiness, worry… It was done.

Mike's kiss melted her freeze. "We've got them," he whispered. "We can do this, Lis. We'll give them as happy a life as we can."

Not the legal guardian. His big heart was in the right place, but the bottom line responsibility would be all hers. "Thank you, Mike. I'm so glad you were here. I love you."

"I know," he whispered, just before her aunts approached with tears and hugs. Big hugs.

Sally looked at Lisa, then at Mike. "It will be harder than either of you think, tougher than facing your fiercest opponent, so remember there's no shame in asking for help. If the road gets too rough, promise me you'll call. We're really just a phone call away."

"Thank you." Lisa's voice trembled. "I will…I will."

Her aunts looked upset, sensitive to her every nuance, and Lisa forced a smile. "We'll be fine. I'll make mistakes, but I'll try not to make them twice."

"'Atta girl. We've had enough doom and gloom," said Aunt Pat in a lighter voice. The woman whipped a checkbook from her purse and began writing. "This is a little cushion from Uncle Ted and me. You'll need it."

"Money goes fast," said Aunt Sally when Lisa began to protest. "That emergency fund your neighbors started won't last long. You'll need to set up a budget. A strict one. So, here's a little more to help out." She started writing, too.

"I'll help her with a budget." Jennifer stepped forward. "I'm taking an accounting course in school this year as an elective. And I sure like money."

Lisa chuckled, glad for the comic relief. Jennifer would be an asset. She weighed every purchase she made with her own earnings as though it were a question before the United Nations. "I-I don't know what to say," Lisa stuttered. "Just thank you. Thank you so much. I'm sorry if you're disappointed..."

"Not in you, Lisa." Sally's voice quivered. "Just...I guess...in life." The woman glanced out the window, avoiding everyone's eyes, simply shaking her head. "I still can't believe it..."

Lisa stepped forward and wrapped her arms around the loving woman. "Neither can we, Aunt Sally. Neither can we."

CHAPTER FIVE

A month after their court appearance, Lisa cuddled against Mike on the living room couch, a large crocheted afghan around them. The children were finally in bed. Jennifer, too, had conked out. The kitchen was clean—a team effort—but once again, they had no leftovers. Either she hadn't yet figured out the right amount of food to insure extra meals or she was afraid to spend enough in the supermarket.

She turned in Mike's arms and stroked his cheeks, loving the feel of the stubble against her skin. He was a man, not a boy. "I feel better when you're here. Just…just hold me now."

His arms folded around her, warm and safe; her eyes closed and her breathing slowed.

"You're falling asleep, baby," he whispered. "Want me to put you to bed? Or better yet, want me to stay?"

She became more alert. "Yes…and no," she slowly replied. I-I don't know. What would the kids think in the morning? What would the social worker think or write if she knew?"

She heard his long drawn breath. "Lis…you're the adult. The guardian. And you're also a woman. Besides, we're getting married in July. Sleeping together is not unheard of. In fact"—he rubbed his hand against the blue corduroy slipcover her mom had made years ago—"we've already put a few dents into this sofa. So don't be a hypocrite. C'mon, honey. I miss you."

And she missed him, but… "I know, I know, but it's different now."

He adjusted his position on the couch and looked straight into her eyes. "How?"

"I-I guess I worry more. With every decision, I wonder how the kids will react."

"For Pete's sake, Lis. I'm here so often I'm like a piece of furniture. They're used to me being in their house."

"But not first thing in the morning." She met his gaze. "Maybe the little ones wouldn't think twice, but Jennifer's sixteen. And she's smart." She waited a beat. "Isn't that self-explanatory?"

"So, let me see. Last month, we were afraid of what the neighbors would think. And now you're afraid of what an almost-grown sister will think? I thought we were the adults."

"Exactly." Why was he being so dense? "You have no sisters, so I'll spell it out." She grabbed his hands and held tight. "Home should be a safe place. I'm afraid of embarrassing her, making her feel uncomfortable. She's not used to an adult male roaming around her house in a tee shirt. Except for her dad. And that's different."

His gentle kiss on her brow made her weak with relief. He wasn't dense, just uneducated about teenage girls.

"I promise, Lisa, our home will be a safe place. I'd protect those kids with my life. As for Jen, I'll kill any boy who touches her."

On the right track, but still a bit clueless. She stroked his cheek, and he kissed her fingers and asked, "Don't you think Jen would get used to me?"

"Sure, I do. After we're married." She saw the disappointment, offered a quick kiss. "This is my decision, Mike. And the answer's no."

She had to stand firm and do what she thought best for her sisters and brothers. But Mike's disappointment made her uneasy, and worse, she sensed the unease ran deeper than a night without making love.

"Is this the new M.O. around here?" Mike asked. "No discussions? You simply make a decision, and that's it?"

"Of course n-not… Oh, God, I don't know. They're my responsibility…and…and…" She began to shake all over and wasn't far from tears. This was about more than conflicting viewpoints. "Maybe your mother's right, and we should wait. I can tell you're angry, and that's not good. We've never had such arguments before."

His kisses covered her forehead, temple, cheek, and finally her mouth, and his love and care enveloped her. "I could never be angry with you for more than a minute, Lis. You're everything to me."

She returned his kisses in full measure and suddenly didn't worry about her mom's slipcovers or her siblings. Opening her arms, she reached for normalcy and pulled him close. "I've missed you, too."

She inhaled the spicy fragrance of his familiar aftershave, loving the aroma just like she loved his firm touch, the sound of his deep voice, the feel of his broad chest that supported her weight with ease. And the powerful shoulders she stroked—all so familiar, all part of Michael Brennan. Her Mike.

His tongue invaded her mouth and heat flared inside her. He whispered her name. He was ready, hard against her. She wanted him, too, all of him, just as they'd joined together in happier days and would in the future, always and forever.

"Yes, Mike, yes…" It had been a long time…

She heard the plastic wrap of the condom and smiled with satisfaction. He'd kept his senses when she had not. A man she could trust. "Love you, Michael."

And then words weren't important as she became lost in her own world—taken to the brink once, then again like the ebb and flow of an ocean wave until at last crashing onto the sand. What a release! Was Mike with her? She blinked and heard his raspy breath, saw his smile, felt more kisses.

"My, oh, my. So good," she whispered and drifted off.

Morning light surprised her. She hadn't slept through the night since the accident. Mike was gone, but the afghan covered her completely, tucked in around her just so. Tender care. Maybe, just maybe, life might make sense again. Hopefully, sooner rather than later. She crossed her fingers for luck and went upstairs to shower. A long Saturday waited with lots on her list to accomplish. Since she'd started subbing in the high school, the weekends were even more crucial for household prep.

#

Jen was still in bed when Lisa got out of the shower. "Your turn, and then we get busy."

"I didn't sleep much." The teen yawned.

"Mike was here late," said Lisa quickly. "Did our talking disturb you?" She held her breath while waiting for Jen's answer, hoping the private conversation had remained private. Jen seemed to ignore the question, however, just looked up with sad eyes.

"Do you think we'll ever be happy again?"

Lisa quickly sat at the edge of the bed. Quicksand always surprised, but definitely took priority over anything else. "Yes, I do. But I think we'll be sad first, like now. I think it's a mix for a long time."

"Well, I think it's *forever*. We can never forget them, so how can we expect to laugh again?"

Time heals all wounds. Yeah, yeah, but she'd be damned if she'd offer Jen clichés. Her sister wanted and deserved more than that. Lisa mentally reviewed her carefully researched file on the grieving process. Research—one of her strong suits.

"There are no rules about this, Jen. We have to accept that we're going to cry hard and laugh little for a long time. That's just the way it works." An idea struck. "Remember when Grandma Molly died, and Mom was so sad for a long time? Remember, she just wasn't herself?"

Jen nodded.

"Mom told me something that made me understand. She said, 'No matter how old you are, a girl is never ready to lose a mother.'"

She could see her sister thinking. Then came the nod. "And she was much older when Grandma died than we are now."

"So, it's okay to be sad. But it's not okay to keep it inside without talking about it." She hugged the teen. "Thanks so much for talking to me. We have to communicate!"

"The word of the day."

Lisa grinned and sighed with relief. She'd met Saturday's first hurdle successfully. "See you downstairs."

She peeked into the other bedrooms. Empty. But the beds were stripped, the linen piled on the floor. The day looked promising.

#

She quickened her step when the aroma of freshly brewed coffee tantalized her. Mike and the little ones were already at the kitchen table, but he stood as she entered.

"Good morning." His deep voice wrapped around her before his lips touched hers.

"It is, isn't it?" said Lisa. "At least a better morning. I slept like a baby last night."

His eyes gleamed, and she felt heat rise to her face.

"Good, I'm glad you're rested because we have a busy day ahead."

"I have my lists."

His wide grin confused her.

"We've got a new item in the number one spot," he said. "We're buying a car today."

The boys whooped with excitement and ran around the room, but Lisa only stared.

"A car? I don't think so when the only vehicle I could afford would probably break down a week later." She rubbed her forehead as another thought came. "And I'm not taking a loan. We have enough money worries. We have to be careful."

Mike had been driving her and Jen to the high school each day since she'd started teaching three weeks ago. But his official off-season training programs would start soon, and he'd spend a lot of time in Boston. She'd probably wind up taking the school bus, riding with the students for a while. Or maybe with Irene. It simply couldn't be helped.

"Relax," said Mike. "We're totally in synch. No loans, and no junk cars, either."

Sighing, Lisa said, "If only the other driver had been insured…"

"Yeah. You'd have collected for accidental deaths and gotten enough for a brand new whatever you want with no financial concerns. Not that you'll have any in a year or two, when my salary takes a jump…"

"I hope so." But she counted on nothing. His whole career could crash in an instant.

His eyes darkened, and she knew he read her mind. She squeezed his hand. "You're the best, but you know the game…anything could happen."

"I never think about the downside, and you never used to, either."

"Sorry," she whispered. "I have to consider everything now. My dad's small life insurance policy provides the only stash of funds I have. Their car was worth less than what they owed, and the entire check went to the lien holder. The neighborhood fund and my aunts' checks don't total enough for a new car. We need the kids' social security to live on along with my salary." Her breath was gone by the time she finished.

His fingers intertwined with hers. "Shush… I called Jason Singer's dad at their dealership and told him what we needed. He's expecting us. A gently used Honda Pilot. Room for seven."

She was familiar with the showroom. In a small city like Woodhaven, everyone became familiar with local businesses. But…

"Why didn't you ask me first?" she demanded.

His brows rose to his hairline. "You had a problem, and I solved it. Sometimes, you need to take action instead of talking a thing to death. You're like a dog worrying a bone."

He might have a point, but still… "And what am I using for payments?"

Funny how the kitchen got very quiet. Even young Emily seemed to know they'd reached the crux of the matter.

"Here's the deal, Lis. You cover the insurance. I'm taking care of the buy."

She stared, didn't blink. Shook her head. "No…"

"It's an early wedding gift. That's all. Stuff your pride in your pocket and get real. You can't even get to the supermarket without a car."

True enough. She'd been depending on Mike for rides for the last two months. "That's really generous, honey, but…"

"No buts. The league's salary, the base for a rookie like me, is more than your mom and dad earned together over several years."

Somehow, she knew that. Just didn't think about it. The money wasn't hers.

"Hey, Lisa," called Brian. "Don't you know anything about football? Mike signed for 310,000 dollars. Isn't that enough for everybody? Forever?"

#

That night, Lisa automatically reached for the black-and-white notebook. Riffling through the pages, reading what Grace had written made her feel closer to the woman. She picked up a pen. The thought of writing her own entries just felt right. Calming. Perhaps therapeutic. Whatever.

April 4, 2009—2.5 months after

She supposed from now on, everything that happened, every topic she and the family would discuss would be measured in terms of before and after.

Hi, Mom and Dad,

Mike bought us an almost-new car this morning, a black Honda Pilot. He called it an early wedding present. I went along with this because…well…did I have a real choice? We desperately need a vehicle. Mike's been driving us everywhere.

The kids think he makes oodles of money. They don't understand that it could end tomorrow. He's a die-hard, try-hard rookie who loves the game. However, he's not the starting QB, so who knows if his contract will be renewed?

Our lives aren't a game. Expenses are real. Even Mike noticed the boys were outgrowing their winter jackets. How could he not when their wrists hang out of their sleeves? Then he studied Jen and Emily. He's starting to understand that raising children is expensive, and admitted the cost of living in Boston will be high. We'd have to be careful for a while.

"But in the long run, we won't have any money worries," he said.

This is what I told him: "I'm responsible for the kids, Mike. Not you. I'm glad to have your backup for emergencies, but you're not taking them on financially."

And you know what he said?

"It's a package deal, Lis. I love you, and the kids are part of you now. End of story."

But I think he's glad that I plan to find a full-time teaching job in Beantown. Maybe he's not as sure of himself as he pretends to be.

She put the pen down and stretched her fingers. Glancing at the pages, she was surprised at how much she'd written. And how much better she felt. Until she thought about moving away.

I don't know if it's right to remove the kids from our home, where they're surrounded by everything familiar, including the neighbors. On the other hand, they're also reminded of their loss everywhere they look. Because you're not here. Maybe a new environment would be better for them.

I know only two things for sure: 1) Mike and I need to have a real marriage, and that means being together all year long; and 2) I have to create a secure and perfect home for the kids. They must feel safe. So we'll be moving to Boston soon after the wedding since the Riders play at Revere Stadium. I hope and pray it's the correct decision, but I'm rarely sure about anything.

Mike is wonderful with the boys. Always tossing a football with them, asking about their homework, making sure they help around the house. He's more cautious with the girls. But one night, Emily climbed onto his lap and fell asleep. When he carried her upstairs, his tender expression left nothing hidden. He viewed her as a precious gift. Maybe everything will work out.

Good night for now. I love you.
Lisa, your lieutenant.

She tossed and turned after putting the notebook away in her night table, thinking about Mike's parents. They'd been quiet lately, perhaps regretting going against their son's wishes in the courthouse. Later, they'd offered perfunctory congratulations on her keeping the children. But Lisa hadn't questioned them. And wouldn't. Irene's words had hurt, but she hadn't deserted them. In fact, she'd taken Emily under her wing, inviting the child to bake cookies with her. She'd give the woman time. If Irene couldn't get past her disappointment, well…that was her problem.

#

Several nights later, Lisa put down her pen and stretched her arms overhead. She had as much homework as the students, and correcting history exams was slowgoing. She glanced at her watch. Nine o'clock on a school night, and no Jennifer. Something about a science fair project with her friend, Stephanie. But how long could a school project take? Jen wasn't the social butterfly she'd been before the accident. Back then, family came in a far second to her friends. Their mom had laughed and accepted it as normal teenage behavior. Since the accident, however, Jen had become a homebody. Hated being at school, never talked much about her friends.

Lisa would have to call Steph's house and track Jen down. Then she'd finish correcting the papers and make lunches for tomorrow. After that, she'd clean the kitchen. In the morning, she had to face a bunch of high school kids who hated her. They'd loved their "real" teacher, who'd decided to have a baby. Was that Lisa's fault?

Suddenly, it all seemed too much. Kids at home, kids at school, here, there, and everywhere, bringing lots of worry and responsibility. Her once-controlled world had been turned on its head. She started to laugh and couldn't stop. A crazy laugh with long sounds and short ones. High notes and low ones. The kind of laugh that's not quite hysteria, but oh, feels so damn good!

And when her laughter ebbed, she noticed Jen and Mike standing in the doorway, staring at her.

That's when she burst into tears.

"What's wrong? What's wrong?" Mike was by her side in a flash.

"Noth-ing." She hiccupped and glared at her sister. "Why didn't you call me? Why so late? I was worried. You can't stay out so late on a school night, Jennifer, especially without letting me know."

"Oh, yes, I can!" Jen snapped back, shocking Lisa. "Just for the record, I'm almost seventeen, and I don't need you telling me what to do. But you'll be happy to know I won't be out late anymore. You know why? Because nobody understands. Not even Stephanie. I talk to her, but she doesn't get it."

Suddenly, the teen deflated, her defiance turning to tears. She plopped to the floor and began crying in earnest. Lisa sat next to her and pulled her close. She remembered the usual emotional upheavals of her own teenage years, but her sister's life was anything but normal.

"Jen, would you rather live with Aunt Sally or Aunt Pat? I bet we could…"

But the girl cried harder and shook her head so wildly that her long hair slapped Lisa in the face. "See! You're just like Stephanie. She doesn't want me around, either."

"Geezus," Mike whispered.

Lisa swallowed hard. "Don't talk crazy. You're my sister. I love you. Of course we want you."

Jen shrugged. "I guess you're stuck with me," she said. "My friends…? They're afraid. When they see me… They're afraid it…it can happen to them."

"That's a hell of a way to treat you," began Mike.

"I wasn't sure about this move to Boston, but now…? I actually want to go with you and you"—she waved toward Mike—"and those brats upstairs."

"And you will," said Mike immediately, "as we planned."

"I've just made an executive decision," said Lisa. "We're all going to talk to someone. A licensed counselor or therapist or whatever they're called. Not Helen, the social worker. She doesn't need to know everything."

"Great idea," said Mike.

"Do you think I'm crazy?" Jen asked, looking horrified. "I talk to Ms. Abrams sometimes, and she doesn't think I'm crazy."

"Ms. Abrams is a wonderful school counselor and is absolutely right," said Lisa. "I think you're in pain. We all are. I think 'crazy' would be to pretend nothing was wrong. So thank you for helping me avoid what could have become bigger problems."

"Oh. In that case, you're welcome. Maybe life will be easier in Boston. When this project's over, I'll be in earlier every night. Mike doesn't have to search me out." She scrambled to her feet and started toward the hallway.

"I appreciate that," said Mike. "We players need our beauty sleep, ya know?" He grinned. Jen giggled. And Lisa sighed with relief.

"One more thing," Lisa called after the teen. "How about getting together with me this weekend to work on that household budget—at least, with whatever information I have?"

Jen whirled. "Absolutely. This is my family, too. I want to know what's going on."

"Absolutely," repeated Lisa. "And I need your help."

Her sister's genuine smile filled Lisa with satisfaction. She'd handled her well. Or, at least, she hadn't made things worse.

After Jen disappeared upstairs, Lisa turned to Mike. "I think I intercepted some real trouble. What do you think?"

"You handled her like a pro." He leaned over and kissed her. A serious kiss. "But be prepared, baby. Those four kids need their own full-time quarterback, and you're it."

"I suppose so," she said with a sigh. "The kids have to come first." But how long until they matured enough so she could return to school? Her goals had been equal to Mike's, and they'd both looked forward to sharing the excitement of their growing careers. Each one supporting the other, each reveling in the other's successes. "One day," she whispered, "I'll go back."

"Count on it."

CHAPTER SIX

Jen accompanied Lisa to the supermarket the next Saturday morning, saying that food was an important line item in their budget, and she was helping maintain the family fortune.

While Jen's reasoning was sound, Lisa privately thought her sister wanted time away from the little ones, a chance to enjoy a ride in their new car while Mike supervised her brothers and Emily. But once at the supermarket, Jen had proven to be an ace, checking or calculating the true unit costs against the aggregate bulk, figuring out sales from sales pitches. No need for a calculator. She did it all in her head.

"You really are hardwired for numbers, aren't you?" asked Lisa as they unpacked the items in the kitchen afterwards.

"Young as she is, I think Emily's a math person, too," replied Jen with a nod. "Must run in the family."

Lisa chuckled. "Maybe I was adopted."

"No way. You look so much like Mom—except her eyes were true blue—that seeing you from a distance…sometimes…I forget." Her voice trailed off, and Lisa was again reminded how a mood could change in an instant; the tragedy shadowed them twenty-four seven.

"Thank goodness we have the new car," Lisa said, purposely changing topics. "How would we ever have done all this shopping without it?"

"Twenty round trips by bus?" suggested Jen, wrinkling her nose. "Carrying grocery bags for two miles would be ridiculous!"

Her sister was right, and even though Lisa had been uncomfortable accepting it, her heart warmed thinking of Mike's generosity. He'd helped them out and also searched for the right vehicle. Now, they had a reliable workhorse, and Lisa expected no repair bills for a very long time.

"You're back!" Emily lost no time in running to Lisa and wrapping her arms around her waist.

"Good morning, ladies." Irene was there, too, her glance taking in their activity. "I brought some simple recipes that stretch money and food," she said, waving several sheets of paper in her hand.

"Simple," said Lisa. "I like that word. Thanks a lot."

"I used them myself when the boys were young and money was tight."

Lisa noticed the change in Irene's inflection. The woman was trying to make a point. It seemed the issues she'd been nurturing since the court hearing were still with her, and one of them was about money. As though Lisa wasn't concerned herself.

"How about taking a walk with me, Lisa?" suggested Irene. "The girls can finish up here. Emily's been wanting to help out, too."

Her suspicions confirmed, Lisa immediately agreed. "I could do with some fresh air." She finger-waved to her sisters and ignored Jen's frown.

A minute later, she and Irene were outside and away from the house. But now Mike's mom seemed to have a hard time getting started. Lisa took a deep breath and jumped in.

"Something's on your mind, Irene, so just spill it. After all," she said with a chuckle, "I'm going to be a lawyer one day, so I'm used to conflicts—at least, in case law." Lisa tried to lighten the mood while sounding confident, but her heart pounded. Her plate was more than full, and she didn't want to deal with anything else. But willful ignorance never worked. She needed to meet trouble head on.

"All right." Irene offered a curt nod. "It's just that William and I…well, we're trying to be both Mike's parents and your parents, too—in a way. Looking out for both of your best interests. I mean…you and Mike as a couple…you want the best for each other." Her statement ended as a question.

"Of course we do. You must know that by now."

"But I'm worried that my son is not ready to support a family, emotionally or financially. His career has barely started. The season isn't as short as it seems. Training is really a full-time, year-round job. Even now, he's going back and forth to Boston to his coaches. If you're depending on him to share the childrearing—the parenting—his career will be over before it begins. He's barely more than a child himself. Just like you."

"Are you kidding?" Lisa halted and pivoted to face the other woman, who must have lost fifty I.Q. points recently. "You think I'm still a child? From the moment the cops knocked on my door, the last remnants of my happy childhood disappeared. I've stood up to my own relatives, fought for the kids in court, organized a household. Does that sound like a child's activities?"

Irene ignored the question and spoke quickly, as if to unload everything she'd been holding back for the past few months.

"Right now, it might seem that Michael's earning a lot of money, but there are five of you to support! And I know my son. He's given you a car; next he'll want to buy you a new house and everything the children need. He already mentioned a new computer for Jen. It's just too much pressure on him."

Lisa's stomach tightened, her usual reaction to unexpected stress. She'd talk him out of the computer. "I know exactly what Mike's earning. And I'm not an idiot about the downside in his career. Why do you think I jumped at that job?"

Finally, Irene paused before speaking but seemed stunned or confused. "You…you're all such a distraction. He could get hurt on the field."

The crux of the matter.

"Any player could get hurt," Lisa snapped. "Football's not for sissies." She stepped forward and motioned to continue walking. "I can assure you, Irene, that when Mike is on the fifty-yard line, his mind is only on the game. So stop casting me as the bad guy here. I'm his biggest cheerleader." She was marrying Mike for his heart, not his money.

"And he's still paying off college loans. He only had a partial scholarship."

Mike's mother was a terrier, holding on to what she wanted, in this case, her arguments to Lisa. "I hear you, Irene, and I understand your point. I have college loans, too." She reached for the woman's hand. "Irene…you know I've loved your son for years and want the best for him. You know he loves me, too."

"You were children…still are. Love's easy before the rent's due and the bills come in." Irene's face hardened. She stared at Lisa without blinking, and in that moment, Lisa saw a stranger. She'd never seen this side of Irene before, the side that viewed her as a threat to her son's happiness and success.

"My siblings and I have an income of our own," Lisa said, her jaw thrust forward, her voice hard. "We're not dependent on Mike for survival."

Irene's eyes quickly tracked to the new Pilot, as if to say, oh, really? and Lisa's frustration zoomed from simmer to boil. She made an effort, however, to restrain her reply.

"C'mon, Irene. Could you live on Hawthorne Street without a vehicle? The car was a necessity, not a luxury."

Irene waved Lisa's words away. "You can rationalize anything. If you love Mike and want him to succeed, then you have to protect him. He'll want to be the 'man.' He'll want to be the provider. He'll want to jump neck-deep into the kids' lives and problems. If he tries to do everything, he won't do anything well. He could easily get hurt out there if he's distracted." She paused for breath. "Now, do you understand?"

Oh, she understood, all right. Irene wouldn't be swayed by any counterargument Lisa had. A stalemate. But her heart broke at another fracture line in the family. Sure, getting hurt in the game was an idea in the back of their minds—hers and Mike's—but they never dwelled on it. Hell no! Mike's love of football overcame any doubts they had.

"Don't project your fears on me, Irene. We don't live that way."

"Then it's time to wise up and face reality. I'm his mother, and I've lived with fear since he was nine years old. Players do get hurt. It's a killer sport."

"Oh, for God's sake," said Lisa, not bothering to hide the impatience in her voice. "Then you should have made him play baseball. I have to believe Mike won't get hurt."

"If you let him focus on his work, maybe he won't."

Lisa froze. Stared at the woman in disbelief. "Are you saying that if Mike gets hurt on the field, it'll be my fault?"

"If he can't concentrate because of you and the children, then yes. So maybe it would be better *not* to get married yet. Let him go to Boston and begin his career by himself without…without…" She turned her head slightly, now gazing over Lisa's shoulder toward the house.

And in that moment, Lisa understood Irene's true motive for the conversation. She wasn't suggesting a temporary postponement of the wedding but, rather, a permanent one. Mike could do better, a lot better than a needy girl with troubled sisters and brothers. Irene wanted a change of bride.

"You've said enough," said Lisa, her voice thick with pain she couldn't hide. "Was your past generosity just a cover for the neighbors? Thank goodness my mom and dad can't hear you now and see the truth."

Irene gasped. Lisa's words had finally hit home, but crushed her own heart, too. With a quickened pace, she left the other woman and headed back toward the house. Irene had been hateful, no doubt about that. Among her barbs, the only the point Lisa agreed with was the need for a warm and secure environment. Irene's first loyalty was to her son, and Mike had to be sheltered from the Delaneys' problems. But to Lisa, all her family needed was to feel secure as they found their way forward.

Clearly, Lisa's job would be to create a perfect home. She'd handle all the family issues alone and protect everyone she loved. She'd do it quietly and provide a smooth path for her soon-to-be husband.

Postpone the wedding? No. That would surely drive both her and Mike to a distraction that never entered Irene's mind.

CHAPTER SEVEN

On July eighteenth, six months after the accident, Mike stood at the altar next to his brother, David, surprised at how crowded the church was on his and Lisa's wedding day. Looking over the congregation, he spotted two of his coaches and a reporter from the area newspaper and a stringer for *The Boston Globe*. He withheld a grin. Local Boy Makes Good? Did they know something he didn't?

Practices were going well; his leg was strong again—as strong as before the break over a year ago—and he was working harder than ever. He sensed his growing confidence and looked forward to the official start of training camp next week. Maybe his status as second backup to the starter would change for the better. On the other hand, the roster would be cut by the end of August. He'd better be on it, even if in the same position.

Shaking his head at the absurdity of news coverage—his was certainly not a society wedding—he continued to scan the crowd.

How had a simple, intimate affair morphed into a full house? He studied the attendees more slowly and had to admit he saw no strangers. It seemed their Woodhaven friends and neighbors hadn't needed a special invitation but had taken time out to wish them well.

Lisa's extended family had shown up in force—aunts, uncles, cousins—and his own family hadn't let him down despite his mother's reservations. She had either come around or was putting up a good front. He really didn't care which. He only cared about the new life he and Lisa would share. Between both families, the front rows were entirely filled—all except for two reserved seats.

On one, a long-stemmed red rose lay on a white silk cushion among sprigs of babies' breath; on the other seat rested a white carnation and a bow tie. Grace and Robert would be with them in spirit.

Mike took a deep breath, rolled his shoulders beneath his white dinner jacket, and stared at the back of the church, simply waiting.

Waiting for Lisa. Waiting for their new beginning.

The soft background music segued to their processional choice, a guitar concerto by Vivaldi. Mike's eyes remained glued to the top of the aisle. Jennifer walked first. The maid of honor, taking her role very seriously, looked beautiful with her hair pulled up in some kind of fancy twist. He watched her approach, this bright teenager, confused and stumbling, trying to make sense of her collapsed world. She and the others had begun working with a therapist, but Mike foresaw a long road ahead. Maybe a lifetime? He shivered. *Don't go there. No drama, no trauma today.*

Jen was college material, and he'd make sure she'd attend next year. He met her gaze and winked. She grinned back at him. Yes! He wanted everyone to share his happiness this day.

He heard a murmur and some chuckles. Gazing toward the rear of the room, he saw his two young groomsmen, identically dressed in white jackets to match his. With their blond hair neatly combed for a change, and cocky smiles lighting their faces, the twins were photo-ready as they strolled toward him. He'd never seen Andy and Brian so self-contained. They spent most of their time engaged with a bat and ball or a basketball or a football, surrounded by their friends. They kept themselves busy. Too busy to think? Mike felt his body tighten. Were the boys living only on the surface, pretending all was well? He studied them again. All he knew for sure was that they were good kids, and he looked forward to coaching them, guiding them…. They already looked up to him, even now, having reached the altar with obviously no clue what to do next. He pointed toward their seats.

A poignant "ooh" and "ahh" hit his ears, sprinkled with whispers of *adorable* and *precious*. Emily. Of course, Emily. With her basket of flowers and a smile that warmed him from afar. A petite princess, perhaps the most fragile of the children, the most delicate, who revealed herself with crayons and paint. *I promise you'll be safe, Emily. You'll be brave and strong again.* He watched her sprinkle her petals with every step. When she reached the front, he nodded at the space next to her brothers. First, however, she blew him a kiss. And his heart squeezed again.

Four traumatized children. Problems and potholes down the road. And he was no shrink. For an instant, his heart stopped beating, and sweat prickled his skin from scalp to soles. What the hell was he taking on? Was he really up to it? Were his parents right?

With that last thought, the music changed. He snapped to attention and finally received his reward.

Lisa.

In unison, the congregation stood. Flanked on each side by her uncles, Lisa floated toward him in time to the music, a short veil obscuring her face. Slowly, she approached, and he soon saw those violet eyes glistening behind the veil, darker than usual and shadowed… She stood before him, now alone, and Mike lifted her netting.

"I love you," he whispered, the one truth he'd never doubted.

She smiled, and the shadows disappeared.

He'd try his best to erase those shadows forever. The key was his career. With hard work and a little luck, he could grow into a star player. The money he could earn would resolve their living issues. Sure, Lisa had said the kids were *her*responsibility, and only hers. But that was an unrealistic and foolish notion. He and Lisa were a couple. A single unit. And he was the one positioned to give them everything they'd ever need or want.

Maybe one day, he and Lisa would start a family of their own. The thought caught him by surprise. It seemed they'd been too preoccupied to have that particular conversation. It didn't matter. They had plenty of time.

First, however, a wedding! Confident again, Mike reached for Lisa's hand, faced the priest, and kneeled. He was ready to steer his new family.

#

"Good morning, Mrs. Brennan."

In the picturesque B and B they'd chosen for their wedding night, Lisa rolled over on the bed, yawned, and stared a long way up at her brand-new husband. Dressed and wide awake, Mike held out a cup of coffee.

Ignoring the tempting aroma, she curled into the blankets once more, her lids fluttering closed. Sweet, lighter-than-air kisses brushed her cheek; a heftier one warmed her temple.

"Did I knock you out last night?" Mike teased, a thread of laughter lacing his voice. Lisa smiled to herself. With all the challenges facing them, their compatibility in the bedroom would never be one. "Did who knock out whom?" she mumbled.

"Feisty, huh? Well, scoot over, sleepyhead."

She complied and felt the mattress sink from Mike's added weight. She heard him rattle a newspaper.

"Take a look. We're actually in an article. Mostly about the football angle, but the writer did include a brief story about your family."

Her eyelids sprang open, but Mike's tone was gentle as he continued.

"I'm sorry about that, sweetheart, but maybe it's the last time that will happen. Once and done. Ya know?"

"Let's hope so," she whispered. Unexpectedly, her eyes filled with tears. "Sorry." She reached for a tissue. "Sometimes the grief hits me when I least expect it, and I cry. I'm sorry."

And then she was in his arms. "Don't apologize. You never need to apologize about that. I miss them, too, Lisa."

Her breathing eased, she became calmer, and a minute later, she pulled away from him. "You're the best man in the world for me. I love you so much, Michael Brennan."

He winked at her, a jack-o-lantern grin on his face. "Good."

"And I think my aunts and uncles feel more confident, too. And their gifts?" She whistled long and low. "I never expected such generosity."

"They love you and want to help."

"I know they want to help Grace and Robbie's children."

"Nothing wrong with that."

"I wish there was no reason to help." Tears dribbled on her face, and she rubbed them away impatiently. "God, I'm such a waterfall."

"Don't worry about it. It's going to take time to feel normal again—whatever normal is. And if a wedding doesn't bring on the emotions, then nothing will."

"For a guy, you're pretty understanding." Now, she had the pleasure of watching him blush, the ruddy hue making him look even more delectable.

"Hey, I'm a macho man," he protested with a grin. "Just ask anybody in the NFL."

He gave the newspaper to her. "I'll probably be in print a few more times during training camp. Every position is important, but everyone has an opinion about their quarterbacks, even a second-stringer like me—and it's not always complimentary. So prepare yourself."

"Phooey! What do they know? You're doing really well. I enjoyed meeting the coaches yesterday, despite their obvious desire to meet me…or should I say, look me over. But that's okay," she said quickly, cutting off his protests. "I know they have a vested interest in you. Professional sports is all about the money."

He looked startled. "For the owners, sure. It's big business. But despite everything, for me, it's all about the game and the team and, most important, the fans. Right now, it seems to be going well. I can't complain, so I won't."

Which meant the coaches were taking note of his talent. His drive. His tenacity. "Every time you come home from practice, you're more excited."

"I've dreamed about the NFL my whole life."

Of course he had. He'd shared those dreams with her as soon as he was sure she wouldn't laugh.

She nestled against him on the bed. "I'll have to start another scrapbook. The current one is bursting."

Mike grinned, suddenly lifting her into his arms and twirling her around the room. "We're heading into a great year, Lis. I forecast touchdowns ahead, in the game and at home. I'll try hard not to let you down."

"Let me down?" she repeated with incredulity. "That's impossible. Not you, Mike. Never you."

#

Training Camp.

At the end of July 2009, a week after the wedding, Mike Brennan and his teammates gathered at Revere Stadium to prove what they could do. They wore their red-and-white short-sleeve practice uniforms for fun in the sun. Boot camp, NFL style. Talking the talk wouldn't do it. Only walking the walk would.

Mike trotted from the locker room to the field and headed directly toward Nick Russo, the QB coach. Easy to find, Nick dressed all in white—his personal affectation—and seemed to glow. "Luke Skywalker with a growth spurt," some of the guys joked last year.

The top of Russo's head was even with Mike's nose, a fact that made the coach happy. "If my quarterbacks are taller than I am," he'd say, "then they'll be able to see over their linemen to find their receivers." Little things, like height, made the man happy, but nothing made him happier than winning.

Mike was graced with the tall gene, the ideal 225 pounds, and the passion. The coaches wanted all three and then some more. He meant to give it to them. Russo and he were both young and had a lot to prove. The coach worked with surety, building a rapport and instilling confidence in his quarterbacks. He expected results. Mike had no problem with that. He had no problem with the heat, the humidity, or the fact that he, like the other eighty players, had just one month to make the cut. At the end of August, after four preseason games, the official roster would number fifty-three. He'd bust his ass to be on that list.

"Your work's cut out for you," the coach greeted him while shaking hands.

Mike nodded. "A batch of new receivers. I know. They swarmed me in the locker room. We'll see what they can do."

The coach chuckled. "You're the QB."

And the players vied for the QB's attention. "I'm just the second backup, but I hear you."

Nick's glance pierced him. "You'll work like you're the starter."

"Absolutely," replied Mike, surprised at the comment to *him*. "I always do." He maintained a quiet, firm tone.

The coach's visual exam traveled from Mike's head to his toes and back up, stopping at his eyes. The man's intensity was palpable. "This is my career, too, Brennan. If you do well, I do well. Hear me?"

"I'm on the field for every play, even if it's only up here," Mike replied, pointing at his forehead. "I'm always thinking about what I would do and when I would do it."

Russo listened, nodded, then asked, "So, how's the wife? Are you in town yet?"

Surprise and guilt stabbed Mike. His words popped out. "Who knew moving could be so complicated? But it'll get done. Don't worry."

"You're not driving back to the country tonight, are you?" The coach's tone suggested a trip to another planet.

Mike shook his head. "Nope. I'm flopping at my old place—it's mine for a few more days. Lisa understands."

"You can stay with me if you need to. No problem."

"Thanks, but we're moving next week." It was reassuring to know, however, that the coach had his back. An alternative to a hotel would eliminate an extra expense. Of course, if he was lucky, he wouldn't be concerned about expenses soon. He'd just heard that the Riders' starting quarterback, Vince Shepherd, was getting a hefty one-point-five mil with another three mil in a signing and other bonuses covering the next two years. One day…one day…

In the meantime, his new family was moving to Charlestown, a working man's neighborhood in the northern part of the city. The area had gone through a face-lift some years back, and they were lucky to have gotten a year-to-year lease on one of the red-brick row houses. He wasn't ready to buy yet in case he got traded or was made a free agent. Their rental offered three large bedrooms, a big kitchen, and with quality public schools in the area, Lisa thought Charlestown would be a good spot for the kids.

Everything was falling into place just as he'd envisioned. "So far, so good," he muttered behind the wheel on his way to the apartment.

Until the next crisis. Lisa's voice echoed in his head.

Not to worry, sweetheart. Team Brennan will make it work.

CHAPTER EIGHT

"I guess we each have a job to do," said Lisa on the phone that evening. "But I miss you."

"It's mutual, baby."

Lisa glanced around the cluttered kitchen. "The place looks like we've had a break-in. Stuff is strewn everywhere. Cartons are half-full. Every time I want to donate something to the thrift shop, one of the kids pulls it out of the giveaway bag. I'm afraid we'll be moving everything to Boston."

"It doesn't matter. It'll be easier on them if they take what they want."

She sighed. "There won't be enough room in the new house."

"Stop worrying. The place is only temporary anyway. If I make the cut—and I'm counting on that—and have a multi-year contract, we'll buy a big house with plenty of room in a great neighborhood. No more renting."

He sounded confident, sure of the future, while she counted on nothing. Guarantees didn't exist.

"Talk to me, baby," Mike cajoled. "How are you doing?"

His voice caressed her, so warm and intimate he could have been standing next to her, holding her, loving her. Unexpectedly, her lips quivered, her throat hurt, and she burst into tears.

"I'm sorry. I'm sorry. Cleaning out their bedroom was…was just awful. Oh, Mike, if the Ladies Auxiliary hadn't helped me today, I'd be a total basket case. Mom's dresses. Her blouses. Every time I touched one, I could smell her perfume. The fragrance lingers… We were all crying, all her friends… And I chose to keep several items. Finally, the ladies kicked me out of the room."

"Sounds like a good thing."

"Maybe, but your mother was crying, too." Lisa sniffed into a tissue. "She's…she's been okay lately. Maybe the wedding turned her around." Irene's heart needed to be made of stone for her not to have grieved again that day. As for the future? Lisa had no idea what to expect.

"I'm so sorry not to be there with you."

"I know," she whispered.

"Maybe I could talk to my coach…"

For a moment, she hoped…but then said, "No. You need to focus on your job."

She heard him sigh with relief and knew her response had been the correct one. The only one.

"Thanks, honey. I really do need to focus—and perform. Everyone's watching. The team needs a strong QB line to back up Vince Shepherd. The press is giving us a lot of coverage. I can't afford to screw up. *My job has to come first.*"

She listened, she heard. All her assumptions were confirmed. Residual doubts began to clear. Michael Brennan was not simply the boy across the street. He was not simply her new husband and brother-in-law to her siblings. When he used the word *job*, he was *not* referring to a new graduate's nine-to-five management training position. He was talking about a talented quarterback in the NFL, where huge amounts of money were invested and where millions of people would be watching him every single time he took to the field. There was nothing simple about it, and he'd made his position clear: his primary responsibility would be to the team.

"I get it," she said. "I've understood for a while now."

"Lis?"

"Yes?"

"Do you really understand the possibilities? If I have a good year, life will be a lot easier for everyone."

It always came down to money. "Don't worry about it, Mike. You're doing enough. Play the game and just stay safe. I'll be teaching again in Boston and will cover the children's expenses. They're my responsibility anyway. We'll manage fine."

"Damn it, Lis. Don't split hairs about the kids. We're in this together and raising them together, so stop worrying."

But worrying was something she did well now. Sure, she wanted Mike's emotional support, his problem-solving skills, his partnership—for herself. The children, however, were hers to feed, clothe, and provide for. Just like her mother had. Grace had used her paycheck for food and clothing while their dad had picked up the mortgage and utilities. The kids' needs— and they had plenty—must not interfere with Mike's growing career. Wasn't that Irene's real message on that walk they'd taken after Mike bought the car?

She hung up the phone and, with renewed determination, continued to attack the kitchen on

Hawthorne Street. Mike had called her the quarterback at home, and she was. Her players and her field might be different, but the object of the game was identical: leading her team to the end zone.

Tenants would be moving into the Delaney house on September first. With option to buy. The place had to be ready for them, and it would be.

"Lisa…Lisa! We can't move." Emily's voice.

For God's sake, what now? She pivoted and turned her attention to the child who was flying toward her, with Andy and Brian following like a miniature posse.

"Well, if you don't pack your stuff, we'll never get out of here," she began.

"Emily's wacky," said Brian. "She thinks—"

"We can't leave," interrupted Emily, ignoring her brother. "We can't leave, Lisa, because…because…Mommy and Daddy won't know where to find us."

Sucker-punched. No breath. A blank mind. Why did the kids always ambush her when she was least prepared? She ignored the packing, the new tenants, even her husband, except to wish she had a playbook as big as his to handle every home situation. The boys' eyes narrowed as they looked at Emily, definitely skeptical about her proclamation, but with just enough doubt to reveal they weren't a hundred percent sure she was "wacky."

"Of course Mom and Dad will know," said Lisa, somehow managing to infuse assurance into her voice. "In Heaven, they know everything." Simple was was good, she thought, and besides, she couldn't think up anything else."Oooh," whispered Emily. "Like God. And Santa."

"That's just about right." Weak with relief, Lisa sagged against the table just as Emily threw herself into her arms.

"You know everything, too," the child said. "I love you, Lisa."

"And I love you…and you…and you…" Lisa said, shifting Emily to one hip and hooking her brothers around their necks with her free arm. "And Jen, also. Where is she?"

"Right here," said the teen.

Lisa turned to the doorway. Her sister stood quietly, eyes red-rimmed, complexion blotched. Lisa sucked in a breath. Jen usually did not keep emotions bottled up. But Lisa should have realized by now that when the important questions stirred the air, Jen wasn't far behind her siblings.

"You heard?"

"They asked me first. Of course, the question is ridiculous, but I didn't know what to tell them," Jen replied. "Their questions are never, ever easy. Who gave them such brains? I'm the one who really wants to move to Boston, so I was going to brush them off with a simple answer. But then I got to thinking…we were so happy here in *this* house…"

More tears rolled down the teen's face. Lisa inhaled, lowered Emily to the floor, and hugged Jen. This sister was a young girl, too. She'd started counseling sessions—they'd all started—but sessions weren't magic bullets. Healing took time. Jen was still grieving, trying to push the pain away while still clinging to a happy but elusive past. Now, Lisa's job was to move them all forward, to get their buy-in once more. They simply couldn't go backwards. She looked from one to the other.

"I cry, too. Just like Jen and you and you and you," she said, pointing to each sibling. "It's okay to cry." She slowed her delivery. "And it's true, we were happy here. But *were* is the key word." She gestured over her shoulder to indicate the past. "Understand?" she asked the younger ones. "Our lives aren't the same now. We voted to stay together, right?"

They all nodded, every one of them. "And that's the most important thing," Andy said.

Lisa took another deep breath, her nerve endings raw. "Does everyone still feel that way?" It seemed she took the temperature of the family every week.

"Yes. Yes. Yes." She turned to Jen, who hadn't replied. "Are you not sure, sweetheart?" She took a breath. "I'm going to ask you again before we make the move. Would you rather be somewhere else, like at Aunt Pat's or Aunt Sally's?"

Her sister's complexion paled. "I knew it! You don't want me, do you?"

"Don't be an ass! Of course I want you. We all do." Being "wanted" had become Jen's theme recently. Was that part of being a self-centered, self-conscious teenager? Or were her friends still acting aloof?

Only the ticking of the clock permeated the silence. Jen's sobs came next. Her whole body shuddered. "Lisa, Lisa!" She blindly reached out, and Lisa grabbed her around. "Sometimes, I feel lost. I really, really want Mommy. That's who I want."

So do I. And Daddy. Lisa was trembling as hard as her sister, trembling from head to foot. "You're not lost, Jen. I've got you. I'm holding you tight."

She motioned the little ones over. "Family hug. We need a family hug right now." Small arms and larger arms, five sets intertwined around each other, pressing with a force that gratified Lisa.

Brian spoke up next. "We went to family court so we could stay together. So, why's everybody crying? We're staying together."

"We thought that staying together was what Mom and Dad would want us to do," said Jennifer in a stronger voice.

The others nodded.

"Okay, then," the teen continued, "let's stick with the game plan. We're the Delaneys, and we're sticking together."

"Exactly," said Lisa, relieved at Jen's recovery. "Get packing. And write in your journals. I find it helps getting through the hardest times."

Crisis averted—this time. But if she had to handle a family meltdown every day, she'd never be able to go the distance.

#

August 1, 2009
Dear Mom and Dad,

We moved into our new home today. It's almost midnight, and I should be exhausted. But I can't sleep. Mike's down for the count, fast asleep next to me. Training camp started three days ago, and sleep is his new best friend.

Leaving Woodhaven was hard. Gail, Sandy, and I ate lunch together on our front porch and watched the movers dismantle our house—we took almost everything. But when my friends had to return to work, we all had a tough time holding back the tears. We've been friends forever, but deep inside, I know nothing will be the same. Gail said they'd call and visit so often I'd get sick of them. As if.

You provided a happy home in Woodhaven, but if I look backwards, I'll be no good for the kids. Sandy and Gail said I was "amazing." Ha! They don't know how unsure I am inside. I tried to smile and joke with them as another piece of normalcy disappeared.

"What's a hundred miles?" I said. "It's nothing! You can even come in for a day."

"Maybe for shopping..."

"Or a football game…" Gail's eyes gleamed. "Jason would love that." Have I mentioned that Gail and Jason are now engaged?

"I'll see what I can do about tickets," I said. "I might have a connection."

Light and easy was working, but then they had to leave.

"Don't you dare say good-bye," I said "Just say see you soon. Because…because I don't know what I'd do without you both."

We hugged so tightly my hands hurt. And then they were gone.

I'm lucky to have such great friends, but logistics count. Sandy and Gail will continue their lives in familiar surroundings while I explore new territory— meet new people, establish new routines, run a big household, and start a new job in a new school with new colleagues.

Overwhelmed at her own words, she wanted to hide under the covers. Sometimes, it was all too much. Just too much.

You can do anything you set your mind to, my college girl!

She grasped the notebook tightly. A talisman. Her dad's voice seemed so real she listened for more but heard only the sound of Mike's gentle snoring.

She continued to write. *For a moment, Daddy, I thought you were here with me. But thank you for that memory. I won't let you down.*

CHAPTER NINE

The call from his agent came five days before the final cut to fifty-three.

When Mike saw the familiar name on his phone's readout after dinner, he stepped out to the backyard, away from the family, and braced himself for whatever happened. His intuition sensed good news; common sense warned not to assume.

"Hey, Scott. Tell me something good."

The man chuckled before speaking. "Those two-a-days seemed to work. Quote: Mike Brennan is a rookie with talent. He's got the mental qualities and character qualities to be a solid player. He's also got leadership qualities necessary in a quarterback. End quote. In other words, Michael Brennan, we've got an offer to consider."

Lisa joined him outside just then. He gave her a thumbs-up, and her shining eyes and sweet smile reminded him of the other Lisa, the Lisa he'd known before the accident. He turned the phone's speaker on and put his arm around his wife.

"Let's hear it."

"The offer's three-point-five mil over four years, guaranteed, plus a mil in incentives and other bonuses. Oh…and have I mentioned that you're now the first backup to Vince Shepherd? You made quite an impression in the preseason games. Your work ethic coupled with all those other qualities was noted. Congratulations."

Lisa's jaw dropped, and even he couldn't speak immediately. Respect. He'd earned the respect of his coaches and, hopefully, the other players. It didn't get better than that.

"Does it sound like a fair, competitive offer to you, Scott?"

"I always want more, but it is competitive. Stay healthy, and next time around, who knows? The sky's the limit."

He caught Lisa's eye and whispered, "I'm taking it." Into the phone, he said, "Done deal. Get the contract drawn up, and I'll sign. And Scott…thanks."

"You're welcome, but hell…I love this job! Love negotiations, and love my players. I've got your back. Don't you forget it."

Mike couldn't suppress a wry grin. "I won't forget you've got a percentage of my gross, either. But it works."

"Damn straight it works. What's good for you is good for me. Sleep tight." And he disconnected.

He picked up Lisa and twirled her around as if she weighed nothing. "Let's celebrate," he said. "All our worries are over."

"You've got to be kidding," she said as he lowered her to the ground. "You think all our worries are over?"

"Can you show a little more enthusiasm?" he asked. "C'mon, let's go tell the kids, and then I'll call my folks."

They reentered the house to find the children gathered in the kitchen, their expressions curious and eager. They must have picked up on the vibes.

Mike grinned and jogged around the room, arms overhead, Rocky style. "We did it," he said. "We're under a four-year contract to the Boston Riders. Backup QB to Vince Shepherd."

"Not we," said Lisa. "You did it."

"But it was our dream," said Mike.

"Who cares?" asked Brian. "Just wow, wow, and wow. My bro plays for the Boston Riders! Can we tell our friends?"

Lisa jumped in. "Have you made some friends in the new school yet?"

Brian shrugged. "I'm not sure." He turned to his brother. "Have we made any friends?"

Andy didn't respond immediately. "It's only been a week, and they all know each other from before. But they'll see about Mike in the papers, anyway."

"But they won't know you're Mike's family unless you tell them," said Jennifer. "And I don't think you should. I'm not saying a word to anyone."

The twins looked at her in astonishment. "Why not? It's fun and important."

"Hmm…let's just say that high school is a complicated place. I can already see that, so I'm keeping myself to myself."

Lisa caught Mike's eye and raised her brow. "Get it?"

"Oh, I get it, all right." Their financial problems were probably behind them, but Lisa wasn't happy unless she had something to worry about. The ghosts and goblins waiting to trip them in the dark.

He punched in the familiar number. "I'm calling my folks. Let them pass the word in Woodhaven, and the whole town can celebrate. *Someone* should have a party."

\#

September 15, 2009—nine months after we lost you
Dear Mom and Dad,
Good news and bad news. First, the good: we can pay the bills now that Mike has a wonderful contract with the Riders. But he's been talking again about buying a big new house next year, with bedrooms for everyone and a man-cave for him, and an office for me. I couldn't care less. The house we're renting is good enough. Actually not any bigger than our house in Woodhaven. But Jen is thrilled. She really wants her own bedroom. I think a bigger house would just be more to clean and take care of. But I'll worry about that later.

Mike thinks I should re-enroll in grad school. I'm happy he has my back, but I told him law school won't work now. The curriculum is a bear, definitely full-time studying, and I don't have that kind of time or energy. At some point, I will return. A dream deferred...as the poet said. But my dream won't dry up or explode. I'll get there, I promise you.

So here's the bad news: I overheard a conversation between the boys a few days ago. They were in their bedroom, sprawled on the floor with their special writing notebooks I gave them. I happened to pass by their door when I heard my name and naturally stopped to listen.

"Why does Lisa make us do this?" asked Brian. "She must like to write."

"She thinks it's therapeutic." Andy sighed. "I hate that word. This writing is harder than writing for school."

"Here—just write what I write: Dear Mom and Dad, We're in Boston. Andy and I are fine. Love, Brian.

"Okay. I can write fast. Here's mine. At least we've got something for Lisa. 'Cause she's gonna ask."

"Wait a sec. Yours is different from mine. You wrote, Dear Mom and Dad, Brian and I are not fine. Love, Andy."

I didn't know what to do, what to say. But I was about to walk in and wing it when Andy started speaking again.

"You know what, Bri? Sometimes I get big stomachaches."

"Yeah. Me, too. And…and here's a secret," he said, lowering his voice. "Lisa's our sister and everything, and Mike's great, but it's not really like having Mom and Dad."

That's when I cried and ran away. I ran away from two beautiful little boys who were breaking my heart. And Mike thinks our problems are over! If I fail with the children, then I've failed at everything that matters. Even my dream career takes last place.

I'll try not to let you down.

Love, Lisa

P.S. About Mike—Except for bruises and aches, he's walking on air. He works hard and doesn't brag. His playbook is huge. How in the world can he memorize more than two hundred different plays? His week is totally football even though he hasn't played in an official game yet. I'll get used to it, and of course, off-season will be better. He's good at distracting the kids, but I can't let him be distracted.

\#

"He's living his dream, but watching my son out there makes me ill." Irene Brennan covered her eyes while Lisa peered at the field from their box seats at Revere Stadium. "I've been a nervous wreck for ten years now. A quarterback's involved in every single play, and he might get hurt."

No kidding.

All of New England was enjoying ideal football weather on this October Sunday. Crisp temperature, but still warm enough. The trees sported their blazing autumn foliage—reds, oranges, yellows blending together and providing a picture-perfect setting for the game.

The noise from the crowd escalated as Mike caught the snap and released the ball hard and fast straight into the hands of his receiver, who took off like a shot into the end zone. Touchdown! Jennifer and the twins screamed nonstop, Emily covered her ears, and Mike's dad stared at the field, a wide smile making the man look younger.

"You can peek now," said William. "He's fine."

"They call him 'Cannon Arm,'" Brian added, grinning at Mike's mom. "He's the best."

"There's more to being the best than playing football," said Irene with a wink for the boy. "But I think he's the best, too."

Irene seemed to have come to terms with her son's marriage, or at least didn't let her disappointment show in front of the children. Good enough for Lisa, who pointed at the field.

"We couldn't have known Mike would be the starting QB so quickly. Vince Shepherd's calf injury will keep him out for a couple of weeks. Tom Knight, the head coach, is spending a lot of time with Mike. And Nick Russo is tied to his hip." As she well knew.

"I try not to, but I worry about injuries," said Irene. "You just never know..."

"I hear you." Lisa had spoken to the kids about giving Mike his space, not jumping on him as soon as he came home. After a full training day of improving muscle strength and aerobic conditioning, he needed to rest.

They didn't get it, and their disappointment rocked her. "It's not fair! He's our brother now. We can so talk to him anytime we want." Andy's dismay left him breathless, and Lisa had to remind him to inhale. Then Brian had thrown a book against the wall. "Mike said we're his kids! He said it. Said he loves us. Why doesn't he want to talk to us?"

"Of course he loves you," Lisa refuted, "and wants to spend time. But here's the thing. He needs his beauty sleep so he's alert the next day." She smiled, tried to take it down a notch. "You guys don't want him to get hurt, do you? When the season's over, you can have him twenty-four seven. Things will be normal again." *Whatever normal was.* "You can still have a catch with him if he has time. Just don't bother him with your problems."

"We don't have any problems. Do we, Andy?"

"Nope. Race ya…" They were gone upstairs in a flash, their conversations to be continued in private. She'd glanced at Emily.

"Mike loves all of us, sweetie. And that's the truth."

Her sister's smile had crept slowly across her face. "I know," Emily said with confidence, "and I love him, too." From then on, however, when Mike arrived home, the child first asked if he'd gotten hurt that day before chatting about little-girl happenings.

Lisa hated herself for being the bad guy. The worrier. The nagger. Before her world had turned upside down, she'd never lost sleep about the danger and injuries common to players.

In the stadium, Andy was comforting Irene. "Mike won't get hurt, Aunt Irene," said the boy, using the courtesy title they'd all decided on. He patted the woman's arm. "Even you said he's the best. He's strong. He's focused!" He grinned at Lisa as he used his new vocabulary word. "Now that we leave him alone mostly."

"What do you mean…?"

"Well, that makes it unanimous," interrupted Lisa with purpose. "We all think he's terrific."

"But we don't see him so much," said Brian, "'cause he has to study videos and do drills and work out with the team and...and everything."

Andy squinted up at the adults. "He's the leader. He has to do everything right so the team will trust him."

"How did you get so smart, young man?" asked William.

Lisa's heart soared. "They are, aren't they?" Her pride echoed in her voice. She pulled them close, one on each side. "They're my boys!"

"And look at you," said Mike's dad. "Just like Gracie."

Oh, my. She'd had no warning. Her heart stopped mid-flight before regaining its rhythm. "Thank you, William, thank you so much. That's the best compliment anyone could give me."

The boys squirmed, and she kissed each one quickly before letting go, amazed at the unfamiliar wave of love coursing through her. Different from her usual affection. *They're my boys!* Maybe it had been growing. Growing slowly. That special connection between parent and child. For the first time since the accident, she felt more like their mom than sister.

#

When the halftime show began, the Brennan bench started to fill up with visitors. Several players' wives introduced themselves, some with their children in tow, wanting to make plans to get together with Lisa, to get to know her and welcome her to Boston.

"Thanks," she responded. "I'll see what I can do. I work full time myself."

"You are busy! Maybe in the evening then…you know, a girls' night out."

Sure. Before or after she cooked dinner, checked the kids' homework, or prepared her own lesson plans? But she smiled and said nothing. After all, she, too, was part of the sorority of football wives, the team was ahead, and a good mood prevailed. She wouldn't spoil it. The hard truth didn't matter much to Lisa. She'd had no time to participate in sponsored wives' activities and no time for cultivating new friendships.

Her visitors said their good-byes, and unexpectedly, Lisa felt Irene's hand squeeze hers. "The Riders have a bye week in the middle of November. How about you, Mike, and the children spend the weekend with us?"

For the second time that day, Irene seemed to be supportive without an ulterior motive. A picture of rural Woodhaven floated through Lisa's mind. A familiar place with familiar people. A touchstone. Her hometown. The phone calls to and from her friends didn't come close to a personal visit. She missed Sandy and Gail, missed them a lot. She nodded at Mike's mother. "Yes. I'd like that, Irene. Thank you."

#

Two days after the game, Emily returned from school, dropped her backpack on a kitchen chair, and announced, "I did what you said, Lisa. Today I started over, like it was the first day of school. No more daydreaming. And I didn't cry all day. Now Ms. Sullivan won't call you anymore."

"That's my girl! I'm proud of you, Em." Lisa and Emily's teacher were on a first-name basis now. That's what phone calls from a concerned adult could do.

The first day of the new school had been tough. The three-story building, walkable from home, was larger than the one in Woodhaven and confusing for new students.

They'd dropped off the twins at their classroom first. Lisa had insisted the boys remain together this year because of all they'd been through. But Emily wanted to stay with her brothers. Fortunately, the grandmotherly fifth grade teacher, Mrs. Cohen, took time to greet the boys and Emily personally. Took time to shake their hands. Her warm smile reassured them, and Lisa understood exactly why her sister wanted to remain.

"Your classroom is directly under theirs. See, Emily? The boys are in Room 302, and you're in Room 202, right beneath them."

She watched her little sister make mental notes—the staircase number, the room numbers, memorizing the landmarks. And when they met Ms. Sullivan, Lisa thought they'd lucked out twice.

"Look, Lisa. She's got long hair like you except blonde. She's pretty. And she's smiling."

"Third grade is going to be wonderful."

Except Em had cried as soon as Lisa left, and had paid no attention to the work. She'd read her own books, drawn pictures, and ignored the "baby arithmetic" on the board.

After Ms. Sullivan's first phone call to the house, Emily had shrugged, closed her eyes, and whispered, "Daydreaming makes me happier than doing boring work. And I draw lots of things. Butterflies…and flowers, and…Mommy, and…and songs. I sing inside my head, like we used to sing at home. And I draw pictures of Heaven."

Her words had Lisa blinking back tears and pulling Emily onto her lap. "I know you miss Mommy—we all do—but you still have to do your schoolwork or you won't learn anything, and if you don't learn anything, you'll be in third grade again next year. Mommy wouldn't be too happy about that. And neither would Daddy."

"But, Lisa," she whispered, "I don't like third grade. Everybody reads out loud and it's so slow. The number work is too easy. I'm like Jen. I like numbers. I don't want to go to third grade. It's more fun to draw like when I'm with Dr. Julie. She lets me do anything I want."

They'd transferred to Dr. Julie Rosen as soon as they'd moved to the city. Lisa didn't want too much time to elapse in their counseling sessions because of the move.

"Well, Dr. Julie's trying to help you. Help us, I should say. She's trying to show us how to…to smile again. Understand, Emily?"

"I-I don't know. But I like going to Dr. Julie every week. I like playing with her dolls and clay and paints. She has huge paper, as big as…as wallpaper. It's a lot more fun than school."

In the kitchen, Lisa took out a carton of milk. With no crying that day, she hoped the phone calls from Emily's teacher would end. She had to believe they were making progress as a family whether Em understood it or not. She was only eight now.

"Snacks and homework, guys."

"The sun's still out," said Brian. "Can't we play outside for a while?"

Better to work off their energy outside than have a lot of noise and cartwheels inside. "You've got one hour, and no arguments later. And stay near the house. Don't leave our street." The sound of her own voice made her wince. Always giving orders. Do this. Do that. She wasn't merely their sister anymore.

When the twins clattered upstairs to change their clothes, she turned toward Emily. "Did you finish your lunch today?"

"Hmm…?

Lisa studied her sister and saw the faraway look in her eyes. "Earth to Emily. Earth to Emily. Come in, Em."

First came the giggle. "I hear you, but…" The child swiveled toward Lisa, joy and excitement emanating from every pore. "I have a secret."

Lisa sat down, trying to ready herself for anything, telling herself that eight-year-olds didn't have big secrets. "Want to share it?"

Emily nodded hard. "I talked to Mommy today."

Oh, God.

"And she talked back to me.

CHAPTER TEN

Not many issues took priority over Mike's efforts on the field during the season. That night, however, Lisa didn't care how many videos Mike had to study, she couldn't keep Emily's revelations to herself. When the house was quiet, she left her own prep work for the next day's history classes on the dining room table and joined him in the living room.

"Can you pause it, Mike?"

His eyebrows rose; he waited a few seconds and complied. "What's up?"

"It's Emily." She filled him in and prayed he'd have an idea.

"You want me to talk to her?"

"What would you say?"

Shrugging, he replied, "Don't know. I'd go with my gut. See what she says, how she looks, try to figure out what she doesn't say. You know—I'd do what I always do. Observe and follow my instincts."

Her nails dug into her palms. Maybe Mike's way was what they needed. But maybe he'd be caught off guard and blow it. She preferred a more measured approach, planning for all possibilities.

"What's your schedule tomorrow night? Maybe we can both have sort of a casual chat with her and see what's up."

He reached for her hand. "Easy, baby. I'll be home by six. Let's do it."

But he didn't get home at six. Or seven. Lisa checked the time every five minutes as she went about the usual evening routines until Jen looked up from her homework and called her a jumping jack. Lisa didn't mind. Her teenage sister was maturing before her eyes. In Woodhaven, Jen had wanted to be with friends half the time. In Boston, she seemed content to stay home. Hmm…and maybe help Lisa stand guard over the family…?

"How was your day, Jen? Everything okay?"

Jen emitted a chuckle. "You're always asking that. I suppose it's because something's always going wrong with one of us. But I'm fine. And next year will be better, 'cause I'll be in college. All the students will be new."

"Absolutely. I'm sorry your senior year isn't as special as it should be. It's got to be hard trying to find friends this late in the game."

Jen shrugged it off. "I don't care so much anymore. My mind's on the goal. I've got to get this high school diploma, and then the next part of my life will begin." Her mouth twisted, her skin blotched. "I-I want them to be proud of me, too."

Lisa's breath caught in her throat as her sister's vulnerability lay open and raw. Jen had confided in her, trusted her. Lisa stroked the girl's cheek. "They'd be so proud of you now, honey, Dad's buttons would pop."

The teen remained quiet for a moment. "Lisa…I'm going to fill out college applications this month. What if

I don't get any scholarships? Where are we getting the money for college?"

Lisa squeezed Jen's hand. "We'll find it, Jen. You can live at home if you're admitted to one of the Boston schools. And with some loans and work-study programs, it will work out. I did it, and you can too."

Jen didn't look convinced. "But if it doesn't work out, if I can't get enough—and you know these schools are more expensive than Woodhaven State—do you think maybe Mike would chip in?"

Just what she didn't want. And how did this evening, which was supposed to be about Emily, morph into a Jennifer time? Sighing, Lisa had to agree with Jen's comment: there was always something going on with one of them.

"As Mom would say, 'Let's not borrow trouble.'"

She checked the time again. Emily's turn would come tomorrow. Hopefully. If Mike ever got himself home when he promised.

#

He was doing the best he could, considering the season was on! Every day of the week led up to game day, and every day of the week was important. Whether it was stretching, lifting, or aerobic activities, he couldn't skimp on any of them. Drills, drills, and more drills. The team that won was often the team in better condition. Then add group meetings, analyzing videos of opposing team plays, reviewing their own playbook, taking apart the opponents' skills and discovering flaws. Not a minute went to waste, but Lisa didn't get it. Maybe she didn't believe it. And that puzzled him. She used to understand everything about the game, including what went on behind the scenes. Maybe she didn't care anymore.

But tonight, he'd be home on time. As promised. And after this big pow-wow about Emily, he'd watch the NY Jets' latest game. He'd be flying to New York on Saturday to play them in the Meadowlands on Sunday. He needed to be ready.

He pulled into the garage and let himself into the hall near the kitchen. A delicious aroma had him salivating. The table was being set by the boys, while Lisa, Jen, and Emily were doing things at the counter.

He blinked. And for a moment, he was a hundred miles away, a lifetime ago. Back in Grace's kitchen, everyone busy, everyone chatting. Family time.

"Hi, family."

And then they were on him. The boys, Emily, a wave from Jen. And Lisa's smile, those violet eyes warm and…relieved. The picture in his mind's eye shifted. This was Lisa's kitchen, not Grace's. He had to remember that.

Jen glanced at the clock. "You lose, Lis."

"Shush."

But Jen grinned and kept talking. "She bet me you wouldn't be home on time. But I knew you would."

He studied his wife. "You bet against me?"

"You were late yesterday," said Lisa. "But I'm glad you're here now. So, let's get started."

A conversation to be continued. She didn't believe he had her back. Or that he rarely made the same mistake twice. She should know better. He washed his hands and sat in his usual seat, across from Lisa, at the head of the table. On this night, his gaze paused on each person, each one quiet now, looking at him. Waiting. For what? He wasn't Robbie. Couldn't sing, couldn't tell stories. Didn't know how to be Robbie Delaney if he tried. But…he led a fifty-three-person team. A warmth glided through him as he took in the tableau.

"Who wants to say grace?"

"Me!" Emily jumped to her feet and plopped back down.

"We see you, Em," said Mike, enjoying a wholehearted chuckle. "And we hear you." Lisa's mouth hung open. Her baby sister, who barely spoke at the beginning, had surprised her.

"Thank you, God, for our food," began Emily. "And for blessing Mommy and Daddy in Heaven, and Mike and Lisa, and God bless Jen and Andy and Brian. And God Bless Ms. Merriweather, who lets me talk to Mommy. Just like this."

Without a moment's hesitation, she stood next to her chair, closed her eyes, and began singing "Amazing Grace" right through two verses before saying, "Amen."

Mike's eyes sought Lisa's, but she stared at her sister, her expression grave. Around the table, he heard sniffles, saw tears.

"That was beautiful, Emily," said Mike. "You're a real Delaney. But I think our food's a bit cold. So everyone, it's time to dig in."

The sounds of family noise took over. Maybe a bit loud at first, but then settling into a norm. Mike sighed with relief. Classic interception.

#

"So tell us more about Ms. Merriweather," said Mike, jiggling the child on his lap. Lisa sat on the blue sofa they'd brought from home, trying to seem relaxed for Emily's sake. But she pressed her lips together to keep them from trembling, a familiar habit he'd recently observed.

The boys were helping Jen clean the kitchen, and he'd suggested that they take their time. Jen's eyes had narrowed, but she glanced at her two sisters and nodded, promising to keep the boys busy. She'd caught on quickly, and Mike had given her a thumbs-up.

And now he and Lisa were alone with Emily. "Is Ms. Merriweather taking over from Ms. Sullivan?" he asked. An innocent icebreaker.

"Oh, no," said Emily. "Ms. Merri is a music teacher. She said to call her Ms. Merri. It's a word joke, and it's so funny." Her eyes shone as she relayed the classroom event, and Mike wished she could be as happy every day.

"So I smiled at her, and she smiled at me." Emily's version might take three hours, but if he prodded, Lisa would kill him.

"And then what happened?" asked Lisa.

Ah-h. He had an ally.

Emily jumped from Mike's lap, eyes wide. "Ms. Merri had a violin. And she put it here," she said, touching her chin, "and played it. And you know what? The whole room was filled with music. Beautiful music." Emily twirled around the room, stopped, tilted her head, and pretended to play the instrument.

"I knew so many songs like from *The Sound of Music*. Remember, we watched it a thousand times? Hmm…maybe not you, but Mommy and I watched it a thousand times." She hummed "Do-Re-Mi." "And I was Ms. Merri's conductor, like in an orchestra." She waved her arms in time to her song.

"Today was the best day in school so far. And then…and then…" she leaned toward them and whispered, "it happened."

Watching Emily rivaled watching a stage play. Except Em wasn't acting. She was feeling it. Feeling every word she spoke and remembered. "What happened, Em?"

"'Amazing Grace'! Mommy's song. Ms. Merri played Mommy's song even though Mommy told Daddy not to be silly, and it wasn't her song. But he said, 'Gracie, you're amazing!' And…and I almost couldn't breathe. Ms. Merri couldn't see me because her eyes were closed, and the bow kept moving across the strings."

Emily darted to her sister and jumped onto Lisa's lap. Mike joined them on the sofa. "You did a great job, Emily. That was a big story to tell."

The child peeked up at him. "I think Ms. Merri was following her heart. She closed her eyes and followed her heart. And…and then I walked to her and sang with her violin. To the very last word, just like I sang with Mommy."

She patted Lisa's cheek. "Mommy was talking to me, Lisa, and I talked back to her."

Twisting in Lisa's arms, she looked at Mike. "I told Ms. Merri that I wanted to play the violin with her, and she said I could. Other kids, too. I brought home a paper about it."

"Is she giving violin lessons?" he asked.

"Uh-huh. In school. Do we have enough money for that? 'Cause I want to play Mommy's song and talk to her. Just Mommy and me. Don't you think the music floats all the way to Heaven?"

He'd majored in the sciences in college, could explain string vibrations and sound waves and distance traveled. But had never measured or considered measuring the number and length of sound waves needed to reach the place called Heaven.

"I think," he said slowly, "that anything is possible." He glanced at Lisa, raised his brow. "Including an extra visit to Dr. Julie."

A hundred visits if it helped. Not that he felt magnanimous, but Em's issues were beyond him. And if his wife were honest, they were beyond Lisa, too. Each one of them, he was starting to understand, had to deal with the unthinkable. Now he saw the effects in real life, not theory. For the rest of their days on earth, each child's story would begin with: *My parents died when I was seven. My parents died when I was nine. Sixteen. Twenty-two.*

He studied Lisa and Emily, gazed toward the kitchen and pictured Jen, Andy, and Brian. Beautiful people. Horrific tragedy. He'd do what he could for them, but for the first time, he wondered if he were up to the job.

CHAPTER ELEVEN

One week after their successful game in Jersey, the Riders lost to the Houston Texans in front of a cheering Texas crowd. More than Mike's body ached. He'd been the starter, and he blamed himself for the loss. A close game—six points. Just one stinking touchdown difference. Why hadn't he released the ball sooner? He needed to trust his wide receivers to be there for the catch. They'd never say it, but maybe the guys were glad Vince Shepherd would be back next week as starter.

After a late flight, he stood in the kitchen doorway, watching his wife scribble on a pad, columns of figures marching down the page.

She was at it again. Her damn budgets. He earned more than enough for all of them. Why didn't she get it? Maybe because he'd lost the game today? His gut twisted. "What's the balance this time? Do we eat tomorrow?"

"Mike!" Her face lit up, and some of his tension dissolved. "You're home. I'm sorry about the game." She came over and kissed him.

"Hmm…this is just what I need…plus a sandwich." He gently rocked her in his arms, his libido roaring to life. Until he walked toward the table and picked up the pad. "You don't need a line-item budget anymore. My money is your money." Except she'd insisted on separate checking accounts. Glancing at her exasperated expression, he knew she wasn't buying it.

"Every family needs a budget," she said, "and our family is no exception. I just laid out a fifty-dollar security deposit for Emily's violin. Fortunately, it's returnable as long as there's no damage to the instrument. Plus there's a twenty-five-dollar monthly rental charge. You talk like there's a never-ending supply of money, and that's not true." She walked to the fridge and started pulling out packages. "Bologna sandwich? Or chicken drumsticks?"

"Chicken's good. And I'm glad about the violin. Emily needs it." He picked up Lisa's pad and saw the sums for Social Security orphans benefits for the four kids, and Lisa's salary. "Put all this in the bank. Save it. Earn interest."

"No," she said, adding some lettuce and tomato to the plate. "We're using that money for general household expenses. You're paying the rent and utilities, and you bought us a car. You're not responsible for the kids' costs, too. I am."

"Damn it, Lisa! You sound like a broken record. You don't have to worry anymore. Haven't I provided for us? Money's not a problem now."

"That's not the point. You're doing more than your share. I have to do mine. Food, clothes…and…elective —"

"Enough!" he interrupted. He'd never recognized her stubborn side before. She was a terrier. Maybe a bulldog. "I'm not *asking* you. I'm *telling* you—be smart and invest the money."

Dead silence. Stony silence.

He'd blown it. He understood that the second she jumped from her seat, before she raised her chin and stared into his eyes. "You *don't* tell me what to do, Michael Brennan. You ask. I'm not one of your teammates looking to you for every play."

What did the team have to do with anything? He was just trying to put her fears to rest.

"In football," he said softly, "we all have the same goal and work together. We should be doing that here, at home, but we're not. You and I are not on the same page with major stuff. Hell, we're not even using the same playbook."

He took his plate and headed for some late-night TV, vowing never to mention finances to Lisa again.

"What major stuff? What are you talking about?"

Her voice stopped him mid-stride. He placed his dish carefully on the coffee table and turned. "How can you not understand? You're so into being a family, but you toss me aside every damn time I want to help. I love you, Lisa, and I'm happy to help out. Don't make money an issue between us. If we're truly a family, then my money is your money. One checkbook pays the bills. That's how it works."

"Not in my family. Separate checkbooks, separate responsibility for assorted bills." She peered up at him. "What else? Are there other items on your complaint list?"

He'd been holding back, trying to give her time and space. But he couldn't turn down an opening. "We need to have fun again." He held up his hand in a stop motion. "I know, I know, we're not like typical young marrieds…but the point is, we *are* young. Twenty-three. Don't you think we're entitled to…to have a social life? Party a little?"

Her eyes couldn't open wider, her complexion as white as a sheet. "My parents are dead in the ground, and you want to party?"

"The first anniversary is coming up. One year. I give you that. But, Lisa, we can't bring them back, and I want us to have a normal life. As close to normal as possible. And that means having friends and fun. I want us to go house hunting together after the season. Boston's our home now, so let's really become part of it."

Tears flowed down her face, and he felt like a heel. "I'm struggling to get through each day," she said, "and I don't even know what fun means anymore." Her hoarse voice hinted at silent sobs. "The thought of another move exhausts me. And I-I…you…oh, God…I'm afraid you married the wrong woman. And I should have stayed back home."

His stomach tightened. He stepped toward her and cupped her cheeks. "You're my one and only, Lis. I'll love you no matter what."

"Maybe," she said, her head tilted back so she met his gaze. "But is marriage supposed to be a roller-coaster ride?"

How the hell would he know? "I've never been married before," he said with a shrug, "but I understand the first year's the hardest for every couple."

"We're no ordinary couple." She deftly pushed his hands away from her and turned toward the stairs. "Enjoy your sandwich. Good night."

#

Lisa ran up the one flight and into the bathroom. She grabbed a towel and clutched it against her stomach. The butterflies inside began their familiar tarantella, and she forced herself to take some deep breaths. She couldn't remember her parents ever fighting. She always pictured them laughing or chatting, no stress. Her aunts and uncles also seemed relaxed and happy.

Now she wondered if marriage to Mike would be one more problem added to her list. As if the kids weren't enough. The sports pages were filled with Mike Brennan stories, all positive accounts. Was he buying into it? Was that why he wanted the big house, the big social life?

One day at a time. One day at a time. Her mantra with the kids had held her steady so far. If no crisis arose in a twenty-four-hour period, she gave thanks. But she hadn't counted on husband issues shaking her fragile balance.

#

"Let's go, Jen!" Mike raised his voice as he waited for his young sister-in-law at the front door. "If we don't leave, the creeping crud will get us."

"I'm coming," came a faint reply.

But Jen took over a minute to finally appear, duffel bag in tow. "I wish we were all going."

"So do I, but not with all that coughing and fever."

The three younger kids were sick and in bed with Lisa supervising. He and Jen were off to Woodhaven for the weekend during the Riders' bye week. Mike had been looking forward to a little family time, but now he also wanted to escape the germs living in his house.

Jen gave an exaggerated shudder. "The twins have a hundred and two. Get us outta here. How could the Riders survive if you were sick? Even though Vince Shepard's starting again, you still have to be his number one backup."

Mike chuckled as they got into his old Camaro. "Keeping track of the team? Well, thanks for your support."

"Anytime."

That was her last word for ten minutes. But as Mike covered the miles on the Mass Pike, he felt Jennifer's glance. A troubled glance.

"What's wrong, kiddo?"

"Nothing."

Right. Teenagers gave him a headache. Especially the female gender. But he'd learned a bit about Jen since he and Lisa had gotten married. And now, he just waited.

"I think I'm a little excited about going back," she finally said. "And a little scared. It's my first time since…you know."

"Since we moved to Boston?"

"Yes."

"For me, too."

"It's different for you. You don't have a reason to be nervous."

Poor kid. He reached over and squeezed her shoulder. "It'll be okay. My mom and dad are looking forward to having us visit. So, don't worry."

But the kid's smile was forced. She wasn't concerned about his folks, so he probed. "I bet your friends will be glad to see you again."

"Maybe…if I can find them."

Just as he'd suspected. She'd had issues with Stephanie and some other friends before the move to Boston. He'd bet she didn't even know their plans.

"I suppose you called some of them before we left?" he asked.

"Yes. Stephanie. But it was almost like talking to a stranger. Just like before we moved. I just *know* she doesn't want me. And she's so close to Mary Beth…

They're happy I'm gone because"—her voice hitched—
"then they can forget about everything that happened
and feel safe again. Now, I'm just a girl they used to
know."

A girl who was more perceptive than most adults.
Surely more perceptive than he'd ever been at that age.

"Let's give Mary Beth the benefit of the doubt. It's
Friday night. Where do you think they are?"

"Steph said she didn't know their plans for sure." A
grin slowly marched across her face. "But I'd guess in
the stands—if it's a home game."

"How about we drive to the high school, stroll
around until you find your friends, then see what you
want to do. If we can't find them, we'll just go to my
folks' house."

She seemed to brighten. "Deal."

But the field was dark when they arrived, and Mike
made a U-turn and headed out. "Sorry, Jen."

"It's okay." But her voice trembled. "We tried. I'll
just call around in the morning."

"'Atta girl. I'm proud of you, Jennifer Delaney."
Whew! The life of a teenage girl was hard.

He pulled in front of the Brennan home, cut the
engine, and began opening his door. Glancing at his
passenger, he realized Jen hadn't moved. She sat
immobile, eyes wide open and head turned, staring
across Hawthorne Street, staring at the house she'd left
only a few months ago.

To his horror, tears started to cascade down her
cheeks. He'd prefer a 102-degree fever. He tapped the
horn, and she jumped. "C'mon, Jen." He nodded toward
his parents, who now stood in the doorway.

"Leave me alone!" she cried. "What do you know
about anything? You don't understand."

Definitely a coward, he pushed his door open, stood
with one foot on the street, one still in the car, and called

to his mother. "Could you grab a coat and come on over?"

"I don't want your mother," Jen shouted. "I want mine!"

He ducked back into the car. "I know, honey. I know."

"And I'm never coming back here again, and you can't make me." She crossed her arms and stayed where she was.

He needed Lisa. "You're tougher than a whole football team, Jennifer Delaney," he began, trying to soothe. "I've got fifty guys who jump to attention when I talk, but you…fuhgeddaboutit." Babble, babble, babble.

Thank goodness his mom had arrived. With frantic motions, he pantomimed tears on his face before Irene pulled Jen's door open. "I'm so glad to see you." The older woman leaned inside and touched her head to Jen's. "I've been waiting all evening for you to get here, honey, because I've got a project for us to do that you're going to love."

Mike watched in disbelief as Jennifer wrapped her arms around his mother. A shiver ran through him. Had Lisa been right after all? Had they taken on more than they could handle?

#

Thanksgiving 2009
Dear Mom and Dad,
We're in Maine with both aunts, uncles, and all the cousins. The kids are having a ball. You'd be so proud of how hard Emily practices her violin. "Twinkle, Twinkle, Little Star" is outstanding! Money well spent so far.

The Riders are in Indianapolis, so we watched the game on television. Mike started in the second half. His passing yardage is phenomenal. He says he barely hears the crowds when he's on the field. The sports writers say he's tough, prepared, and smart. He is smart…about football.

Lisa sat on the bed in the "dormitory"—the large attic bedroom her aunt had turned over to the five Delaneys for the weekend. Alone by choice, away from the tumult, she had automatically reached for her journal, the one her mom had started. Thanksgiving was a family time, a ladies-in-the-kitchen time. The football game had been a welcome distraction for her and, she suspected, for everyone. Their cheers could have been heard for miles when the Riders won the game.

She glanced at the gold ring on her left hand, a solid piece with diamond-shaped facets. Mike wore a matching one, but not when he played ball. Nothing could interfere with his sense of touch, with his skin directly against the football.

I look around this family gathering, and I miss you so much. Despite all the noise and conversation, the game and cheers, we are incomplete without you. There's a hole in the family, a hole in the house—even in this house that isn't ours. In my daily life, I'm too busy to cry. But during the quiet moments, inside the cracks of time, the yearning for you overwhelms me still.

Everyone says the first year is the hardest. If they're referring to marriage, they're right. Recently, Mike and I… Well, it's been rocky. If they mean coping with loss, they're right again. Not to mention a first full-time job. First time running a household. First time for the family living in a big city. A lot of firsts this year. A lot of adjustments. I often want to hide away.

Her memory teased her—those exciting days as a grad student in the heart of Beantown and her ordinary life back then. She planned to meet with her advisor and reenter the law program next fall. Her detour would finally end, and she'd be back on track.

She put her pen down and reread her words, the fingers of her left hand drumming on the notebook. Under the dull ceiling light, her wedding band lacked its usual luster. She stared at it for a long moment, then raised it to her lips and bestowed a kiss for her phantom husband. Her heart thudded at the description. "Phantom husband" fit Mike perfectly during the season. He seemed to come and go, and she could barely keep track of him. Their normalcy was everyone else's abnormal. Their marriage certainly didn't mimic that of her own parents' marriage, nor, she suspected, Irene and William's relationship, either. Of course, neither of those men had played in the NFL!

She reminded herself that the first year was the hardest. So, next year would be better, especially after she returned to school.

PART II
LOST DAYS

CHAPTER TWELVE

On a warm May evening in 2010, almost a year and a half since the accident, Lisa placed two pizzas in the middle of the kitchen table and waited until everyone had taken a slice. "I have good news and I have bad news," she began.

"No bad news," Jen said immediately, her pizza dropping to her plate. "I don't want any more bad news. Not ever again."

Lisa squeezed Jen's hand. "It's nothing traumatic…just that I met with my grad school advisor today."

"That's so cool," said the teen. "Why'd you scare me like that?"

"I don't even know what you're talking about," said Andy with his mouth full.

"Me, neither." Brian's voice.

"What's an ad…advisor?" asked Emily.

She couldn't win. Lisa rolled her eyes and glanced at Mike, whose shoulders were already shaking. His return glance had them both laughing out loud. It wasn't the first time the kids had innocently set them off, and Lisa had to admit they needed more laughing moments.

"So, here's the deal," she continued, aiming her remarks at Mike and Jen. "The good part is I can go back without losing credits for the one term I've already completed. The bad part is that I have to wait until next spring instead of the fall because of the way courses are scheduled. Classes travel together, so I'd pick up in the second term where I left off."

"Lisa! Do you know what this means?" asked Jen, a wide grin covering her face. "Next year, we'll be students together at Boston University. That is really so cool. Yay, us!"

"I agree," said Mike. "That is very, very cool, Lis. Congratulations."

Despite all the "cool," she wondered at the heat rising to her face. "Thanks. Thanks a lot. I'm disappointed with the delay, but I'm…content. After talking to my advisor, I'm beginning to think that someday, I really will have the initials J.D. after my name." She looked at the boys. "That means *juris doctor*, a doctor of law."

Her advisor, Attorney Eileen Kerry, had been encouraging but realistic. "I'm a wife and mother, too," she'd said. "And the juggling's not easy. You're coping with a lot, but I'll reserve your place in next year's entering class. I'll be available for you at any time. I hate to see a good mind go to waste."

The attorney's compliment had warmed her through and through. When she'd thanked her and said good-bye, the woman hadn't seemed in a hurry for Lisa to go.

"Also think about your current career," she'd added. "Teaching a high school class—and getting results—could be just as challenging, maybe more so, than practicing law."

Teaching? A great career for someone else. She gave her students her total attention, but her heart had been set on becoming an attorney since she was a kid watching courtroom dramas and cheering when justice triumphed.

After the meeting with her advisor, she'd meandered down Commonwealth Avenue in a daze. She'd finally done it. She'd taken the first step—a major step—toward turning her professional goal into a reality. *Mom, I'm going to make you proud of me.*

"Hey, Lisa?" Andy's voice broke into her daydreams.

"Hay is for horses. What?"

"If you went to see your ad-vis-or today, that means you cut school. How come I can't cut school?"

"Because I said so!"

"Ouch." But Mike gave her a thumbs-up and locked onto her brothers. "No cutting school or you're grounded from sports. Forever."

The boys glanced at each other, nodded in silent understanding, and kept eating their pizza.

She turned to Mike. "How do you do that?"

Brian spoke. "We're not pissing him off." He nodded at Mike. "I wanna play real ball when I get to high school, not just at the Y. I wanna play everything. Football, basketball, baseball. So does Andy."

"Yeah. We're not taking any chances."

"But you're not afraid to tick me off? I'm your sister, and I'm the boss!" She wondered if Mike was holding more sway simply through gender or by some type of osmosis. "And by the way," she added, "the correct words are want to, not wanna. I also don't like that other word you used."

They sighed, exaggerated sighs. "You're a girl. You don't understand anything."

A gender issue after all. Or so the boys thought. Mike glanced at the ceiling, whistling tunelessly, and Lisa poked him.

"You'd better clue me in, big He-Man, because I need to know everything that goes on in their heads." It was the least he could do. A discussion wouldn't take too much of his time, especially in the off-season.

"I'd be happy to provide pointers on raising boys," he said. "Or you could ask my mom. She's experienced." He grinned and tousled each boy's hair.

Pointers. About all she could expect. How about some hands-on help supervising homework, getting them ready for baths and bed, putting lunches together in the mornings? He'd never volunteered to take any of it on.

She clenched her jaw, cracked knuckles. Drew a breath. She imagined their custody courtroom scene as they'd waited for the verdict, and buried her frustration. In the end, the kids were hers. The judge had given her the ultimate responsibility. A wise decision. The one time she'd asked Mike to take her place at a teacher's conference, he'd been late, and the boys' teacher had left for the day. His good intentions needed a lot of follow-through. She couldn't count on him to shoulder the work equally on the home front.

"Pointers would be nice."

#

Wednesday, September 23, 2010
The Boston Globe—Sports
BRENNAN IS THE MAN
FOR RIDERS

Mike Brennan is the new starting QB for the Boston Riders it was announced today after 35-year-old Vince

Shepherd's retirement from pro football. The succession came as no surprise after QB Shepherd was slammed to the ground and sustained a third concussion in Sunday's game. Brennan took his place and brought in a win with a bullet pass to Darrell Sommars, who ran the ball to the end zone after the two-minute warning.

Shepherd will recover, but "Enough is enough," he said on Tuesday from his hospital bed. "If I don't kill myself on the field, my wife will do it for me."

The Riders are in good hands. As a backup QB, "Cannon Arm" Brennan has garnered attention as one of the NFL's rising stars. With his arm strength and quick release, his fast feet and smarts, he's both a crowd pleaser and a management pleaser. In his last full game, he threw for 226 yards and completed 19 of 23 passes for a win.

"We're getting real comfortable with him," said Sommars, the wide receiver who caught Brennan's last pass for the winning TD in Sunday's game.

"I'm looking forward to the challenge of leading this team to many victories," said Brennan. "Vince Shepherd has been a great help to me since I was recruited, and I don't want to let him down."

Talented and modest, too.

#

Mike's career had shifted gears, reinforcing his love for and dedication to the game. There was nothing in the world he'd rather do with his life than play in the NFL. Maybe when he was old, say, forty or so, he'd come up with another plan, but for now, at twenty-four, he was in the best place at the best time for making his mark.

At the kitchen table in their Charlestown rental that evening, he began folding the paper, Andy and Brian standing on either side of him.

"Wait! What do they mean by modest?" Andy's nose crinkled as he spoke. "That's a girl's word. We brag about you all the time. Don't we, Bri?"

As usual, the boys' world view put him in a good mood. He leaned back in his chair, ready to riff on the article with them.

Lisa's horrified, "Oh, God. You don't really brag, do you?" made him pause. And listen.

"Remember, we talked about this," she continued, her index finger wagging at the twins. "If you're making new friends only because Mike's your brother-in-law, then you're not making real friends. Dropping his name to impress people is called…well…name-dropping."

Brian shrugged. "It doesn't matter, Lisa. We got each other, so we don't need anybody else, and besides…"

"…we're gonna move again anyway," inserted Andy with a shrug. "So, we'll hafta meet new kids and make new friends in the new school."

If Lisa's complexion got any paler, she'd become a ghost. When she didn't bother to correct the boy's pronunciation, Mike handed the paper to Andy. He needed private time with his wife. "How about you and Brian updating the scrapbook now?"

"Yes, sir!" The boys scrambled upstairs to their room, which housed the "official" record of Mike's career.

Taking charge of Mike's scrapbook was a job the twins had given themselves and took seriously. A healthy diversion for them, something "important" they could do and enjoy at the same time. More significantly, Mike thought it nudged them forward rather than backward into dangerous, emotional territory. Distractions worked to refocus their minds.

He watched Lisa slip papers into the kids' "mailboxes," devised from stiff manila envelopes and labeled with their names. He and Lisa had one, too. He still couldn't decide if his wife's organizational skills were sublime or absurd, but he knew they worked for her. As Lisa had explained, the kids were trained to put all school notices into *her* mailbox, and that was the whole point. He'd vote for anything that made life run more smoothly.

Alone with Lisa now, he saw that "smooth" wasn't on her agenda. He sat back in his chair, knowing he'd need awhile to convince her of the move. Adapting to new ideas had become difficult for her, something he'd learned since their marriage, when he'd had to talk her into that!

"Come on, Lis. Out with it." Her beautiful face— that shadowed face—it got him every time.

"This house is working out fine, and I don't want to move and uproot everyone again. You heard the boys. The kids will have to change schools…and what about Emily's violin…and—"

"This move will be the last. I promise. Emily can continue with Ms. Merri privately. Imagine how much better she'd be with one-on-one lessons."

A gamine smile lightened her face. "Em is good, isn't she? I mean…she started only last year, but even I can hear the maturity she brings to it."

"Even you?" The modest person around here was Lisa. "Honey, you sing like a bird. You've got an ear for music. I'm following your lead with Emily and her violin. I trust your opinion totally in this."

Half a truth. He didn't need Lisa to tell him that the violin meant to Emily what a football meant to him. By fourth grade, he'd thrown that ball with his buddies every day after school. Emily, now in fourth grade, practiced her instrument every day, too, without being prompted.

"We may be young, Lis, but we're not stupid. Owning a house is an investment," he continued. "We'd have a tax write-off. Paying rent indefinitely makes no sense at all." Warming up to his subject, Mike prepared to unload the big guns.

"Isn't that exactly what your folks thought? Isn't that one of the reasons they came to Hawthorne Street? And when you sold it to your tenants last year and paid off the mortgage balance, you still came out ahead. The profit went right into the bank. As it should have."

Her brow furrowed, and she remained quiet. Score one for him. She was listening. At least, her practical side—about ninety percent of her makeup these days— was on the alert. In financial matters, it was a hundred percent.

"There are other reasons, too," he continued, "reasons that make sense. We need more room. Jen's in college now but lives at home. I know, I know." He put up his hand to forestall her protest. "It was her choice to stay, and we didn't push her to a dorm. But she's got no place to study, no privacy here. Sharing a room with Emily is not helping Jen. She's coming home later and later from the college library, and we're both uneasy until she walks through our door."

He watched Lisa pace, rubbing her hands together, twisting her fingers against each other, twisting her wedding band—all her usual nervous mannerisms. His instincts screamed for him to hold her, comfort her. He found himself halfway to his feet but then reclined again. If he cuddled her and sprinkled kisses, she'd accuse him of trying to manipulate her. She'd done it in the past over money issues, like when they'd bought their new bed. He hadn't wanted to stint on a mattress; she thought cheap was good enough. They'd ended the argument having fantastic sex before buying a top-of-the-line mattress, so she might be onto something, but he didn't think so. She just needed to be held.

"And then there's me," he said quietly. She turned sharply, her brows raised. He nodded at her. "Yes, me. I've been wanting a home gym with a treadmill and weight training stations as well as a hot tub."

"What are you talking about? You've got a professional training center at the stadium to use any time, night or day."

"True, but I'm playing complete games now, every week during the season. Football's a tough contact sport. The latest research shows that the effect on a guy's body after playing a single professional game is equal to him being in a car accident."

Her natural color disappeared. Her eyelids fluttered. "A…car…?"

He ran to her. Stupid, stupid choice! He shouldn't have told her. In a moment, he held her in her arms, supporting her entire length and weight. "I'm sorry, Lis, so sorry. I was simply trying to make my point."

"But is it true? Verifiable?" she whispered, "Or are you just trying to get your way?"

Keep your cool. He tamped down his anger, but damn it! She could frustrate him like no one else on earth. He worked hard. He was trying his best to support her. And then she accused him of…of selfishness? Of being a me-first selfish husband. Before their marriage… No, he amended, before the *accident*, she was the sweetest, funniest, happiest…and most trusting woman. They seemed to be working out of different playbooks now.

He led her to their living room and continued to support her as she lay against him on the old blue couch from Hawthorne Street.

"I'm not answering that question, Lis," he said quietly. "You'll have to make up your own mind about my motives and…character, I guess. As far as I'm concerned, I'm the same guy now as the guy you married. The same Mike Brennan from Woodhaven, Massachusetts."

"Is that how you really see it?"

"Yup."

Lisa shook her head, sighed, and didn't meet his eyes. "People change. Circumstances change. The Mike Brennan from Woodhaven was not a starting QB for the NFL. Nor did he live in a big city with four kids and a wife."

"Who he's trying to support as best as possible. In every way possible. Like he promised at the beginning. So give me a break here, Lisa. I am telling you again that this house is too small for us and does not give us any equity. Not one penny. And we need to invest."

Seeming to regain her strength, she pushed against him to a sitting position. "Okay. You've made your point, and I'll admit you make sense." She squeezed his arm. "I'm glad you told me about needing the gym to keep you safer…"

"Don't turn into my mother," he joked. "Let her be the one to worry. Let's you and I try to have fun."

A smile. He got a smile from her.

"So how many bathrooms am I going to have to clean in this…this mansion we're buying?"

He chuckled again, relieved that his instincts were still on target. And that Lisa was still using her rational brain. He knew she'd come around. "You're not cleaning any bathrooms. We'll get a cleaning service. In fact, we'll get one now."

"Oh, no, we won't. I'm not wasting money on something we can do ourselves. Saturday is cleaning day around here."

She sure hadn't married him for his money, or even potential money. In the old days, they'd talked about their dream careers and their challenges. Never about the money they'd earn. She wanted to fight for justice; he wanted to throw a ball. He had the impression she still thought his money was irrelevant, more like a necessary evil, despite the four kids. Well, it wasn't irrelevant anymore.

"I'm the starter now, Lis. If all goes well, my next contract will be higher. Do you understand we have no money problems? We can afford a cleaning service. We can afford to buy a townhouse in the Back Bay or in Beacon Hill," he said, naming the two most expensive neighborhoods in Boston.

"Beacon Hill?" she whispered. "That's for blue bloods, not for working-class people like us."

She made his head spin with her need to find problems. Shifting on the sofa to look directly into her beautiful eyes, he said, "What world are you living in? Blue blood is out! It's all about green these days—the color of money. And our money spends just as easily as anyone else's, even those families living in Beacon Hill."

"I don't know, I don't know..." Her voice trailed away for a moment, her hands restless. She focused on her college graduation photo hanging on the wall. "I can't wrap my mind around that much money. I'm going to law school so I can defend folks who need a voice. Not to live an elegant life."

She was harder to coach than the ten other starting players on his team. But at least the starters hung on to his every word. Lisa resisted every word, always questioning, examining. A lawyer without a degree. He took a deep breath and tried another approach.

"What did you think was going to happen as my career grew?"

She rose from the sofa and began to pace. "Well...I don't know. I guess I didn't think about later on, but you make a good point." She eyeballed him. "I suppose I had a few other things on my mind," she defended herself, "like taking care of four kids and just getting through the day."

"Which you're doing amazingly well," he said calmly, praying for patience.

She crumbled. Instantly. Her lips trembled, her chest heaved, and tears rolled. "Do you really think so?" she squeaked.

He was by her side in a second, his arms around her. "Have I ever lied to you?"

Shaking her head, she whispered, "Bottom line? No."

"With the *kids*, you get an A-plus." He allowed his voice to linger, hoping she'd pick up on what he didn't say. *He* missed her.

"Every single day," she began, "I ask myself what my mom would do, what my dad would advise. I never know if I'm good enough." Her sobs lessened, and she wiped her eyes with her sleeves, exactly like one of the twins would do.

Mike had his answer. Lisa hadn't heard his unspoken question at all. Her head and heart were so focused on her sisters and brothers she had nothing left over for him. Time. Energy. Interest? No wonder he'd been feeling lonely.

Back off. He had to back off or be miserable. Grace and Robert had died less than two years ago. The kids required a lot of attention, both physical and emotional. Sometimes Emily wouldn't let Lisa out of her sight.

And yet…and yet…despite his rationalizations, a sharp pain pierced his gut. He wanted Lisa's attention, too.

Coughing, he stepped away from her, squared his shoulders, and inhaled slowly, deeply.

"I'm calling a Realtor to start the search, and we'll move when the school year ends. By that time, I hope you'll be able to wrap your mind around *our* life—yours and mine."

CHAPTER THIRTEEN

"Moving is a great idea." Jennifer grabbed her jacket the next morning and glanced at Lisa. "I would love a room of my own—a quiet place—without an ongoing violin concert, a place with some privacy. School is tough this year, you know?" She leaned down and pecked her sister on the cheek. "Gotta go. Are you coming?"

"I'm right behind you."

Jen rushed out the door. College life suited her. Her sister had made a big deal about Jen's high school graduation and invited all the relatives to celebrate. Everyone had come, which was nice. But Jen had been happy to leave high school behind. She was ready for a fresh start, new friends, and to explore possible careers, preferably those that paid well.

During this first semester at Boston University, Jen and Lisa left the house for school and work at the same time. Mike had the honor of getting the little ones fed and out the door before he went to the stadium. Lisa said it was his most important responsibility with the twins and Em. And his only one. Every other minute he spent with them was fun time.

Jen didn't see it that way, but gut instinct urged her to keep quiet. Aside from the morning rush, the kids and Mike had little time together, so they used it to mess around, toss a football or jump rope, with Emily the "expert" in rope jumping. The younger ones basked in Mike's attention. In Jen's opinion, their time together was more important than Lisa understood.

She was eighteen now. No more social security payments came into the house for her. Legally, she was able to live on her own. But now that she could, she didn't want to leave. Dr. Julie said Jen was "integrating" the pieces of her life, that she recognized she still had a family, just with a different configuration. Whatever.

Forty minutes later, she slipped into a seat at the back of her first class, Creative Writing. Her least favorite subject, the only one she didn't like. She'd wanted to get the two required writing courses out of the way quickly. During the summer, she'd completed Expository Writing. At least, in that course, she'd read some good short stories on which to base her own essays. In this class, everything she wrote had to come from her own brain. Her imagination. She hated the idea, considered it an invasion of privacy. The journal she kept at home was for her eyes only, the way personal writing should be.

She'd quickly figured out that despite using a common prompt for their essays—such as a photo— each student's interpretation revealed part of themselves. The thought gave her hives. She didn't care about her grade at all, as long as she passed the damn course.

Sighing deeply, she raised her eyes to the professor at the front of the room, wishing she were in her accounting course or calculus class or economics or…or…anything else. Her finance program pulled at her as strongly as the force of gravity.

As though he'd read her mind, the instructor said, "There are no grades on the essays I'm returning to you because they are the first you've written this semester. Most of them contain plenty of suggestions in the margins. In red!"

Jen groaned along with the rest of the class. No grade. Now each of her future essays would carry more weight, and she'd have to spend real time on them.

"These essays were a warm-up based on personal experience. I've found there are fewer blank minds that way."

Jennifer had to agree. If the prof hadn't suggested a few life topics, she would have stared at an empty page for hours, wondering what to write. She tuned in again.

"I've chosen a few of the best to be read aloud anonymously. Remember, only your code number is on the sheet. No one will read their own work in front of the class."

What a relief. Jen couldn't imagine anything worse than having to reveal herself to a room full of strangers and… Oh. My. God. Someone was reading her essay right now! A smooth tenor who seemed to know where to pause, when to have his voice rise and fall, and how to make each word count. She stared down at her desk, eyes burning, ears burning, wishing she were a million miles away.

The Longest Journey

Most journeys are measured in miles. My longest journey began and ended in the moment my parents died in an auto accident almost two years ago. On that day, I left childhood behind and clawed my way up, up, up to adulthood. At least, I tried to. My older sister wasn't home, and the three younger kids ran to me first on that terrible, life-changing day.

The deep voice continued reading in what became the tomb-like silence of the classroom. Nothing rustled. No one moved, coughed, or whispered. Jen peeped sideways. Every student sat angled toward the speaker, a tall, wiry guy who needed some meat on his bones. The fault made her feel better, for whether he knew it or not, the guy was revealing her soul to the class—and she didn't even know his name.

She identified the concluding sentences:

Although the distance between Woodhaven and Boston is one hundred miles, I measure my journey in light years. The wounds of childhood still bleed, and my journey continues.

She didn't expect the deathly silence afterwards; she didn't expect the outbreak of applause. She wanted to run, run, run. But if she did, everyone would know the story was hers. She clutched the sides of her desk and just breathed. Inhaled. Exhaled. Then she dared a peek at her classmates and recognized the truth. They all knew. She was the only one not clapping or looking around the room to identify the writer. One by one, the glances of the other students rested on her.

She stood and gathered her books together. "So much for anonymity," she said, her voice trembling. "I'll be dropping the course." She headed for the door.

"No! You can't do that." The tenor's voice. His tone hard now, and insistent.

Jen swiveled and stared at the speaker, at the boy who'd dared read her work. Boston University was a top-flight school, filled with bright students, bright minds. But this guy had no authority to speak to her like that.

She glanced toward the professor, who nodded sympathetically and said, "Mr. Collins has said aloud how we all feel. The class will be richer for your presence, but of course, that's up to you." The man glanced at Collins, leaned against his desk, and seemed to be waiting.

"We don't even know your name," said the reader. "I think of you as 'the quiet girl,' the one sitting in the back of the room for two weeks with nothing to say. But I won't think that anymore. You're bursting with things to say, and if you don't, you might explode. You can't leave."

His dark eyes beseeched her, but Jen shook her head. "Sorry. You're wrong, and this class is not for me."

In fact, his reasoning was total bullshit. Jen had a journal at home to write in. She had a logical mind; equations turned her on. Sure, she still cried and wept sometimes, maybe a lot of times, but she hadn't "exploded" in a long time. And didn't plan to. Why had he used that word? Furthermore, she wasn't going to discuss anything with nosy Mr. Collins, especially in front of twenty-five others.

She pressed her lips together and headed for the door.

"I bet the class is a requirement for your degree," called Collins.

She jerked to a stop. He was right. And now, backed into a corner, her insides began to churn like molten lava ready to explode.

#

"I wanted to kill him," Jen said later. "I was shaking. Like I'm shaking now just thinking about it."

In the living room that evening with Jen and Lisa, Mike listened to his young sister-in-law. He watched Jen look down at herself, her arms trembling. The girl stood, then sat, not knowing where to alight.

"Want me to go to class with you?" he offered. "I'll set the guy straight."

Her horrified expression! He worked hard not to laugh. "Kiddo, the guy was making a move. It was a powerful pickup, maybe awkward in front of the class, but he's got the hots for you. That's what this is all about."

Two sets of eyes widened. He glanced at Lisa. "What?"

"Men! Is that the only theory you could come up with? Is it always about sex?"

"With men, yes."

"He's too skinny," offered Jen. "And he's too smart. But he's got eyes darker than midnight, eyes that really pay attention to you, and a speaking voice…oh, my God. He could be an actor, a real actor in a Broadway play." She shook her head, then stared at the ceiling. "When he read my stuff, his pitch, his inflections…reminded me so much of Daddy."

Her voice broke, her chin hit her chest, and Mike knew she was on the verge of a meltdown. In this family, meltdowns happened, less frequently now, but… he was almost used to them.

A rustle of sound caught his attention. Three little people sat crossed-legged on the threshold of the room. Their appearance strengthened his decision to move the family to a larger place, where privacy could be found. But now, the younger children's presence distracted Jen, who looked annoyed.

Brian jumped up before his sister could scold. "I can sound like Daddy, Jen. Remember when we used to eat supper and he did jokes?'" The boy disappeared for a second, then returned with two spoons and gave one to

Andy. The boys held them to their mouths like microphones and made eye contact with their audience:

Brian: "My Gracie is so amazing, she fattened up a turkey one Thanksgiving with corn and chestnuts…I never saw a fatter turkey."

Andy: "So, you had a great Thanksgiving dinner?"

Brian: "Nah. Gracie didn't have the heart to kill it, and now the bird comes back every year for a good meal."

Mike cracked up. He couldn't help himself. The boys had nailed it, and Mike could clearly picture Rob and Grace Delaney at their dinner table, laughing it up while Robbie ran his comedy and captured the audience. To his horror, however, Lisa burst into tears. Jen followed. Then one by one, Emily, Andy, and even Brian, who'd started the whole thing, began crying. The twins had done too good a job.

Unexpectedly, Mike choked up, too, pulled under by the grief around him. His defense was weak today.

#

Monday, December 20, 2010
The Boston Globe—Sports
PLAY-OFFS AHEAD
MIKE BRENNAN BORN TO LEAD

In his first season as QB, Mike Brennan clinched the Riders' position in the play-offs after yesterday's win against the New York Giants.

"He's growing into himself," said Coach Nick Russo, "and we want to keep him centered." The coach grinned. "That would be under center, but no pun intended."

In this writer's opinion, Brennan looked and played like a veteran, not like a typical first-year starter who needs two or three seasons to become an elite NFL quarterback. Brennan is already there. He's a decision-maker who can throw and scramble.

"Mike's confidence is contagious," says Darrell Sommars, wide receiver, whose thirty-five-yard reception scored the final TD of the game. "Before you know it, everyone feels like a winner. Like we can get places as a team."

Excitement is high in Beantown with legions of fans eager to cheer their "Cannon Arm" quarterback and their home team to victory. No one expected a bite at the Super Bowl after the change in quarterbacks early this season, but Brennan made it happen. The new QB's already made history in this town—in his first year.

#

On Monday morning after the game, Mike browsed a copy of *The Boston Globe* while on the plane flying back home. Amazing how the club had gotten copies of the paper so quickly. He didn't question it, he simply enjoyed reading the story.

Just as much, he'd enjoyed the celebration at the hotel last night. For the first time, the very first time, he'd felt like a celebrity. The play-offs rated as big news. The coaches had relaxed for the moment, and the team's owner had offered a gracious toast to the players. A plethora of wives were there, too, beaming smiles at their husbands all night, asking about Lisa.

His wife never went to the away games and hadn't been there last night because of Emily. His parents agreed to babysit for any weekend at all, but the little girl got hysterical at the thought of being separated from Lisa, even with Jennifer promising to stay home.

He was getting tired of Lisa and him not coming first. Tired of explaining to his teammates and seeing them pretend to understand. Maybe some of them did. No one's life was perfect. But he would really have liked Lisa at his side last night. He did enjoy the back-slapping, however, the good feelings that permeated the club, the anticipation they all shared about the play-off game next Sunday. He joked with the men, greeted the wives, all the while thinking about Lisa.

He hoped next week would be different. Whether they won or lost, he wanted his wife to be at the Miami play-off game in two weeks. They'd talk about it tonight, after dinner, if they could find a quiet spot in that small house.

He felt better after stepping into the kitchen after the flight. Across the doorway was a large banner saying *Welcome Home, Hero*, with smiling faces all around. On the table sat his scrapbook with the latest stories already cut and saved. The boys had been busy. A note from Lisa—*special dessert tonight*—which meant she was going to the Italian north end of the city for ricotta pie.

For a moment, all his irritation vanished. His personal home team loved him, supported him. Maybe Lisa wouldn't be averse to going with him to the play-offs. Maybe an extra visit for Emily with Dr. Julie would do the trick, and Lisa would relax and actually enjoy herself. A lot of maybes. Sighing, he reached for the phone and dialed his parents. If he lined up Auntie Irene and Uncle William, as well as Jen, as babysitters, he might stand a good chance of taking his wife out of town.

At seven that evening, Mike looked around the festive and messy kitchen table, loaded with leftover lasagna, eggplant parmigiana, as well as the ricotta pie. Lisa almost apologized for not resisting the homemade meals once she entered the grocery and inhaled the wonderful aromas.

"I wish you'd do it more often," he said, winking. "You work too hard. Now, you look relaxed and so pretty."

She still blushed at compliments, and when she peeked up at him with those eyes, now soft and loving, the last two years disappeared like quicksilver, and he saw the unfettered girl who'd opened the front door to him that first time on Hawthorne Street…was it almost seven years ago?

"Lisa." He breathed her name.

Her blush deepened, and he was filled with satisfaction. The evening ahead looked promising—a commitment to the play-offs was only the beginning.

"About the next game," he began, his attention totally on Lisa.

"The play-offs!" A twin chorus with a lot of young boy chatter——opinions, fortune-telling, and wishful thinking. Mike should have remembered that, in this family, everyone had something to say about everything. He made a chopping motion with his hands, and the kids shut up.

"My folks are set to come so you can go with me to Miami." He paused for a beat. "It's two weeks away. How about it? I've missed you the entire season."

Lisa held up a finger. "I'd love to…but let me think."

Mike felt himself smile. She actually looked eager.

"The Christmas break is next week, and I've got to be back at work on Monday, January third. My resignation's not in effect until the fifteenth. Yay, law school."

"Take a vacation day," he said quickly. "We'll probably fly back on Monday and be here by the time the kids get home from school."

"Hmm…that might work," said Lisa. She looked at her brothers and sisters. "So, you all heard that?"

"No problem," said Jen. "I can take care of them. Your folks don't even have to come, Mike."

"Yeah," said the twins, eyes gleaming. "We'll be good. Right, Jen?"

"Not right," said Lisa. "Irene and William will come, and you'll be on your best behavior. Got it?"

The boys quieted down. But one little girl's frightened voice spoke.

"No, Lisa," said Emily, walking around the table to squeeze onto her sister's lap. "You can't go. What if the plane crashes, and you and Mike go to heaven, too?"

Lisa's eyes widened, her lips thinned. She clutched her little sister and began rocking her. Mike knew where this conversation was going and didn't like it. Maybe another man would have had more patience, maybe another man would have cuddled Emily on his lap at that point and reassured her that all would be well. But Mike couldn't do that. Mike *wouldn't* do that. How could he promise that nothing bad would happen to the plane, or to Lisa or him in any way? They could be robbed at gunpoint simply walking down a street. Who knew what the future held?

He glanced at Lisa. "This is ridiculous. It's been almost two years. Isn't she making any progress?"

"Of course she is," Lisa replied softly, nuzzling Emily. "In fact, I'll ask Dr. Julie about this on Wednesday."

He rose so abruptly his chair crashed to the floor. "Is Dr. Julie in charge of our everyday lives? You're supposed to be the QB at home, Lisa. If you let the weakest player take the lead, you'll be nowhere."

She was on her feet now, too, eyes blazing. "I am responsible for the health and well-being of these children, and that has to come first."

He'd touched a nerve, and it sizzled. But there it was. Spoken out loud, and they'd all heard.

"I've never once asked you to choose," he said. "But this trip is important to me. And it's happening before you go back to school at the end of the month. There's no scheduling conflict."

"No fighting! No fighting!" Emily's cries broke the immediate silence as a watershed sluiced down her piquant face, her cries turning to sobs and her narrow chest beginning to heave. Mike saw it all and, in one smooth motion, tucked the girl under his arm and held her over the sink as she threw up.

Unless he took Emily with them, he'd be going to Miami alone. Damn it.

CHAPTER FOURTEEN

Not without trepidation, Lisa resigned from her teaching position. Giving up her salary bothered her, but she'd husbanded the profits from the sale of her parents' house. Her ability to budget would pull them through with a monthly portion toward household expenses. When she graduated from law school and started her career, she'd more than make up her expenditures with higher earnings—after she repaid her school loans. Now, at the beginning of the spring semester, with excitement strumming through her, Lisa marched up Commonwealth Ave and reentered full-time studies as a law student.

She stopped off to see Eileen Kerry. "Welcome back," said Eileen warmly. They chatted for a moment, and the advisor wished her good luck.

"Thanks. Fortunately, the football season is over. Unfortunately, the Riders lost the play-offs, but at least Mike's more available to be with the kids."

"Well, good. We never talked about your husband when we met. Is he an announcer, a sports writer or…or…something else?"

Lisa crashed to a mental halt. Then her thoughts raced. She was registered under Delaney, but had she truly never mentioned Mike to this woman? And should she now? She hadn't had this issue when she was a student the first time. She and Mike hadn't been married yet, and besides that, Mike had been a no-name ball player right out of school. She could postpone the inevitable with Eileen, but with all the media coverage, the truth would come out eventually.

"Hmm…well, he's definitely part of the Riders organization. Mike Brennan. Delaney is my maiden name."

"Brennan…Brennan. Sounds a bit familiar, but I have to confess," said Eileen, "I don't really follow football and don't read the sports pages. Should I know him?"

A piece of luck. "That's wonderful, Eileen. I mean—I'm here to study and become a lawyer. Not be a celebrity wife. Mike's the quarterback, and I suppose millions of people know his name." She glanced toward the doorway and back at the woman.

"Ah-h. I get it. My lips are sealed, Ms. Delaney."

Lisa leaned against the desk in relief. "Thank you so much! I so appreciate that."

At the end of the day, she was more than grateful about Eileen's ignorance of the game. Her confidence flagged for the first time since she'd made the decision to return to school. She'd forgotten how the coursework had consumed her that first semester. Sure, she had the ability to master the curriculum, but would she have the time it required? Content in the doctrines and rules of torts, property law, contract law, plus participation in moot court would command all her time and energy. She'd have to draft briefs and present oral arguments before a panel of faculty, lawyers, and students.

"So it's a good thing I kept Delaney on my records," she told Mike as they prepared for bed. "I saved you the embarrassment of having a wife who might fail."

"You? Fail? That'll never happen."

She pointed to the stack of books lying on her dresser. "These are only the ones I can carry. I'll need to be in the law library most of the time doing research." Wringing her hands, she said, "Have I made a mistake? There's so much to do right here at home."

"I thought we were partners, Lis. Today ran smoothly here. You'll have to trust me to organize the house. I'll get the kids off to school. I'll train at the stadium, and I'll be home by three o'clock. I'll also hire a cleaning service once a week. Don't worry, it'll all work out."

"A cleaning service? I thought we agreed that Saturdays…" But she'd be studying on the weekends, too.

"The kids have their chores, but heavy cleaning isn't one of them."

Of course, he was right. She reached for his hands, looked into his eyes. "Mike, I'm so scared."

He held her close. "You've been scared before, honey, and survived. Besides, I've got your back." Then he kissed her, and nothing else mattered.

#

A month later, at the end of a cold and dark day, Lisa entered the house after using the law library, and followed the sound of male voices into the kitchen. Six guys and a poker game. Cash lay all over the table; takeout cartons and longnecks sat everywhere. The twins and Emily were still in their school clothes and dirty dishes filled the sink. Was this what Mike meant about "having her back"?

"Uh-oh. Your wife doesn't look happy," said Nate Dixon, who happened to glance up at her arrival. "We'll clean up. Don't worry."

Right. "I'm going to hold you to that." She didn't need this…this disappointment. Looking hard at her siblings, she said, "Get upstairs, undressed, and ready for bed. You've got school tomorrow. Have you done your homework?"

"Yes, yes, and yes, and we're having fun. Why can't we stay and watch poker?"

Because I said so! She refrained, but barely. "Because it's late and you won't get up in the morning. Go. Now!"

Emily went, the boys lingered, muttering about her ruining their fun.

"It's my fault," said Mike. "I lost track of the time." He glanced at his watch. "Nine thirty. It could be worse." He gestured at the twins. "Go on. Your sister's right. The evening's ended for you."

With a lot of mumbling and dragging of their feet, they disappeared. Lisa walked into the living room and collapsed on the sofa, a comfortable old friend. She closed her eyes and let her head fall back on the cushion. Tired. She was bone-weary tired. And she had to work on a writing assignment that night.

The boys were starting to resent her, and Mike seemed to have become another kid, but bigger. A kid who needed friends around him and constant activity. This wasn't the first time his buddies had come to the house. They usually watched football videos and studied other teams. But this was the first poker game, and she'd bet there would be others. She couldn't deny him his friends, but pigs would fly before she'd clean up that God-awful messy kitchen.

Her stomach rumbled. It had been hours since she'd eaten anything, and she was hungry. Against her better judgment, she dragged herself back to the game.

"I don't suppose you saved some dinner for me?" she asked, peering inside the fridge.

"I'm not sure," admitted Mike. "Sorry, Lis. We all just kinda pounced, but the kids got as much as they wanted. Jen, too. I guess I messed up."

You sure did, Michael. You sure did. She reached for the jars of peanut butter and jelly, noting the men about to deal their next hand. "Order some extra next time, will ya?"

But her stomach knotted. She'd become nothing more than an after-thought to her own husband.

#

Gracie and Lisa's Notebook

May 30, 2011—almost two and a half years since we lost you

Dear Mom and Dad,

I've finished another semester of law school! One full year is done. Mike tried his best on the home front, but it was tough. When Emily got sick, she wanted me to stay with her but had to settle for Mike. I hated not being there. In the evenings, Mike had to supervise while I rushed through dinner and cracked the books again. But the semester's over!

I can't figure out if Andy and Brian are turning Mike into a big kid. Or if his teammates are. Or if he's been one all along. Maybe athletes think of life as a big game. They're treated like rock stars in the media and by the public. Mike definitely has a spotlight on him. Maybe I shouldn't be surprised, but I didn't anticipate this distraction. Mike's always been a regular person to me, but I guess we're not living an ordinary life anymore. Someone in this family must hang on to common sense, and that someone is me. No surprise.

The F-word around here is Fun. Mike's bought enough toys and equipment to stock a school. So wasteful. However, I do appreciate his purchase of new winter clothes. The kids outgrow everything so quickly! I guess my disapproval shows because they all tell me to "go with the flow." Big vacations are on the agenda.

What kind of values will your children have as adults if they're indulged so much? This lifestyle has become too real. I want you to be proud of your children now and later. I want to do a good job for you. Mike just wants to make them happy. And now that includes a violin for Emily. He's talking to Ms. Merri about buying one before we move.

I'm glad the younger ones adore Mike, but they still need some mothering, too. I'm also glad summer is here. We all need time together—without a schedule.

#

Gracie and Lisa's Notebook
July 18, 2011—our second anniversary
Mike and I are spending our anniversary unloading cartons in the new house, a four-story brick Tudor in Beacon Hill. Mike loves the place, but it's overwhelming me with so many empty rooms in need of furniture. It's got an elevator inside. Can you imagine that? I agreed that owning a home was the right thing to do, but I think I've fallen down the rabbit hole with Alice.

Despite losing the play-offs last January, Mike's looking forward to the new season. Training camp's just around the corner. He's anxious to get started. I think he'd play for a fraction of what he's earning. Maybe one day, Jen will be ready to give us some financial advice— she is so into her business program! In the meantime,

Mike's money is sitting in a simple savings account. He's been approached by plenty of financial advisors but hasn't found anyone he trusts yet.

He tried to buy a house for his brother and sister-in-law, who are expecting their first child. David was insulted, and the brothers had a heated disagreement, which was very disturbing because those two never fight. In the end, Mike forced a down payment on the couple.

Your younger ones are in Connecticut with Aunt Sally and Uncle Steve this week. Jen and I dropped them off yesterday. Emily wouldn't let me leave, but Aunt Sally managed to distract her. Emily's violin is the key. She still thinks you can hear her playing and that she's talking to you. I say nothing. Who am I to doubt? All I know is that it helps her.

Lisa's hand trembled. She dropped her pen, and in a moment, she was sobbing, her head resting on her arms at the desk in the master bedroom. She didn't often break down anymore, but at this moment, when she was tired and uprooted again, when going through cartons of family items started memories flowing once more, she couldn't hold back the tears.

Mike and I—our second anniversary—but something's not right. We haven't spent much time together this year. Law school interfered a lot. And there's always so much supervising to do with the kids. Everybody needs a piece of me. If I'm with the boys, I should be with Em. If I'm with Em, I should be paying attention to Mike. If I'm with Mike, I should be with the kids. Maybe I should have gone to Miami with him last January, but Emily...

Crying was a good release as long as no one saw her. She took a deep, shuddering breath, then another.

And felt better. Almost as good as she felt after making love with Mike. Hmm…talk about a release. Too bad they communicated better in bed lately than in real life.

I'm doing the best I can, so don't worry. Thankfully, the boys provide comic relief.
Love, Lisa

#

Mike stood in the doorway of the master bedroom in the new house, watching Lisa stow her journal. She'd been crying again. It seemed to him that every time she wrote in the damn notebook, she cried. The therapist encouraged writing. Mike thought it pulled Lisa backwards instead of forwards, but he wasn't a shrink. He could be dead wrong. Maybe she was just tired. Moving days were a lot of work, even with hired professionals to handle the furniture. He stepped into the room.

"I think we've earned a good dinner tonight. How about Mama Rozetti's?"

"Good choice, but I'm too tired and filthy to go anywhere." She looked him up and down, then shook her head. "I don't know how you do it. You're as dirty as I am, worked as hard or harder than I did, but you never get tired."

He grinned. "Clean livin' and good lovin'." He leaned down and kissed her. "Happy anniversary, Lis. Bet you thought I'd forget."

Her blushes always gave her away.

"I wasn't sure with all this turmoil around us. But I'm glad you remembered. How about celebrating here with a pizza or Chinese? I'm hungry. But after I shower, I'm going to sleep."

He and Lisa needed to have a serious talk before he started training camp next week. Staying home that night actually seemed like a good idea.

An hour later, he watched Lisa sit back, replete after dinner. Jen was with them, too, the only Delaney sibling around, but she quickly excused herself and returned to her new suite of rooms on the fourth floor of the townhouse. She'd said it was better than a dorm. Perfect for a college student. He and Lisa agreed about that.

"Training camp starts next week," he began. "Then preseason games in August, and then…well, you know the drill. We need to square away a few things."

"I'm one step ahead of you. I've already left a message with Eileen Kerry that I'm dropping out of school."

"What?" She'd blindsided him. "Wait a minute, Lis. That's a big step, and I have a better idea."

"No housekeepers. I don't want a housekeeper living in."

"Not living in. Someone who's more like a nanny. She'd make the lunches, be here at three o'clock…" His wife wasn't listening, had tuned him out. He clasped her hands. "Talk to me, Lisa. Why not?"

The shadows were back. Those big eyes of hers so expressive in their sadness. "Because hiring a stranger is no substitute for family. If I can't do the job, then maybe the kids would have been better off with my aunts and uncles."

"They would have been split up."

"Nothing's easy, everything's hard," she whispered. "Even when you took over last semester, we had sticky times."

"Sticky times" was actually an understatement. After the first poker game, Lisa had demanded daily reports. She didn't trust him, and he resented it. True, he'd screwed up once or twice. One time, he'd come home late. The kids had gone into the backyard, where the boys found privacy to relieve themselves. When he'd arrived, Emily was crying. He'd been too late to help her, and she'd wet her panties. He'd made each child a set of keys the next day. He wasn't proud of the incident, but…stuff happened. However, he hadn't expected Lisa's decision to leave school. He couldn't allow it to stand.

"Mishaps don't count as long as they're resolved. And I took care of the kids. In the end, they were in good hands. They were happy. Stop being so critical! And stop acting like a martyr."

"A martyr? No. Don't insult me. I'm just doing what I have to do."

"We're *both* doing what we have to do. We're both missing out on what should have been carefree days. Right now, my career sustains us, and…."

"I would have been right up there with you if not for the kids," she interrupted. "Are you saying my own goals mean nothing?"

"No! I promised you when we got married that one day you'd graduate. I meant it then, and I mean it now. So, let's make a deal." *The sooner she got that damn degree, the better.*

She cocked her head, eyes brightening. Good. At least she was listening.

"Let's try a nanny for one semester, no long-term commitments. We'll do the interviewing together. We'll go through a licensed, accredited agency and ask a ton of questions. Let's see how it works. If it doesn't, then I won't say another word if you want to leave school." He spoke quickly, reminding himself of other times when he'd had to come up with ideas and solutions on the spot. Would Lisa give this one a chance?

She licked her lips, looked at the ceiling, then at the floor. She was thinking…and tempted. "All right. We'll try it for one semester."

"That's all I ask." Really, for her sake. Nothing else seemed to make her happy.

"Try what out?" Jen had entered the room.

"A nanny, so Lisa can stay in school. Football season is here."

"A nanny? Not for me!"

"Of course not for you."

"I could take next term off and stay with…"

"No!" Mike and Lisa interrupted simultaneously. "But thanks for the offer."

Lisa stared at Jennifer, and Mike saw the pride his wife had in her younger sister. Lisa's smile, her sparkling eyes, the clear forehead. No furrows or wrinkles.

"You're a wonderful girl, Jen," she said. "You've come far. Mom and Dad would be so proud of you."

At that moment, Mike felt proud of himself. He'd brought Lisa around to his nanny idea, and now he'd go off to training camp with a clear mind. The kids and Lisa would start a new school year, and a nanny would organize everything. Problem solved.

CHAPTER FIFTEEN

After two weeks of employing Tillie Kingsley, Lisa couldn't imagine why she'd ever had any objections to a helper. Reliable, sweet, and energetic, the woman from Jamaica with the lilting accent had after-school snacks ready for the kids and dinner in full preparation each evening. Tillie showed up every day at noon for light housekeeping and laundry. Most important, she was there when the twins and Emily got home.

Mike had installed a nanny-cam system. Totally legal, and totally necessary for Lisa's peace of mind. Mike had had no objections, either, but with Tillie now in the family, they could have saved their money.

By mid-October, Lisa was deep into her second-year curriculum of law school, well into drafting briefs for her Constitutional and Employment Law courses, and working hard in her Juvenile Justice seminar and Juvenile Rights Advocacy course. The work didn't daunt her. In fact, her spirits were high. She could glimpse her goal. If she could get through this second year, then she'd rock on to the third one.

On a glorious autumn evening, she arrived home later than usual to find Tillie still at the house, waiting for her. With one glance, Lisa knew trouble had arrived on their doorstep. The nanny was wringing her hands.

"I'm so sorry, so sorry. My grandmother needs me. She is with the cancer in here." Tillie tapped her chest and coughed to illustrate. Tears streamed down her face, reminding Lisa that the grandmother had raised Tillie. In essence, her nanny was losing a mother.

"I'm so sorry," said Lisa, giving her a hug. "When do you leave?"

"In one day. Tomorrow. I am sorry, too. The children—they are so fine. Good boys and a sweet little girl." Tillie departed amid hugs and promises to write, and Lisa called the agency, requesting another nanny.

"Just bad luck," said Mike that evening. "Stuff happens in people's lives."

"True enough, but does it have to happen all at once? Andy was running a temp earlier, which means Brian is sure to get sick, too."

In the middle of the night, both boys were burning with fever and coughing. Lisa stayed with them, dozed on the floor, and missed school the next day. She took the kids to the doctor and urged Mike to stay at a hotel. He couldn't afford to catch the flu, not in mid-season.

It took two full days before the fever broke. Then Emily felt warm, and the cycle began again with three children at home in bed in different stages of sickness.

In the end, Lisa missed a week of school, including two exams. When she took her makeups, she knew the results wouldn't be up to par. A heavy knot settled in her stomach when she saw her scores. She had failed one of them. For the first time in her life, Lisa Delaney had failed an exam.

The second nanny arrived, and Lisa breathed a sigh of relief. She could vindicate herself at school if she could concentrate only on her courses and allow Tillie's replacement to take over the house.

Brenda Owens knew her way around a kitchen. She could make basic meals taste special. Lisa was delighted.

"Maybe we lucked out twice," she said to Mike as she dug into a shepherd's pie two weeks after Brenda had started working for them. "This is good!"

Mike's hand covered hers, his fingers stroking. "I'm afraid there's a problem, honey, although it's not with the food."

Her appetite vanished. Mike wouldn't kid around about this. "What? What's wrong?"

"I viewed the nanny cam. Two young men have been here, probably her sons, and that's against the rules. I also found cigarette butts on the front step."

The tasty shepherd's pie turned to cardboard in her mouth. "Strangers in the house? Were the kids here?"

"I don't know for sure, but they weren't on camera."

"That's it then," she said. "We can't take a chance. This experiment is over."

"Not so fast. Let's talk to her. Maybe her sons didn't know the rules and just popped by."

"Not likely. Your heart's too soft, Mike. We've got to keep them safe."

"Do you think I'd let anything happen to those kids? I like Brenda, though. I'd like to hear what she has to say."

Lisa shrugged. "She's a mom. She'll cover for her sons."

"She can't deny the camera."

She didn't. But tears pooled and the woman's voice broke. Her boys always asked her for money. "Ten dollars, twenty dollars. I don't even tell them where I work anymore. I'm sorry. I don't know how they found out."

Someone at the agency? But Lisa had no proof.

"We're sorry, too," Mike said. "But we have young children here, and we just can't be worried about this."

Mike reached into his wallet and gave her five twenty-dollar bills. "It'll help until you get your next assignment."

A deep quiet settled over the kitchen after Brenda left the house.

"If I fail another test or miss another deadline," began Lisa, "I'll be put on probation. I need to speak to my advisor." A river of disappointment drenched her, and she began pacing. "I'd rather drop out while still in good standing. With 'good standing,' I could try to go back someday." School could be postponed. The kids' welfare had to come first.

Mike reached for her hand. "Maybe the third try will be the charm."

"I'm not sure…I just can't go through this…this roller-coaster ride again. High hopes and dashed ones. It's too much."

"You've been a powerhouse, Lis. I'm so sorry our deal didn't work out. But I'm not sorry we gave it a try. Are you?"

She had to think about it. "It was always a risk, but now I'm more frustrated than ever. I'd even started counting down the semesters." She rubbed her eyes against incipient tears. "Damn, damn, damn. It could have worked…it just didn't. But now, you won't nag me about housekeepers land nannies. Th-that's a plus." Her voice quivered; her breath hitched. And Mike's lips bestowed kisses along her temple and cheek.

"I'm sorry," he repeated. "I don't know what else to say except this: when graduation day comes and you do receive that diploma, I'll be in the front row cheering the loudest."

Sometimes, her husband could be so sweet. But the excitement was gone. Her little-girl dream, gone. Her professional identity was painfully disappearing. "Thanks," she whispered. "But I'll expect pom-poms with that cheer."

"You bet."

She could feel her smile wobble as she relegated law school to the distant future. Maybe dreams were always defined with "someday."

#

At the beginning of December that year, 2011, the Boston Riders stood at thirteen and one in the AFC. Super Bowl talk was whispered and sometimes spoken aloud—before the speaker was hushed. Superstition permeated professional sports, and Mike never pushed those boundaries.

As usual, the twins had preserved every article about him and the Riders that appeared that season, the whiff of Super Bowl making the task extra special. They'd been throwing a football after school, themselves, and wanted to play on school teams. A bone of contention with Lisa. The sport was too dangerous for her brothers. They were too light, too skinny, too young, too everything. But Mike knew they had good hands, sensitive hands, and were quick to jump, catch, run, and anticipate the ball. Positive traits for the game. Potential talent to work with.

Lisa monitored the kids like a hawk, as if they were two years old. It was nonsense. But ever since dropping out of school again, she'd been acting like a…well, maybe bitch was too strong, but it was close. Maybe she was "displacing" her anger. He grunted at the psychobabble he'd picked up in conversation around the house. Dr. Julie was still part of their lives, but she couldn't undo the nanny experience fiasco.

He left Revere Stadium on an overcast chilly Wednesday after an intense strength training session and a hot shower and headed for his new SUV parked near the entrance. He'd spend the evening watching videos of the Pittsburg Steelers in preparation for Sunday's game. A home game. The whole family was planning to go, Lisa and the kids as well as his folks, who'd come into town the day before. He looked forward to seeing them all under one roof—his roof.

"Hey, Brennan. Wait up."

He watched his wide receiver trot over.

"A bunch of us are going to the north end for a good meal and good talk," said Darrell. "Wanna go?"

He was tempted. Good, hot, Italian food—his culinary weakness—was actually an excellent choice with its blend of carbs and protein. More than that, however, he was tempted by the company. In fact, he'd prefer the company of his teammates that evening.

The thought surprised him, and he nodded at the other man. "I'll call Lisa," he said, reaching for his cell phone.

Sommars' eyes widened and a grin spread across his dark face. "Never thought you'd leave that woman. We're at Mama Rozetti's, and we always have a private room. Know the place?"

Mike nodded. "One of my favorites. See you there." Sommars ran off and Mike punched in his home number and got Emily.

"I'll tell her, Daddy Mike. She's only making spaghetti anyway…"

Daddy Mike?

"Em, can you find her?"

A minute later, Lisa got on.

"I'll bring a couple of lasagnas home for tomorrow," he said, "but what was the Daddy Mike thing all about?"

"Do you really have to ask? Oh…never mind. Forget I said that. I'm not a shrink, but I'll let Ms. Julie know."

"Don't bite my friggin' head off."

"Sorry. It's been one of those days, always something with the kids. I'm trying my best, but I'm not the answer man."

It's not my fault. "See you later." He hung up and started the ignition, glad for the change of company that evening. He preferred the company of an upbeat bunch who thrived on winning, who thrived on possibilities.

An hour later, Mike looked around the table they'd commandeered in the restaurant's back room. He couldn't remember the last time he'd laughed so hard or listened to so many earthy jokes, so much salty language—the kind he tried not to use at home. The F-bomb and Emily certainly didn't mix, and self-monitoring had become habit. But here, the warmth and camaraderie felt natural. He fit right into this fraternity of professional athletes, except that he was the only married player in the room.

Shrugging off the observation, he dug into his meal, sipped his longneck, and jumped into the conversation. About Sunday's game. About women. Finances. Pittsburg. Careers. Women again. The Steelers. Attendance at the stadium. The Steelers again. Not a word about the Super Bowl.

"I like the way you think," Mike said. "The season is played only one game at a time."

"Hell, Brennan. I've heard you say that so often I hear your voice in my sleep."

Mike's grin turned into a laugh, and seven other guys joined in before attacking their meals again.

"We gotta win this one," said a defensive end. "It's a home game, and we'll have eighty thousand people in the stands. Do you want to lose in front of that crowd? Besides, my folks are driving up from Atlanta."

Now, that was commitment. "My folks are coming, too," said Mike, "as well as Lisa, the four kids, my brother and sister-in-law. The only one not coming is my nephew, but he's only a month old."

"That's nice, Mike. Nice that Lisa and the whole family will be there."

Discreet eye contact passed from one man to the other after the last remark. Intuitively, Mike understood his personal life had been a topic of discussion at some point. He shrugged that off, too. If positions had been reversed, he'd wonder why the wife of the starting quarterback attended only some of the home games and none out of town.

He stood and pushed his chair in. "Study those videos tonight. I want to win." Nodding toward the front of the restaurant, he added, "Besides, you owe me. I promised Mama Rozetti I'd say hello to her customers, which means you don't have to!"

Their chuckles followed him through the door as he started his meet-and-greet with the diners. The Riders were a bunch of great guys. He knew they sometimes went out clubbing in the evening, too. He saw nothing wrong with a good meal, music, dancing, a little fun. He should hang around with them more often.

#

The Steelers were kicking their butts. Especially Mike's. If he got sacked one more time… Damn, their defense was all over him like sauce on a pizza. He'd barely caught the snap before they brought him down right in the pocket. Where the hell were his guards? Probably overwhelmed, too.

Pittsburgh had definitely prepared. And Lisa would be covering her eyes. A recent behavior, so different from when they were both in college.

Nerves were showing on his guys. *Keep your head, Brennan. Exploit Pittsburgh's weaknesses.* If ever a team needed a steady leader, the Riders needed him right now. *Turn the game, turn the game around.* And from the recesses of his mind, from his intense study and preparation, an answer came to him. A rarely used play, but worth the risk when trailing by thirteen points and having only six minutes left in the last quarter.

Mike took his place on the line of scrimmage, forty yards from goal. For this particular play, he stood six yards behind center to receive the snap. He signaled his guards for a shotgun offense. If his teammates were surprised, they kept it hidden.

His center hiked the ball. Mike caught it, scanned Pittsburgh's defense, and spotted Sommars, who looked as ready to receive as he'd ever been. Mike threw the ball in a straight line. His wide receiver ran to meet it, jumped, caught it, and drove toward the goal, three Steelers after him, and…crossed into the end zone.

Touchdown! Noise from the stadium surrounded him. Do crowds really go wild? Yes!

The score was now 28-21. Mike's heart burst with hope when the special kicker scored the point after, bringing the score to 28-22. All they needed was one more TD. Six little points to tie the score. With four minutes left in the game, their first job was to stop Pittsburgh from scoring so that the Riders could take possession of the ball again.

Pacing the sidelines now, Mike could only pray for an interception. If the Riders' defense was hot, the ball would be turned over. The Rider guards were taking down the Steelers' QB as many times as Mike had been sacked. Good. No yardage gains. And then…and then…oh, oh…how beautiful! His prayers were about to be answered.

Mike watched Nate Dixon intercept a pass at the Steelers' thirty and move the ball to the Steelers' fourteen before he was tackled. Yes! Yes! He punched the air. They were alive. They owned the ball. And eighty thousand screaming fans knew it. Mike and his offensive line trotted out to the field.

He was filthy, he was hurting, he was euphoric. The oval-shaped ball was an extension of himself. He no longer saw the crowds nor heard their roar. He saw one hundred yards of grass and teammates. Some blocked, some protected him, and others moved in their pass patterns, trying to get free. The Steelers' defense rushed through his line to sack him, and the opposing secondary raced back to cover his receivers.

Not one of his guys was open. His only chance was to squeeze through a hole in the line and run for the goal himself. Zigging and zagging past defenders, he ran toward the side and doubled back toward the middle, eluding defenders until he barreled through their linebacker and fell hard into the end zone. His body hurt. Like hell. Quarterbacks weren't built to take the punishment of a bruising linebacker coming at them full force. He didn't care. He was flying! Elated from tying the score, he now heard the frenzied fans cheering their QB.

Tied score! Then bad luck. The special kicker missed the point after, but good luck followed. The Riders won the coin toss and had the first crack at scoring in overtime. After two minutes of play, they drove the ball far enough downfield to try for a field goal. The kicker kicked, the ball flew between the goal posts, and the game was over. A sudden death victory in overtime. By three little points. It was enough.

Victories were always sweet. But some wins were sweeter than others. For Mike, this was major.

"There's nothing like a hometown victory in front of a great crowd," he said into the microphone later in the press box. "Thanks, Boston, for being with us. And thanks to the entire team. Offense. Defense. Everyone was on top of their game at crunch time. The Steelers were tough opponents!"

The announcers wanted more specifics, but he gave credit to the entire team. He was already thinking about their next game. The Riders now stood at fourteen and one. If they wanted to maintain their position, he had to be prepared for the following week. And the week after that.

Mike waved to the crowd and made his way into the locker room. He'd use the hot tub, get a massage, and be driven home. Lisa and the kids would get there before him. Life was good. And if he needed more treatment for his bruised body, he'd use his own hot tub in the basement gym he'd designed in the new house. Maybe Lisa would join him. He felt himself stir and had to laugh. Some parts of him weren't bruised at all.

He looked forward to going home.

#

Lisa stared at her winning quarterback. Mike's smile might become a permanent motif. Her husband was on top of the world, and Lisa wondered what that felt like. She was job searching again, but her heart wasn't in it. Teaching was definitely second-best for her, which wouldn't be fair to future students. So guilt resided in her gut. But Mike…he was still in the zone, still high from the win despite the bruising he'd taken.

"Congratulations, champ. A good day's work." She kissed him and was twirled around the room.

"The Mistress of Understatement," he joked. "I'll never get a swelled head at home."

The kids had been too excited to sleep, and now the boys rushed him with a babble of talk, rehashing the game and the actions of their hero. Then they each ceremoniously shook his hand. It was a man-to-man moment, and Lisa didn't know whether to laugh or cry. "Lis…" Jen called softly, nodding at Mike and the twins. "See what I mean? It's not always about chores."

Lisa startled. Where did that come from? Jen found it easy to criticize when the bottom line responsibility was someone else's. Her glance landed on Emily, who, despite her best efforts to stay awake, had drifted off on the couch in the family room.

"Hey, hero—do you have enough energy left to carry her upstairs?"

Mike's smile grew. His eyes gleamed. The man lived in a different stratosphere than the rest of them today.

"Come on, boys," he said. "You're going into bed also." He lifted Emily and tucked her in his arms as though she weighed nothing at all. Rousing, she hugged him. "You won! You won. You can do anything."

"For you, princess, I can do anything. Go back to sleep."

She instantly closed her eyes and did fall asleep, as though she were hypnotized. When Mike laid her on the bed, Emily didn't stir. Lisa rarely saw her youngest so relaxed. So content.

As they left the girl's room, Lisa squeezed Mike's arm. "I think you make her feel safe. She never falls asleep so easily, and it's wonderful to see. Thank you."

Could Jen be right about Mike's relationship with the kids? He was not the guardian. But could his influence on the children's development be greater than Lisa had assumed?

"You're welcome, and I hope it's true. But don't give me too much credit. The game ended late, and she could have just been tired."

True enough. But more likely, her husband didn't want the blame if something went wrong next time.

"The kids are settling in bed. Why don't you and I just celebrate?" he asked, leading the way downstairs again.

"Sure." She could do that. "I'm celebrating that the countdown's almost over. Only two more games left in the regular season. We're almost home free from concussions, pulled tendons, and other miscellaneous injuries. I'm happy."

He burst out laughing. "Is that how you measure the season?"

Nodding, she replied, "I'm getting to sound like your mother. Frankly, I'm glad the season's coming to an end."

"You've gotta have more faith than that. I'm fine."

"You just like the fourteen and one standing."

"What I'd really like is if you'd come into the hot tub with me. I could use another soak."

She yawned. Bad timing, but she couldn't help it. "I'm so sorry, Mike. I've got a subbing job tomorrow at my old high school, and I've got to get to work on time, which means early." She saw the disappointment in his expression. "Sorry," she whispered again. She gave him a quick kiss and started for the stairs again.

"Hey, Lisa," he called.

She paused in flight and turned toward him.

"You don't need to work a temp job," said Mike. "In fact, you don't need to work at all. Stay home and kick back a little. And maybe we can begin to have some fun. Remember, we talked about that. Don't you think it's time?"

Maybe he'd talked about it. "Fun? I can't even relate. But I suppose it's a legitimate question from a guy who spends his life playing a game."

His mouth tightened; his complexion got ruddy. "That's not fair…"

But she was more than two years past fair. "I know it's not fair. Of course I wish we could be like any other couple! But we're not. My staying home won't control the grief. It won't make the hard times disappear and guaranty fun, fun, fun. And besides that, I'd go crazy." She gripped the banister and shook her head. "I wish we had only sunny blue skies overhead. But we don't. And you knew that when we got married. I told you it would be hard…and…and I'm so worn out."

"So, what's wrong with taking it easy for a change? Get some extra energy, some extra sleep."

"It's wrong for me. I'm not a lady who lunches or who knows how to decorate this huge house. But I'm also more than the quarterback's wife, more than a substitute mother. I'm smothering beneath those jobs. I am so lost and don't want to be lost. I remind myself that I am Lisa Delaney, and I need a life, too!"

Silence surrounded them, pounded in her ears.

Mike's arm lifted. He pointed at her. "Try out Brennan once in a while. Lisa Brennan. See if it fits. See if you can get used to it. And while you're at it—call the damn decorator and learn something. Make us a home."

He turned and headed for the basement, the hot tub, and she couldn't produce another word. Not one word to call him back.

Not fair. I take care of everyone and protect you. I am making a home. The girl I used to be is disappearing, but I'm doing the best I can. Walking slowly toward the master bedroom, her thoughts whirled, the last one echoing. *I'm doing the best I can.* It had become her refrain. Was it a mantra to relax her or a crutch to lean on?

#

Soaking in the hot tub was exactly what he needed. The irony was that his ego hurt more than his body at the moment. He'd gotten scared about that being lost stuff. But hell, she'd been rough on him.

Lisa *Delaney*. They'd been married two and a half years now, and she still thought of herself as Delaney. He wondered if she hyphenated it with Brennan when she signed her name. In the end, however, it really didn't matter what she wrote on a piece of paper. What mattered was how she thought of herself and how she thought of them as a couple. Of course, she couldn't forget her roots, but without Rob and Grace, and with her marriage to him, her family had changed. She didn't get that. Lisa still saw herself and the kids as one unit. Sometimes, Mike actually felt like an outsider, and it hurt. The six of them needed to blend as a family, with him and Lisa in synch as the parents. The only time he and Lisa were in total accord now was when they made love. Thank God for that. But good sex wasn't enough!

Whoa! He slipped under water as he reached that conclusion. The big picture. He always looked at the big picture. *Team Brennan* was not a team, and that had to change soon. Seemed it was up to him to make it happen.

CHAPTER SIXTEEN

Lisa didn't know why Mike wanted to accompany her to her therapist's office, but she wasn't happy about it. Dr. Julie Rosen had become her safety net. In her office, Lisa could complain, cry, or explode at the fates without having to worry about anyone overhearing—child or husband. In fact, she could be a child herself for a little while. She treasured the sessions, which were only twice a month now, and didn't want to waste a moment. Tonight would be a total waste.

She moved down the corridor at a steady clip, leading the way in the building of psychological specialists. Mike knew how she felt about sharing, but he hadn't backed off about going with her tonight. She'd questioned him.

"After two years, why now? The doc's not going to reveal secrets of the deep." She'd lowered her pitch and imitated a horror film voice-over. "In fact, there's nothing I talk about that you don't know—if you've been paying attention." But she'd felt her skin heat up and turned away quickly to hide the lie. She talked about plenty of stuff Mike couldn't guess at including her anger at her parents' deaths. And hated herself for it.

"I'd like five minutes for the three of us together," Mike had replied. "Is that so difficult? Besides, I simply want to meet the great Dr. Julie."

"Her diplomas are hanging on the wall. You can see them in the waiting room. This is my last session, Mike, and I want every minute of it."

"My timing sucks, I agree. But that's too damn bad. It's important that I go."

He'd respected her privacy until now, and she allowed his intensity to sway her. So here they were, entering Dr. Julie's territory. The woman opened her inside office door and greeted them with a smile.

"I'm happy to meet you, Mr. Brennan." She glanced at Lisa. "Did you need a ride tonight?"

"No. Mike insisted on coming, and I reluctantly agreed. He's never asked before, so something must be on his mind."

"Oh?" Her attention turned fully on Mike.

"There's a lot on my mind, but nothing more important than Lisa. She says she's feeling lost, so I figured we need some kind of road map before we both disappear. She respects you, so I thought I'd tag along."

"Then let's go inside and get comfortable."

Mike would take over if she let him. After they were seated around a plain coffee table, Lisa spoke up. "Mike wants me to stay home and not to have a job, and that's how it started."

"Time out," said Mike, making the familiar T gesture with his hands. He leaned forward in his leather chair. "First of all, I want my wife to be happy, and I want her to feel secure. My goal is for her to think of us as a couple, but she doesn't. She's more loyal to her parents than she is to me. She thinks she's carrying all the responsibility at home, and that I don't understand what she's going through…"

"He doesn't. He thinks he does, but he doesn't," said Lisa.

He glanced at her but continued speaking to the grief counselor. "If I don't understand, it's because she doesn't tell me," he replied. "I'm used to taking charge. I'm the go-to guy on the team, and I should be the same at home. We should be past all the emotions by now. It's been two and a half years. There should be more progress."

"He thinks we're on a timetable!" Lisa cried and swiveled toward him. "It doesn't work that way. How many times have I told you that grieving is a process? Everyone's timeline is different."

"I get it," he conceded, "but could you give me just a little hint? Are we in for five years of this? Ten years? When are you going to be happy again? When do I get the old Lisa back? When will you stand firm with Emily and go to a game out of town?"

He turned toward the counselor. "We have a play-off game this weekend. And if we win, there's one more to go. The play-offs are no small thing. If we get to the big game…damn it. She doesn't have to work."

Lisa shifted toward the shrink. "He thinks the world revolves around him, about what he wants." She stared at Mike. "The 'old' Lisa is gone. Gone forever. I'm not the same girl I was before the accident. No one remains the same after going through such a trauma. But I'm still my parents' daughter. I was taught to work and earn and not be a spendthrift."

His eyes narrowed as he studied her. "I get that. I really do. The problem is…I barely recognize you anymore. You shut me out a majority of the time, and that's what I don't understand." He turned toward the therapist. "I'm crazy about the kids, but for some reason,

I'm not truly hands-on unless Lisa needs me. She doesn't trust me to really be the dad."

The pain on his face! She'd rarely seen that dark misery in his eyes, the tight mouth and jaw. But…

"I trust you, Mike…but not as much as I trust myself. And sometimes, I don't trust myself. So, it's hard. You're more like an older brother. You know, someone who plays with the kids but then turns them over to the parent—the truly responsible one."

"My God," Mike whispered, studying her as if she were lying in a petri dish under a microscope. "You think so little of me."

His complexion had paled; his eyes went blank. Lisa's stomach did its familiar dance. This time, she had no one to blame but herself. "I love you, Mike. But the children…well, raising them is on me. It's my responsibility."

Mike rose from his chair and pivoted toward the door.

"Mr. Brennan, this office is a place where issues are brought up and get aired out."

"I suppose so," he said, turning around. "It's also a place where folks can get blindsided. Isn't it ironic that fifty-three men hang on to every word I say, follow every drill, follow every play without a problem? And one little woman has a hard time trusting me. What does that say about this marriage?" He stepped toward the door.

"Where are you going?" Lisa asked, panic rising. "You can stay."

"I'll be outside. You can talk privately. The way you wanted." He took another step.

"Hang on a moment," said the therapist, writing something down on her pad. She looked from Lisa to Mike. "I'm a grievance counselor, Mr. Brennan. I specialize in helping individuals or families going through the trauma of loss like your wife and her siblings are doing. I'm not a marriage counselor. The issues you're bringing up require someone trained extensively in couples therapy and family counseling. So I've written down some referrals."

"Marriage counseling?" Lisa asked, confused. Their issues were about grief and childcare. The kids came first and took up all her time. But Dr. Julie was looking at her now.

"Considering that tonight's your last session with me, maybe it's time to focus elsewhere in your life."

Lisa couldn't believe it. Dr. Julie was saying she needed a different counselor? If she couldn't continue with Julie, she wouldn't go anywhere.

"Just for the record," Mike said to the psychologist, "why is tonight Lisa's last session with you?"

"It's up to Lisa to share or not."

Lisa avoided his eyes, but telling him wouldn't change the facts.

"Well, Lis?"

"I'm not making much progress anymore," she said quietly. "I've hit a plateau, and I need a break."

"A break? Then where the hell does that leave us?"

#

In the car on the way home, Mike pulled over into a store's parking lot, shut the engine, and snapped on the reading light.

"We need to talk while I'm not driving and before we get home."

"All right. Good idea." Her words were chipper but her mouth trembled.

"I wasn't kidding in her office, Lisa. I'm not willing to live like this until we're old. We need to be a couple, on the same page, at least most of the time."

"You're not even home six months of the year, both mentally and physically. How could we be a real team?"

"Lots of players have families, and they do just fine."

She glared at him.

"I know, I know. They didn't start out like we did. But I'd like Mrs. Brennan to really feel like Mrs. Brennan, not Ms. Delaney. Know what I mean?"

"I actually do, but knowing up here"—she pointed at her temple—"and believing it in here"—she pointed at her heart—"are two different things."

He saw a glimmer of hope and smiled. "That's my girl."

"The children…" she began.

"I was thinking about them, too," he said. "And I have a suggestion." He took a deep breath, hoping she'd agree. So much was at stake. "Would it relieve any pressure on you and make us feel more together if everything were legal with the kids? If I petitioned the court for co-guardianship with you? I've got no problem with that. I love them, too."

Her eyes widened, her mouth opened, but words wouldn't come out. She rubbed her throat.

Jesus, she couldn't get air. "Breathe, baby. Just breathe. We won't talk about it."

Her chest heaved. He heard her suck air, saw her take two big breaths, and then she was fine.

"Don't shock me like that. And for God's sake, don't say a word about that idea to the kids."

So he had her answer. "Why not?"

"It'll only confuse them more. Give me a minute." She closed her eyes and he waited. When she turned toward him, he didn't know what to expect, but he didn't expect to hear her say, "In the end, the legalities don't matter. The kids really belong to Robbie and Grace. I never forget that I'm just their placeholder, trying to do the best I can. For them and for you, too, whether you believe it or not."

He heard her pain. Her mouth quivered, and like a heat-seeking missile, he was there, kissing her softly, nuzzling her. Trying to provide whatever strength he could while he figured her out.

"Placeholder? Now, you're really scaring me. No matter how much you miss them, Lis, your folks are not coming back." What the hell had been accomplished with the grief counselor if his wife was still living in the past or worse?

"I'm not crazy. I know they're gone. But I have to keep them alive for the kids. Emily…sometimes, she calls me Mommy. Pictures of my parents are becoming distant photos to her. Maybe to the boys, too, and that's not right. So, I try to do what my mom and dad would want me to do every time something comes up. And I tell the kids to make Mom and Dad proud."

And she placed an unnecessary burden on everyone. It wasn't fair to the kids or to herself.

"No wonder you're so exhausted," he said. "you're trying to be a mind-reader, and that's impossible. You simply need to be yourself, not an imitation Grace. The kids need two strong parents now, flesh-and-blood parents, who they can go to every day. For better or worse, they have you, and they have me."

Maybe if this issue was resolved, other issues would fall into place. Maybe she wouldn't feel lost anymore. Maybe the Delaney name would become less holy.

"It's a nice theory," Lisa said, "but parenting is twenty-four seven, and you're not around enough. Even when you're home, you're watching videos or calories or working out. Look, Mike, the family court said the kids were my responsibility, my relatives believe it now, and it's getting better. I'm not spoiling what's working."

"But it's not working! You and I…we…aren't working very well." And this conversation wouldn't change that. However, he still had an ace. Dr. Julie had referred them to marriage counseling, and he pulled out the sheet of referrals.

"What about this? I'm willing to go. To work on making a change."

"I told you, I'm taking a break."

He let the paper drop from his fingers and watched it float to the floor of the car. Her response confirmed his greatest fear. He came in last on her agenda. Their marriage didn't warrant her attention. It wasn't important enough.

#

She'd make it up to him by caring for the house. She threw herself into decorating, an activity that would make Mike happy while it made her miserable. She knew nothing about styles—contemporary, traditional, Mediterranean, Colonial, French—a million decisions hinged on the basic choices. Window treatments, art work and wall hangings, floor coverings… She drowned in it all. She interviewed two decorators, each of whom showed up elegantly made-up and dressed in pencil-straight skirts and high heels while Lisa greeted them in a sweater and jeans, her hair clipped at her nape.

The decorators' reactions to the house were identical. Their eyes shone with the challenge of an almost blank canvas. An almost empty house. With an almost unlimited budget—according to Mike. Not according to Lisa. If the costs didn't kill her, her own ignorance would. But…she reminded herself, she was trying to make Mike happy. Not in a million years had she ever thought she'd be researching home décor. She dug into her new project, superficial as it was, knowing it would take a long time.

At the end of the month, Lisa filled the new house with family for their first Christmas in Beacon Hill. The urge to see her aunts and uncles, to hug the men and kiss the women, had been overwhelming, and she'd issued the invites before she could change her mind. They'd get sleeping bags for all the kids and send them upstairs to Jen's "dorm." The bedrooms would go to the adults.

"It will be the first time in three years we'll all be together at the same time," she'd said to Pat and Sally. "And this house is big enough—you'll be comfortable."

Whether she'd touched a chord of guilt or yearning, or mere curiosity, she didn't know. But they all came. Mike's family showed up on Christmas Day, too.

A full house. A new house. Still with the old furniture. But it did the job.

As she scanned the long dining room table, she was at peace for the first time in a long while. The coffee and desserts were almost gone, the adults were catching up with one another, discussing the forthcoming play-offs and the Riders' chance at the Super Bowl. The twins and Emily were happily engrossed with their cousins just as any children would be. She'd made the right decision to hostess this holiday. The kids were reveling in family and familiar songs from the old days. A round of "Row Your Boat," where Emily's name was substituted for Merrily.

"I remember! I remember." The child beamed and started another verse herself. Still petite, Emily looked younger than ten and a half going on eleven. At times, Lisa didn't know if her sister was a true late bloomer or was old beyond her years.

When the round was finished, Emily disappeared with a warning that she'd be right back and don't move. True to her word, she returned with violin in hand and garnered her relatives' attention immediately.

"I've never heard her play," whispered Pat. "After all this time."

"We've heard her play plenty," said Brian, wrinkling his nose.

"Yeah. A lot!" chimed in Andy.

The visitors chuckled but looked at Lisa.

"Two and a half years, all with Ms. Merri," said Lisa. "We were lucky. She loves her teacher as well as the instrument. That's all that matters."

Lisa watched Emily take the violin out of its case, examine it, pluck a string, tighten it. Finally, the girl looked at her audience.

"I worked on this especially for Christmas. I heard Ms. Merri play it on the very first day. It's a present for everybody, but especially for Mommy." She tucked the violin under her chin, raised her bow, and shared her gift.

"Amazing Grace" had never sounded better to Lisa. Never sounded sweeter. Never sounded as beautifully performed as her little sister was performing it right now. Em had certainly improved, and Lisa hadn't really noticed.

Neither had anyone else. Mike looked stunned, as though he'd just been sacked. Jen's eyes could not open any wider. Even the boys were quiet. As for her aunts and uncles…not a dry eye anywhere.

Emily bowed the last note, then held the instrument at her side. No one had moved. "Do you think Mommy liked it?" she whispered.

"Liked it?" roared Uncle Steve. "She loved it."

The applause built to a crescendo, words of encouragement thrown in.

Emily's smile could light Carnegie Hall. "Wanna hear something fun?" she asked, jumping into "Rudolf," then "Frosty" and had everyone singing.

"She's not even using sheet music," whispered Lisa.

Mike nodded. "Sensitive hands. Sensitive heart. Talent. I told you she needs private lessons. I'll pay for them and no arguments."

Lisa hesitated. Mike was spending too much already. She'd love to cut the furniture budget.

"Thank you, Mike, but Emily's lessons will be our treat. We insist." Pat and Ted were beaming at their youngest niece. Lisa sighed with relief. One argument avoided.

"Are you finished yet, Emily?" Brian asked when his sister stopped playing.

Each boy was holding a silver tablespoon. Lisa laughed and pointed it out to Mike. Naturally, the twins would want some attention from their aunts and uncles, too. And they got it after telling a bunch of jokes, talking into their "mics."

"I've got something to share," said Jen, looking at Mike's mom.

Lisa wondered what Irene had to do with this mystery. One thing she knew for sure—if Irene suddenly produced Doug Collins as a surprise Christmas guest, Jen would kill the woman. The guy from her writing class had become part of their dinner conversation whenever Jen was home early enough to eat with the family. With every new installment, Lisa didn't know whether to laugh or cry as she listened to "what that skinny dumb guy had the nerve to say to me." If this was a courtship, as Mike had said, it was certainly a rocky way to begin.

But the front door remained closed as Jen, carrying a large, rectangular box about a foot deep, walked toward Irene. She looked around the room and took a breath so deep Lisa could hear it. Then she tapped the box.

"This is the secret project Aunt Irene and I started about two years ago when I was acting crazy. Going crazy. That was…a very bad time.

"But Mike's mom had this idea…"

She then removed the cover and, with Irene's help, carefully unfolded and unveiled a colorful patchwork quilt of many squares. As more material was revealed, Lisa's eyes filled and words wouldn't come. Couldn't come. She knew those fabrics. But Andy said it first.

"Daddy's ties! You used Dad's ties."

"And Mommy's apron!" exclaimed Emily. "The red-and-white snowflake apron. And her red-and-green Christmas apron, and over there's part of her pink sweater with her name on it."

"Everyone is on this quilt," said Jen. "All of us."

Their dad's ties formed a sunburst around the enlarged photo in the center. There, Grace and Rob smiled at each other on their twentieth anniversary. In the corners were photos of the children. Their names marched across the quilt. Colorful and warm. Exactly descriptive of their family.

Lisa wrapped her arms around her sister. "It's magnificent, Jenny, simply magnificent." She hugged Irene and thanked her. Then she glanced at Mike, noting his somber expression. He smiled when he saw her and approached, but directed his attention to Jen.

"Great job, kiddo. Just don't let it get you down."

A half smile appeared on Jen's face. "I know what you mean, but I…I just had to do this. It felt right."

"Ahh…" Mike's eyes gleamed. "Going with your gut," he stated. "I understand completely. And now…?"

"And now the job is done." Jen glanced toward the relatives, who were crowding around the quilt. "It was a labor of love," she said softly. "But now, it's done."

Closure. The word sprang into Lisa's mind as she listened to her sister. *Grieving is a process, but it's time to move on.* It seemed Jen, who at one time provided Lisa with sleepless nights, had found a measure of peace. Lisa heard it in the younger woman's voice, saw it in the determination of her jutting chin. Jen would soon be twenty years old. She was smart. Ambitious. Beautiful, too. On the cusp of adulthood. Of course, she was looking ahead to wonderful things.

Just as Lisa once had.

This time, however, nothing would get in the way of a Delaney daughter's dreams.

An hour later, the visitors slowly dispersed to the bedrooms. Before saying good night, Lisa's uncles stood close and spoke to her and Mike quietly.

"You both were right, and we were wrong," Ted began.

Steve agreed. "We can see how happy the children are to be together, and the two of you deserve the credit. You're a wonderful couple. We just wanted you to know that."

They shook hands with Mike, again wished him luck in the play-off game next week, and kissed Lisa. "You're Grace's daughter through and through," whispered Ted before heading upstairs.

And I can't let her down.

She and Mike watched the men leave the room. "They were right about one thing," said Mike.

"What's that?"

"The kids. They're doing better. They're happier and more confident."

"For once, we're in total agreement, Mr. Brennan."

"But we still need to work on the 'wonderful couple' part. I haven't forgotten, so think about that." With those words, he walked away.

She froze. More conflict lay ahead. "Merry Christmas, Mike," she whispered. In the season of peace on earth, she longed for peace at home. Why was that so difficult? What was she missing?

CHAPTER SEVENTEEN

His first Super Bowl.

With lots of nail biting and a couple of Hail Mary passes, the Riders had won their play-off games and had gone to the 2012 Super Bowl. And now, after a long sixty minutes of inspired play, the winning QB and his team stood in the Atlanta stadium watching the Lombardi Trophy being presented to the owners of the Riders. Millions of people had watched them accrue yard after yard, down after down, touchdown after touchdown. Mike could barely believe he was standing there, victory behind him.

His folks were in the stadium, his brother, too, in the reserved section. He was well represented, but not by Lisa. He tamped down the anger and shrugged. He should be used to her absence by now. He should be used to celebrating without his wife and traveling alone. But it still stung. Snow had been threatening when he'd left Boston a week ago. Winter in New England always threatened snow. There was no way Lisa would leave and have Emily worry about planes and cars and creatures that bumped in the night.

He heard his name over the sound system. Then a chorus from the stadium. "Brenn-an. Brenn-an," they chanted. MVP? Was that what they were saying?

Oh, man. This was a moment he'd never forget. The colorful crowds, the noise, the press box, the coaches and owners and teammates. He walked toward the podium as if in a trance. Took the microphone from the announcer. Found himself thanking everyone. Giving credit for the teamwork perfection of the offense and defense. Everyone was important. As he spoke what could have been trite throwaway lines, he realized he actually believed what he said.

"A team is only as strong as its weakest link. I'm happy to say that the Riders are connected by a strong chain. Each man depends on the other, and that's how we do it."

No big secret there. Theory was great, but truth lay in the execution. Every quarterback in the NFL was probably listening to him now, but he wasn't worried about leaking secrets. If they had the talent, it would show. If they didn't, it would show, too. He'd been a starting QB for less than two seasons, but any doubts about himself disappeared. The writers called him a leader who respected his team, able to get the best out of each man because the respect was reciprocated. It was the only way to win.

If he were truly respected by the Brennan home team, Lisa would have been in the stands today, despite Emily. He understood more than ever that he was merely a backup for her. He was more than a convenience, but not an equal partner. He was sick of it.

He'd just received the highest accolades an NFL quarterback could earn. A Super Bowl! A God-Almighty Super Bowl. And the winning quarterback would party alone that night.

Or...maybe not.

He waved to all the fans. Someone out there would want to make him feel good later on. He'd turned down dozens of offers in the past. Not worth mentioning. Not worth thinking about. He was thinking now.

#

Later that night, after the official celebration in the team's private ballroom, Mike made his way into the hotel lounge. Brightly lit around the carousel bar, darker at the tables, the place hopped. One big party was underway. A few of his teammates sat at a corner table, surrounded by admirers. He made his way over.

"Sit right down, Mr. Quarterback." A beautiful blonde with a purr like dark honey.

"Don't mind if I do," he replied and received her thousand-watt smile. The temperature in the room seemed to rise as high as Sommars' eyebrows.

Mike held back his threatening scowl. Darrell had no business judging.

As though reading his mind, the wide receiver said, "Hey, man. Didn't expect to see you. So, what're you drinking?"

He caught the waitress's eye. "Sam Adams, Dark. I'm from Boston." He turned to his newest partner. "What would you like?"

"Do I have to say Southern Comfort because I'm from the south?" Her drawl caressed that dark honey in a Scarlett kind of way, but her sense of humor reduced her to real-people size.

"I'm Mike Brennan," he said, extending his hand.

"I know. Cassie O'Hara."

"O'Hara? You're kidding. I was just thinking…"

Her eyes lit up. "You northern boys get real snookered by the accent. It's so cute to see."

And that was enough for Mike. Ms. O'Hara's I.Q. had just plummeted, or maybe it was her social skills. There was no denying the light touch as her fingers stroked his bare arm.

"Hey, Cassie. Aren't you going to introduce me?" Another blonde, just as pretty. "I want to meet the star of the show."

"Then that would be me." Darrell stood up and beamed at the newcomer.

What a hoot! Mike began to laugh, drank his ale, and forgot about anything but having a good time. In thirty minutes, there were two dozen belles at his table. Sure, the same thing happened up north after a game, but he usually wasn't around to notice.

He could have had any of them. Or all of them. One by one, the guys departed with a new friend, but Mike remained. The girls were nice. Certainly attractive. Certainly willing. And he was certainly tempted. Hell, no one deserved to celebrate more than the winning quarterback.

How honorable did he have to be? Even now, he would rather have celebrated his first Super Bowl with Lisa. If life at home didn't change, however, he didn't know how he'd feel in the future.

#

Wednesday, February 8, 2012
The Boston Globe
RIDERS RULE!!
THOUSANDS PACK DOWNTOWN TO CHEER
TEAM

A snowstorm of confetti and paper couldn't hide the grin on Mike Brennan's face yesterday as he cradled the Super Bowl trophy like a baby. He and the entire Riders team led a parade through Boston with Mayor Dan Taylor, team owner Jack Mowery, and head coach Tom Knight. Each man took a turn hoisting the Lombardi Trophy as they traveled the 1.5 miles to City Hall in duck boats, Boston's famous amphibious tourist vehicles.

It was only the second Super Bowl victory in the team's fifteen years as a franchised operation. Boston police estimated that over a million people came to celebrate from all over the New England states.

"And we'll be back again next year," said one exuberant fan. "The Riders are on a roll now, and I'm planning to take another day off from work in '13."

#

All would have been well at home if the pictures on the front page hadn't included Mike with his arms around the twins, one boy on each side of him. Lisa hadn't known they'd cut school yesterday along with hundreds of other kids. Mike hadn't known, either. But when the parade had reached City Hall, the boys were in the front of the crowd, jumping up and down to catch his attention.

Caught it they did, and after a quick conversation with his coach, Mike urged them to the float.

"Your sister's going to kill you," he'd whispered.

They shrugged. "She worries too much."

He didn't comment. Just said, "Wave to the crowd, boys. And behave."

That night he sat on the family room sofa watching Lisa pace the floor and listening to her mutter about dumb luck. It was blind, dumb luck that had kept her brothers safe in that melee.

"They're just asserting their independence," he consoled. "It's perfectly normal at their age. And besides, they were together."

"To egg each other on." She looked at him. "I can't let it go, or they might do something stupid again."

If she weren't so serious, he'd laugh. "It was the Super Bowl victory parade. Of course they wanted to see it. And of course they're going to do stupid things again. That's what being an adolescent boy is all about." He told a few stories about David and himself growing up. "It's all normal. My folks survived, so you can lighten up."

Foot in mouth again.

"Easy for you to say. I've never done this before, and I'm feeling my way. And just when I think I'm getting the knack, the kids change again. A new stage to contend with. Regardless…you heard my uncles at Christmas…I'm Grace's daughter."

Grace's daughter. Not his wife. The truth hit him once more like a well-aimed football to the gut. And once more, a knot formed in his stomach as a trap tightened around him. She didn't want couples counseling, she didn't want to allow him fifty percent authority and responsibility for the children, so let the pieces fall where they may now. His temper flared.

"You're also Michael's wife. How about me being Lisa's husband? Just us. Just family. No other labels. Let's try. It's spring semester, and I've got more time, like last year. I can pick up the slack at home since you're teaching again. I'm experienced now. You can trust me."

Her eyes sparkled with hope—a glimpse of the old Lisa, the Lisa he'd fallen in love with. He felt himself grinning like a Cheshire cat right back at her.

"Really?" she asked. "You're right about this time of the year."

"Having the boys with me at the celebration yesterday felt good. I love them, too. You should know I love all four kids."

She almost hurled herself into his arms, kissing him like they were still in college, kissing him like their good times were just starting.

They never made it to the bedroom. Instead, they made love on the floor under the watchful eye of Rob and Grace, who smiled from the center of the quilt now hanging on the wall.

Michael's wife and Lisa's husband. Team Brennan. He wished their ideas meshed more often. About the kids. About the game. About their lifestyle. How could she question his love for the kids? He was getting tired of having to pick his battles.

"Hmm…Mike?"

"Yeah."

"How'd you like to work with the decorators? I'm very willing to share that job!"

#

Her husband had a passion for football. Jen's was for financial management. Then there was Emily and her violin. More than a passion, perhaps, her survival tool.

Lisa had been rehired at her prior school as a long-term sub. As she made her way through the corridors to teach her second-period American history class, she allowed herself one sigh of regret over her aborted education. One day…one day…she'd follow her own passion, but that day hadn't arrived yet.

She entered her classroom with an unusual enthusiasm and energy. It was time to think like a professional educator, or at least give it a good try. The spring term had just started. Maybe she could up the game and keep these teenagers interested.

"You can put your books away," she started, "because today I have a story."

Instantly, the students settled in and waited. And that's when Lisa made her first discovery. *Story* was a magic word.

"About ten years ago, the principal of a high school refused to permit the students in a journalism class to publish two articles in the student newspaper. The articles dealt with divorce and teenage pregnancy." She filled in a few more details.

"So, I'm asking you a question today: Should students writing for a school newspaper be subject to censorship by school officials? Or should they be protected by First Amendment rights?"

With her students in hot debate, the forty-five class minutes seemed to take only five. They'd brought up library book censorship issues, as well, and when the bell rang to change classes, they ignored it. She finally had to hustle them out the door.

"We'll pick up tomorrow," she promised. Now, she had to figure out how to combine the regular curriculum with constitutional debate to ensure she'd cover all the required material by the end of the term. A happy challenge. She wanted to do this.

In the teacher's lunchroom later on, she learned that word travels fast in a school building.

"My math students were buzzing about you today, Lisa."

Lisa turned toward Katie Roberts, an enthusiastic teacher only a few years older than she. "I hope in a good way."

"I'd definitely say so. I think you hit on something with them. So, whatever it is, keep doing it."

Lisa felt the heat rising to her face. She definitely wasn't used to compliments at work. "I love to debate legal issues, so I thought I'd give it a try with the class."

Katie's eyes shone. "Isn't it exciting when you find something that works well? When the kids really respond? That's the high point of teaching."

Well, Katie Cohen was born to teach. Lisa hadn't gotten excited about it before today. "I guess it can be pretty wonderful," she replied.

"I know you're just starting out, but you might want to consider getting your master's degree. Most classes are in the evening or on Saturday, and your salary will go up afterwards."

Katie had no idea what Lisa's true goals were because Lisa hadn't shared them with anyone. Her dreams were her own business. Now, she was tempted.

They sat together with some others, chatting, eating, reading the newspaper. From the corner of her eye, Lisa spotted the picture of Mike and the twins on the front page of yesterday's paper and groaned. She hadn't shared her personal information here, either, but somehow, she suspected that, little by little, the teachers had found out about her relationship to Mike. Her checks were mailed to the house under Delaney-Brennan. Most Bostonians knew their quarterback lived in Beacon Hill. From school secretaries to teachers was not a huge leap.

She focused on her sandwich.

"The staff buzzes, too," said Katie softly, pressing Lisa's hand and darting a glance at the newspaper. "And a lunchroom is a place where gossip collects."

Lisa nodded. She could either hide or face it head on. But if she outed herself, there would be no going back. She'd be a semi-celebrity from this day forward, something she'd tried to avoid. Glancing around the room, she identified a number of co-workers who'd become friendly to her during her tenure there, offering assistance, answering questions about procedures or students. She was comfortable with them…and by God, she could use some friends in Boston.

She sat back in her seat and said, "So, how cute are my brothers on that front page?"

CHAPTER EIGHTEEN

Gracie and Lisa's Notebook—Christmas 2012
Dear Mom and Dad,

We're back in Woodhaven for the holidays this year with Mike's family. We can only stay a few days because Mike has to prepare for his play-off game—two years in a row! But even so, we've all reconnected with long-time friends. Between attending Midnight Mass and the twins' bike ride through the old neighborhood, everyone knows we're in town. Irene and William have been keeping their door open to visitors—all ages welcome. Very generous of them.

Lisa put her pen down, walked to the bedroom window, and pulled the curtain aside for the third time. Like a jagged tooth that teased her tongue, the house across Hawthorne Street pulled at her soul. Another family lived there now, but to Lisa, the home belonged to her proud parents and to them all. She heard Mike calling from downstairs and allowed the material to drop into place.

"Just another minute," she replied, snatching her pen once more.

It's been almost four years since you left us, and it's still difficult to look at our house. We were happy there.

She remembered that hopeful, upbeat world where anything was possible, full of family and fun. She wanted that again, but now snatched at bits and pieces of "happy." A moment with Emily, making love with Mike, motivating a class of students.

She ran downstairs to her husband, ready to catch up with her long-time friends.

#

The local karaoke club was only half-full when Lisa and Mike arrived. The noise from a back table increased significantly when they walked in. Looking over, they spotted a group of familiar faces and made a beeline to their old friends.

Within five minutes of receiving warm hugs from the guys, Lisa understood that, to them, this reunion was just as much about football as about friendship and pride. Mike had become an honest-to-goodness hometown hero, and with another Super Bowl possibility next month, he'd taken on the image of a superhero. She studied their awestruck faces as they examined the big, diamond-studded Super Bowl ring he always wore on his right hand when not playing. He'd accomplished every little boy's dream, and his friends were proud of him.

She gave and received tight hugs from her girlfriends. Sandy didn't want to let go. Compliments and questions followed. About the kids, about living in Boston, about being an NFL wife.

"I know you're disappointed about postponing law school again," said Sandy, giving Lisa her full attention. "I felt so badly for you with the nanny situation. I'm hoping you enjoy your teaching job at least a little?" Her voice rose in question.

"If it were me," Gail interrupted, "I wouldn't work, period. Mike earns enough to support everybody."

Lisa laughed along with the crowd and smiled at Sandy. Her friend was smart, intuitive, and caring. They were still close, but phone calls were a poor substitute for sharing time in person.

"Teaching's not my first choice, but it's gotten better. Forget about me," said Lisa. "You all look pretty darn happy yourselves."

Gail grinned and stood. "Bobby and I are expecting our first," she said, patting her stomach in that protective way pregnant women do.

"Congratulations." Mike's voice aimed at the couple. "My brother has a toddler. A terrific little boy."

"We know all about him, Uncle Mikey," teased Rick, Sandy's husband. "David and Nancy drive in from Cambridge about once a month for the weekend. Got to make Grandma and Grandpa happy."

"Thank God for David and Nancy," joked Lisa, sipping a glass of wine and hoping her humor came through. "Mike and I are *so* not ready."

"Which is totally understandable," Sandy said. "You're still raising a crop."

Mike's bark of laughter had a tiny edge to it. "That's the truth. And the crop is growing up just fine. We're proud of them all. But someday, someday soon"—he raised his glass toward Lisa in a toast— "here's to staying young enough to have some of our own."

Her glass slipped and almost fell. Breathing became difficult. Of course she understood his desire for children. She wasn't that selfish. But how could he discuss this private matter in public when he knew darn well she couldn't handle another child now?

Later…when their lives became calmer and the future held only blue skies. Later…when the thought of starting their own family excited her instead of generating tears. She needed some freedom first. A chance to catch her breath.

She forced a smile and reclaimed her glass. "I'll toast to the future and to feeling young again."

#

The door of the eatery opened and another group of chatting people entered and searched out seating.

"Speaking of the crop," said Sandy, "isn't that Jennifer over there with that tall drink of water?"

Lisa's head snapped toward the doorway. "Holy cow, that's Doug Collins. Jen's brought him around a few times but doesn't say much about him, either good or bad. But the guy doesn't give up."

Mike peered at the couple and put his drink on the table. "Collins. How the hell did he find her in Woodhaven? He's got it bad."

"He's a big boy," Lisa interrupted.

"Their relationship's interesting," said Mike. "Remember that first essay? She wanted to kill him." He began walking toward the couple. Lisa rose and pulled at his arm. "Don't you dare embarrass her."

He turned and placed his hands on her shoulders, pressing gently but firmly. She got the message and sat back down. "Come on, Lis. Try trusting me."

Five minutes later, the younger couple approached Lisa's table, Mike with them, grinning from ear to ear.

"I keep forgetting what a small town this is," said Jen with a big sigh. "And I'm so glad we live in

Boston." She waved at the group. "Hi, everybody. This is Doug Collins on his way back home after skiing in the Berkshires. He just happened to notice the turnpike exit to Woodhaven and decided to take a chance and call me."

"Not quite right," said Doug. "I exited on purpose. Mike may be famous, but his parents are still listed. Ask Google."

"Meet Jennifer's nemesis," said Mike, his arm around Jen. "But I like him."

"Want to join us?" asked Lisa.

"Sure. We're starving," Doug replied.

"We're just about to order," said Lisa as Doug added two chairs to the long table.

Jen pointed at the karaoke machine. "See that apparatus? I'm going to be the first one to use it."

"No kidding?" Lisa couldn't have been more shocked if Jen had said she'd be swimming the Atlantic naked in winter.

"Yup," Jen replied, not seeming too happy about it. "I'm going first to get it over with." She pointed at Doug. "He dared me."

"And she accepted," said Doug. "Payoff time is near."

Lisa laughed. Her friends began to chuckle. "Dared you to sing?" Lisa asked. "Well, that's no problem, is it, Jenny-girl? You can show him."

Jen winked, then waved to someone and wandered off.

"You're in for a disappointment if you think she'll embarrass herself," Lisa said to Doug. "My sister has pipes."

"Your sister is wonderful," he replied, "except she doesn't believe it. She's put you on a pedestal."

"What? That's not true." Lisa glanced at her sister, remembering her criticisms from a while back. Jen hadn't heard Doug's remark, but it seemed the guy had more to say.

"Yup. She talks about you all the time. I think she lives in your shadow."

"Dr. Freud, I presume?" snapped Lisa.

Collins shrugged. "I know what I hear, what I see."

Had Jen said Doug was an English major? Maybe creative writing or theater? Some liberal arts area that would give her logical, mathematical sister a case of hives. Or would it capture her imagination?

"We can make this more interesting," said Mike, sitting back in his seat, seemingly relaxed and having fun. "I'll double dare Doug to try it." He nodded at the song machine.

The young man grinned, his eyes on Jen as she returned to the table. "I accept."

"I heard that, and it's not necessary," said Jen quickly. "I know he can carry a tune. Hell, he can read the phone book and make it sound like Shakespeare."

"Glad you noticed, Jenny-Henny-Penny."

Mike's questioning gaze caught Lisa, who shrugged, realizing the details of her sister's relationship were unknown to her. Her stomach tightened.

"So, what are you going to sing?"

Jen brightened. "Thank goodness it's Christmas. I'll just do "Jingle Bells" or some other holiday song programmed in the karaoke machine. I bet the audience will join in. And then I will have fulfilled my part. The string bean won't be able to nag again."

Not such a string bean anymore. Doug had filled out quite a bit. Jen either hadn't noticed or wasn't giving Doug the satisfaction of having noticed. Lisa's thoughts flew awry. Relationships weren't her strong suit. She and Mike seemed to ride a roller coaster even when they were both trying to do their best.

The club was now almost full, their waitress had brought their food, and the disc jockey lit up the karaoke area. "To keep you in the holiday spirit, we're going to start the evening with a sing-along of holiday tunes."

"He stole my idea!" complained Jen.

"It's Christmas, Jen. What did you think he'd do? But listen up. He's still talking." Doug put his finger over her lips.

"And while we're all singing," continued the DJ, "those people who want the spotlight can look through the track listings and write down their song choice on a slip of paper. You'll get up to sing when I call your name."

As though heading to the guillotine, Jen made her way to the song book.

Lisa turned her attention to Doug. "So, what power do you have over my sister?"

"For God's sake, Lisa!" Mike interrupted. "Give the guy a break. She invited him here."

Lisa shrugged. "But my question remains. And I want to know the answer."

"Well, well, well. Now, that's proof you're still a lawyer," Sandy interjected. "And Doug, I feel sorry for you."

"Don't worry about me," replied Doug. "Jen's worth it. After two years, I'm still peeling away the onionskin. I don't understand everything about Jennifer yet, but I will."

"The onionskin? Sounds like psychology talk. Is that your major?"

"Minor. It's helpful when I watch a movie or read a book. Helpful for what I want to do later on."

The young man wanted to know people inside and out…real and fictional. So maybe he was a theater major, an actor. Good Lord, what could be worse?

"I'm a writer."

She groaned. Writing was no way to make a living. "Are you any good?"

Mike choked on his drink and turned to Doug. "It's her sister you're involved with, but you have to get through Lisa first…and me."

Lisa squeezed his arm. Doug's gaze rested only on Lisa when he replied.

"I've completed two stage plays, and now I'm working on a screenplay. One of these days, you'll go to a theater and see my movie up there."

"Right," she muttered. The guy needed a reality check. Hadn't he ever heard about starving writers who thought success was just around the corner, just one script away? Jen could not possibly be serious about him.

Mike, however, was already extending his hand. "Welcome to my world, Doug, where you either have the chops or you don't."

For crying out loud. A second ago, Mike was supporting her. Had his opinion changed in a moment? He shouldn't encourage the guy.

But her husband had already captured the younger man's attention. For the first time since arriving, Collins's smile disappeared, his slouch evaporated as he straightened in his chair. The expression on his face was appropriate for a funeral.

"Thanks, Mike. I intend to make my own touchdowns."

Doug Collins seemed to be as passionate about his career choice as Mike had been. She'd talk to Jen. A writer? Jen liked security. She was the one who'd pounced on the budgets from the beginning. She'd hate living her life unsure of the next script, the next sale.

"Relax, Lisa," whispered Mike. "They're still undergrads. Not even old enough to order a drink. You're borrowing trouble."

Maybe. But she and Mike had only been eighteen when they'd met. She'd opened her front door, and her life had changed forever. Jen needed to have her eyes wide open.

A verse of "Deck the Halls" was ending, and the DJ spoke into the microphone. "For those new to karaoke, there are no rules, except not to break my equipment. In karaoke singing, only the background to popular songs is prerecorded on each track, so whoever comes up here tonight will take the place of the lead singer. And remember, folks, we're here to have a good time. If you can't clap because the singer did a great job, then clap because the song is over!"

The crowd chuckled, and suddenly all eyes were on Jen, standing alone at the microphone. She scanned the crowd and said, "This one's for my big sister."

Lisa leaned forward, wondering what Jen had in mind. But when she heard the introductory notes, she knew what was in her sister's heart, and a corner of her own started to tear.

"Stand by Me." Jen's voice, with its smoky jazz delivery, was a natural for Ben E. King's song. Her sister was as pitch-perfect as she'd ever been when the whole family used to belt out songs, singing and laughing until they couldn't breathe at all.

The verses, the chorus.

...stand by me....

Jen caught her eye and waved her over. Lisa didn't think twice, didn't stop, didn't pause—she just went. She harmonized, and she carried the melody, sometimes weaving in and around Jen's voice.

...won't be afraid....

Stand by me.

A weight lifted. She was a girl again, back home with her family, singing their hearts out. Mike used to be there, too, not singing, always saying he'd ruin the harmony, but she wouldn't have cared if he had. Not in those days.

And when it was over, it was Doug Collins who asked, "Who do you ladies think you are? The Von Trapp Family?"

Jen and Lisa looked at each other and burst out laughing.

"No," they cried in unison. "We are the Delaneys!"

Whistles and catcalls came from her old friends. Other patrons applauded wildly. Gail cried out, "You will always be the Delaneys. Grace and Robert are up there with you. They live through you."

#

Mike winced at the reminder. It seemed that the entire world conspired against him on the question of Lisa's identity. He had to admit, however, that she looked and sounded wonderful up there with Jen. Joyful memories filled his mind. So many dinners in Grace's kitchen, so many impromptu concerts afterwards. A sharp longing pierced him. Startled him. It wasn't often that he yearned for yesterday. No profit in that. Only pain. But seeing Lisa up there, singing with her sister, brought it all back. That damned auto accident had wrought huge collateral damage. No one sang anymore.

#

The girls returned to the table while another patron took to the stage, causing Mike to wince. "Everyone thinks they've got a voice."

"Especially when they have a few too many belts in them." Doug nodded toward the performer.

"Lisa and Jen are naturals," said Mike, snaking his arm around Lisa's chair. "You were both great. Maybe you should join a glee club or a choir or something back in the city. Have a little fun for a change." As soon as that F word left his mouth, he wished he'd bitten his tongue. Fun was still not part of Lisa's agenda—as far as he could tell.

"I wish," said Lisa. "But the last time I looked, there were still only twenty-four hours in a day."

An excuse. If she wanted to join a chorus, she could do that. He was home at night; so was Jen. A weekly rehearsal was just as important as a weekly therapy session. And as for their social life? Hell, it didn't exist. He had the time and money now. They could easily afford a dinner out and a show or movie plus a babysitter. His wife wasn't even trying to meet him halfway.

She had a trust problem, but he wasn't getting into that again. Especially not here. Not with everyone in good spirits.

Sandy and Rick Bennett stood, glasses in hand. "We'd like to propose a toast to Lisa and Mike," said Rick. "First, it's great seeing you guys again. Make the trip more often."

"Hear, hear!"

"We know your lives haven't been easy in the ways that matter most," Sandy said, "so tonight, we drink to the Brennans, to a successful play-off game and Super Bowl, and to a super family. Remember that we miss you in Woodhaven."

Mike watched Lisa's tears trickle as the love and comfort of longtime friends poured over them. She made her way around the entire table, hugging every man and every woman. For the first time, he wondered if they'd made a mistake moving to Boston. Maybe Lisa would have had an easier time here with a "phantom" husband—as she'd called him—but with the support of friends she didn't have in the big city. Not that she'd bothered to seek out new friends, he reminded himself, certainly not the players' wives. He and Lisa lived in a magnificent house, in a magnificent city that provided magnificent opportunities, but Woodhaven still held her heart.

Mike loved Boston. Loved the team. He was close with some of the guys. They had no "off-season," not if they wanted to stay on top. They played cards only after a day of training at the stadium. They worked at the game full time, year-round. They reviewed videos, worked with coaches to stay in shape, and had small-group practices with whomever was available. He'd gone out for a meal more often lately and to a few clubs, too, enjoying the noise, the people, the camaraderie.

Now, he looked around the small-town karaoke club and thought of his life in Boston. Two different worlds, with him straddling both. In Boston, women swarmed the Riders as soon as they walked through any door. Beauties who knew how to pay attention to a guy. In Woodhaven, friends swarmed him and Lisa as they did now. And that was great. But thinking about his life a hundred miles east made him smile. Excitement rushed through him.

He should be living that good life! He was only twenty-six years old. He was decent-looking and had legions of admirers. For God's sake, he was the star of the show! A celebrity—and he barely enjoyed it.

Lisa probably didn't think about the groupies on the road and in town. She had to be aware, had to. But they'd never discussed it. Maybe she had no idea how much temptation he resisted on the road, like that night he won his first Super Bowl. Volunteering the information would seem like a threat, and that was no way to have a good marriage. If only she would take joy in his accomplishments. If only she'd go on the road with him at least once in a while and cheer the team on.

He'd love to show her off. Show everyone that their QB had a beautiful wife and a strong family behind him.

"If we make it to the big game in Miami," he said, stroking Lisa's arm, "I expect you to go. I'm tired of traveling solo. I want you with me."

Startled, she had that deer-in-the-headlights look. "Can we please take it one game at a time? You know, with Emily, I can never promise anything in advance."

Of course he knew. And hated it. "Get the shrink in on this right away. I'm not taking no for an answer." Mike didn't have a lot of faith in the woman, not after she'd allowed Lisa to stop the sessions. He wanted to be wrong this time.

Maybe he'd wind up going solo again. But he wouldn't make it easy for his wife.

CHAPTER NINETEEN

Monday, January 20, 2013
The Boston Globe—Sports
RIDERS GO TO MIAMI
CANNON-ARM BRENNAN DOES IT AGAIN!

The Riders held the lead from the first quarter of the play-offs with a hot defense. Three interceptions gave them possession for most of the clock, scoring two touchdowns right out of the box. Then, in the second quarter, the Redskins pushed back. But Dave Steinberg intercepted and stormed the field from his own end zone straight for a touchdown. That was just the first half!

The Boston Riders are prime-time players. They have offense, they have defense, they have a running game, they have a throwing game.

"It's all about trust," Brennan says. "Trust in each other, in our coaches, and staying focused. Having 80,000 cheering fans yesterday was pretty good, too."

But trust is only half the story. The other half is about leadership, and Brennan's one of the best in the game. Maybe his success has to do with his style. It's quiet. He gives the best of himself to the game, and expects the best from others. He leads by example. They don't want to let him down. You want proof? Brennan's taking Boston to the Super Bowl again!

\#

Grace and Lisa's Notebook—January 21, 2013
Dear Mom and Dad,
Evening has fallen quickly, as usual during our winters, and it's already dark outside. Two memorial candles provide the only light, a soft glow that comforts me. Mass cards are propped open near the candles. It's been four years since our personal holocaust, four years since we lost you—and I am still drowning.

I walk along the edge of two worlds: Delaney vs. Brennan. Mike returned from his successful play-off yesterday, totally pumped up about having another bite at the Super Bowl. I'm happy for him. I truly am. But these days are also about you. While Mike was away, we went to church, celebrating the mass we offered for you. Of course I understood that he had to go with the team, but he never mentioned you before he left last week and not yesterday, after he came home.

I know his mind is on the game, but I'm afraid he acts more and more as though you're now part of the past. A detail. According to him, we should have moved on. Made more progress. Especially Emily.

Her hand cramped from gripping the pen. Anger simmered and slowly rose again to the boiling point. Jumping to her feet, Lisa paced the length of the kitchen several times, took some deep breaths, and returned to her chair.

The four years sometimes feel like a hundred and sometimes feel like a day. I get confused. Time seems elastic, stretching and contracting whenever I think of you and what happened to us.

Mike was supposed to be my strength, but I depend mostly on myself now. Our outlooks are different, especially about how to handle the kids. I had such a good time in Woodhaven over Christmas, so happy to be with my friends and share memories. Maybe we should have stayed there.

Maybe Mike and I shouldn't have gotten married.

She reread the last line and crossed it out. Their relationship wasn't that bad, was it? Life had become more stable with routines at work and home. She enjoyed her own job a lot more since she'd begun coaching a debate team for the school. Her siblings were doing what they were supposed to do. Jen, now twenty years old, was on her way to a great career; the boys, at thirteen, were accident-free despite their winner-take-all attitudes in whatever sport they played; even eleven-year-old Emily was coming along—slowly. Of course, Mike wanted to push her.

One thing she knew for sure: they were all surviving day by day, and that was the goal.

#

Mike waited two days until his aching body recovered from the play-offs and the kids were busy with homework before bringing up the trip to Miami.

"Have you spoken with Emily and Jen about the Super Bowl weekend?"

"I did."

"And?"

"Of course, Jen is fine. But Emily wants to ask you some questions."

"Great. I'm all about discussion. What does she want to know?"

She shook her head. "I'm not sure—maybe about how airplanes stay in the air…? Science was not my best subject. So this conversation is all on you."

He'd majored in the life sciences in college, with a lot of physical science on the side. Made dean's list, too. No problem here.

He and Lisa walked upstairs to Emily's room, stood in the doorway until she finished the piece of music she was playing. Although she'd played "Amazing Grace" for the family, the girl was beyond songs he could recognize easily. He did recognize melodies from Tchaikovsky and Mozart from time to time, but he couldn't name any titles. Now, she seemed to be annoyed with herself.

"My bow strokes need more work. I need to improve the spiccato."

Sure. Well, every vocation had its own vocabulary. "What does your coach say?" asked Mike.

"Ms. Merri?" A dimple popped up. "You called her my coach!" She placed the instrument on her bed and stared at her hands. "I'm not ever playing football or basketball or any ball, not even with my brothers anymore."

"Good decision, Em," he said. "But we need to talk about the Super Bowl."

"I know." She dropped her gaze. "You want Lisa to go to Miami."

"Yes, I do."

"Together with you?"

"No. I go the week before the game. She flies down later."

Her head snapped up; her eyebrows almost touched her hairline. "You won't be on the plane together?"

He sensed her fear, squatted on the floor in front of her, and took her hands. "We're on separate planes both ways, sweetheart. Flying is very, very safe, but God forbid something does happen, you won't be left alone. I promise you that."

She wrapped her eleven-year-old arms around him, tucked her head in the crook of his neck. He stood up easily, her weight still feather-light.

"I love you, Daddy Mike."

"And I love you, Emily."

"That's good." Then she wriggled out of his arms and picked up her violin.

"So, we're okay with the Super Bowl?" Mike asked.

Her eyes clouded, her forehead puckered. "I don't know yet. I'm still scared."

"But you'll try to be brave, right?" he coaxed.

Lisa knelt by her sister. "You think about it, okay? Talk with Dr. Julie. But it's your choice. We're not forcing you to do anything you don't want to do. No one's going to be angry with you."

Mike bit his lip. They left Emily to her music, and went back downstairs.

"You've given her a way out," Mike said as soon as they were out of earshot. "She was almost there. She was focusing on being brave, and you blew it."

"Blew it? You were pushing her. And I don't want her getting sick over this."

"She *makes* herself sick, and nothing will change if she doesn't take any steps forward. You build confidence by facing the things that scare you."

"She's building confidence with her violin because she so good at it."

"The violin? You've got to be kidding. She loved playing from the first moment. The violin doesn't scare her; it's not a fear to overcome. She'll probably be playing concertos before long, but that's a skill challenge she wants and has nothing to do with what we're talking about. She needs to overcome what frightens her. She needs to develop courage and be brave. Tell that to the damn therapist. Let her earn her money."

He grabbed a beer from the fridge and turned toward his wife. "The bottom line, Lisa, is that I want you with me. Last year, I swallowed it—your absence. But this year? No. It's the Super Bowl, Lisa. The biggest day of the year across the NFL nation. I can't do any better than that. I'm coming through for us, and you're going to be there! Now, you figure out a way."

#

With her smart phone in hand, Lisa sat in the reserved box in Miami with Mike's parents, following the football action with part of her mind while the other part was back in Boston. Silence had pounded against her ears after Mike's ultimatum, and in that moment, she'd known everything between them was on the line. Intellectually, she couldn't blame him. She'd also want her family with her at such an important event. But emotionally…she couldn't throw Emily to the four winds.

Instead, she bribed her. The child now had her own phone where she could touch base with Lisa whenever she wanted to, even on the plane. Very extreme, very expensive…but Lisa had no choice. After the weekend, when they were all home again, Em would see that traveling was a normal thing to do and would accept it.

A first step to finding courage. That was the hope and should certainly satisfy Mike's request.

Jen jumped in to plan a Super Bowl party for the kids. Doug would be there, too. She'd hugged Lisa, urged her to go. "I'll handle Emily. You go with Mike. He needs you there."

Her in-laws were on their feet, screaming, Lisa scanned the field. The Rider's wide receiver was zig-zagging toward the end zone, two defenders after him. But touchdown! And they were ahead by six. She joined in, excitement flushing through her, and she forgot about everything else, especially when the kicker made the point after.

She finally allowed herself to absorb her surroundings, the colorful crowd, the energy, and the Florida sunshine in mid-winter. She grinned at Irene. "Really fabulous, isn't it?"

"I'll say. And if—if the Riders win…

"…Yeah. I know. Mike will make the history books along with Terry Bradshaw and Joe Montana. Two back-to-back wins." She pressed Irene's arm. "He's really talented. Special."

"As long as he stays healthy!"

Her phone vibrated. "Hey, Em. Did you see that?"

"Yup. Everybody saw it on our big screen. Everybody was cheering. It was very noisy because we're having a real party, not just Brian, Andy and me."

Lisa gripped the phone as her body tensed. A real party? "Where's Jen?"

"I-I'm not sure. There's a lot of people here. Maybe the kitchen. I'm upstairs. Can you come home now instead of tomorrow?"

Lisa took a deep breath, visions of disastrous teenage parties taunting her. But not Jen! Not Jen. She was a mature twenty.

"Emily – please find your sister, and I'll stay on the line with you."

"Okay."

Finally, finally, Jen's voice. "Hi, Lisa. Why are you calling in the middle of the game?"

"What's going on there, Jen? What's this party about?"

"Just some friends from school. Doug's and mine."

"You didn't ask me first."

"I didn't know. It just kinda grew."

Damn. The worst kind. "Is everything under control or do I have to fly home now? Or I could call Officer Ramos to check on your guests."

"For God's sake, Lisa. I'm not a baby. Everything's fine. It's a party, not a riot. Don't you trust me?"

"I don't know, Jen. What I do know is that Emily is hiding in her room. And she shouldn't be. You should have called me." She inhaled deeply. "I want them out—now."

"The game's not over!"

Lisa took a deep breath. "This isn't a joke. I will not allow Mike's beautiful house to be trashed by a bunch of kids who are there without our permission. You've got five minutes before Officer Ramos is at the door, arresting them for trespassing. Have you got that?"

The dial tone buzzed in her ear. She called again and got Emily. "Everything's fine, honey. They're all leaving. But if you don't want to watch the game, you can practice your fiddle."

She heard the giggle and sighed in relief. Em would survive, but the phone slipped from Lisa's sweaty palm. She should have stayed home.

#

Dirt covered his uniform. His knee ached so badly that he limped to the microphone. He glanced toward the reserved box where his family sat. Lisa's presence dissolved the pain, and Mike grinned as he hoisted the Lombardi Trophy over his head.

In the Miami stadium, the Rider fans roared with approval. Their team, their win—their second win. They knew what their quarterback had just accomplished, of the elite company he'd be joining. The cheers continued throughout the entire arena.

Wow! All he'd focused on was the game, but…wow! He took it in. The packed arena. The color, noise, and happiness, all totally overwhelming. Humbled, Mike's breath hitched in his throat in that surreal moment.

He finally focused and gave a short speech of appreciation. For his teammates, for the Riders organization, for the NFL. He complimented the opposition. He raised the trophy toward Lisa and his parents. Gave a shout-out to 'the kids back home," promising to spend more time with them now. He wanted to hug the whole world on this crazy and fabulous day. This, this was joy. Hope. Love. A new beginning because…

Lisa had come to the game.

Except her mind was elsewhere. At the after party that evening, she smiled, kissed him, kept checking her phone, and didn't hear a thing he said.

He kept her at his side, made sure she chatted with everyone on the team. She knew some of the men and their wives already, and he gave her credit for feigning interest and making everyone feel special. Like a politician's wife.

But he knew the difference between the real Lisa and the actress.

He handed her a glass of champagne. "Have a drink. Relax. Tell me why you're miles away."

Her brow shot up. "I'm right here. With you. Like you wanted."

"Yeah…" he said slowly. "Like I wanted, but you didn't want…and obviously still don't."

She stood in silence for a moment. "I didn't hide it. If my folks were alive…it would be different."

"That's not news."

With a flourish, she stepped away from him, champagne spilling from her glass. "You want news? Well, here's some. Jen had a party today, and not just for the kids. Emily called during the fourth quarter, and I threatened Jen with the cops. I think all is well, but"— she reached into her purse—"I'm calling the house again."

Crap. He didn't want to think about children, his home life. He didn't want to fight with Lisa. He snatched the phone from her. "Let it be. I spoke with the boys ten minutes ago, and they didn't say anything."

Her eyes seared him. "They wouldn't. You walk on water, and they're not making waves."

She'd never get it. He and the boys were real together. They pummeled and played, and he checked homework. He reminded them to help their sister. If something were wrong at the house, they would have told him.

Music filled the room. He looked around at the excited faces. His coaches were in heaven; the team's owner had congratulated him and thanked him. The Riders rocked. And he rocked with them. There'd be another parade in Beantown in a few days, something he looked forward to. But now a shadow overrode the celebration.

"Before you turn victory into total defeat," he said, "we're ending this conversation. You've got the hang of this party—meet and greet. Smile. Pretend you're happy for us. For me. It shouldn't be too hard. Your husband's a hero."

She gasped, and her head jerked back as if he'd slapped her. One hand covered her mouth before she pivoted and scurried away. He tracked her path to the exit and didn't follow.

#

We can't go on like this. Lisa inserted her key into the house lock after her morning flight from Florida. Mike would follow later on his prearranged flight with the team. Hard-core Rider fans would be at Logan Airport to welcome them back. Heroes all.

She and Mike hadn't spoken much after the party. Wrong place, wrong time, wrong subjects. Her heavy heart had kept sleep at bay, and she'd risen at first light, anxious to get back home.

The house was quiet. Seemed Jen had gotten everyone off to school. One step toward redemption for her. Mike hadn't seemed too upset about Jen's homegrown Super Bowl party. Either the possibilities hadn't registered, he didn't care, or he was more concerned about his own party. Sighing, Lisa knew she couldn't blame him for that.

Blame. Blame. Blame. With every step up the stairs, the word echoed.

Was their relationship only about conflict? Daily life had become more stable. She enjoyed her own job more since coaching the debate team for the school. Her brothers and sisters were doing what they were supposed to do. Jen had made a mistake yesterday, but she wouldn't make it twice. They were all surviving one day at a time. Good enough for her.

She lifted her suitcase to the bed and began unpacking, paused, and sat down. Really? Was just surviving good enough?

We can't go on like this.

\#

Maybe they shouldn't have gotten married.

Mike dozed on the plane home, knowing he'd be "on stage" once the team landed at Logan. His mind should have been on the meet-and-greet and the fans who waited. It should have been on the teammates who'd made it happen. It should have been on the bonus and his future with the Riders. But like a bear to honey, his thoughts turned to Lisa. Did she have regrets?

Admittedly, he was the one who'd pushed for a wedding after the tragedy. He hadn't bargained, however, for a partial marriage. And that's what they had.

It was late afternoon by the time he walked into the house. Seemed pretty quiet for his gang. Maybe the kids had after-school activities? He stepped toward the kitchen and then heard, "Surprise!"

A big cake, homemade congratulations cards, and framed Super Bowl articles stood in the center of the table. An aromatic pile of pizza boxes waited on the counter. Most important, a family of young, happy faces surrounded him and attacked with hugs, kisses, slaps on the back, and high fives. God, he loved these kids.

Lisa stood behind them, nodding, smiling. Only her eyes were shadowed.

Good. The family celebration was about her siblings and him. But it might have been her idea. An olive branch? Like last year? Was she concerned about them—Lisa and Mike—and open to some honesty? He hoped so.

They couldn't go on the way they were.

\#

The game had taken a toll, and after homework was done, no one protested an earlier-than-usual evening. Mike yawned and was not embarrassed.

"Before I conk out, I need a count on who's attending the parade on Wednesday. There's a VIP section blocked off. You'll miss school. So, who's going?"

"Me, me, me." Hands shot up.

"Emily! Great. You want to go this year?"

"Yes. Yes, I do."

"Then include me," said Lisa. "I'll take another day off."

"Not necessary," said Mike slowly, looking from Lisa to her sister. "Emily's older now. She'll be fine with her brothers and Jen."

His wife wanted to argue. He saw her expressions change quicker than kaleidoscope images, but she finally remained quiet. Discretion in front of the kids won the day. But that evening, he knew it wasn't over between them.

Lisa was waiting for him in their bedroom, already in her nightgown, but pacing. "About Emily…"

He held up his hands. "Not tonight. I'm tired. I want to sleep."

"But you need to make arrangements tomorrow."

"And I will. She wants to go. And I think she should. Without you."

He heard her inhale, ready to protest. He shook his head and preempted her. "You know, Lis, I once thought we'd do everything together. Act as parents to your sisters and brothers together, and someday have children of our own. But you…you don't let me in. And I don't like it one bit. We were supposed to be a team."

"You act like a kid…and the judge—"

"Forget the judge for a minute." He stepped closer to her and spoke slowly. "The real question is: how many years is the accident allowed to reverberate? For how many years is it allowed to control you?"

She froze, and he knew he'd hit her sore spot. Her Achilles' heel. If he didn't know better, he'd think she was undone…or frightened.

"I'm the guardian," whispered Lisa. "You heard her in that courtroom. I have to take care of them as my parents would want. I can't screw it up!" Her decibels escalated, her fear easy to read.

"How can you be so smart and so ignorant at the same time?" asked Mike. "I was in that courtroom, too. The judge was talking about making the paperwork legal and living like a family. In real life, couples work together. A family lives together. The judge knew that. She hoped that would happen with us.

"For what it's worth, coming from me—and I know you don't value my opinion on these things—but you're *not* screwing up the kids." Hope gleamed in her eyes until he added, "But you *are* screwing up our marriage."

Her chin came up. "It takes two people to do that, Michael." She turned away and went into the ensuite bathroom, closing the door behind her.

#

She sat on the floor and cried. She cried until no more tears came. She cried until she heard a tap on the door. "Lis? Are you all right?"

"It's open. I'll get out."

He stood in the doorway, looking very tall from where she rested. But she didn't move.

"I remember the day the police showed up at my door. I ran into the bathroom then, too, and vomited until I was empty." Her parents were lost forever. And now Michael would be gone, too.

He extended his hand. "Come on, stand up."

She stood on her own, and a crooked grin appeared on Mike's face. "'Atta girl. Uh…are we still friends, or do you want me to sleep downstairs?"

She jumped back. "Friends or not, after what you've been through?" She pointed at their bed. "It's yours. Use it." She nodded at the chaise lounge near the window. "I'll—uh—sleep over there."

His brows rose. "Suit yourself."

"I'll be fine. Go to bed."

An hour later, she gave up on the narrow day bed and crawled into her own. It was king-sized. Enough room for both of them without interference. Maybe she'd build a wall of pillows down the middle. Mike would say she was good at building walls.

CHAPTER TWENTY

A week later, at the end of February, Mike sat behind the wheel of his BMW on his way to meet the guys at one of their new hangouts, The Players Club. Here everyone was a "player," although not necessarily an athlete. The common denominator among patrons was full pockets.

He and Lisa had a tacit détente since the Super Bowl especially since Emily had enjoyed herself and had come to no harm at the parade. With a big brother on either side of her, it wasn't surprising. He wondered why Lisa couldn't see how beautifully the kids were doing. She chalked up the parade as Mike having gotten his way and was stressed until the kids arrived back home.

When he'd grabbed his jacket a few minutes ago, she'd barely looked up and didn't ask about his plans for the evening. He guessed she was too busy supervising homework or preparing for her debate team.

He shrugged and stopped for a red light. Soon it wouldn't matter. They'd stay together in the house until the end of the school year. Lisa's request, for the kids' sakes. Hell, he'd given it his best shot, but it wasn't working. He still could hardly believe it. He'd once thought they'd become closer as time passed. Instead, she cut him out, and her actions demeaned him. Either she didn't understand or didn't care.

Hanging around with his teammates allowed him to pretend. Pretend he was free. The light turned green, and ten minutes later, he pulled into the club's parking lot and exited his car. Other young professionals were making their way to the front door. Each time it opened, he heard the tinkle of glasses and murmur of conversation. Exactly what he wanted and needed.

Lisa. They'd communicated well only in bed, and damn if he could figure out what that really meant. Love? Habit? Nervous release? Every time he thought about it, he grew more confused. The sooner they cut their losses, the better.

He pulled the club's door open and was surrounded by party sounds—music, laughter, noise. His spirits lifted, and Mike made his way inside.

#

"Mike, over here."

At the bar, Darrell, Dave Steinberg, Tyrone Fox, Nate Dixon, and about half the guys who lived in the city were keeping a seat warm for him. Mike joined them and ordered a beer.

"They're setting up a place for us in the back," said Darrell.

"Good." Other patrons had recognized them and were coming over, shaking hands, talking about the big game. Mike smiled and chatted. Fans made the business, the big business known as professional football, and none of the guys minded a brief hello.

As they retreated to their own room, a fellow Mike didn't recognize joined them.

"Bruce Jamison is a financial planner," Darrell began. "A financial advisor. He's been working with a lot of pro athletes, not just in football. Let's face it, guys. We earn a lot of money, and most of mine is either sitting in a bank earning a little bit of interest or I've spent it."

Mike noted the nods around the table. He belonged in that group but remained still, not wanting to show his cards, at least, not yet.

"Hell, I've spent more than I've saved," said one of the newer guys.

"That's why I've been talking to Bruce at his office," continued Darrell, "and brought him here so you could meet him and get educated about money. We need it." He grimaced and sat down.

Just how much had Darrell invested and in what? Not that Mike had a sophisticated knowledge of the markets. Even his twenty-year-old sister-in-law knew more than he did, and he had almost seven years on her. Mike's interests lay elsewhere. His responsibilities to the team took up most of his time and concentration. So his money sat in a bank, earning basic interest, which was a shame. He could do a lot better.

Of course, he also bought things with it, like his BMW for winter and the Corvette for summer, the house in Beacon Hill, a new car for his dad, a down payment for his brother, winter coats and ski equipment for the kids. The kids' stuff was just chump change. He'd bought jewelry for Lisa—diamond earrings, a diamond bracelet. She'd smiled and thanked him, but he could almost hear her calculating how much money he'd spent…or wasted. No one could accuse his wife of being a gold digger.

Now, he was curious about this investment advisor. Mike had just earned an eighty-eight-thousand-dollar bonus for winning the Super Bowl. He could play the market with that and see what happened.

"So tell us a little bit about yourself," Mike invited after finishing off his longneck.

Jamison spoke well, and Mike listened, recognized the prominent investment house he represented, managing one hundred million dollars in investments balanced between managed money, tax-free bonds, and annuities. The words spun in Mike's brain.

"And I never had a client complain about me!" The man chuckled, ate dinner, and distributed business cards before disappearing.

Mike tucked one in his shirt pocket.

Darrell stood, took a step toward the bar, and turned back to Mike. "There's a lot of chicks hanging out tonight. Are you going home or staying around?"

An easy question. What was there at home for him?

"Oh, I could use a little conversation…a little noise…a little music."

His friend looked away for a moment. "I hear ya'," he said, "and I'm sorry."

Mike shrugged. "It is what it is. Rocky times happen with every couple. It'll pass." Not that he believed it. He and Lisa had an understanding.

"Yeah," said Darrell. "In the meantime, you can count on us."

"I intend to, pal. I intend to." He headed toward the bar. And later, called a cab to take him home.

#

Two weeks after the dinner, Mike made his way through the business district to Bruce Jamison's office with a blank check in his pocket. The man worked for one of the largest brokerages in the industry, a name familiar to anyone wanting to invest. To Mike, that was an endorsement in itself. And then there was Darrell's financial statement, which Mike had seen last month. All good signs.

An hour after first shaking hands, Mike left the man's office, the blank check still in his pocket. He wasn't ready to hand over eighty-eight thousand dollars. Little things had niggled at him during the visit—the man's small office, the gaudy jewelry including rings to rival Mike's Super Bowl rings. Most important, Jamison's boast of performing miracles with money.

Mike believed in miracles on the gridiron. He believed in Hail Mary passes. He believed in medical miracles. New discoveries in the labs, new therapies for patients. And the miracles of healthy babies. But he didn't believe in financial miracles. Money trees didn't grow in the backyard.

Jen once said that, someday, when she handled a large portfolio-a hundred million or more-she'd have the largest office in the firm! A corner office with windows. And she'd be respected by everyone. Although he didn't know if she was being realistic, he could picture Jennifer in exactly those circumstances. And his picture didn't match Bruce Jamison's environment.

Mike made split second decisions each time he touched the ball during a game: pass, throw, or run with it. Today, he ran and took his check with him. But he'd learned something. He'd spend part of the off-season doing due diligence, educating himself on financial matters. Ignorance was costing him too much. Ironically, Lisa, who valiantly budgeted their expenses, couldn't criticize him for past financial failings. She understood big finances less than Mike did.

#

As spring came slowly to Boston, Lisa scoured the real estate section of the Globe. She'd have to find a new place for her and the kids to live, and that wouldn't be easy. Or affordable. Not to mention another change of school for the younger ones. The understanding with Mike about their future had not left her heart lighter one bit. But it clarified the future.

Once more her constant companion, a yellow legal pad, lay next to the newspaper as she worked on a new budget. She had to be practical, but the thought of asking for alimony induced a wave of nausea. The thought of telling the kids about her separation from Mike made her queasy as well. They'd hate it. They'd hate her. Maybe they'd hate him too. Such a mess. They weren't a long-term couple who stayed together for the sake of the children. The kids weren't even Mike's.

Her hand paused. Her breath caught. Mike would not agree with that thought. He'd argue about legal nonsense. Exhaling slowly, she admitted what she'd always known: Mike loved her siblings.

Naturally he did. He was one of them. An older sibling, a playful big brother. Not a dad.

The kettle whistled just as she heard the key in the door and approaching steps.

"Still up?"

"Going over a few things. Want some tea?"

He pulled out a chair and glanced at the table top. "Good God, Lisa. Are you still driving yourself crazy with your budgets? I thought that was over."

Carefully returning the kettle to the stove, she asked, "Changes are coming again, Mike. You know that. And I have to be prepared."

He reached for the pad.

"Stop that!" She tried to grab it, but was too slow.

"Toiletries, school uniforms, lunches…." His eyes scanned the list. "Rent, gas, electric…." He twirled toward her. "What the hell is this all about?"

"We talked about it…

"And you think I'd leave you in poverty to worry about-about toiletries?" His pitch rose with an inflection of disbelief.

She winced, then said, "Lower your voice. The kids don't know."

"Yeah. We have to work that out. But this…this is ridiculous." He threw the tablet across the room and watched it fall to the floor. "I just earned a wad of money on the big game. It's yours. All of it. Money's not a problem for me."

"That's because you have it!"

"And you don't?"

"I didn't earn it!" She picked up the kettle and poured hot water into two cups, and on the countertop. "Oh, what's the use? You never understand anything."

She hated when his eyes gleamed like they did now.

"Try me," he said, pushing his chair back and stretching his long legs to full length. "Let's get down to it." He leaned back and waited.

She stared at him totally confused. "We've been through it all before."

"Summer hasn't come yet, Lisa. Try again." His gleam became a challenge.

"Oh, pul-ease. I'm too tired to play games."

"I dare you. In fact, I double dare you."

I dare you. From the old days. When they were carefree and young and happy. Lisa Delaney did not run away from dares.

"Where to begin, where to begin." She paced the kitchen. "Of course, the accident. No parents. And I took on the kids, and you know what happened? Lisa got lost.

Cooking, cleaning, monitoring, working, round and round and round, lost in the mundane. And I never knew how well I took care of them, and you thought I was terrible and babying them. And all I could do was try, but deep down inside, way down…you know…that place where the truth lives?" She grasped the back of a chair, her fingertips turning white. "I didn't even want to take them on. I was so scared." Her voice hitched; her throat quivered. "But I had to," she whispered. "They turned to me. They needed me. And I loved them. So what was I to do?

"But you?" She pointed her finger at him. "You always criticized me, my parenting—how and why this and that—and you bought them things, big things. Skis and skates and computers and games. Can that make up for a mother or father? You think money's the answer to everything. And I don't understand that. You weren't brought up that way. And that's just for starters."

She was panting now and tasted salt on her lips. Rubbing her face, her hands got soaked. And Mike brought her a tissue.

"God, Lisa, you were once my biggest cheerleader, and now I can't do anything right. I'm not a shrink. I thought money would make you feel secure, but obviously not." He crouched in front of her. "What can I do to help you? To help us?"

The clock chimed midnight. "I don't know. The answers have to come from inside me. And sometimes…still…I'm overwhelmed. Look outside. It's late and dark, and tomorrow the sun will rise, and then the day will turn to night again, over and over. But I can't find the rhythm. I try so hard, but everything's out of kilter. And I have to be vigilant. My folks were wiped out. The kids…you…could be, too."

"Oh, geez…"

"Love's a scary word, don't you think? There's so much punch into that one little syllable. Sometimes I'm not sure what love is anymore. Or how it's supposed to feel. Because if what I'm feeling is love, it doesn't make me happy, and I think love should make people feel happy. Don't you?"

"Go on."

"Remember that picture? The one of my college graduation?"

He nodded and remained silent.

"Yesterday, I stared at that picture," she continued, "and I thought, *That's what happy looks like!* I was young, with everything ahead of me. Mom said, 'Follow your dreams,' and I tried. You know I tried. But instead of following a dream, I was just going through the motions. I miss Woodhaven. I wish…I wish…"

"Yeah. We all wish, but nothing's the same back there. You know that."

"The heart yearns. The head knows better." She sighed and shrugged. "I'm sorry, Mike. Nothing's turned out the way we thought, the way we wanted it. I don't even like football anymore."

He grunted. "I noticed."

She rose. "I'm so sorry about that, and about not…not…wanting more children in the near future. You deserve better."

"Well…maybe we both deserve better."

#

For Jennifer, each day that spring seemed to last forever until she could get home and check the mail. In early May, she pounced on the envelope she'd been waiting for, ripped it open, and read. Barely breathing, she twirled toward the back of the house, to the kitchen, where she expected the rest of the family to be at dinner.

"Lisa! Mike! I got it, I got it, I got it." She sang her own tune and continued her crazy dance as she waved the letter at everyone.

"My summer internship with Fidelity. I got it!" She paused long enough to make her point. "I'm going to be assisting the manager of a growing mid-cap fund. Isn't that great? Do you know what this means? It means I'll probably have a job with them when I graduate next year. Then I'll get my stock broker's license…maybe one day I'll be managing a fund, too."

"Of course you will!" said Lisa immediately. "You can do anything you want. Just follow your dreams."

"Amen," Mike said. "One day you can manage some of my capital."

"What's a mid-cap fund?" asked Andy.

"Capital, like Washington, D.C.?" Brian's voice squeaked.

"The boys sure take after you, Lis," Jen said while dancing again. "I'll be balancing your checkbook for the next fifty years. I'll probably have to take care of all you guys."

"Don't worry about it now," said Mike. "I've been taking an investment course online. Learning a lot. And being cautious. Who knows? After football…anything's possible."

"Wow. That's great. And Mike…there's something else." She walked close to him and kissed his cheek. "That's a little thank you for all you've done for me. I know you've covered the school costs my scholarships and work-study job didn't. My suite upstairs is better than any dorm could be. I…I don't know how to put a price on all…" She began to choke up.

"Stop right there," he replied, his complexion ruddy. "You did all the work. I'll be proud to watch you graduate next year."

Mike was such a great guy. A great big brother, and she really loved him. But something wasn't right between him and Lisa. She hoped they could work it out. Damn! They *had* to work it out.

"Are you going to call Doug and let him know about the internship?" asked Lisa.

"Hmm… I'll wait until tomorrow when I see him. He's totally wrapped up in his play."

"Writing requires a ton of concentration," said Andy. "Look at all the time I'm spending with the school newspaper."

"You got sucked into the editor's job," said Brian. "Not me."

"Whaddaya mean, not you? You said you'd write the sports column for me."

"Because you begged me, not because I want to."

Jen couldn't help grinning. She glanced at Lisa, who made eye contact with her, and they both broke into old-fashioned giggles. The boys would never change. Funny, loyal, but with their differences, too.

"About Doug and his new play…" Jen began, and received their undivided attention. "I may have forgotten to mention that *The Broken Circle* is being produced by the Theater Department in the fall. It's not often that the university stages a student's work. Isn't that amazing?"

"I'll say. So, he wrote another stage play? Not a screenplay?" asked Mike.

Lisa waved her arm in a dismissive motion. "He's just following his artistic muse. If he starts writing poetry, you're in real trouble."

Heat surged through Jen, all the way to her fingertips. Her cheeks burned, and she knew she'd turned red. She calmed herself with a deep breath before saying, "I actually think he's brilliant, Lisa, and I don't appreciate the sarcasm. He's worked his butt off on this play. He's just as excited as you were when your brand new debate team made it to the state quarter-finals last year."

To Jen's horror, Lisa's eyes filled with tears. "Sorry, Jen. I'm so sorry. But a playwright? If you and Doug go on together, you'll be supporting him, maybe forever…"

"And that decision would be mine," she said quietly. "Only mine. Maybe you should worry more about yourself."

No one spoke. Lisa paled to alabaster, then stood, using her hands on the table to push herself up. "Finish your dinners." She left the room, and seconds later, Jen heard the front door close as her sister left the house.

She started to run after her, but Mike's hand on her arm made her pause and say, "Do you want to go?"

"No. Let her be. Maybe the only privacy she can get is outside, away from us."

Jen wasn't sure that's what Lisa needed; she didn't know *what* Lisa needed. She wasn't sure about anything anymore, not even how to talk to her big sister, the rock of their family.

PART III
FINDING HOME

CHAPTER TWENTY-ONE

Despite her words to Mike, Lisa yearned to go home. To a familiar place. To the safe place she'd left behind. Where her real friends lived and where her parents were buried. She longed for the town where life was smaller and slower and calmer. No NFL. No Beacon Hill. A place where she knew who she was and where she fit. The gorgeous townhouse in Boston, with its marble fireplaces and leather sofas, a Baccarat chandelier, and a Roche Bobois entertainment center, had been Mike's choice, and Lisa had allowed herself to be pulled along.

The idea simmered for a week. Woodhaven. The more she thought about it, the more she liked it. She could easily find another job. The school system was great, so the kids would be fine. Of course, there was no Boston Symphony youth group for Emily, but there was a magnet school for music. The boys could play on other teams.

During the second week of May, she took a day off from work and got behind the wheel. She had high hopes for a new beginning in her hometown. Maybe she'd go house hunting today. She remembered to leave a note on the kitchen table for the boys and Em saying she'd be home late that evening. No details needed.

Two hours later, she exited the Mass Pike and drove the familiar road into town. Maple and oak trees shimmered in the breeze, showing off their spring green. White birches dotted the landscape, too. Lisa smiled, feeling at peace. She drove past the central police station, the courthouse, the auditorium. That courthouse…where a blindfolded Lady Justice proudly stood with her scales balanced evenly in her hands. A second inspiration for Lisa's dream of law, and the reminder caused a flicker of pain.

She took her time meandering through familiar streets, past shopping areas, a supermarket. Main Street contained a mix of businesses and shops and eateries. People earned their livings here just like they did anywhere else, in a variety of venues. She drove past the school where she'd subbed after her parents died, and later past the high school from which she'd graduated. Maybe she'd surprise Sandy and Gail with a visit. But for now, she was simply getting her bearings…or procrastinating her visit to Hawthorne Street.

Lisa had visited Irene and William on occasion, but today, she wanted to absorb the place where she and her family had been so happy. Surely, it would bring comfort.

After making a quick pit stop, she finally nosed down the familiar street, a tree-lined street with plenty of shade and sturdy wood-framed homes offering safe harbor. She crawled along, looking from left to right, at the familiar houses sheltering families she knew.

Of course, they were familiar. Yet they seemed smaller than she remembered. She noted details she hadn't paid attention to years ago—the uneven sidewalks, the potholes—winter's gift to New England.

When she was halfway up the street, she parked the car. On her left, Mike's old home. On her right, hers.

With a *For Sale* sign out front.

Her mother-in-law must have forgotten to mention that fact when they'd last spoken. But it didn't matter. Her heart raced as she studied the sign. Was this an omen of some kind? A good omen?

She clutched her purse and got out of the car, the Lexus's door closing behind her with a satisfying thud. A Realtor's name and number were lettered prominently on the poster, but Lisa ignored the information and decided to ring the bell. If these were her old buyers, they wouldn't be shy.

They weren't. A friendly greeting and conversation about their move to Houston, Texas. They'd just started boxing up their things. Sure, she could take a look around, and if she knew anyone who wanted to buy…?

"I'll keep it in mind," she said. "And thanks. Thanks a lot." She stepped inside. "I appreciate…uh…" She choked up. "I'm a little homesick, I think."

"Take your time, Mrs. Brennan. No problem."

She quickly regained her balance. Maybe it was the boxes lined up everywhere. Maybe it was the unfamiliar furniture. Or maybe she'd gotten used to the townhouse. Her memory had lied. Like the others on the block, this house, too, was so much smaller than she remembered. She climbed the stairs and walked from room to room, memories whirling. She and Jen had shared a bedroom until she went off to law school, giggling together one minute, fighting for closet space the next. Good times. Across the hall, the twins' room had held bunk beds, their walls covered with racing car paper. Now, their room was painted pink.

She continued the few feet down the hall to the master bedroom and slowly pushed open the door.

Standing on the threshold, she inhaled deeply, her feet unable to step into the room. Memories assailed…

"Robbie, did you hear the story about my Uncle Harry?"

"No, Gracie. What about your uncle Harry?"

"Well, he didn't want to marry my cousin, Mary…

"Why not?"

"Well, because Mary was related to Barry, and Harry…

She couldn't breathe. Not in, not out. She began to rock and grabbed the doorframe as a gray cloud descended. Somehow, she slid to the floor and inhaled a huge gulp of air. Then another. Her head cleared just as she heard her hosts calling her name. Grabbing the wall for balance, she rose to her feet and stepped farther into her parents' room, scanning the corners, the walls, the closet doors. And wondered if she'd indeed lost her mind.

Grace and Robbie weren't here. Not even a trace. This house wasn't the Delaney house anymore.

She felt a sob rising in her chest. What had she expected to find? Why had she gone inside? If she couldn't bear it, how could she possibly live here? How could she bring the kids here? Hawthorne Street was out of contention.

"Mrs. Brennan?"

Lisa forced a smile on her face and went to greet the woman. "I'm coming. Thanks so much."

"We're not rushing you, but you've got company. Mrs. Brennan, from across the street, is waiting outside."

#

Irene? Lisa frowned. She hadn't intended on visiting Irene today. Mike had told his parents about the news of their impending divorce, and she understood

Irene and William were disappointed. They'd need time to accept it.

Mike's mother was standing next to Lisa's car, fingers drumming on the fender. Not a good sign.

Might as well get this over with. Lisa's chin went up as she approached her mother-in-law. "Hello, Irene."

"If you are considering buying back that house, I won't let you."

"I'm sorry you're so upset."

"Upset doesn't begin to cover it. But I'm telling you, Lisa, you can't move back here. I'm not going to wake up and be reminded every day that Grace's daughter ruined my son's life! No, I won't. Not even for Grace's sake."

"I'm not buying it," Lisa said quietly.

Irene seemed to collapse against the car. "Thank God for small favors. The sooner Michael's done with you, the sooner he can start a new life. You were his siren song. He fell in love with you and only you. And how did you repay him? By making him miserable. He deserved better… Oh, oh, I knew this would happen. I knew it would be too much. Your relatives should have taken those children."

"Out of my way." Lisa stepped toward the driver's side of the car, feeling as though she were walking under water, Irene's words echoing from afar.

Irene blocked the door. "Oh, no. I'm not finished. See what I mean? Even now, you don't want to listen to anyone."

"You're attacking me, Irene. Why would I listen to more?" She hoped her words were coming out faster than her thoughts. Was this what people meant by an out-of-body experience?

"He's crushed, Lisa. He loves those children, but they're not his. And you never gave him children of his own. I love those children, too, but they're not my grandchildren. You never gave me grandchildren…"

Her visit to Woodhaven had turned into a nightmare. The sun was just about overhead, about noon, but the day felt a hundred hours long.

"You have grandchildren, Irene. Through David and Nancy, so count your blessings. My parents will never have that pleasure. And this conversation is officially over. So please get out of my way."

She bent down to open the door, but Irene said, "Whatever made you go inside that house? What were you looking for?"

How could the woman not understand? How could she not know that I'd give anything to find a trace of my family…a flavor, an aroma, a song…a memory…hidden in the cracks of that house. I wanted to find peace! What other answer could there be?

But to Irene, she merely said, "I didn't find it. And if you don't get away from my vehicle, I'll simply run you down."

"You've really lost it," said Irene before she walked home. "Do those children even know where you are today?"

Lisa started the car and roared away, now anxious to leave Hawthorne Street, sorry she'd ever gone there. So much disappointment among the ashes. She had no appetite for food. No thirst for a drink. No desire for company. She braked hard at the corner and counted to ten. Maybe later, after her next stop, she'd call her friends.

The gates of the cemetery were wide open. Without hesitation, she followed the gently winding road to the place where her parents lay in eternal sleep. Lifting the two wreaths of flowers she'd brought from the front passenger seat, she got out of the car.

The sun warmed her, the quiet calmed her. Until she studied the headstones. She placed the wreaths carefully and traced the names with her fingertips. *Robert Delaney. Grace Delaney.* Still so alive to her, but too elusive to help. It wasn't the first time she'd come here, of course. But as her tears streamed, she realized it was the first time she'd visited without an entourage. Was privacy the true reason for her trip to Woodhaven? She'd needed privacy to chat.

Hi Mom. Hi Daddy. Bad news today. Nothing is going right.

Nothing?

Well, Jen is great—she has a nice boyfriend—and the kids are healthy.

Good.

They do their homework.

See? Good job, Lisa!

Wrong. I'm doing a terrible job. Mike and I are getting a divorce, and I don't know what to do next. You always told me to follow my dreams. Well, I need more direction than that! I keep dropping out of law school. Who knows if I'll ever be an attorney? Mike's out of the house several nights a week. He might have a girlfriend. I don't know what to believe. We haven't told the kids yet, but they'll hate me. As for Mike's mother…well, you should have seen Irene a few minutes ago…

Lisa plopped down on the grass, grabbed fistfuls of dirt and pebbles, and slammed them on the ground. Over and over until her knuckles hurt. But she needed to talk to those who would listen.

I have a second-best career, Mom. No marriage. No home of our own. Not even Hawthorne Street. Your children are not in great shape. Help me!

Your career, Lisa? Surely you have bigger goals than that. I've told you how I met Daddy and how he made me laugh. There went my big "show biz" career and began the best career I could have had. And I taught you all to sing.

Lisa burst into tears. She missed their laughter. Their outlook on life. She missed the music and carefree good times. With Michael Brennan, she felt old and worn.

Mike and I don't laugh much.

After your father and I got married, I never looked back. I made music with the family. You can make music with Mike.

Times have changed, and besides, Mike can't hold a note!

Ah, Lisa. The boy was crazy about you. You harmonized perfectly.

That was before…before we lost you. And before I disappeared too. He doesn't understand how hard I'm trying to make you proud. And not make mistakes. Your other children…need you!

You've kept our babies together. We are very, very proud of you.

It was her heart speaking. Of course, it was. But maybe she'd lost her mind. A calmness descended, and her tears dried. Exhausted, she remained sitting on the grass.

"Lisa, Lisa!"

Real voices? Or her imagination? Warm hands rubbed her arms and back. Female chatter, low and comforting and familiar.

"Hey, girl. What's going on?"

"Come on, Lisa. Talk to us."

Sandy? Gail? How? When?

"Irene called me," said Gail, kneeling beside her. "She was worried. She saw the wreaths in your car."

"And you peeled out of Hawthorne Street leaving rubber behind."

Irene, worried? "That's impossible," Lisa replied. "Lexuses don't squeal."

Suddenly, she was laughing, and holding on to her friends, who were holding on to her. They began to giggle, enjoying one of those absurd moments when hysteria bursts through for no reason at all.

"I'm so glad to see you." Taking each of her friends by the hand, Lisa rose to her feet. She started humming "Stand By Me."

"Oh, let's do it for real," said Gail quickly, "even if I can't sing on key."

Arms around each other, they swayed and sang a chorus right there in the cemetery. Gail hadn't lied about carrying a tune, but it didn't matter to Lisa.

"We sure gave your folks something to laugh about," Gail said, nodding toward Grace's and Robbie's resting places.

"They loved it. I promise you, they loved it." Lisa's eyes watered and she rubbed them with the back of her hand.

"Don't you dare start crying again," warned Sandy. "I can't take it."

"I miss you both so much," Lisa said. "Did Irene tell you about Mike and me?"

"Yes. And we're so sorry to hear it," said Sandy. "Sorry and surprised, Lisa. You've never mentioned anything—"

"But on the other hand," Gail interrupted, "his life in the NFL is probably not too…what's the word? Humdrum, shall we say?"

"I don't think he's cheated, if that's what you mean," Lisa said quickly, "but frankly, we're both miserable. We make each other miserable, so, I'm…I'm thinking about moving back here with the twins and

Emily. Jen is happily employed and has her own life now in Boston."

To Lisa's surprise, her friends remained quiet for a moment too long.

"That's a very big decision," Sandy finally said. "Take some time to think about it. Teenagers don't like change. And you and Mike are hitting them with a big change."

Her friend stepped closer and squeezed Lisa's arm. "I'd bet money that the kids don't feel the same way about this place as you do. They were so young when you moved. Seven? Nine? Their childhood and most of their memories are intertwined with you and Mike in Boston."

Soft words, true words Lisa hadn't considered and didn't want to hear. She began to shake.

"But it's not our decision," said Gail. "If you do want to move back, we'll help you find a place. In fact, there's some new construction on the west side of town. A development called Cranberry Cove. You'd love it."

Lisa felt a smile emerge and a warmth fill her. Her friends would stick by her no matter what she decided. "We're talking to the kids within the next week or two and we'll see what happens. In the meantime, I'm treating for lunch." She glanced at her watch. "Hmm…a late lunch."

"I'm sorry, Lis. I have to get back to work," Sandy said. "I used my lunch hour to come here."

"And I have to get back ASAP. I left little Bobby with a neighbor."

They bestowed kisses on her and rushed to their cars. Lisa tracked their hasty departure, instantly aware they'd moved on with their own busy lives and routines. Jobs, husbands, a child. Their friendship had remained strong, but they wouldn't be at her beck and call if she returned. The three of them had grown up, and she couldn't turn back the clock.

She paused as the thought seeped into her soul. Had she spent the last four and a half years looking backwards instead of forward? She got behind the wheel and headed to the highway. *You can't go home again.* Thomas Wolfe had it right. People and time didn't remain static. So, Woodhaven was out. Boston was in.

She stepped on the gas.

CHAPTER TWENTY-TWO

A spotless kitchen greeted her when she arrived home. Not a crumb on the counter or floor. Not a plate left in the sink. Even the dishtowels were folded and stacked. Whew. Maybe she should leave the house more often.

She heard faint sounds from above and glanced at her watch. Almost eight. On the early side to prepare for the night. When she looked up, Mike stood in the kitchen doorway.

"They're good kids, Lisa, and smart." He waved his arm. "They cleaned up for you. And I guess for me. They sense something's wrong, and we need to tell them."

She swallowed hard. "You're right," she whispered. "It's just that procrastinating is easier."

"But it doesn't get the job done. Summer's coming. Training camp and preseason games. I'll be busier with the team soon, and we need to get our act together."

He was right about that, too, and she had to look ahead. "Well, I've made one decision. I'm not going back to Woodhaven."

His head jerked back. "Woodhaven? Are you nuts? Why would you have even considered it? The kids live here now. And so do you."

His response flew at her so fast she needed to take a breath before replying. "You're having a great night, Michael. Three correct conclusions within five minutes while I've agonized for months to get there."

His eyes moved slowly from her head to feet and back up again. "Where were you today?"

Lifting her chin, she met his gaze. She had nothing to hide no matter how much he
ridiculed. "Woodhaven."

"Geez! Why?"

He'd never understand that with all his decision-making, he'd plunged her headfirst into extra chaos after the custody battle. Their quick marriage and the move to Boston had instigated turmoil on top of grief. But it didn't matter anymore.

"I went to Woodhaven to visit my parents."

Now his eyes widened, any trace of fatigue gone. "Okay," he said slowly. "How did it go?"

"Better than expected." Considering her run-in with Irene and the tour of her old home.

"You're almost smiling," he said, amazement lingering in his voice. "It must have been a heck of a visit."

"But I'm not going back."

"Great decision, Lis. How would I have seen the kids regularly?"

She'd never thought of that. Her surprise showed, and he could read her like a book—as he often said. Oh, well…

"Dammit, Lisa. How selfish can you be? I don't care what in hell those legal papers say, I'm taking the kids part of the time." He walked toward the basement door. A workout waited.

She collapsed onto a chair. He'd been thinking ahead, as usual, and she'd been looking backwards. Her futile attempts at apartment searching had been just that. Half-hearted. Woodhaven had been the constant lure. Until now.

Grabbing *The Globe*, she scanned the real estate section. Then reread it slowly. Nothing was getting past her.

#

Irreconcilable differences. It's just not working out. Convenient catch phrases to describe reasons for a divorce, but not language the kids would understand. Or want to understand. So, Mike took a different approach after dinner during the same week Lisa visited Woodhaven.

"Hang on a minute," he began in the moments between the table being cleared and the kids disappearing upstairs. He got their attention and motioned them to sit down again.

"What's going on?" Andy asked, his eyes narrowing and his gangly arms braced on the table.

Mike's eyes met Lisa's. Her lips were pressed together, but she nodded.

"Well, something is going on," Mike began slowly, "so we need to sit here for a while and talk about it." Three pairs of young eyes were glued to him, and he took a deep breath. "Your sister and I need a little break from each other." He spoke quietly and soothingly, but he needn't have bothered making the effort.

Brian jumped to his feet. "No breaks! No divorce!" he yelled. "That's what a little break means in the end. We don't want any breaks."

"Here's what we can do," said Andy, his intense gaze traveling between Lisa and Mike. "We already thought of it because…because…things don't feel right in this family. And we're not stupid."

"Right," said his brother. "Listen to Andy."

"Brian and I will go back into our old bedroom, and Lisa can have the top-floor suite—Jen's probably not there for much longer—or you can keep your master bedroom, Mike. Everyone can have a big place all of their own."

If only it were that simple.

He glanced at Lisa. Wide open, her violet eyes were almost black. Her mouth made an O.

"I'm afraid, boys," she began, "that's not the answer. I-I know this isn't easy…I'm looking for a new place nearby."

Emily hadn't said a word yet. Mike wondered how much of a setback this would be for the sensitive girl. They might be kids of his heart, but he had no authority, as Lisa had so clearly pointed out during their marriage. The hell with authority. Lisa would probably screw it up. He wasn't letting the kids go without a fight.

"I have an idea, too," said Mike directly to the teens. "You guys know we're a team, so even though we can't arrange this legally, how about reserving all day Saturdays and Monday afternoons just for us? No exceptions."

"But I want you every day. I want you 'legal.'" Emily walked toward him and wrapped her arms around his waist. His lids closed, and he swallowed hard.

"You've got my phone number, sweetheart. You can call me any time at all," he said, "even when I'm at the stadium. Andy and Brian, too. You guys come first."

But the girl stepped back and shook her head. "I don't think we do. Not us. Not Delaney kids. Because we keep saying good-bye to parents, and that's not a good thing."

Her words rang out as clearly as a church bell on Sunday morning. Total silence followed. The twins, without a word spoken, instinctively took their places on either side of their younger sister, their complexions pale and mouths compressed. In silent accord, the three left the room together.

Staring after the kids, Lisa said, "It's your house, Mike. Don't move out. It's not necessary. I've been thinking… Summer's coming. We can visit my aunts and uncles until I find a place."

"No. You and the kids stay here. I'll check into a hotel for a while."

"Bad idea. Paparazzi."

True. And he wasn't up to dealing with the photographers yet. "Then I'll stay with David and Nancy until I find a condo."

"They've got two little kids—"

"So I'll live in the basement."

"Don't be ridiculous. I think we're more mature than that. I'll take the boys' old room until I rent an apartment."

His staying would give the kids the wrong signal. A new apartment would uproot them again. "I'm going for a run." He moved toward the front door.

"That's better than a bar, I suppose."

He let the door slam.

#

Death by a thousand cuts. A simple explanation and the most accurate. That's how Mike explained the separation to his parents and to himself. They'd been aware. He'd told them more than a week ago that things weren't good at home. But no details.

A thousand cuts. Lots of details. Some cuts left a deep mark. Like the day the boys told him they were keeping his official scrapbook with them. They weren't handing it over to him or anyone else when he moved. The press releases about him and the Riders were still their job. No one had to articulate their reasons. As long as they had the scrapbook, they still had Mike. He'd said it was an excellent idea and grabbed each of them in a bear hug. Great kids. None better.

Lisa was right in some ways. They didn't hate each other. But hurt ran deep with Lisa. She blamed him for "charging in on a white horse" after her parents were killed. For thinking he had to "rescue" her. She wouldn't have gone along with it again. Not with him or anyone. That was another conversation. But he'd spoken up, too.

"You've never asked me what my life is like on the road. You've never bothered to go with me. But do you ever wonder about it? Do you know how many opportunities I've had? How many women throw themselves at me? But I've never betrayed you. Not once.

"So when we talk about who's been cheated in this marriage, I'd say it's me. You shut me out of what's important. I wanted the joy of being a dad to your sisters and brothers, but you insisted on creating a wall, a line I couldn't cross. Until I'm forced to interfere. I wanted the responsibility of supporting this family, but you always threw your own money—orphans' money—in my face. Give me a break! And I wanted to have children with you, children of our own. But…no. Again, we do what Lisa wants."

So what if she'd cried? "I'm no good for you," she said between tears. "Not what you need."

"And what would that be?" he asked.

Her broken smile almost killed him. "What you need," she'd said softly, "is a wife with no baggage." She paused a beat. "And I know you won't have trouble finding one."

They couldn't live together anymore. They were destroying each other. And neither of them was happy.

It had taken him three days to staunch the bleeding from those thousand cuts—or at least slow it down enough to make an articulate phone call.

His parents' sorrow, the pain he heard in their voices—but then his mother's, "I knew this wouldn't work," led him to The Players Club and to a bottle of single malt. It was a good place to hang out for a while, at least until he settled into some new digs. Yeah. New digs. A bachelor pad. A luxury condo on the waterfront sounded good. The warehouse conversions had become a big deal in the Boston real estate market over the last few years. He'd choose one with three bedrooms in case the boys and Emily wanted to stay for the night.

He nursed his drink. He loved the big townhouse, but the kids would be miserable moving again. Ironic that Lisa would have to stay in a place she'd never liked because it was best for her siblings. Swimming through a fog. That's what they were all doing.

Now, he banged his glass on the bar and nodded at the bartender. "Fill 'er up."

#

Wednesday, July 8, 2013
The Boston Globe
ALL AROUND THE TOWN

Super QB Mike Brennan has been seen All Around The Town on most weeknights at the city's hottest spots including his usual, The Players Club. During the holiday weekend, reliable sources placed him in the Hamptons, New York's summer playground on Long Island for that city's young urban professional crowd. He's on the move. But is he making a move on

someone new? His elusive wife, Lisa Delaney-Brennan did not accompany him on his vacation in the Hamptons. She was absent when he spoke at the gala fundraising dinner for Boston Children's Hospital last month.
Here's the question: Will Lisa Brennan be at the stadium this season rooting for her man…or not?

Check back on these pages as All Around the Town follows this story.

#

The single life had beckoned, the life he'd never had the chance to embrace before. Ha. He figured he'd have to get used to it. The holiday weekend in the Hamptons was a start. Fast and fun. He'd gone with a teammate and wound up hanging with some guys from the NY Giants. The teams weren't in the same conference, so no harm, no foul. And who cared when every last one of them had women on their minds and in their sights? It had been a great weekend, and he hadn't been left out. He was beginning to enjoy blondes. They'd eased the pain for a while.

In his new condo along Boston's waterfront, Mike gave the gossip column a quick glance and headed for the business section. He didn't need to read celebrity news about his life. He'd lived it for three months now, handling reporters with a "no comment" comment. He'd bought the new digs quietly through his lawyer and his real estate contact, but it was only a question of time before the news would leak, and the paparazzi would besiege him again. An announcement of his and Lisa's separation via the Riders organization would come at the end of the month during training camp. The piece would state only the facts. No details about reasons. Nothing about the kids.

How long would it take this empty million-dollar apartment to feel like home? He'd bought big, with a mortgage, so the kids could stay over whenever they wanted. They'd already visited and approved. The boys and Em were armed with cell phones with all his contact numbers listed. Damn! If only Lisa could have seen them as truly one family. But she couldn't get past her fears and what she saw as responsibility to Robbie and Grace. Not to mention the legal paperwork. So what if the kids weren't his by decree? Paper didn't count in real life. The boys and Emily had been unanimous about that.

His conscience niggled him. She couldn't count on him, she'd said. Maybe he didn't know how to give her the emotional support she needed. Maybe he really was Peter Pan. How many men played games for a living? And he intended to keep at it until he was too old or too injured. Maybe he was still a boy.

Or maybe their lives had been based on too many schedules—school, football, music lessons, work. So much to do in twenty-four hours they'd simply forgotten to schedule in the marriage part. Their fourth anniversary was next week. Not much to show for it and certainly not much fun.

He sighed. It was so easy to blame the other. He'd had dinner with David and Nancy a few times and loved playing with his niece and nephew; he inhaled them. His brother called him almost every day just to talk, to check up on him, more likely. But that was okay. Their relationship had always been solid, except for the time Mike had wanted to buy the couple a house. Now, David worried about Mike's finances, and Mike had grinned. "I'm still employed at a damned good wage."

Later that day, he'd be leaving for Nantucket, where his running back, Jack Miller, had a place. They'd do some fishing, eat fresh lobster, and run miles around the island. They'd also get blitzed. Sounded good to him. But he had to get back early Saturday in time for the twins' baseball game.

He also planned to host a kickoff party for the Riders' gang and their wives, a time to bond, and something he'd never done before. The work would have been too much stress for Lisa. Stress! That's what caterers and cleaning services were for, and he'd hired both for next week. His spirits lifted at the thought of the party. Of getting himself back on track. He'd work hard, preparing for a game, and play hard in between.

That's what single guys did, that's what celebrities did, and it was about time he enjoyed the good life instead of feeling like an old married man. He'd turned twenty-seven last month. Old? Hell no! His life was just beginning.

#

On Saturday morning, Lisa drove to the field early, the boys anxious to warm up with the rest of their team, anxious for Mike to watch them. Afterwards, they planned to go off with him for the rest of the day and do guy things—whatever that was. But Lisa had her doubts about the entire arrangement.

"Mike might not come today," Lisa said. "Isn't he in Nantucket?"

"I reminded him before he left," said Brian. "He knows."

But it was a gorgeous Saturday. Why would he want to leave a beautiful beach and ocean for the hot city?

"He's with his pals," she said. "He might forget. I really wouldn't count on him."

The way they could count on her.

"He'll be here. At least by the third inning. That's what he said."

She bit her tongue, thinking of the endless number of games she'd attended through the years, cheering for her brothers. Winter basketball and summer baseball, she was there. True, she'd managed only a couple of Brian's football games last year, but that was the best she could do. As with Mike, she'd closed her eyes whenever Brian was on the field. She was her brothers' biggest fan, but she would have skipped today's game if she knew Mike would definitely show up. He'd already kept the boys overnight after a couple of Saturday games, however, and might not have felt the urgency of seeing them today.

With a John Grisham novel in hand, Lisa made her way to the bleachers and chose a shady spot to enjoy the story while she waited for the game to start at ten. Jen was sleeping in after a party night with Doug and some new friends she'd made at her internship placement.

The day was all hers—a luxury. Emily was away at a music camp run by Itzhak Perlman and his wife in Long Island. Thanks to Ms. Merri for pushing Em to submit an application, including a disk of her playing. According to Jill Merriweather, if Em were accepted, she'd be nurtured and mentored with a faculty-to-student ratio of two to one. The teacher had insisted it was perfect for Emily.

But of course, Em had been very nervous about leaving the family for six weeks. Stay or go? Stay or go? Lisa and Mike had been in accord this time. The child needed to develop both musically and emotionally.

"And she deserves the chance," said Mike. "In case you hadn't noticed, Em is as true to her instrument as I was to football." His eyes gleamed when he'd looked at Lisa, and she'd known he'd fight her if she disapproved.

This time, however, she didn't argue, simply asked a question.

"Did you say she was far ahead of any other child in the school's orchestra?"

"Yes. Not only in technical skill but her musicality…her interpretation is…so sensitive, so unusual for one as young as she is."

She'd met Mike's gaze. "Do you see any downside in this?"

And despite Ms. Merri's presence, he'd said, "Thank you for asking my opinion. It's the first time."

In the bleachers, Lisa sighed a contented sigh. The day ahead had no conflict, no stress. No thinking! A day of happy things. *Summertime, and the livin' is easy…* She hummed to herself as she opened her book. Summer. It used to be easy; it used to be the best time of the year. She and Mike…so long ago. *Nope! Don't go there.* Since he'd moved out—what, two months ago?— she tried never to look back. Maybe she should have done that years ago like Jen had done as soon as she'd finished that quilt. Somehow, Jen had stopped dwelling on the past as soon as she'd sewn her last stitch; somehow, she'd successfully focused on the present. As Lisa was doing now. Or trying to.

One thing she knew for sure—Mike's absence made the house a stress-free zone. No more arguments. No more disappointments. No more gossip about him and her.

All was well now. Except at night when the house was too quiet. And the bedroom too lonely. And she found herself reaching out for him. So puzzling. But she missed their intimacy.

She buried those thoughts and opened *The Street Lawyer.*

#

Lisa could pass for eighteen today. She was still a knockout. And still his wife. If appearances meant anything, she was better off without him. From twenty feet away, Mike absorbed the picture Lisa made relaxing in the shade with her book. Her long dark hair was piled high, shapely bare legs extended to the packed ground beneath the bleachers. Cute sandals on her feet. He could spot her in a crowd at a hundred yards. Five yards was a gift he didn't want or need.

Lost in her book, she hadn't noticed him yet. Good. He didn't want to see the frowns and creases that would form, the caution that would shadow her eyes when she spotted him. Or was it anger? He remained where he was for a moment, looking at the "old" Lisa, enjoying the view and the early memories. Then he walked to the fence where the team was gathering in their dugout.

"Hey, Mike!" Andy's grin said it all. "You didn't even miss the first inning."

"Lisa thought you'd probably forget about us," added Brian.

"Only because you were out of town," Andy said quickly, glaring at his brother.

Mike made a mental note about Andy taking on the peacemaker role. They'd talk about it later. His research on children and divorce reassured him that Andy's behavior was a common one. Mike had figured out that if studying videos prepared him for a game, studying about children's behavior after a divorce would prepare him for now.

"Coach says I'm pitching today," said Brian, shaking out his arm.

"And I'm catching for him."

Smart coach. The twins didn't even need hand signals when they could read each other's minds. Andy had the composure to study the opposition hitters and call the right pitches. He'd set up his team's defense like a field general. But all eyes would be on Brian. Another good fit. Brian loved center stage.

His young brothers-in-law looked so professional in their red-and-white uniforms that, if it weren't for their smooth faces, Mike could almost forget they were young teenagers. "Remember what I always tell you?"

They nodded.

"When you're working out there, ignore the crowd. Concentrate. And remember to have fun."

Their identical grins cracked him up every time. He waved and headed to the benches. To Lisa.

#

If he thought his Foster Grants and baseball cap allowed him to appear incognito at the public field, he was in for a surprise. Lisa sensed his presence from the first moment he approached the neighborhood venue. She also heard the quiet chatter, then the hum of recognition as spectators realized their quarterback was simply one of the regular folks that day, ready to watch the national pastime right along with them. She prayed he'd ignore her and find a seat far, far away. He could handle the spotlight like the veteran he was; she hated it. And who knew if the paparazzi would show up. Lots of celebs were out of town now. Mike could be fodder.

She stared at the printed page. Grisham had become her lifeline.

"Good morning, Lis."

"Hi." She kept reading.

"PMS?"

"F-U."

"Lisa! Lisa, Lisa. You are in rare form this morning."

She finally tipped her head back. "I was blissfully happy. Calm and at peace. Why are you ruining that?"

"So why'd you stay around? You could have dropped off the boys and left." He did sound puzzled.

"Because I couldn't count on you showing up!"

"But I'm here. Aren't I?" A quiet delivery. A confident delivery.

"Well, score one for you," she said.

"It's not a contest, and I'm not keeping score. I've always been there for the kids. Unfortunately, you just never noticed."

Then why had she done all the work? All the planning? All the worrying? "I'm not having this conversation. I've finally found some tranquility. Why don't you go sit somewhere else?"

She scanned the sets of bleachers. "Damn it. Look. Right by our team's dugout," she said, pointing. "There are a couple of stringers covering the game, maybe from *The Globe*. I've lost track of the schedule, but I think this is an All-Star game. And it won't take a moment for them to discover you. Damn, damn, damn."

Mike stood. "If you're so miserable, go home. This was supposed to be a fun day for everyone, and I'm not letting you spoil it."

Like you've spoiled other fun times. That's what he meant.

"You're so unfair," she said, her fist clenched. "You have no idea of the pressure…" What was the use of talking? He'd never walked in her shoes. Never tried to. She took her book and made her way to the visitor's benches. She didn't care where she sat as long as it wasn't with Michael Brennan.

CHAPTER TWENTY-THREE

Grace and Lisa's Notebook—August 12, 2013
Dear Mom and Dad,

We couldn't do it, Mike and I. We couldn't make music together the way you two did. And I know you're disappointed, and that's the one thing I've tried so hard not to do. Disappoint you.

Mike's now living in a beautiful condo on the waterfront that must have cost a fortune. He insisted that the kids and I remain in the house. He really wanted to prevent another school change for them. Maybe it's his conscience or maybe plain common sense.

She brought them up-to-date on the kids' summer activities.

You'd be proud of all of them. As for me...I've given myself the gift of leisure time this summer. For the first week, I slept until ten. Can you imagine? No teaching, no school. Just three siblings! Leisure time is a wonderful luxury. It's funny how I can walk through this house now and notice how lovely the dining room set is, how rich the woods are in the entertainment center. And the kitchen! It's really a fabulous place to work. Granite counters, the latest appliances. I'm experimenting with new dishes just for fun. Too bad the boys will wolf down anything without complaint. No honest feedback there.

As she wrote, her thoughts swirled. Had she been closed-minded before or truly distracted by responsibility? Had she resented Mike's earnings because she'd felt like a charity case? Had every new beautiful piece of furniture exacerbated the wound? She sighed. Perhaps she'd had too much pride. However, one truth stood out. When they'd moved here, she had no desire, time, or energy to learn about home décor. Her energies had gone elsewhere, and she regretted that now. She and Mike could have worked on the house together…during the off-season…if she could have found time.

Round and round. She wondered if Mike thought about details of their past too. Did parting really make the heart grow fonder? Or was something else at play? After the Woodhaven debacle, she wouldn't vote for nostalgia anymore, but rather on a new perspective.

One more thing…I joined a community chorus. It's a lot of fun. And I'm making new friends. We sing excerpts from Broadway shows, films, rock, pop, and jazz. I'd love to do a tribute to Ella. Maybe someday. Eventually, we'll have a concert, but I'm not sure I'll have time to continue after the summer. My schedule will be tight again. I'll be teaching, Jen will be a senior with a full load of college work, and the younger ones still need supervision. Remember the Super Bowl party…?

Lisa replaced the notebook in her night table, closed her eyes, and calculated another two weeks of freedom before the school year started. She wouldn't waste a moment of it.

#

What should she wear? It wasn't a date, simply a Friday night out with Jen, Doug, and Jen's friends. Lisa's presence was totally her sister's idea, a sister who'd nagged and nagged until it was easier to agree than argue. Lisa would be the old lady of the group.

"So what?" Jen had argued. "It's been almost four months. You've got to start going out sometime. And besides, you're not old!"

A simple black knit dress, a chain belt low on the hips, big hoop earrings, dark hose and heels. Eye shadow. Lipstick. Why hadn't she had her hair cut yet? Inserting two fancy dress combs, she pulled her too-long hair back from either side of her face and let it flow loose past her shoulders. She finger-combed her bangs, and with a last glance at herself in the mirror, left the master bedroom she'd once shared with Mike and raced to find her siblings.

"Are you both still going to Brian's game?" she asked Emily while Andy removed a pizza from the oven. Brian had cajoled her into permission for playing middle school football. If the coach had eyes, he'd keep her brother on the bench. He sure wasn't the biggest teen there. She could only hope.

"Yup," said Emily. "Andy doesn't mind me tagging along."

"She doesn't ask stupid questions in the middle of a play."

"'Atta girl." Lisa high-fived her sister. "I've got to leave now." She adjusted the oven dial to "off" and left the second pizza to stay warm. "Clean up after yourselves, will ya? Leftovers in the fridge."

"Sure." Andy scrutinized her from head to foot. His mouth tightened and he turned away.

"What's the matter? Don't I look all right?"

"You don't have to go barhopping. Come to the game, or we can skip it and go to the movies or something. How about a family night?"

"Fine with me," said Emily. "Besides, you're not divorced yet, Lisa. You can't go out."

"I'll be with Jen and Doug."

"And lots of guys," said Andy. "You're pretty. They'll be hitting on you."

Who knew little brothers noticed? More important, why was every change so hard? "Let's back up a second," she said. "Mike is on his own, too. Don't you think he goes out with other people?"

"Not girls. Just his teammates. They go to the Italian north end to eat."

She bit her lip. Her brothers and sister adored the guy. They had no clue. And she wouldn't tell them. "That's true some of the time. But remember he went to the Hamptons and to Nantucket during the summer? And now, there are the away games."

"We're not stupid, Lisa. We know there's always groupies hanging around after a game. But Mike wouldn't cheat on you. At least," he paused, "not on purpose."

She closed her eyes, buying a little time. "Mike is a good man. I'm a good person, too."

They brightened.

"This isn't about someone cheating. It's about not being able to live a happy life with each other. And it has absolutely nothing to do with either of you or Brian or Jen."

She stood on tiptoe to kiss Andy's cheek. Then, she kissed Emily. "I'm off. Be good."

"How do you know you'll live a happier life separately?"

She raced to the front door, grabbed her red pashmina, her purse, and pretended not to hear the question.

An hour later, she was part of a large group seated at a round table, ordering drinks and food, taking in the Irish flavor of A New Beginning, the name of the club. The other tables in the place were filling quickly, and the noise level had risen. A piano player provided background music, and a polished dance floor waited to be filled.

"Top Forty tonight," said Jen. "This place has a really good DJ. He'll get everyone on their feet." She peered at Lisa from under her lashes. "Not that most of us need any help."

"Hey, don't look at me like that. I can dance."

"Trust me, you're going to."

And she did, at first with Jen's male friends who were…respectful. Jen must have put them up to it, but even her sister couldn't stop them from asking a few questions about Boston's prominent QB. She hardly cared. The DJ proved himself, and Lisa felt wonderful moving to the music, thinking about nothing at all. It had been a long time between dances.

They adjourned to the lounge area after dinner. Little by little, her group became separated, the guys on the prowl, girls on the prowl, too.

"What's the best pickup line you've heard tonight?" A low voice behind her, close to her ear. Unfamiliar. Lisa shifted on her barstool. Tall, slender, brown hair, brown eyes, straight nose. A great smile. She took a breath.

"Why, yours, of course."

The man threw back his head and laughed. "Prove it by dancing with me. You're good. Better than your partners. I noticed you out there earlier."

She smiled. "Thanks. Is that your criteria for asking a woman to dance?"

Sipping her wine, she thought, *I'm flirting. With a man who isn't Mike.* Guilt, thrill, pleasure, pain. She kept her smile on.

He held out his hand. "Come and find out."

She went. He moved to the beat. A natural. And it was fun—for a while. For as long as the Top Forty rocked. When it slowed down, she did, too. And he. But his body was too slender, aftershave too sweet, conversation too practiced. He was a player with a gimmick and an eye for someone new. She preferred earthy, broad shoulders and a wide chest. She preferred straight talk and a small-town pace.

The evening waned. Cinderella was ready to go home, leaving the prince behind. She said good night to her partner, to Jen, Doug, and the others. She needed house slippers, not glass slippers. She made her way to the door, pulled it open, and stepped outside.

"Lisa! Lisa Brennan!"

She twirled toward the voice, and the flashbulbs went off.

"Oh, no!" She covered her face, probably too late, and returned inside. She'd been caught by paparazzi at other times, but Mike had always been with her. Where was Jen? Was there a back door? But, shoot, she didn't want to wind up in an alley. She reached for her cell phone and automatically pressed the Riders' car service number. A mistake.

"So sorry, John. I touched the wrong button. I'll just call a cab. Thanks."

She hung up before he could reply, searched for a cab company—oh, she loved her smartphone—and began to dial.

Her cell rang. Mike's name in the readout. She sighed and answered. "Stay where you are. I'll be there in five."

Damn. She wasn't a princess waiting to be rescued. She was a mature woman who could handle her life.

He arrived in ten. When she saw the passenger door open and heard Mike's familiar whistle, she made a beeline for the front seat and practically fell into his arms while the photographers had a field day.

"You shouldn't have come," she said. "I was calling a cab."

"Nope. You did the right thing, calling the car service. Absolutely the right thing."

"It's all your fault, anyway! Who said you had to be a hot-shot quarterback?"

"Who said…?"

"I can see the headlines now: Brennan rescues Brennan. I wonder who tipped them off. And for the record, I can rescue myself."

Mike began to laugh, then laughed some more. And she hadn't heard that carefree sound in such a long, long time that she shut up, leaned back, and floated on the music Mike made.

Single life seemed to suit him.

\#

October 19, 2013
The Boston Globe
PONZI SCHEME UNRAVELS
Local Financiers Involved

Mike scanned the headline, heart beating rapidly. His investments were under his own control, but he recognized several names, including Bruce Jamison's, and that meant bad news for his friends. Damn it! His phone rang. Joe Siegel, his lawyer, got right to the point.

"Did you see today's paper? Are you affected?"

"No, no. By the skin of my teeth and a gut feeling. But that's no way to make decisions…is it? That's just luck."

"Whatever works, my friend. I'm inundated with calls, but I wanted to check on you. You never did tell me who you decided on for investment and planning help."

Mike felt heat rush to his face. "I'm embarrassed to say that I never went to anyone. My savings are just sitting in the bank and in a few mutual funds."

A low laugh came through the phone. "Normally, I'd bawl you out, but today we're filing claims with the Security and Exchange Commission, the Attorney General's Office, and the federal government on behalf of a lot of other athletes. Glad you're okay. Gotta go."

The man would be busy. Too busy. And his own friends…Darrell and Nate…they would have lost everything. He should have told them. Should have said something. But what? Based on a hunch?

The phone rang again.

Darrell was sobbing. "I had all my savings in there with him. Everything. We shoulda known, Mike. We shoulda known."

His pal assumed Mike's funds were involved. Mike paused for a second before replying. Now was not the time to tell him the truth.

"How could we have known?" he asked softly. "Jamison had lots of credentials." As well as two-thousand-dollar suits and jewelry.

"He wore expensive clothes…worked for a famous place. He had to be making money."

"Call your lawyer, Darrell. And if you need anything, let me know."

Mike gasped for air. Had to get out of the condo—as big as it was— before the walls closed in. After throwing on some sweats, he grabbed his keys, ran down the ten flights of stairs, and began jogging, all the while tallying his assets and liabilities.

He'd be negotiating a new contract soon. More money. He was still young at twenty-eight, but his career was physically limiting. His body had taken some punishment since college play. Hell, he ached after every game. The gridiron was a battlefield where everyone played to win, and the current season was no different.

His divorce loomed. Lisa's absence in his life seemed unreal, another kind of ache he'd get used to. As his teammates said, Mike was in transition. He'd partied, met lots of pretty women, but no one had been special enough to bring back to his place. He needed to open his mind.

He jogged along the wharves, inhaling the fragrance of ocean—sea salt mixed with the tang of kelp and seaweed. So different from Woodhaven. Different from Beacon Hill. Coastal air couldn't be confused with anything else. Tomorrow was game day. Technically, he was supposed to be resting, but he took a deep breath and picked up speed, his legs finding their own steady rhythm as he ran block after block.

He could have been wiped out financially. The thought brought on more sweat. The kids! Their college accounts. He groaned when he recalled how he'd laughed at Lisa's budgets and her frugality. Made fun of her and Jen as they labored over their yellow legal pad.

Not anymore.

His steps slowed as he turned down a familiar street and came to a stop at Lisa's door.

#

Lisa put up the teakettle and opened the newspaper. The black headline made her uneasy, and she began to pace. Jamison's name rang a bell. Had Mike mentioned him? She snapped her fingers, remembering. A business card. She'd seen the man's business card on Mike's dresser.

This would be a blow not only to his pocketbook but to his pride. He liked rescuing others, but he'd never admit to needing help himself. She gazed ahead, not seeing anything around her. Just needing a minute to catch her breath.

The kettle whistled. The doorbell rang. She shut one and opened the other.

Mike stood on her threshold, jogging in place, dripping with sweat. A crease developed in his forehead as he faced her. "Got a minute?"

"At least ten." She opened the door wider and stood aside. "Let me get you a towel. Or do you want to shower? You left stuff downstairs in the spa. Sweats, socks. It's all there." She was babbling.

"Sounds good. I'll take a cab later."

She cocked her head, not believing the implication. "Did you run all the way from your place?" Miles of streets.

"Yup. I needed to think. And right now, I'm thinking a shower's a good idea."

She waved her arm. "Well, you know the way."

"That I do."

He disappeared into their finished basement while footsteps pounded on the stairs from above.

"Was that Mike?" asked Andy, with Brian right behind him.

"Where'd he go?"

She pointed. "He's taking a shower. We need some private time today."

The boys eyed each other, then grinned at her. "Sure. Take as much time as you want. We don't even need to talk to him."

She could have cried. Fourteen and still hoping. "I love you guys, but we stick to the truth here. Mike and I are having a finance discussion, not a family discussion."

"Then change topics," ordered Brian, "and try harder."

"We're sick of worrying about you," Andy said. "You stay out too late."

"He's right." Brian always had his brother's back. "But at least the new guy down the street isn't going to call you again."

"What are you talking about?"

"We told him you were still married..."

"...and not available."

Pivoting in unison, they ran back upstairs, leaving Lisa with her mouth agape. The twins egged each other on, demonstrated more chutzpah than a single child, and more immaturity. They got into trouble more often and were twice as challenging to her. On the other hand, they'd have each other's backs for a lifetime.

She retrieved the newspaper and sat down with her tea. Mike knew where to find her.

And he did, wearing a clean navy running suit. "Water still hot?" He nodded at the teakettle.

"Sure." She reached for another cup. "Sorry, I don't have any bran muffins or..."

He waved her concerns away. "I've got something on my mind."

She poured the water and placed the tea in front of him. "I read the papers, Mike. I know about Jamison. I hope they throw away the key to his cell." Shaking her head, she continued, "You worked hard for that money. No one knows the cost and the effort behind the glamour."

Standing again as her anger grew, she walked across the room and back. "I'm afraid you won't recover all your funds. Ten percent if you're lucky. I'm sorry. And of course…we'll sell this beautiful house, trade in the cars…you can raid the kids' bank accounts…"

She sensed the stillness. Not a sound from Mike. Instead his eyes followed her path back and forth until she stopped.

"I thought you hated the house."

Was that all he'd heard? "Not hate…well, maybe. I was more overwhelmed by the price, neighborhood, and the upkeep. But it is lovely, and…I guess I got used to having cleaning help."

"So…it was just too much, too soon?"

"I think so, but that's in the past. We need to get a Realtor as soon as possible."

"No, we don't. But sit down a sec. I've got a question."

She complied and watched his jaw tense, his eyes darken as they met hers. "Do you think," he began, his words slow and deliberate, "that in the end, all I am is a dumb jock? And that's why you never trusted me with finances?"

"A dumb…? No! Not at all. Never. I just thought you were living in the moment, enjoying the moment. God knows you'd earned it! But you always thought about the children and…and about me. Maybe you bought so many gifts to make us feel secure. I don't know. I'm certainly no shrink."

He sat quietly and said, "But I only got a partial scholarship to Ohio State."

Instead of a full one. "Don't you remember the competition for that aid? And the thrill of winning the partial?" She pictured him sharing the news. "We celebrated."

She moved around the table to where he sat, pulled a chair close, and took his hands. "Don't do this to yourself. Think about how you've managed your career and your money. You've got no debt. You didn't squander on houses in Italy or jet planes or who knows what. And if I haven't said it often enough, I'm truly aware you've provided wonderful support for my sisters and brothers. You've made our lives easier. So, thank you."

Nodding, he walked to the sink and stared out the window for a moment. With a snap of his wrist, he turned on the spigot, washed his face, and grabbed a paper towel.

"Thank you for this conversation, Lisa. It means more than you know."

"The only mistake you made was trusting Jamison."

"Had that been my only mistake, we wouldn't be separated." He pulled out his phone. "But as it turns out, Lis...I didn't trust him, didn't give him a dollar. We're not selling the house or anything else."

"What?" Her chair toppled when she stood again. "You let me stew all morning..."

"Sorry."

No, he wasn't. She saw the gleam in his eye, the smile he tried to hide.

"We got down to a few basics, didn't we?" he asked. "A civil conversation. But I am calling the car service before you throw that tea in my face." With those words, he bounded upstairs to visit with the boys and Emily for a few minutes.

She watched him take the steps two at a time, still moving like a panther, smooth and graceful. Her hands became restless, her fingers moving with an itch to touch him. And that would have to stop.

They'd been friends today. Calm and kind. If circumstances had been different, she might have put on some music and asked that big cat to dance with her.

#

That night she reached for the notebook. Flipping through the pages, she saw how many fewer entries she'd made lately. Unusual for her. She depended on the journal—on her parents—to get her through the roughest times, and there always seemed to be rough times.

But today, Mike had eclipsed her folks.

A civil conversation about serious matters. Mike's question. Her similar question from months ago teased her. Why hadn't they had meaningful conversations when they lived together? She bit her lip. The past was the past. At least they'd made progress and would have an amicable divorce instead. A lack of bitterness would be best for all.

Lisa's Notebook, October 19, 2013
Dear Mike,
Neither of us wants to make the same mistake twice, so I'm writing to you as a friend who'd like you to live happily ever after next time around. I suggest you consider the following:

When you get married again, you should have rational discussions as we had earlier today. Make sure you ask for your wife's opinions, and make sure she hears yours before making decisions. You shouldn't ignore each other's ideas. A marriage should be a fifty-

fifty relationship. I always felt I had the minority share and had to fight to be heard.

Most important, you need to be each other's best friend. Respect. Trust. We had it once, in the beginning, but…I think they never had a chance to bloom.

I wish you much better luck ahead.

Short, but with an arrow in her heart. She'd need to take her own advice in the future. How would Mike react if he read it? Hmm…lawyers needed imagination to prepare for opposing counsel's arguments. She closed her eyes.

Mike would call her bossy. *So what? Someone had to be in charge.*

He'd call her stubborn. *He might have a point there.*

He'd say she put the children before their marriage. *Ouch. That one stung with its measure of truth.*

He'd say she made money an issue when it needn't have been. *Only half right there. Delaneys weren't parasites! They'd pay their share.*

Hmm…maybe this little exercise wasn't such a good idea.

CHAPTER TWENTY-FOUR

The following Saturday morning, Mike stretched out on his sofa and autodialed the house in Beacon Hill. Lisa picked up.

"My lawyer's nagging me to find out who's representing you."

"Well, hello to you, too. Just tell him I don't want anything. You've already been more than generous through the years. He can just write something up, something simple."

He massaged his temple. "That's a lot of baloney. One guy can't represent both of us, or it's a conflict of interest."

"Massachusetts is an 'equitable distribution' state. That doesn't mean equal, it means what the court deems as fair. So, since I'm not fighting for anything, whatever the court decides is fine."

He needed an aspirin. His body ached from his earlier workout, and now his head chimed in. Why couldn't she just be an ordinary greedy woman his lawyer could handle?

"It's mid-season, Lis. I don't have time for a lot of back-and-forth."

"Okay, okay. Here's an idea I could live with."

"Shoot."

"Just grow the college funds for the kids. They're smart, Mike. And Emily might require… Of course, I'd make sure they take on-campus jobs, but it would be wonderful if—"

"Already done." A no-brainer. And he was happy to provide the funds, but she sounded embarrassed discussing it. "Speaking of college…are you ready to go back? You could do it now."

"I'm thinking about it, but I've still got three kids in the house."

"They're almost self-sufficient, so that excuse doesn't wash with me. You've always needed to plan every detail before you act."

"So what's wrong with that?"

"Nothing. It's just an observation.

"Well, here's another observation. A funny thing happened on my way to law school."

"Go on."

"I discovered that working with high school classes can be rewarding, especially after I introduced debating into the curriculum. So, now I have a personal career conflict."

"Oh?"

"The administration is very happy with our showings in the statewide tournaments. They're pushing me to go for a master's degree."

He wasn't surprised. Once Lisa put her mind to a task, it got done. "If I say something, Lisa, will you promise not to jump down my throat?"

A pause. "Sorry. Can't do that."

"Then I'll take my chances." He inhaled, then said, "Why couldn't we have calm, meaningful conversations like this and the one last week when we were together?"

"Because when we were together, we couldn't breathe."

He heard the soft click on her end and stared at the phone until the dial tone squawked. He didn't know what the hell she was talking about. And he didn't know why the hell he cared.

#

At seven o'clock that evening, Lisa examined herself in the mirror and saw a witch. Not a very original idea, she admitted, but she looked the part with her long hair and pointed hat. She'd chosen a clingy black dress with a side slit and high heels to add a little sex appeal. Long red beads added interest. She reached for her cape and broom. She would do.

She had her bases covered. The twins had two scary movies to watch later on. Emily would probably retreat to her own room by then.

She would have been surprised at the boys' willingness to stay home if Brian hadn't played in a school football game the night before. Under the lights, it was still cold in late October in New England, and the forty-eight-minute game, which always took two hours to play, had gone into overtime. Andy had written the sports column for his school paper late last night. Brian ached this morning. Both boys had slept until noon before ambling to the kitchen for breakfast. Very unusual for the twins to move in slow motion.

Now, Lisa headed downstairs, broom in hand, and found the kids in the family room watching television. "You're all set? There's sandwich meat in the fridge if you get hungry."

The bell rang. Andy ran for the door.

"You look beautiful," said Emily, walking slowly around her sister. "I think too beautiful to be a witch."

"I agree with you, Em."

Lisa whirled. Mike stood there. "You scared me. What are you doing here?"

"He's got a bye week, Lisa. No game tomorrow."

"I'm watching scary movies with my boys." He glanced at Em. "And girl, too, if she wants."

"I'll scream a lot."

"Perfect," said Mike. "That's exactly what we need pre-Halloween."

Sounded like fun to Lisa. "Well, have a great time, everyone. I'm off." She gathered her purse, checked for her cell and Katie's address.

"My car's right outside," said Mike. "I'll drive you over and save you the trouble."

"Thanks, but I've got good directions," Lisa said, waving a paper at him. "Besides, I'll need a ride home afterwards."

"No problem. With two movies, I'll be up late."

He seemed sincere enough, harmless enough, just a friend doing a favor for a friend. But…why? What was he thinking? They were finally establishing their own lives like reasonable adults and having excellent conversations about important matters. They'd made great progress, but now he was stepping over the line. Definitely mixing them up.

"It's just weird, having you drive me."

"It's practical—and safer. Look outside. It's pitch-dark and you've never been to her house before. You don't have a GPS, you don't know where the place is, and you're driving alone—wearing a sexy costume. That's what's really weird."

Her laughter bubbled as she pictured herself behind the wheel. "Points to you. Getting directions from a cop while wearing a witch's hat and holding a broom…it's just funny. Okay, pal. You win. Let's go. I'll buy a GPS." She started for the door.

Mike jingled his keys and turned to the kids. "Behave yourselves until I get back."

"Have a good time," said Emily.

"Have a *great* time," added Brian.

"Yeah. Don't rush. Have fun." Andy's words.

"I specialize in fun," said Mike, following Lisa into the night.

#

It did feel weird, sitting next to Mike on the front seat while he drove. Such a familiar setting, going back to their teenage days when his car ran on a wing and a prayer.

Mike tapped the wheel of the SUV. "Not quite the old chariot, huh?"

"Mind reader."

"You're easy."

Because he knew her too well. "We're going to Cambridge," she said, studying the directions.

"That's simple enough. Punch the address into the GPS or give me the specifics later on. In the meantime, tell me about your friend, the hostess tonight."

"Katie? She's a terrific math teacher, and the kids love her, even the ones who find numbers difficult. Totally inspirational. She really encouraged me in the beginning."

"So, you actually made a friend?"

"I guess I did. A good friend."

"Like a Sandy and Gail type?"

She had to think about it. "I think it's developing that way. And tonight I'll meet her husband for the first time. He's at MIT. They have no kids yet."

"Katie's the only name you've ever mentioned since we moved to Boston. You need more friends."

"And when did I have time?" she snapped. "The summer theater group was great, but the season goes fast."

"Hey. I'm not criticizing. Everyone needs friends, and you sounded happy talking about Katie."

"I guess you should know. You've got millions of them."

Silence filled the car for a moment. "Do I really?" Mike finally replied. "Have you checked the Riders' roster this year? Some of my players were picked up by other teams and moved away. Nate's injured again. My job's to hold the guys together and make sure they play as a team. I'm the kingpin. But at the end of the season, I go home. And they go home. Boston is a second residence for most of them. That's the way it works."

Once again, he was throwing her a wild pitch. What did he want from her? "But some of the guys do live here, so if you're looking for sympathy, forget it. *Lonely* is something you don't believe in."

"You're wrong, and we need to talk about that. You and I need to be friends again. It's important."

She shook out the paper with the written directions and turned on the reading light. "Are we on Mass Ave? Look for Drummond Place and take a right."

"Yes, ma'am."

"I agree with you. I'm glad we're not enemies,"

"That's a start. But we're not friends, either. You don't trust me, not even as much as you trust Katie, so we can't be friends. At least, not yet."

"There's the house. The one with the shining pumpkins on the porch and on the pathway to the front door. Look at the ghosts in the trees." Tonight was for partying and meeting new people. Not for serious conversations. "You can just drop me off…"

He pulled into a convenient spot and opened his door. "I'll walk you in. I'd like to meet Katie and her husband."

"You're not crashing this party! Go home. I'll call." She exited the car and slammed the door.

"Lisa! I'm not in costume. I can't crash."

"That's worse. You'll be recognized, and who needs that? Remember the nightclub? Someone tipped off the paparazzi. Katie doesn't need that here."

One look at the stricken expression on his face and she wanted to call back the words.

"Point taken," he said, backing up and leaning against the hood. "Go on in. I'll just watch from here to make sure you don't trip in those killer shoes."

"I'm sorry to be so harsh," she said. "I'm just trying to find my way."

"And I'm a pariah."

"Don't be so dramatic." She scanned the modest neighborhood and gestured to Mike. "This reminds me of Hawthorne Street. The house on Beacon Hill is beautiful. Really. But I would've felt more comfortable in a neighborhood like this from the beginning."

"You haven't changed a bit," he said, "regardless of everything that's happened."

"I don't agree at all. But it doesn't matter. It's really you who've changed, Mike."

He made an impatient gesture. "Are you sure, Lisa? Are you very sure? Look harder."

She marched toward the front door, leaving him at the car. Of course he'd changed. His life wasn't ordinary. In fact, was exceptional. As for her, he might have a point. She was still a working-class girl scrambling to make a happy life for herself and her family, just like always.

A husband was family.

She halted on the porch, her breath catching, her mind racing. She'd always made excuses, always had her reasons, but in the end, *she'd put her husband's needs and happiness last on her list.*

Her shoulders slumped; she leaned against the porch column as she faced the truth. *There was plenty of blame to go around.*

She didn't feel like partying anymore, but she couldn't disappoint Katie. Marching back to the sidewalk, she waved Mike over.

"It's your lucky night, kiddo. I had a change of heart. Come meet my friends."

"What about paparazzi?"

"Wear a mask."

#

"It really was a great evening," said Mike, his arm around Lisa as they walked to the car at midnight. "Katie and Jonathan were very gracious about an uninvited guest."

"Especially when Jon realized he knew your brother," said Lisa. "I thought MIT was huge."

Mike shrugged. "They've both been there for ten years. Bound to happen."

"Walk slower, please…these shoes kill…never again…"

In one quick movement, he scooped her up.

"Mike!" she squealed. "What are…?"

In two big steps, they were at the SUV. He used the remote to open the door and carefully placed her inside. He trembled from want. Lisa in his arms again, for the second time that night. They'd had one dance, one slow dance at the party, and she'd felt so good against him, she'd fit so right. Her familiar fragrance almost blew him away, but he'd said nothing earlier, and he'd say nothing now. The risk was too great.

He entered the driver's side. "Seat belt on?"

"Uhh…"

He watched her buckle up.

"Of course," she replied. "Heck, I just forgot."

"Probably for the first time in your life." So, he'd had some effect on her. He started the engine and pulled away from the curb. Neither of them spoke for a while.

"You know what?" asked Lisa. "I'm surrounded by children all day long. I really enjoyed getting out, being with adults. My own peers."

"I understand completely," Mike said. "And I'd put pin-the-tail-on-the-cat right up there on the adult activity list. And how about the costumes? Yours was conservative!"

Her light laugh gave him courage. "You were the most beautiful woman there."

"Well, thank you, Mike. But compliments aren't nec—"

"Shh. They are when they're sincere. Maybe I should have given you more."

Her hand covered his. "Please don't go there. You and Jen always accuse me of looking backwards too much. And you've both been right. I've learned that it's too hard emotionally and doesn't change anything. You and I are moving forward now."

She didn't see the difference, so he'd have to point it out. "Only the accident was out of our control, Lis. Our marriage was not."

They'd both screwed up. He knew that. *There was plenty of blame to go around.*

After turning the last corner, he doubled parked in front of the house and scanned the street. No one else was out this late…or early.

He heard Lisa unlatch her belt, felt her prepare to leave.

"One more thing before you go…"

"Yes?"

She'd given him her full attention. From the streetlamp's light streaming through the window, her skin looked luminescent, her mouth generous and inviting. He took a deep breath.

"Are you free next Saturday night?"

An eternity passed. Her brow furrowed. "Don't you have a game?"

Game. Buffalo. He was an idiot. "You won't believe this, Lis, but I forgot."

"You…you…forgot?" Her mouth fell open and laughter emerged, slowly at first but gathering speed until its delightful sound filled the car. He had to join in. Lisa's rare laugh was as catchy as a hit tune. Soon they were breathless.

"Oh, that felt so good." She unlocked her door.

"Hang on." He exited first, walked around the vehicle, and opened her door. "Let's do this right," he said.

"I can manage," she said. "And as for next week, I'll be watching the game."

"Good." He wrapped his arm around her back and led her to the house. He'd take one step at a time. But…

"Lis?"

"Yes?"

"You're more beautiful today than when we met." He leaned over and kissed her gently, thoughtfully, and relished her response. Thankfully, his wife was not passive.

"Now, I'll say good night."

CHAPTER TWENTY-FIVE

Monday, November 4, 2013
The Boston Globe—Sports
NFL Injury List
Boston Riders:
Mike Brennan, QB, bruised ribs
Tony Aiello, DE, separated shoulder
Jack Miller, RB, broken ankle
BRENNAN OUT FOR 2-3 WEEKS,
OFFENSE AND DEFENSE WEAKENED

All eyes are now on Chris Carter, the backup QB for the Riders. According to head coach Tom Knight, Carter is the QB who will lead the team while Brennan'sout. Two-time Super-Bowl-winning quarterback Mike Brennan is recovering from severe bruising suffered at Buffalo last Sunday.

Injuries are plaguing last year's number one NFL team. Fortunately, Brennan should be back soon. Aiello and Miller are key players with major injuries. They won't be back this season.

#

Lisa had turned Sunday afternoon into a family football day, and all her siblings and Doug were with her. When Mike went down, an audible cry filled the room. Her heart pounded; her eyes stayed glued to the screen.

"Get up, get up. You can do it," said Brian to the television.

Mike tried to rise and staggered, and then almost fell before being put on a stretcher.

How could a man of Mike's build survive the impact of a defensive end weighing in at almost three hundred pounds and whose only goal was to sack the QB?

"He always comes through," she said. "Every week, he takes some bruises, but he's basically in good shape afterwards."

"Of all the games you decided to watch," began Jen, "this one shouldn't have been it."

Or maybe she should have cheered every game. "I guess I can't control everything. Life's a risk. But oddly, I'm not as frightened as I was before."

"Quiet!" cried Andy. "They're announcing it now."

A minute after hearing about "painful bruised ribs" needing several weeks to heal, she grabbed her cell phone and hit QB coach Nick Russo's number.

"Bring him to the house to recover," she said. "Not to his apartment, where he's alone. The team's doctor can visit him here—with detailed instructions."

She listened, then said, "I'm grateful nothing's broken. We'll be ready for him tonight. And thanks."

Turning to the family, she gave orders. "The immediate needs are small bags of ice or bags of frozen peas or carrots. So, boys, check the downstairs freezer to see what we have. Jen, you and Doug go to the store for ice and ibuprofen. He's in a lot of pain."

She turned to Emily. "You and I are going to turn this family room into a nice place to recover."

Jen grinned. "My sister's in lieutenant mode again."

"Is that another word for bossy?" asked Lisa.

"It's a good kind of bossy. We get things done. And we do it together."

Jen's compliment gave Lisa a sweet moment. She glanced from one youngster to the next. All four smiling. Looking at her with love and expectation. Maybe she hadn't done a lousy job with them after all.

But she hadn't done it alone.

Conscience pinched. Mike had wanted them to blend into one family. One ordinary family. They hadn't done that…because of her. He'd never fully enjoyed his great success. Not because of Emily's fears but because of Lisa.

She hadn't given him what he needed. Her fault!

They shouldn't have gotten married in the first place. His fault!

Somehow, love wasn't enough, and their broken marriage seemed to rest on her shoulders. So she'd given him his freedom. A chance at that good life he wanted. Parties in the Hamptons, friends in Nantucket. Adoring women everywhere.

When the chips were down, however, he'd landed on her sofa like a homing pigeon. Her heart ached. Was it too late for regrets?

#

Mike lay on the couch in the large family room the day after the game. His job was to heal, and healing would take longer than he liked. But he believed the doc's estimate was correct. Every inhaled breath was painful. Moving was painful. Coughing and sneezing were painful to a fault. Good thing Lisa hadn't acquired a cat, a definite allergy for him.

After the Halloween party last Saturday night, he'd planned to romance her. Court her, as his dad would say. Make a new beginning. Slowly. A nice restaurant. Dancing. A museum. A café on Newbury Street. Or a stop at a trendy store.

She'd responded to his kiss. He sensed a change, and that gave him hope.

Then came the sack from Buffalo's defense. And here he was, barely able to walk, let alone dance. Lisa's phone call to his coach had been a welcome surprise. Her call to her school was another one. She was taking the week off, except for after-school practice with her debate team. The twins would be home by then, and Mike wouldn't be alone.

Her choices amazed him. Totally unlike the Lisa he knew. Taking time off because of *him* was unheard of. She barely went to a Super Bowl because of missing work the day after, not to mention leaving Emily behind.

But that was in the past. Lisa had certainly welcomed him back to the house and family for now, and being with everyone he loved was exactly where he wanted to be. And certainly more fun than he'd have alone in his condo. But it was difficult to romance Lisa while propped on a couch! Especially while breathing was painful.

Emily walked toward him with a glass of water. "Lisa said to take the pain meds now. And then you can cough more easily." Her brow wrinkled, and she bit her lip. "We don't want you to get an infection."

"Thanks, sweetheart. Can you ask Lis what this is? I don't want narcotics."

"She made me a bet you'd say that!" She leaned closer. "Don't worry, it's not bad drugs."

Laughing would help clear his lungs but hurt too much. He reached for the ibuprofen and downed them while Emily took out her violin. "Want me to play for you, Daddy Mike? Or do you want to go to sleep?"

Under the weather or not, the tears he blinked back then could have happened with Emily at any time. "You are the best child in the world, Em. I love you."

She dimpled. "I know, and I'm going to play you something fun. I'll save Mozart for upstairs." Instantly, she picked up her instrument and filled the air with "My Favorite Things."

Perfect choice.

Lisa walked over when her sister had finished. "Great job, Emily. But right now Mike's not going to do his favorite thing. Time to prevent pneumonia and get air moving in the lungs."

She turned to him. "Come on, big boy. Let's stand up. You've got to cough, laugh, or just breathe deeply."

Easier said than done. "No problem." He stood, inhaled, and felt as though a knife sliced through him.

"Lean on me." In an instant, she held him around. "Bad, huh?'

He remained silent. *Let's lean on each other.*

"Oh, boy. Maybe we should use the recliner now. Better than a sofa. You'd sit taller, and I'll give you a new bag of ice."

"I think I'll walk a bit. Go downstairs to the treadmill. Might be better for the lungs."

Her eyes narrowed. "Treadmill? Are you nuts? That will lead to the strength training machines… You can't rush this recuperation. I don't care how badly the team needs you. I don't care what the team doctors say. I've done my own research, and this injury takes time to heal. You breathe twelve to fourteen times a minute, and those injured ribs are forced to move. So if you dare," she said, wagging her finger in his face, "just dare to do stupid things…"

His mouth claimed hers, cutting her off mid-sentence, his pain forced to the back of his mind. He exhaled only when she leaned in.

"There's no one like you, Lis," he murmured. "From the first time you appeared at your front door… Now, my love, all I need to know is whether that door is still open?"

So much for a long courtship.

She remained in his arms as though she belonged there. Which she did. "We're not the same people we were back then. Young? Yes. But certainly not innocent with the world for our asking. Sometimes, I guess love isn't enough. I do know we can't repeat the past."

He kissed her again and gasped.

"Ice! You need ice." She shoved a bag of frozen peas at him, but then stroked his cheek and laughed. "I'm always in a tizzy with you."

He gave his best shot at a smile. "I hope that's good thing."

"A fun thing," she admitted. "But there's also the serious part." She began her usual pacing while he leaned against the kitchen table.

"I'm listening."

"After the Ponzi scheme hit the papers, and you visited me, I took out my journal. I was surprised how less often I've written in it. But that night, I did write in it and addressed my note to you."

He stared, blinked, and cleared his throat. His nerves tingled. A good-bye letter? A goodluck letter? A tell-off letter? "Do you want to share those thoughts, or don't you think I'd want to hear them?"

"Neither of us has a choice if…if I understand what you're saying, and you really want to…to try again.

Maybe I communicate best by writing, and maybe that was part of our problem. But now…yes. We need to face the heart of the matter—together."

"I agree. Everything on the table. And I'm betting we don't need a referee."

Her quick smile reassured him. "I hope not. But…but I'm a little nervous."

He bit back his laughter and asked, "Not the intrepid Lisa Delaney?"

A shadow appeared, diminishing the gleam in her eyes. "It's Brennan," she whispered. "I'm Lisa Delaney-Brennan."

Hope blossomed. "Yes, you are. It suits you well." And me. "Why don't you go get that notebook?"

She glanced at the wall clock. "The twins will be home in a minute, and I've got to get ready to feed the masses. But don't worry. We'll have an empty house every day this week while the kids are in school. Time for us. Just you and me."

She wouldn't renege, and her game smile melted his heart. "Imagine that," he said. "Lisa and Mike all alone? Now, there's a unique idea, and one that'll work.

#

"Should we cut out this article, too?" On the floor of the family room that night, Andy Delaney's face was a picture of concentration. Wrinkled nose, furrowed brow, pursed mouth, the young teen was clearly puzzled about saving "bad" newspaper stories for the scrapbook. And Mike had to admit, the coverage was pretty grim with photos of his sack and him on the ground. The story included the Riders' future games and the question of Mike's return to the field.

"What do you think we should do?" asked Mike.

Andy raised his head and looked his brother-in-law in the eye. "I think we have to," he admitted slowly. "Because it's the truth, and we're keeping a record for you. It's got to be real and have everything."

"Give me five, kiddo," replied Mike, raising his hand to slap Andy's. "I like the way you think. You're exactly right. You'll be a good reporter."

He received a cockeyed grin for his compliment before the boy picked up his scissors and began cutting. Footsteps down the stairs preceded Brian's arrival.

"Here, Andy. I got it done." He checked his watch. "In record time, too." He handed some binder sheets to his brother, but his eyes were on Mike. "Feeling better?"

"Better will take time. Did you write a story for the school paper?"

"Nope. It's our math homework."

Our math homework? "What the heck does that mean?"

Andy's grin should have reassured him but fell short. "Don't worry. Math's easy for us. Brian does it tonight, and I'll do it tomorrow. We've got the same teacher this year."

What a scam. "And your sister knows nothing about this?"

Andy shrugged. "You know how it is sometimes. You can't breathe around here without her knowing about it. But she doesn't need to know everything."

"Andy's right," said Brian. "I hate that she's always talking about making Mom and Dad proud of us, and that we should always let her know what's going on so she can make sure we did the right things."

Mike had known it was only a matter of time before adolescent rebellion would hit the household. The twins were just about the right age when kids started giving their parents a few heart attacks. Whether Lisa deserved it or not was beside the point. But he sensed an underlying issue here.

"Mike?"

"Yeah?" He had to wait a moment for Andy to form his question.

"Do you think," he began, "that my mom and dad are proud of us anyway?"

An easy question, but if Lisa thought she had a handle on the twins…

"Andrew Sean Delaney—I don't just think it, I know it! No question about it. Your parents would be very proud." Mike motioned the boys over. "We need a man-talk right now. Just the three of us."

He couldn't remember the last time he tried to take over any serious parenting responsibilities. Certainly not since Lisa had dropped out of school the second time. She'd made it perfectly clear that because she was teaching again, she could handle being in full charge of her siblings. It was her job…except when she needed his backup. Problem was she didn't know when she needed it.

"Regarding the math homework," he began, "there's a big difference between doing what's easy and doing what's right. Around here, we do what's right..."

And if the boys were quieter than usual that evening, he didn't think Lisa noticed. Boys needed men in their lives, and he was glad the twins trusted him. Despite his injury and pain, he ended the day with a win. And a win in this case would reverberate for a lifetime.

#

Darkness fell early, typical of a winter evening in New England. One by one the young Delaneys said good night and disappeared upstairs. Soon only table lamps illuminated the family room, creating soft shadows. Lisa stretched out on the sofa. Mike lay on the recliner. Neither fell into a deep sleep.

When he groaned, she immediately brought more ice packs, ibuprofen, a fresh glass of water. He watched her care for him with tender hands and the patience of a caring nurse. Or a loving wife.

"Sorry to put you to so much trouble," he said.

"You've been a model patient so far, Mike. I didn't think you had it in you to be so...so patient." She grinned. "Okay. Not very punny, but Em would have laughed."

Nodding, he said, "I'm not an idiot. I want to get well as soon as possible. And Em still loves her 'word jokes.'"

"So when the team doc comes around tomorrow," Lisa continued slowly, "and says you need to be on the fifty-yard line this Sunday, that the Riders are counting on you, and the fans are going to be so-o-o disappointed...what are you going to say?"

He rolled his eyes. "You set me up for that, didn't you?"

"I did. Because you know they're going to tell you to 'man up' and all that nonsense."

"Lisa, darling...that idiocy comes from irate fans, not my coach."

"Really?" Genuine surprise mapped her face. And he wondered what other misconceptions she harbored.

"Oh. Okay then," said Lisa. "You'll do what's right."

The words echoed. Isn't that what he'd told the boys? He inhaled and winced. "I've always tried to do that, Lis, especially with you."

In the silence that followed, Mike watched Lisa's pursed lips and thoughtful expression slowly change. Her jaw set; her back straightened. She'd made some kind of decision.

"I know you tried," she said. "And I tried, too. I was just thinking…we're all alone right now, and what can be more private than a conversation at midnight?"

Her notebook. She was talking about the letter she'd written to him.

"A perfect time. I'm not sleepy at all." How could he be tired when his heartbeat galloped and his skin tingled? This was it. The chance to recapture the life he'd dreamed about when they were younger. "Go for it, Lisa. I'll listen to every word."

She pulled over a chair and took his hands in hers, her slender fingers pressing his larger ones as though she either needed his strength or wanted his attention.

"I've been your friend since I was eighteen and loved you almost immediately. You and I were best friends…and inside"—her hand tapped her chest— "I still want to feel that way. I want you to be happy. But here's the big thing—the thing I'm scared about.

"I know I've made a lot of mistakes, so if you can't be happy with me, then please find the…the right person. And please, this time, have a marriage that's fifty-fifty. Where you ask her opinions and she hears yours before you both make decisions. I…I always felt I had to shout to be heard, but was dragged along anyway."

Tears began to roll down her face. He wanted to speak, but she said, "No. Hear me out."

He nodded.

"That's the key. My parents had a great relationship. They were each other's best friend. We had that once, Mike, in the beginning—the love, respect and trust. But…I…I think, because of all that happened, trust never had a chance to bloom.

"And if we start again, you and I…our marriage…our relationship…has to come first. The sharing. The decision-making. It…it's taken me quite a while to figure that out."

Of course the marriage had to come first. But his file cabinet of memories clicked through issues: children, house, Delaney money, stubbornness, not supporting his career. His and Lisa's relationship seemed to come after everyone else's needs. But—

He reached for a tissue and gently wiped her face. "Don't be so hard on yourself, Lis. We were no ordinary couple and no ordinary family when we got married. Barely twenty-three years old with four children and a pile of grief. Come on, how could we have been prepared for all that came later? Our families tried to tell us, and I understand all that now, but back then…I thought I could handle everything, take the lead, and together make a happy home. With a happy wife."

"I know. I know you wanted to lift me up and make my life easier. That was love talking." She inhaled deeply, her fingers twisting together. "I want to ask you something important. It's…it's regarding the kids… Oh, Mike, did we do the right thing?"

A no-brainer for him, but not for Lisa. "Yes. In my opinion, yes. Look at them now. They know who they are, who they can count on. So, yes. We did the right thing." Hopefully, he assuaged any lingering doubt she harbored.

"But it came at a cost to us," she whispered. "And the truth was I sort of wanted them to go to my aunts. And maybe things would have been different."

A double guilt trip. She was haunted by the reverberation of that big decision.

"I was one hundred percent in favor of taking the kids. Let it go, Lisa. Your alternate universe wouldn't have been carefree. The children would have lived right here with us in a shadow world, and been our main topic of worried conversation. We would have been affected anyway."

Silence. A myriad of expressions flitted across her face. "Oh, my God. Mike…you're right. They would have been constant companions. Phantoms. So I guess, in the end, we were between that proverbial rock and hard place. Each choice came with big negatives."

He saw her pain, heard her pain, and wanted to wrap her in his arms but couldn't. Breathing was an effort.

"We've made mistakes along the way," she said. "You and I."

"Who doesn't make mistakes?"

Lisa slowly nodded. "I guess so, but here's the upside." When her gamine grin peeked out, he sighed with relief. "We know the best and worst of each other now."

Chuckling, he agreed. "No bad surprises anymore."

"Surprises? Oh…I almost forgot. Wait right there."

He watched her race up the stairs and laughed, then winced. Where would he want to go?

A minute later, she walked toward him, more slowly than when she'd left, her hands behind her back. "This is for you." She handed him a long envelope. A legal-looking thing.

He turned it over in his hands, reading the return address. Woodhaven Family Court. Puzzled, he looked at her. "Have they contacted you?"

"No-o. But I…I think it's time we contacted them. The guardianship document needs to be amended." Crying again, she gulped her words. "And that's the biggest gift I can give you."

Trust. Total trust. Without which a relationship was doomed.

"I accept." He opened his arms, and she was there. "Welcome home."

EPILOGUE

Seven months later—June 2014
Woodhaven

The front porch of Irene and William's house was crowded with family, just the way Lisa liked it and expected it on a warm June evening. They'd visit the cemetery tomorrow, but for now, she was content to watch the sun set low and shadows grow long. She couldn't help herself, however, from gazing across the street.

The Delaney house.

Once upon a time, it had been theirs. Now it wasn't. But she'd be ever thankful for those five years in that home. If not for moving to Hawthorne Street, she would never have met Michael Brennan.

She looked at each member of her family, every one strong and healthy and doing what they should be doing. Jen starting her first professional job, the boys starting ninth grade, and Em, starting seventh, would also audition for the Boston Youth Orchestra. Busy, busy. All of them challenging her. No problem now. "Ask Mike" had become a phrase she enjoyed using.

Her husband would be starting another season soon. Maybe another winning season to make up for last year. And as for her…this time, a choice between two positives had kept her up nights.

"Hey, guys, I'm going to need your help this year. Again."

Seven pairs of eyes focused on her. Mike's gaze zoomed in with laser precision, and a wide grin began to form. "What your sister's trying to say is that she's back in law school again. And please, God, let her finish this time!"

Laughter, groans, and cheers greeted the announcement. Lisa laughed, too. She and Mike were on track again. Two careers and then, hopefully, children of their own. Her dreams had once more sprung to life, and she was young again. Not eighteen, no, but certainly twenty-eight wasn't old! Right now, a wonderful future beckoned, and she'd appreciate every moment.

Team Brennan was back!

"I'll be going into family law," she explained. "I think I can make a real difference there. Like the judge did for us."

"Congratulations," said Irene.

"Makes sense." William's voice.

She enjoyed their approval, but nothing eclipsed the pride in Mike's eyes. "I propose a toast." She lifted her glass and gestured toward her old home. The others did the same.

"To Mom and Dad," she began. "Thank you for loving us, believing in us, and for the gifts of laughter and music. Your children are singing again, and you can finally rest in peace."

"Amen. Amen."

Closure.

The Delaney kids were absolutely fine.

The end

HELLO FROM LINDA

Dear Reader,

Thank you so much for choosing to read ***The Broken Circle***. I hope the story kept you turning the pages and elicited a sigh of satisfaction at the end.

If you enjoyed this book, I would truly appreciate your help in getting the word out to other readers. You can post a review wherever you bought the book whether at Amazon, BN, Apple or Goodreads. Short is good! A sentence or two about how the story makes you feel is perfect. You will have my everlasting thanks for your time and effort.

If you're looking for more heartfelt family stories, try ***The Soldier and the Rose*** and ***Family Interrupted***. I promise you an emotional roller-coaster ride with a positive ending.

And if you're craving a lighter romantic read, check out my Sea View House series. The first book, ***Her Long Walk Home***, is **FREE**! Two excerpts follow this letter.

I welcome you to visit my website at www.linda-barrett.com for news about upcoming books and what's going on in my writing world. You can also sign up for my newsletter while you're there.

With many thanks,
Linda

QUESTIONS AND TOPICS FOR DISCUSSION

THE BROKEN CIRCLE

- At the beginning of the story, Lisa is faced with the choice of either raising the four children or distributing them to their relatives and returning to law school. Is there a right or wrong choice? What would you have done?
- If Mike had been given joint guardianship right after their marriage, would that have eased the way for Lisa?
- Lisa's memories of her parents are only positive—laughing, singing, and good family times. Were Lisa's memories realistic?
- Did Mike provide support for Lisa, or was he just another person to take care of?
- How did Lisa's view of money impede her relationship with Mike?
- Do you think Lisa should have postponed the wedding and stayed in Woodhaven with the children?
- How did Lisa's insistence on "not letting her parents down" almost cost her own happiness? Is a child's perspective, even a young adult child's, realistic?
- Can romantic love die under the weight of obligations to others who depend on you?

MEET LINDA

Linda grew up in Queens, NY and earned her B.A. and M.S. at Hunter College. She's also lived in Massachusetts, Texas and currently resides with her husband in the Tampa, Florida area. "Enjoying different parts of the United States has been a wonderful experience, and I've made life-long friends everywhere."

Linda's written fifteen contemporary romances, three books of general fiction focusing on families in crisis, and a memoir about surviving breast cancer twice. She's won industry awards such as the Holt Medallion, the Award of Excellence and the Write Touch Reader's Award through Romance Writers of America. To learn more, please visit her website: www.linda-barrett.com.

LINDA BARRETT BOOKS

NOVELS—ROMANCE

Starting Over Series (coming in 2018)

True-Blue Texan (Bk 1)
A Man of Honor (Bk. 2)
Love, Money and Amanda Shaw (Bk.3)
The Inn at Oak Creek (Bk.4)

Flying Solo Series

Summer at the Lake (Bk. 1) — Free!
Houseful of Strangers (Bk. 2)
Quarterback Daddy (Bk. 3)
The Apple Orchard (Bk. 4)

Pilgrim Cove Series

The House on the Beach (Bk. 1) — Free!
No Ordinary Summer (Bk. 2)
Reluctant Housemates (Bk. 3)
The Daughter He Never Knew (Bk. 4)

Sea View House Series

Her Long Walk Home (Bk. 1) — Free!
Her Picture-Perfect Family (Bk. 2)
Her Second-Chance Hero (Bk. 3)

NOVELS—WOMEN'S FICTION

The Broken Circle
The Soldier and the Rose
Family Interrupted
For Better or Worse – A boxed set of all three WF
novels at a discounted price

MEMOIR

*HOPEFULLY EVER AFTER: Breast Cancer, Life and
Me* (true story about surviving breast cancer twice)

READ AN EXCERPT FROM *HER LONG WALK HOME*
(SEA VIEW HOUSE SERIES—BOOK ONE)

CHAPTER ONE

"Will she use the ramp or try the stairs?"

Bartholomew Quinn, proud founder and Co-President of Quinn Real Estate and Property Management, leaned forward in his oversized leather chair and peered through the large front window of his Main Street office. A young woman faced the building, her dark hair neatly gathered behind her neck. She wore a long dark skirt and a red sweater. In her right hand, she held a cane. Bart watched her glance flicker between the two paths. Ramp or stairs? Either might be considered a challenge for her, but… He caught her determined expression as she made her choice.

"Atta girl," he cheered.

Quickly transferring the cane, the woman placed her right hand on the railing. Her chin jutted forward as she raised her right foot to the first step, her left following only a tad more slowly.

Quinn had become familiar with this girl's background through a trustworthy friend. Now he'd seen her in action for himself. In just a moment, he'd depend on his gut instinct to fill in the blanks. He had the knack, those "people skills" folks talked about, instincts which had never let him down. He'd know her well by the time their conversation was over.

A sea breeze brought the flavor of the ocean to Bart's nose and he inhaled with joy. Another summer season was poised to begin in Pilgrim Cove, his favorite place on earth. He'd spent his entire adult life here—and he'd be buried here—God willing—many years from now. He was young! Seventy-six years young, and people in this town depended on him.

He and his buddies had never let them down. They were always ready to meet, greet, and befriend newcomers as well as summer folk. Or, as his granddaughter Lila would say, they were always ready to meddle—especially him. Well, his lassie might have a point. But he wasn't so sure. So far, all his "meddling" had turned out well.

And now, Rebecca Hart had come to see him. His anticipation sizzled as he walked down the hallway to greet her. Hopefully, Sea View House would be sheltering a new resident.

#

Becca chuckled to herself as she evaluated Bart Quinn. The old guy had definitely kissed the Blarney Stone more than a few times, but he still had it—that gentlemanly courtesy of his generation. He'd put her at ease immediately. He treated her as though she were like anyone else. As though she hadn't been watching the runners at the finish line in Boston instead of running herself. As though the Marathon had never happened. Except, of course, it had, and she wasn't one to wear rose-colored glasses. Leaning across Quinn's desk, Becca stared directly at him.

"My cousin, Josie, and I checked into the Wayside Inn last night, but I can't afford to stay there much longer. So I'd like to see this house you have where the rent is so reasonable, I can't believe it's true." If there was a mix-up, she'd need to find another place right away. "My graduate professor at BU insisted I contact you. He said his friend at Harvard had some clout with this office."

The light in Quinn's blue eyes rivaled the sun's. It sparkled and blazed as he rubbed his hands together. Becca sat hypnotized. Was Quinn a man or an oversized leprechaun? His fist banged the arm of his chair.

"You're talking about Daniel Stone. We call him The Professor. Comes back every year since his first stay in Pilgrim Cove. Now that was a story…was it last summer or the one before that, when he came to Sea View House? He'd lost his wife, ya see, and was in a grievous state." Quinn's head moved from side to side as he made sorrowful sounds. "I gave him the upstairs apartment, the Crow's Nest. But waiting for him downstairs was Shelley Anderson and her two little tykes. Ah-h. That was no ordinary summer, no sir-ee. And now they're a family, everybody together." His index finger pointed directly at her. "Sea View House holds the magic."

Magic? Baloney. But she'd bet her last nickel he could regale her with stories until the sun went down. She didn't have time for stories.

"Very nice, Mr. Quinn. But what I need to know is whether you've got a cottage for me to rent this summer. Easy access would be needed."

"True enough, lassie. But you did well coming up those steps. I watched from that window."

Her body stiffened. "You spied on me?" She adjusted her angle slightly to peer over his shoulder. Sure enough, she saw a swath of Main Street through the glass. She glanced over at Quinn and sighed. "Why aren't I surprised? I bet you don't miss much around here."

"You'd win that bet, my girl. This town is special to me. And will be to you, too."

"You mean you've got a place for rent? A house that will suit me?"

"Haven't you been listening, lass?"

He posed the question with such wide-eyed innocence that her lips twitched. Between the irascible Bart Quinn and her own one-track mind, she was in no better position than Alice was in Wonderland. The twitch became a smile, then a giggle, and she found herself laughing aloud, as though she'd finally gotten the joke.

And then the tears came.

She reached for the tissue box Quinn slid toward her and dabbed her eyes. Strange that she wasn't embarrassed. "Well, that was a first."

"The laughing?"

"The crying, too."

The man seemed surprised.

"They have meds for the physical pain, Mr. Quinn. No tears there. As for the rest, well, as my mother taught me from the beginning: *Life hurts. Deal with it.*"

Studying her for a moment, Bart Quinn finally said, "Well now, respecting all mothers of course, I've got a different slant. I say, *Grab the brass ring and enjoy the ride.*" He rose from his seat, searched in a drawer and came up with a set of keys. "Let's go, my dear."

"Go where?"

"Where else would I bring a friend of a friend of Daniel Stone's than to Sea View House? Right beside the ocean where you'll hear the sound of the surf, the call of the gulls and where you'll find your own healing."

#

Becca was about to tell him that her healing came from physical therapy not from ocean waves, when two small tornadoes blew into the room. The first was blonde, her long hair woven into a French braid which probably started the day neatly plaited. The other whirlwind sported dark waves, framing a sweet face. Cinderella and Snow White. Totally adorable.

"Guess what, Papa Bart!" said Cinderella. "No school 'til Tuesday, so Sara can sleep over." The child's infectious grin coupled with her attitude easily confirmed her as a twig on Bart Quinn's family tree.

Sara stepped forward. "If that's okay," she added quietly.

This girl's entrance had been embellished by her friend. Sara seemed more reserved and sensitive. A classic beauty who'd mature into a stunning woman one day.

"Sara, my girl," began Bart, "would you condemn me to a quiet house when we could be playing a hot game of-of—" the Quinn glanced at Becca then back at the child—" …Candy Land instead?"

A frown lined Sara's brow. "Candy Land?" she asked, her voice laced with incredulity. "That's for babies. Poker is more fun. Isn't your penny jar still full?"

Bart looked at the ceiling, then at the girls. "Ach. What will Ms. Rebecca think of us now? You've gotten us in trouble, you have." He looked at Becca. Two other pair of eyes followed suit. "Better a round of cards than leaving them to their little computer machines all night. Agree or not?"

Oh, she agreed. These children couldn't appreciate their luck. A loving grandfather, probably good parents, too. Even the quieter one knew she was welcome here in the middle of a business day. Secure, confident children. They'd have no idea how other kids lived. Kids who hoarded a penny. Kids with no dads or granddads. Kids with a mom who worked all the time. Kids like Becca.

She couldn't have found better entertainment than Bart Quinn and the girls if she'd paid for a ticket of admission. But she hadn't come to be entertained. She tapped her watch. "Your granddaughters are delightful," she said. "But time is flying." Bracing her hands on the arms of the chair, she stood, took a moment to find her balance, and reached for her cane. "I'm ready when you are."

"I've always been ready," said Quinn. Turning toward the little blonde, he said, "Katie, love, tell your mom I'm away to…

A pretty blonde woman, definitely Katie's mom and definitely pregnant, walked into the room at a good clip, a leather tote bag on her arm.

"Wherever it is," she said, "you'll have to take the girls. I'm showing Butterfly Cottage, and then I've got a doctor's appointment which I must keep or feel Jason's wrath."

T.M.I. "If you don't mind," said Becca, "I'll be waiting in my car—right out front." She'd have considered another Realtor at this point if her curiosity about Sea View House hadn't been peaked. Not to mention that low, low rent. And if she'd known another

Realtor. The kids were cute, but really, was this any way to run a business?

As if she read her thoughts, the other woman smiled and extended her hand. "Hi there. I'm Lila Parker, Chief Cook and Bottle Washer around here. Where's my granddad taking you today?"

Becca shook her hand, glad to see no sign of pity or sympathy. "He calls it Sea View House."

Lila's brows hit her hairline, her eyes widened to saucer size, but a small grin started to emerge, too. "Perfect. It's a special place." She cocked her head toward Bart. "He's in charge of that special property, never tells me about possible residents. It's all hush-hush until it's done."

Becca didn't care about mysteries, but walking was easier than standing, and she stepped toward the door. "I'll let you know how special it is…if I ever get there."

"I hear ya." Bart and the girls followed her. Once outside, the man installed the kids into his back seat and opened the front passenger door for Becca.

"Honestly, Mr. Quinn, it's easier for me to drive. That is, to get into the car on the driver's side. My right leg's fine."

"Then I'll keep you in my mirror. We'll take it slow so you can look around as you drive."

Becca opened her door and threw her purse inside. She'd left the seat in the far back position she'd used to exit the car. Now she'd have enough room to manipulate her prosthetic left leg while getting in. She sat down facing the street, then turned and shifted her weight toward the front, her right leg going inside. She guided the left. The sequence made sense. Her physical therapy was paying off, and she'd be continuing it in Boston and at the medical clinic in Pilgrim Cove. If this house worked out. Or if Quinn had something else.

With a little luck, forethought and care, she'd become the woman she once was. She'd become whole again. Or almost. Whole enough for a marathon? Whew. If only… She chased the thought away. More important on the survival scale, she'd need a job. A respiratory therapist at Mass General needed strong legs to run around the halls, treating patients on every floor. She'd been building a career at the prestigious hospital, with two promotions behind her and supervisory responsibilities on her plate, too.

Now her small savings would trickle away in no time. There was a chance, of course, that she'd receive some money from that charity fund set up after the marathon. But how much could that be? A few dollars? Even a few thousand wouldn't make a real difference in the long run. She'd have to rely only on herself. Her finances were tighter than a balloon's knot. A reality that tied her stomach into a dozen knots.

As promised, Quinn drove slowly, providing her with that opportunity to look around. From the man's office on Main Street, she passed a bank, barber shop and the nautically designed Diner on the Dunes. She spotted Parker Plumbing and Hardware. The name seemed familiar. That Lila woman? Then she saw the beautiful greyhound—on a leash. She glanced up. At the other end of the leash stood a tall, lean, good looking guy. Behind the pair was a pet store. Adoption Day. She glanced again at the grey. Talk about running…

They made a left onto Outlook Drive and another left onto Beach Street. Bart honked and pointed with his hand out the window. Then he pulled into a driveway. Becca slowed down, looked around and took her time before pulling in behind him.

She hadn't known what to expect, but Sea View House was bigger than anything she could care for. A salt-box style. Weathered wood. A large sloping roof.

Two stories with a third window above…maybe an attic. A white wooden fence surrounded the front yard on Beach Street.

Disappointment flooded her. What was the man thinking? She could never take care of a house like that. She hoped Quinn had another property to show her. Something small and easy. She rolled down her window and remained inside the car. With her first breath, she tasted the flavor of ocean and sea grass. She inhaled again, more deeply this time. No mistaking that definitive aroma existing only at the shore.

She looked at the big house. A house right on the beach. Not that she'd swim…how could she? But she'd hear the waves. She'd see them, too. And that view…the pleasure of that view…that elusive horizon where ocean met sky. Tempting. So tempting. So different from the confines of a hospital rehab wing where she'd spent the last seven weeks working to recover.

"Needing some assistance after all, lassie?" Quinn was at her car door.

"What else do you have to show me?"

And with that question, she'd reduced Bart Quinn to silence.

#

So what if she'd jumped to conclusions. The house was divided into two apartments, and Bart had the first story in mind for her. While Sara and Katie scurried ahead, Becca walked more slowly down the paved driveway to the back of the house which faced the water. There, a spacious covered porch opened to a backyard with a low cement wall placed at the sand line. Inserted into the wall were tall boards.

"We'll remove those, of course, now that summer's here. But they're handy protection for the house when winter winds blow the sand."

"Makes sense," said Becca, "not that I have any experience living at the beach."

"Then you're in for a treat this season. You'll come to love our peninsula with the ocean on one side and the bay on the other. There's always a breeze here. Know what I call this place?" Bart didn't need the sun to make his eyes gleam. "I call it our finger in the ocean."

He made life in Pilgrim Cove sound like a fairytale, but Becca held back. Walking on soft sand would be a challenge. But…with this shady back porch, she could simply step outdoors and feast her eyes on the mighty Atlantic. Not live cooped up in a city apartment three stories above the street. The place she shared with Josie had no elevator and remaining there was not an option. Compromise. Life was now about compromise.

"We'll have the porch furniture out here in a jiffy," said Bart as he unlocked the door. "And anything else that needs to be done."

Wide planked oak floors ran throughout the house, chintz covered couches and chairs, and in the kitchen, ample counter space. Three bedrooms. Three! Well, Josie and her boyfriend could visit—an easy enough trip from Boston. She hoped her mom would visit, too, maybe stay for a week or more. But she didn't count on it. Her mother had missed work after the Marathon. She lived in the western part of the state near the Berkshires and had stayed in Becca's apartment while Becca was in the hospital. She probably had no vacation days left, and she'd never sacrifice a day's pay.

Becca shrugged. She was on her own in Pilgrim Cove. *Deal with it.*

"We'll install the grab bars in the shower and anything else you think you'd need. Maybe a tall stool at the counter here? Easier to sit and stand again." Quinn paced the kitchen, looking for possibilities. "Would that suit?"

Suit? Becca's heartbeat quickened as she looked around. Outside, she'd have the sun, sea, porch, and a steady breeze. But inside this weathered ship, she'd be surrounded by sturdy walls, a cozy fireplace and halls— wide halls—with elbow room. No problem using a cane or wheelchair. Sea View House. An island of safety. And privacy. She'd get stronger here. Return to normal. Oh, yeah. It would suit.

"How much, Mr. Quinn?"

He jumped back as if she'd slapped him. "How much, lassie? Why there's no charge for Sea View House. Not for you. This beauty is let on a sliding scale, part of the William Adams Foundation, who was shirttail cousin to John Adams, himself, and wasn't he the second President of the United States?"

The man spoke faster than she could hear, but she got the part about "no charge." She didn't buy it. Everything in life had a price. "Would you repeat that more slowly—about the rent?"

"No rent for you. The sliding scale, you see. By unanimous vote of the Board of Directors of which I'm President."

Unbelievable. "Just to be clear, Mr. Quinn. Are you saying that this beautiful house—at least the first floor—is rent-free for the entire summer?"

"The first floor is called The Captain's Quarters, and that's exactly what I said, Ms. Rebecca. Rent free. The question is, what do you say?"

"I say, where do I sign?"

Quinn laughed his big laugh. "Not to worry. I'll bring the papers around after you move in. I'll also bring the Sea View House journal where you'll write your story."

Ahh. She knew there had to be a catch. "I'm no writer. Besides, the bombing's been in all the newspapers."

"Grammar doesn't count, girl! But stories do. It's a record, you see, about finding the magic again. You'll be able to catch up on all the folks who've stayed here before you. Like that professor you mentioned from Harvard who lived upstairs. Some other folks who've stayed here live right in town now. You'll probably meet them soon."

Not interested. Becca stared into the man's eyes, her gaze demanding his undivided attention. "Let's be perfectly clear, Mr. Quinn. My goal is to work hard and get strong enough to support myself later on—when I figure out how. I'll write something for you, but I'm not here to make friends or socialize. I had plenty of company in town after…after the bombing. Lots of attention and therapy. Sometimes too much. Everyone was terrific, but sometimes the place seemed like a madhouse to me. Now I need to be on my own. Independent." She wouldn't put it past him to send a few neighbors over just to stir things up.

"We'll do all we can to help you," said Bart. "Modifications and all. You'll be able to move in tomorrow."

Logistically perfect, but she sighed. He hadn't acknowledged a word about her wanting to be left alone.

#

Friday night and child-free. Adam Fielding, DVM, locked the door to his veterinary clinic, his newest retired greyhound at his side, and wondered what to do with his unexpected leisure time. Evening was a killer. The loneliest time of the day, the time when memories of Eileen were the strongest. Her laughter…that dimple tucked beside her sweet mouth…he'd loved pressing kisses against it. He missed cuddling on the couch, playing with her dark curly hair, wrapping the strands around his fingers. Their daughter had inherited that feature. He missed Eileen's intelligence—her fast quips and thoughtful suggestions, strong support for a debt-ridden young veterinarian just starting out. He yearned for his loving wife, his perfect wife. The perfect woman for him. He spoke to the grey.

"Neptune Park's probably opened for the season, but I'll save the carousel and Ferris wheel for Sara."

Ginger whined in agreement. Adam leaned over and scratched behind her small folded-back ears. "Of course, Katie will come along." The intelligent dog, parti-colored with a white background and fawn patches, tilted her head, listening to Adam's every word. After a month with him and Sara, the grey had adapted well to being a house pet and was ready to adopt out. But Sara had other ideas for the pretty canine.

"No, Daddy. Not this one. She's special. I love her. Please…"

His daughter didn't have to beg. He'd give her the moon if she'd asked for it. As for the greyhounds…they were all special, at least to him. Each one faced a huge adjustment after living in a kennel since birth and after a life at the track. As he'd done with others, Adam had taken Ginger home from the rescue center, helped her to adjust to family living—house, car, kids, stairs, bed—until she'd be ready for adoption.

He shrugged. So now they'd have another personal pet. No problem. Dogs and cats got along, and the mighty Butterscotch ruled his roost with confidence. Sara's devotion to Ginger was odd, though. His daughter normally used her energy and wits finding good homes for abandoned pets. She knew they couldn't keep every rescue brought into the clinic. It seemed, however, Sara and Ginger had an understanding. They were a duo. From his own observation, Sara's love for the grey was being returned twice over.

Love. Easier between a dad and daughter or between a child and a puppy than between a man and a woman. He'd tried romance again after Eileen, a sensible relationship with Katie's mom. But they'd called off the engagement after Jason Parker returned to Pilgrim Cove. With one glance at Jason's love-stricken expression, Adam had recognized his own yearning for Eileen. He'd bowed out. Gracefully, too. And never looked back.

But their daughters remained inseparable—sisters of the heart. And now Jason and Lila were expecting a sibling for Katie. He wished them well. Sometimes, everything worked out. Pilgrim Cove was too small a town in which to hold grudges, and no one harbored any.

He meandered next door to the house he shared with his daughter and her changing menagerie. His stomach rumbled when he went inside, but he had no appetite for cooking or being alone that night. Dusk hadn't fallen yet, and the evening stretched out before him. The Friday night Happy Hour coupled with dinner at the Wayside Inn would suit. He'd probably run into a few friends or neighbors and have a congenial evening.

Friendships in a solid community suited him now, too. He wasn't getting involved with women again. He'd focus his energies on being the best dad a little girl could have. Sara had been cheated of a wonderful mother, and Adam would make it up to her. Between caring for his daughter, running his animal hospital and planning the addition of a new greyhound rescue and fostering center, he wouldn't be lonely or bored. The expansion excited him. He had the start-up funding from his own savings and a bit from the Boston Greyhound Foundation where he volunteered his services. He was waiting for word about other funding, a big chunk, from a state sponsored animal foundation. Life was good. Good enough anyway.

After a quick shower, he slapped on some cologne, grabbed a clean jersey and jeans and headed out.

#

Thirty minutes later, Adam stood at the bar, nursing a longneck with Rachel and Jack Levine. The couple had married recently and decided to live in Pilgrim Cove, Rachel's home town.

"I didn't realize the Inn would be this crowded," said Rachel. "We were trying to avoid the hoards at The Lobster Pot tonight."

The Wayside Inn boasted a restaurant, bar, dance floor, spacious lobby and guest rooms while somehow retaining the picturesque New England flavor at the same time.

"The summer season's the money season," Adam said.

"On a holiday weekend, every place is crowded," said Jack, "We should've stayed home."

"Well, I'm glad you didn't," said Adam. "My daughter's with Katie, so I'm on my own."

"Maybe not for long." Rachel grinned and inclined her head toward two attractive brunettes several seats down the bar. "New in town. No gold bands. Let's welcome them to Pilgrim Cove." She shifted from her seat, starting to match action to her words.

"Whoa, Nelly. You're not the welcoming committee." Jack wrapped his arm around his wife, and Adam breathed a sigh of relief. The man had his back, whether he realized it or not. Adam had no desire for small talk with strangers.

"Why not, Jack?" protested Rachel. "We're in Pilgrim Cove, not Manhattan. It's the start of summer, and everyone's on vacation and in a good mood. In another month, I will be too."

"Some of us," drawled Jack, "work twelve months a year. Like Adam and me."

While the couple bantered, Adam glanced at the two women who were now following a hostess toward a table. Something was off. He focused harder and continued to track their progress.

"The pretty one's got trouble. Big trouble," he muttered just as the woman shifted toward him, her head on an angle. She met his gaze, and her chin rose. Her brown eyes darkened to the color of bitter cocoa, then as swiftly as she engaged him, she turned away.

He burned. Whether from embarrassment or anger, he couldn't discern. He couldn't think! The woman's eyes were as dark as Eileen's, her shoulder length hair as dark and wavy as Sara's.... Adam needed air.

#

"The last thing I expect or need is to be hit on. Did you see that guy?" Becca leaned across the table toward her cousin. "But I think I scared him off."

"Sure, I saw him," said Josie. "Hard to miss tall, hazel and handsome. Easy on the eyes. But he was all about you, cuz. That is so cool!"

Meeting a nice guy in a bar might have been cool in the old days—not that this guy seemed "nice" at all. He'd studied her like a specimen on a petrie dish, and she wouldn't put up with that. If she ran into him again, she'd say so. But more important was the big picture. Today began her new tomorrow. The old days were gone.

"I don't need anyone in my life, Josie. I'm not in the market for pity or being second best. I'd rather be alone."

"Oh, please." Josie waved away her protestations as if slapping a gnat. "You're only second best in your own mind. That guy was looking and looking hard."

"Until he saw me walk."

"You're imagining things."

But she hadn't imagined that. He'd stared at her so hard, she'd felt the burn. And then she'd met his gaze and gave as good as she got. She'd be willing to bet her bottom dollar—which was about all she had—that the only looks she'd receive from now on were those of curiosity and pity. Her hands clenched into fists. Not for her! She'd deal with them like she'd dealt with tall, hazel and handsome tonight. Just return their stares with one of her own.

READ AN EXCERPT FROM *FAMILY INTERRUPTED*

CHAPTER ONE

CLAIRE BARNES

Houston, Texas
September

"*Bellisima! Brava!* Your best work yet, Signora Barnes. Maybe you give Leonardo some competition?"

I rolled my eyes and grinned at my instructor. "Leonardo can rest easy."

Dr. Colombo teased, exhorted, or flirted with his students on a regular basis, especially the talented ones, but comparing my work to the *Mona Lisa* was going too far, even for this powerhouse.

I stepped away from my easel and focused on a portrait of a young girl peeking sideways under half-closed lids. I'd called it *Girl with Secrets*. The child held secrets I wanted to know.

"Your daughter, yes?" Colombo asked, his voice a deep rumble.

DNA didn't lie. I nodded and said, "On the outside, Kayla's mine, brown eyes and blonde hair, but inside, she's her dad, an unquenchable extrovert. Sometimes my daughter's surrounded by more friends than my house can hold." My pride in Kayla overrode the mock complaint. "She's twelve-and-a-half, almost a teenager—almost grown up, as she likes to remind me."

"Ahh." He sighed as if he understood. "I have two daughters, Signora, and I know how they too much wanted to be women but were not ready, *never* ready in the eyes of their mama."

The man had nailed it, nailed my heart. I wasn't ready for Kayla to grow up and fly away, especially with her brother applying for college this year. I wasn't ready to let either of my children go.

"This portrait of your daughter.... It is...is..." Colombo waved his arm this way and that as he searched his English vocabulary. "Exceptional!" His voice rang out, eyes shone. The young student at the next easel walked over and stared.

"Holy Toledo, Claire," she whispered. "Your kid could step right into the room. How'd you do that?"

Surprised and uncomfortable—I was just a student like the others—I wondered how to respond. Capturing Kayla's image had come easily. I knew every smile, nuance, and angle of her face. I knew how she looked when she was happy or sad or puzzled. The work hadn't been *that* difficult to execute.

"I'm her mom," I finally said as if that explained everything. To me, it did. A few of the students nodded. Others seemed to be waiting for more, which I guess was not surprising. I was old enough to be their moms!

"I know all Kayla's moods and expressions," I said. "I can picture her rolling her eyes at her dad's bad jokes.

And I've seen those dark eyes shine when he walks through the door each night."

My classmates seemed glued to my words, so on I went. "And her hair...it's so thick and long, she still needs my help combing it after a shampoo." I thought about how I could never resist kissing her neck and laughing when she groaned, "Ooh, Mom."

Pointing to Kayla's hair in the painting, I said, "See the rich auburn color here? In the summer sun, it glows like a banked fire. Maybe next time, I'll paint her outdoors."

I finally shut up, and in the quiet room, I felt the other students' eyes on me and forced myself not to squirm. Being the center of attention was Jack's specialty, not mine.

"Don't be too impressed," I quickly added. "I've sketched her hundreds of times. Maybe thousands." I was trying to be modest for the sake of my classmates, but dang, I found it hard not to celebrate. *See, Jack? I told you I had talent! And the validation feels damn good.*

My endless drawings through the years had meant less to him than the bottom line of our construction company. But when I turned forty-five last year, I knew I couldn't keep waiting for Jack's promise of "one day." I'd seized my own moment and enrolled in the University of Houston's MFA program.

I was a second-year student now, and whatever artistic gifts I possessed were being revealed under the guidance of a marvelous staff. No instructor, however, could match the gusto and intuition of Professor Colombo. Like the original explorer, this Colombo also led his crew on a voyage of discovery. *Create like Michelangelo! Find the heart, the soul of the stone, and chip away the rest. Fall in love with your subject, and it will show.*

The teacher had a point. I certainly loved *my* subject.

"So, Signora, we will spotlight *Girl with Secrets* in the *galleria* next month, at the exhibition."

I pivoted toward the man so sharply I almost tripped. "Exhibit? But I'm not ready." Was I? Sure I was living my dream, learning and improving, but didn't I need more experience and confidence before showing my work in public? If I'd spent the past twenty years painting instead of decorating model homes for Barnes Construction, I would have been more than willing to exhibit.

"With respect, Signora Barnes, you do not decide who is ready." Colombo swept away my protest with no hesitation. "I, myself, handpicked the twelve artists in this class. I studied the portfolios from last year. You are more than good enough. Art is to be shared and enjoyed. To touch the soul. Claire—or Clara, I may call you Clara? Good. Let me tell you something else, a secret between us."

He glanced around the room while I stood alert, heart racing at being the focus of his pointed attention. Handpicked for his class? I'd had no idea. When he turned to me again, his gaze holding mine, a frisson of electricity danced down my back. His index finger covered his mouth for a moment, reminding me that this was a private conversation.

"You are my most promising student in a long time," he began. "Your hands transform what your heart feels and your eyes see." He tapped his chest. "The emotions here, inside, are on the canvas too! Do you think everyone can do that?"

I took the question seriously. "Well, not the man on the street, but the other students...?"

"You are not listening, Clara! Am I speaking with the 'other students'?"

As his words began to sink in, my excitement soared. My attention focused exclusively on Colombo, and my classmates seemed to disappear, leaving the professor and me in our own private world. The man was implying I was extra special, wasn't he? Oh, Lordy, I hoped so. And then I'd tell Jack. And maybe we could hire a decorator, someone to replace me at work. If that happened, I could finally devote more of my time to art and less to business. Could the day get any better?

"Thank you. Thank you." I'd finally found my voice. "I appreciate everything you've said and done. I know I've improved as an artist because of you." *Take a breath. Calm down.* I turned my attention back to my painting of Kayla. Despite all the compliments, evaluating my own stuff was difficult, especially at this professional level. Sometimes I was too critical, sometimes too soft.

"All right, Professor. I'll agree with you. It's pretty good."

"Very good, Clara. Excellent."

During the past month, I'd started trusting Colombo's judgment despite him being a showman. His own work had impressed me—his use of light and shadow in particular—and the Art Department had been delighted to attract this visiting professor. Now I felt lucky to be studying with him. Even privileged. I knew my talented classmates felt the same. But to be called his best student in a long time?

I scanned the room for glimpses of the others' work and realized my fellow students had already put away their easels and were leaving the studio.

Quickly checking the wall clock, I felt my stomach tighten. "Oh, God, I'll be late. And Kayla has a dental appointment." Forgetting about my schedule and kids was unlike me. Had I encouraged the professor's compliments? Our lingering after class?

Pushing those thoughts aside, I quickly became a focused mom again. I carried Kayla's portrait to my private studio space, threw my smock on a chair, and shouted a goodbye to the professor while running toward the staircase. Down, down, down, until I exited the building to the parking lot, digging for my car keys at the same time. Finally, I thrust myself into the driver's seat and revved the engine. Back to reality. Back to Jack, the kids, my domestic life, and my working life. Tomorrow was soon enough to face Colombo and his compliments. A handsome Colombo with his dark mane of hair touched by wings of silver. I wondered how many art students, both in Italy and America, had produced his portrait while studying with him. My fingers reached for a phantom pencil.

#

I followed the restrained campus speed limit but hit the gas as soon as I reached the interstate. Twenty-four miles stood between the University of Houston and home. I gave myself fifteen minutes. The miles disappeared until sirens blared and lights flashed in my rearview mirror. Damn, damn, damn. I slowed down, pulled over, and prepared to smile my widest. Jack always said my smile was my secret weapon. I didn't necessarily agree but was prepared to give it a try if it meant getting Kayla to her appointment on time.

I rolled down my window and beamed.

"License and registration, ma'am." No twinkle, no smile, no sense of humor. Pure cop face.

I handed over the documents and used my cell as I waited for Houston's Finest to check out my identity. I had to leave a message at the house but wasn't really surprised. If Ian had to watch his sister, he'd be sure they shot hoops in the driveway or kicked a soccer ball on the lawn. God forbid he'd set a good example by doing homework right away. So irresponsible. I sighed a frustrated sigh. A mother's sigh.

"Ma'am, you were clocked doing eighty in a sixty. That's twenty miles over the limit."

I could do the math. "Any chance of turning this into a warning? I'm usually excellent at following the rules." *Smile.*No answer except for the scratching of his pen. Five minutes later, I was on my way with a ticket nearing two hundred dollars and an invitation to driving school. For the rest of the trip, I crept at posted speeds until, with a sigh of relief, I finally entered my subdivision and turned left around the lake toward Bluebonnet Drive.

As I approached, I saw a small crowd milling on the corner, blocking my street. In the mid-distance was a revolving red glow. My body tensed, every muscle taut with strain at the possibilities. I lowered my window when I saw my friend Anne Conroy waving at me.

"She's here," Anne called over her shoulder while rushing toward my vehicle. "Pull over. You need to park right now."

I didn't like how she looked. My hands began to tingle, but I followed her directions.

"There's been an accident, Claire."

"What? Who?"

Instead of answering, Anne opened my door and pulled me out. "It's Kayla. She was hit by a car. The EMTs are lifting her into the ambulance right now."

My worst fear.... I took off like a track star. A path opened as I headed for the gurney. Around me were familiar faces I could barely recognize because I saw only one face. Kayla. My beautiful Kayla, lying on that narrow bed, her complexion snow-white, forehead swollen, head enlarged, and blood oozing from her ears. Her stillness frightened me most.

"I'm here, baby-girl. Mama's right here." I leaned over her and kissed her cool cheek. No response.

"Ma'am, we've got to get her in the truck."

One medic spoke to me while the other was arranging stuff—tubes, IVs, and God-knows-what. They hoisted the gurney, and I jumped in beside it while scanning the crowd for Ian. Where was that boy? Then I saw him, right in front of me, sobbing aloud with tears running thick down his face.

"I'm sorry, I'm sorry, but we were only throwing a football," he cried, his voice cracking. "That's all...."

"You should have been doing homework," I snapped.

He ignored me and pointed at a young woman sitting on the ground, a stranger. "She was driving and...and..."

Glancing at her, I took a mental snapshot, certain I'd recall the details later. I didn't care about the driver then. Instead, anger, fear, and dread filled me, and I lashed out. "How could you have let this happen? You were in charge."

"But it wasn't my fault! I've told you a million times I'm not a babysitter. Maybe if you were home more, Kayla would be okay. It wasn't my...fault."

Because it's my fault. My fault for being late. That was the bottom line. My son and I were at odds again, and remorse filled me. "I'm so sorry, Ian," I whispered. "It's all right. You'll be okay. Kayla will too." *She had to be.* "Hang out with Anne and Maddy for awhile, and I'll see you tonight."

"Gotta close these doors, ma'am," said the EMT, suiting action to his words.

For a moment, I worried about leaving Ian but later was glad I did. My son didn't need to witness or hear the conversations that followed.

\#

Kayla lingered for five days. Jack and I slept at the hospital, neither of us wanting to leave. We drank strong tea, wrapped ourselves in warm blankets, and had quiet conversations with the staff.

When I mentioned to Jack how kind the nurses were, he shrugged and stepped closer to Kayla's bed. "It's part of their job." His words were abrupt, curt, and cold, a rarity for my husband.

"But only kind hearts become nurses in the first place," I argued, as if making my point would make everything better. It made nothing better.

Six weeks had passed since Kayla died, but I still remembered the name of every medic on the unit. I still pictured the IV bags with their liquids dripping into Kayla's arm one drop at a time, the orange chairs Jack and I dozed on, and the plantings between the parking lot and Kayla's hospital wing. Most of all, I remembered holding Kayla's hand, stroking her cheek, and talking, talking, talking, praying she'd hear my voice and smile. I remembered that insulated hospital world in detail.

But I couldn't remember my daughter's funeral.

Vague recollections of friends and family surrounding us at the service were all that stayed with me. I'd watched their mouths move but heard nothing. I'd seen nothing. Usually, I'd notice particulars—the cut of a blouse, a change of hairstyle, a newly framed picture—but my powers of observation disappeared that day. All gone. Just like Kayla.

Friends said that Jack and I had been amazing. What nonsense! We were numb. Paralyzed by the unthinkable. They described Jack catching me as I fainted at the cemetery. I didn't remember falling, but they said I'd collapsed the moment our daughter's casket was lowered into the ground. I believed them. I'd become a zombie, one of the walking dead.

At home, meals arrived, coffee brewed, and the refrigerator and house remained equally full. Our loved ones surrounded us, stayed with us, supported us. My parents. Jack's parents. Their lips trembled and pain etched their faces.

But no one managed to answer the one question that mattered: how could a vibrant twelve-year-old kick a soccer ball one day and lie in a coma the next? The question haunted me still. I knew there were reasons. Cause-and-effect type reasons. But I hadn't been able to accept them. How would I ever cope with this nightmare? The memories...the memories...

When Kayla was five years old, she'd said, "Mama, if you turn the number eight on its side, you know what you get?"

"What?"

"Infinity!"

A grown-up word. She'd giggled, eyes beaming, so proud of herself for surprising me. I hadn't known how she'd come up with the word, but I'd been pretty sure her brother had some influence there. *Infinity*. An appropriate description for the days that now came and went, unremarkable one from the other, simply periods of light and dark I sometimes noticed through the windows of my diminished home.

So, six weeks later, I was still a mess. Jack too. Not sure about Ian. He'd been hanging out with his friends almost twenty-four/seven. Maybe if I started cooking—really cooking—again every day, he'd find his way home for dinner. He loved meatballs and spaghetti. Heck, he used to love anything I'd put on the table. A growing boy needed nourishment, and we all used to laugh about our skinny boy devouring more than his dad. He'd filled out some this year.

Jack finally returned to work yesterday because he'd been afraid to leave me alone sooner. He'd taken calls at the house after the first two weeks and depended on his staff to keep Barnes Construction going. He had great employees, but we all knew that my Cracker Jack was the engine driving the company. It was his baby, his creation, and certainly his success. I sensed he was anxious to get back to work full-time while I, on the other hand, had no heart for anything, not even painting.

Thirty minutes after Jack left, the doorbell rang. I sure didn't want any company, so I peeped through the sidelight curtain, ready to ignore any social caller. But I couldn't ignore a FedEx delivery. Occasionally, items for Barnes Construction were shipped to the house. This item was a pretty large box, which the driver pushed over the threshold for me.

Return address: University of Houston, Art Department. I hadn't stepped onto the campus since that horrible day. I hadn't contacted the department or the registrar to officially drop out of school. Maybe they wanted clarification. I opened the outside envelope and extracted a note:

Whenever you are ready, Clara, come back. I am keeping your last painting here. You have much art still to make, and I am saving your place. CC.

The man would have a long wait. None of it mattered anymore. Only Kayla mattered. I didn't open the box, didn't look at any of my portfolio items. Instead, I dragged the carton into the guest room and closed the door. I brushed my hands together and walked to the kitchen. My college adventure was over. Maybe someday, I'd have the courage to retrieve *Girl with Secrets*.

I spent the rest of the morning alone, looking through photo albums, torturing myself. Jack called me every hour.

"How're you doing?" he asked.

How did he think I was doing? "Fine."

But of course, I'd never be fine again.

After four phone calls, I threatened to ignore his number on the Caller ID. We finally compromised. He'd stop phoning if I promised to take a walk. He said I hadn't gone out of the house since the funeral. Somehow, I also promised to track Ian down, cook a real dinner, and then make love to Jack that night. I promised a lot of things because when you lived in a time warp, nothing mattered. Not even promises made.

As it turned out, however, I did take a walk in the afternoon. Maybe the milder temperatures and gentler sun lured me, or maybe it was the general quiet with everyone else at work or school. I thought a solitary walk would be a perfect first venture outside. Unfortunately, one of my neighbors spotted me, a neighbor I didn't know well, and I wanted to retreat but couldn't.

"I'm so sorry, Mrs. Barnes...Claire," she said, full of sympathy.

I just nodded. A tiny nod. I pressed my lips together and began to stride past her.

"Sometimes," she continued, "it's hard to accept God's will."

I jerked to a full stop. My heart pounded, my vision blurred. God's will? God's will? I screamed silently. What had my innocent child done to deserve this fate? I whirled and stared at the woman for what seemed hours. Her self-righteousness oozed like the slow-running sap of a sugar maple tree. My palm itched. My fingers curled. Her cheek would make a good target. *Don't do it, Claire! Don't do it....* But I was in my time warp, watching myself from afar as I lifted my arm and smacked her across the face.

"That was God's will too," I said and walked off, confirming I was a long way from acceptance. If there was such a thing.

#

When Jack arrived from work, a home-cooked meal waited for him. Ian sat at the table too, thanks to my meatball bribe. The men ate with gusto. I managed one bite to ten of theirs and hoped Jack wouldn't notice. When their first hunger pangs had been satisfied, I announced, "I might go to jail."

Ian's mouth made a perfect O.

"You might what?" asked Jack. But when he heard the story of my walk, his blue eyes glowed, and his grin stretched across his face. Then he swung me around, laughed, and cried. "I couldn't survive without *both* my girls, and you're coming to life again. I love you so much, Claire. We'll get through this. Somehow, we'll get through." Then he looked at me with his I-have-a-great-idea expression.

"It's been more than a month, Claire. How about coming back to work? The company needs you. More importantly, *I* need you. You know how the economy sucks, and I might have overreached, but we've contracted to build in the Eagle Ranch subdivision. We've got four brand-new models for you to work your magic on."

I felt myself shrivel. Jack depended on me to dress up our models to their best advantage. I supposed I could manage the decorating part, but interacting with all the people involved in the business? Making intelligent conversation with Realtors, decorators, home buyers, vendors, and municipal departments was beyond me. I couldn't focus for more than ten seconds on anything but the family photo albums I'd browsed through that day. I couldn't fathom how Jack managed to handle his responsibilities.

"Sorry," I said, shaking my head. "I'm not ready." When I saw his disappointment, I added, "But I am ready to keep my promise about this." I snaked my arms around his neck, tugged him toward me, and tilted my head back. His eyes brightened again, and our kiss sizzled at first contact.

"Yuck. I am so outta here." Ian grabbed his backpack and left the room, calling, "I'll be at Danny's."

"The kid has great instincts," mumbled Jack, his lips on mine again.

I wanted this raw encounter with Jack. I'd been thinking about it on and off all day, knowing I needed it more now than when I was twenty-one. I didn't know why. Didn't care about the reason. Not then, anyway. I just wanted the numbness to go away, if only for a few minutes.

Interlocked, we headed toward our bedroom, automatically kicking the door shut before pulling at our clothes. I was desperate to be skin-to-skin, touching, rubbing, stroking. Feeling! Feeling Jack's muscles move under my fingers. Borrowing his warmth, his strength. He knew my hot spots...just where, just how.... I knew his, too...just where, just how....

We twined closely around each other on the bed, our limbs weaving like yarn on a loom enveloping each other, so in synch, so frantic that soon there was no rhythm at all. And then, and then...oh, God...approaching that point of no return...vibrating through shimmering reds, scarlet and crimson, heading toward the neons, gold and hot orange...until the sun shattered, and we shattered. Together.

Our first communion since Kayla died.

I burst into tears.

Jack was still trying to catch his breath, but he reached out and coaxed me against him, across his chest. A very familiar position. "Aww, Claire. Don't cry. You're all right. You're all right."

No, I wasn't. "I shouldn't feel this good. Kayla—" But I hadn't thought about my daughter for the past ten minutes. Had it taken the most basic of human instincts to break through my grief? As though in punishment, a new wave of grief surged through me. *I'm sorry, sweetheart.*

"We can't bring her back," Jack whispered. "But it seems that you and I are still alive." He spoke slowly, emphasizing each word. "In fact, we're very much alive. That was good, Claire. And healthy for us. So keep it on your to-do list, will ya?"

I couldn't blame him for wanting to reclaim as much normalcy as possible in our abnormal world, and intimacy had always been a healthy part of our marriage. However, my tears kept dribbling onto Jack's chest.

"If you keep on crying, my love, then I will too. And we'll both go back to being zombies like in the beginning."

"I still feel like one," I said between sobs. "I think I always will."

"No, no. I don't think it works like that. It's not forever. But in the meantime, I like having a naked zombie in my arms."

Jabbing him, I said, "No jokes."

"I'm just trying to—"

"I know, Jack. I know. You're trying to pretend we're okay."

"What's wrong with pretending for awhile if it works? I have to believe we'll get there someday, that we'll be strong again someday."

Granted, my numbness had disappeared during our sexual encounter as I'd suspected it would. But I didn't believe Jack and I would ever be strong again. I didn't care about "someday," a nebulous time in a hazy future. My heart was breaking now.